Imagine Summer

Imagine Summer

A Novel

SHELLEY NOBLE

wm

WILLIAM MORROW
An Imprint of HarperCollinsPublishers

IMAGINE SUMMER. Copyright © 2021 by Shelley Freydont. All rights reserved. Printed in the United States of America. No part of this book may be used or reproduced in any manner whatsoever without written permission except in the case of brief quotations embodied in critical articles and reviews. For information, address HarperCollins Publishers, 195 Broadway, New York, NY 10007.

HarperCollins books may be purchased for educational, business, or sales promotional use. For information, please email the Special Markets Department at SPsales@harpercollins.com.

FIRST EDITION

Designed by Diahann Sturge

Library of Congress Cataloging-in-Publication Data has been applied for.

ISBN 978-0-06-295360-5

21 22 23 24 25   LSC   10 9 8 7 6 5 4 3 2 1

To Jerry, whose friendship was a journey of discovery for us all

Imagine Summer

Chapter 1

As a child, Skylar Mackenzie's imagination always got her in trouble. Now it was making her a fortune. Well, maybe not a fortune, but enough. More than enough. And it kept growing.

Skye clicked out of the month's expense spreadsheet and stood up, stretching with satisfaction. She was tired, but it was worth it.

She pushed the desk chair under the desk and grabbed her bag before taking a last look around her office, the smallest room in the two storefront spaces that made up Imagine That and Imagine That Too.

She walked through both areas every night, making sure that the lights were turned off and that everything that needed to be unplugged or put away was. But really she did this just to bask in the residual hum of ideas and art still hanging in the air. It was remarkable what good energy people could make if they only would.

The results of that evening's adult Pipe Dreams class, an unbridled hour of pipe cleaner creativity, were lined up on a shelf ready to be picked up or added to at the next session. Some were two-dimensional, like paintings; others defied gravity to rise in the air.

Every one of them was amazing.

Skye smiled, knowing that at least two of the people participating in tonight's class had been executives from a Hartford advertising firm who had asked her if she'd ever thought about designing de-stressing workshops for corporations.

She'd practically laughed in their faces. She was dead on her feet most nights. With just the two stores and the upcoming summer discovery weekend, she was swamped. She didn't even have time or energy for the people who meant the most to her.

Who knew that a crazy idea she'd thrown out in the pub one night after a couple of beers would turn into this? Skye's announcement of "I want to open up an idea store" was met first with silence, then "Why the hell not" from her mostly on-again significant other, Jack. Seconded enthusiastically by her best friend, Maya, and her husband, Sonny, who merely said, "Huh," and after an elbow from Maya, added, "Sounds great."

So she did.

First a book, toy, and activity store for children, it quickly expanded into the vacant store next door, which was refitted to include several Creativity Without Borders areas for children and adults alike. Maya took on the day-to-day running of the store, and the discovery sessions were led by a bevy of volunteer and hired docents and artists. Which left Skye to keep everything working smoothly, scheduling workers and workshops, ordering supplies, balancing the books, and everything else.

She switched off the lights, set the alarm, then turned left out of the store, taking one last quick peek through the glass window. All was quiet. She blew at strands of hair that had escaped her ponytail and smiled to herself in her window reflection.

"Onward and upward," she said to the night and turned down the sidewalk toward Mike's Dog and Pony Pub to meet her friends.

She spotted Jack first. Tall and lanky, he was leaning on the bar in conversation with Mike himself, who bartended on weeknights, and Skye paused just to appreciate the view. Maya called Jack a lean, mean, furniture-designing machine, unlike Maya's husband and Jack's partner, Sonny, who was built more along the lines of Thor.

Skye scooted onto the free stool beside Jack and kissed his cheek. He smelled like soap; his hair was still damp from a shower and curled at the ends, dampening the frayed neck of his favorite T-shirt.

"Hey," Jack said. "Sonny and Maya are in the back booth. I just stopped to shoot the breeze with Mike."

Mike slid Skye's favorite microbrew toward her. "I'm trying to get his advice on some tear-off coupons to put up during Discover It Weekend. Jack said he'd come up with something with some real pizzazz."

Jack leaned back to reveal several paper napkins with scribbling on them.

"Looks like you succeeded," Skye said and took a well-deserved sip of beer.

"A beer on the house? I couldn't say no," Jack said and waggled his eyebrows at her.

"Well, I wouldn't say no to you ordering a burger and sweet potato fries," Skye said. "And me tasting a few. I'm starving, but I promised Aunt Roxy and Hildy I would have dinner with them."

Jack gathered up the napkins, folded them into his T-shirt pocket, and slid Skye off the stool. She just had time to grab her beer before his arm was around her waist and they were making a beeline for their usual booth.

There were way too many empty tables. It was midweek but it *was* summer. Each year the burgers and beer got better, but the foot traffic got worse. Once the college students left for home, downtown became a virtual ghost town. It filled up again at midsummer when the tourists flooded in, but that was mainly because the town beach had a perfect view of the Newport Fourth of July fireworks without the Newport traffic and parking restrictions.

The Fourth was only a week away and though the weekends were beginning to pick up, the local businesses were still feeling the bite during the week.

But the town had a plan, starting with Skye's Discover It Weekend. Enough fun to appeal to families and sophisticated enough to bring in the big bucks. But it was taking a huge amount of planning as well as the physical refitting of the old family camp by the river to accommodate the two hundred participants. Lots of planning—and even more persuasion to convince Herb Pritchard to delay the camp's sale until after the summer.

Fingers crossed everything would come together with time to spare. And the improvements that Skye was making would add sale value to the camp for the Pritchards.

"All done?" Maya asked when Skye slid into the dark green banquette across from her.

"Ye-ep. And I must say we had a very good June. And thanks to you, by the way."

Maya frowned. "Me?"

Skye noticed that Maya had pulled her normally straight hair onto the top of her head into an explosion of shiny, black curls. When had she starting curling her hair? Was it possible that Skye hadn't noticed?

"What did I do?" Maya asked.

"Sundays in the Park with George?" Skye said. "Brilliant. Story hour with George Zenakis, he of the silvery voice, accompanied by Tizzy Lane's homemade ice cream *and* a goldendoodle. It was bound to be a success."

"And messy," Sonny added in his rumbly voice.

Maya snuggled comically against him, her petite, small-boned figure practically disappearing into his six feet of muscle.

"Amazing how much ice cream a dog can wear after an hour of quiet reading," Maya said and smiled adoringly at her husband.

Skye and Jack exchanged looks. Their friends were laying it on thick tonight.

"Well, here's something else to think about," Skye said.

Bea Clark came to take their order. Bea had been the Pony's barmaid "since forever" and knew everybody's favorite beer and their most deeply hidden secrets.

"You're not eating?" she asked Skye, pulling her pencil out from behind her ear. "Oh right, it's girls' night at Roxy's. Tell them I said hi." Bea took their orders and stuck her pencil, which she hadn't used, back behind her ear and headed off toward the kitchen.

"What else do we need to think about?" Sonny asked. "We've got a pretty full bill already. And you know, Jack and I do have to work on stuff that pays sometimes . . ."

Maya elbowed him in the ribs. "I pay you."

"You sure do, babe."

"Could you two—" Skye noticed the orange juice at Maya's place instead of her usual microbrew. She lifted both eyebrows in question.

Maya and Sonny turned as one to grin across the table.

"We're pregnant," Maya said, then hiccuped and burst into tears. "Happy tears," she managed before throwing her arms around Sonny and sobbing while Sonny gently patted her back and shrugged at the other two.

"That's incredible," Skye said, then thought, *What a stupid thing to say*. They'd been trying for several years already. "That's wonderful," she amended. "I'm so happy for you." She cut a look at Jack, who took the cue.

"Oh, yeah. That's great."

Skye rolled her eyes at him. "So tell us everything. When

are you due? Are you going to find out if it's a boy or girl? We'll have to have a shower," she effused, while her selfish side thought, *Oh God, please don't tell me you're going to have to quit work.*

But even if she did, Skye was really happy for Maya. She had been so patient, had tried not to let the fact that nothing seemed to happen get her down. She'd even discussed the subject of adoption with Skye a couple of times, Maya saying she was afraid Sonny wouldn't go for it.

Well, hell, now they could do both.

"Here's to new Baby Daniels," Skye said and lifted her beer bottle.

Bea came back with the salads. "What are we celebrating?" she asked, neatly placing three bowls on the table.

Skye looked at Maya.

"We're pregnant," Maya practically sang.

"Well, honey, that is good news. When's the shower? I gotta get over to Newport and get some baby yarn. Blue or pink?"

"Don't know," Maya said. "We're going to be surprised."

"Well, okeydokey then," Bea said. "Rainbow yarn to the rescue. Back in a jiff with your meals." They watched as she stopped at several tables on her way to the kitchen. Then the smiles and waves from the other diners.

"One thing about a small town," Sonny said. "Everybody knows your business."

"It's like a big family," Maya said, her eyes swimming again.

Yeah, thought Skye. "It is."

They all toasted the new addition and Skye peppered the

expectant couple with questions until the food came. Then she picked at Jack's fries while she listened to Maya happily describe their plans for a nursery, shopping for the safest car seat . . .

Skye needed to get going, but she didn't want to cut Maya's exuberance short. She knew that as soon as she left, the two men would turn the conversation to other important topics like wood types, truck repairs, and who was favored for the weekend game.

But she couldn't wait any longer without being late. She took a last sip of her beer and motioned for Jack to scoot over. "I hate to leave all this excitement, but Hildy's making brisket and I don't want to keep them waiting. Congratulations, you two."

"See you later?" Jack asked as she got out of the booth.

"Yep. Your house or mine?"

"Mine. I want to get this design done for Mike. I think he's just a little concerned about business."

Mike and most of the town, Skye thought. Only a few of the more upscale businesses were doing at all well, including hers. But she and the chamber of commerce had great hopes for the future. Now just to implement them.

"Are you coming in tomorrow?" she asked Maya.

Maya frowned. "Of course. Why wouldn't I?"

Skye shrugged.

"I'm good. I'm not sick, I'm pregnant!" Maya warbled into a falsetto.

Skye laughed. "Then I'll see you tomorrow."

"Wait, what were you going to tell us that needed thinking

about before I stopped you with my most perfect announcement?"

"What? Oh, just that two execs from the Lexington Advertising Agency in Hartford dropped in to check out the workshops."

"Just dropped in," Jack said drily.

"Whoa," said Maya.

"They felt the need to de-tense with a little macramé?" Sonny asked.

"Pipe cleaner art. They wanted to know if I'd be interested in doing corporate events."

"Wow, what did you tell them?" Maya asked.

"That I'd think about it. Now I gotta run." A quick kiss for Jack and Skye was headed to the door.

"Corporate events, huh," Sonny said, frowning at his wife. "You know, once the baby is born you'll have to cut back hours, not add to them."

"Oh, don't be so last century. I can do a lot of work from home. And Imagine That is a perfect place to raise a baby."

"Just don't let Skye go off half-cocked."

Jack couldn't agree more. Corporate events. The thought alone made his blood run if not cold, at least lukewarm. First they tell you, *sure, son, you'll be free to work on your own designs,* then suddenly you only have time to do the classic designs, and before you knew it they would take over your work and your life and you'd be working for them and doing everything their way.

"What do you think, Jack?"

That he'd given up his family because he wouldn't make furniture his father's way and he'd be damned if he'd let Skye's business be swallowed whole by some corporation.

"He'll be supportive of whatever Skye decides, won't you, Jack?"

"Oh no you don't," Sonny said. "I'm not losing my partner to some harebrained scheme to turn uptight executives into navel gazers. Nope, not happening."

"I agree," said Jack. "I haven't put up with all of Sonny's bad advice for the last five years just to get sucked back into the world of working for someone else."

"*You* wouldn't be working for them. They'd be coming to *us* to enhance their work efficiency," Maya argued.

"Nope," Sonny said. "You're going to be busy with the baby, and Jack and I got more orders than we can complete."

Maya threw her napkin at him. "You guys are just complacent. It's not like we're going to drop everything for power suits and four-inch heels."

"You're darn right there," said Sonny. "Four-inch heels are for one place only."

Maya blushed.

"Don't say it out loud," Jack said.

"But you'll be supportive," Maya said.

"Aren't we always?" Sonny asked. "But we have our own business. She can't have him."

"She already does, doesn't she, Jack?" Maya shot him a sly smile.

Of course Skye had him, but Jack didn't need to announce it in front of everyone. He would just let things take their course. That was the best way to deal with life. Things were fine the way they were. It was enough for him. But were they enough for Skye?

THE WALK THROUGH town to the beach was one of Skye's favorite ways of relaxing after a day well spent. It was close to eight, dusk, not light, not dark but hovering somewhere in between.

She blew out a deep breath. Breathed in again. Ironic that someone whose business was to encourage people's creativity in order to de-stress would so often be stressed herself. It came from owning a business, she guessed, that and being responsible for employees, and from somehow becoming an activist for the local business community.

She was happy to do it for people she cared about. She owed her creativity and her success to Aunt Roxy and Hildy and to the town. Her sense of belonging, too. *Everything*, if she thought about it.

Skye stopped when she came to the stone seawall just to enjoy the view. To her left the town beach was empty except for a few lingering gulls. Beyond it, the last of the setting sun glittered on the surface of the swells. Below her, a cluster of cottages sloped down to the shore.

The little neighborhood known as Sunny Point had started as a private beach community decades ago. Now it was a mix of permanent and vacation homes, summer and academic rentals, constructed in "early higgledy-piggledy" style, according to Roxy, crammed closely together wherever and in whatever direction there was room.

Skye turned right and hurried down the sidewalk until she reached the drive down to Roxy's cottage, her feet accelerating of their own accord at the promise of dinner.

She passed several cottages, some lit up invitingly, others dark and closed until the following week. Large and small, their cedar shingles had weathered to deep grays and browns, delineated by crisp, and not so crisp, white-trimmed windows and doors.

All the cottages were quite old, having withstood the test of time by being built by trusted local builders on a slight rise above sea level. They were protected on one side by glacial boulders, and on the other by smaller jetties, coves, and inlets that laced west along the shoreline to the actual point that gave Sunny Point its name.

The drive fanned off into a number of narrow lanes that disappeared into the maze of cottages until it reached the row of beachfront houses. Aunt Roxy's cottage sat at one end, where the drive ended at a path that passed by a peaceful cove to connect with the rest of the residences closer to the point.

Jack's cottage was just on the other side of the cove, and if they stood in their yards, they could yell a conversation at each other across the water.

"Better than Skype," Roxy often said.

"And louder," Hildy would add.

Roxy's three-story cottage was large enough to house an extended family. Something that neither Roxy nor Skye had, the family having dispersed or died out several generations ago.

Like the other beachfront "cottages," the front of the house faced the ocean with a small front lawn of warring zoysia and chickweed that sloped down to a white sand beach. And for the less active, there was a set of wooden stairs a few feet away.

The back side of the house faced the drive with parking slots for family and a guest or two, a main entrance, and a side door that opened directly into the kitchen.

Usually Skye walked around to the kitchen door, passing through Hildy's garden of abundant excess, where vegetables and flowers mixed and tumbled together and made a home to butterflies, bees, and the occasional mosquito.

Tonight Skye knew Hildy would be busy with last-minute preparations, having banished Roxy—who was something of a liability in the kitchen—to another part of the house and out of her way.

So Skye rang the back doorbell and stepped inside.

"I'm here," she called.

Roxy's "Come on in" echoed in her ear, followed by the door to the entryway closet opening and an angular figure unfolding into the hallway. "I swear that closet is getting smaller," Roxy said, straightening to her full height.

Roxy was Skye's mother's older sister. Tall, taunt, and thin, she was the only one of the Kyle family who was a real redhead.

She always wore her hair pulled up but left unattended on the top of her head, whether intentionally or through lack of concern was still a mystery, though she'd been known to call it her Katherine Hepburn look.

"What were you doing in there?" Skye asked, attempting to peer around Roxy's shoulder.

Roxy tossed an old pair of Wellingtons back into the cavernous closet and brushed her hands on her plaid work shirt. "Hildy set me to cleaning out the winter boots and coats to make room for . . ." She trailed off. "I don't mind having Hildy living here. Actually don't tell her, but I love the company. And God knows we can use the money from turning her cottage into an Airbnb.

"And I thank you for the brilliant idea, and helping us get started, but if she thinks I'm going to open *my* home to strangers, she's got another thing coming."

"Is she thinking that?"

"Not exactly, but she said we should be prepared to take in any overflow from Discover It Weekend."

"No, Aunt Roxy. We've got enough places in town on the Where to Stay list, so that should never happen. She's just yanking your chain."

"And she does it so well. I don't know how we've stayed friends for so long."

Hildy stuck her head out of a door down the hall. "My brisket," she said drily and disappeared again.

"She's got you there," Skye said. Hildy and Roxy had been neighbors and friends for decades; total opposites in most things except loyalty and energy. Hildy was short, stocky, and pleasingly soft with hair gone naturally gray and cut to frame her face so as not to get in her way while she gardened and cooked—and did all the domestic chores that she loved and Roxy despised.

"Indeed, and . . ." Roxy cupped her hand to her mouth and shouted, "I don't know what I would do without her, but don't tell her I said that." She dropped her hand and grinned. "I swear we have as much fun as we did as neighbors, and since going into the B and B biz, she's got more interest in life than she's shown since Emmet died.

"So I have to clean out the occasional closet." Roxy shrugged and closed the closet door. "Come on back. I have a nice cab breathing on the porch."

Roxy turned to lead the way, just as car lights flashed in the window by the door. The car came to a stop just outside and two doors slammed.

"Is Hildy expecting guests tonight? Didn't she put a lockbox on her cottage so she wouldn't be bothered by people all the time?"

"Yes, she did," Roxy said. "And they're not due until tomorrow." A knock sounded on the door. "Maybe someone is lost."

Skye stepped out of the way while Roxy went to answer the door.

A young woman stood in the doorway, blond hair making a nimbus of curls against the lowering sun. It was an interesting effect, but it left her face in shadow, making it impossible to see her features.

Roxy opened the door wider. The woman's face came suddenly into view.

And Skye's world went out of focus.

Amy. Skye's half sister. *Little Princess Face.* It's what Skye's father and stepmother called her. Delicate pointed chin, wide blue eyes, slightly turned-up nose. *Little Princess Face.* Skye could choke on the words just thinking about them.

Roxy hadn't moved or managed to say anything.

Amy's gaze flitted from Roxy to Skye and back to Roxy.

"Aren't you going to invite me in?"

Roxy stepped aside.

"Why are you acting so strange? It's me, Amy."

Skye could only think, *Is something wrong with Dad?* Is that why she came?

She must have said the words out loud because Amy's head snapped toward her. "Nothing's wrong. I came to see you. I thought we could be friends again."

Skye was faintly aware of someone still standing outside. Amy must have brought reinforcements.

She stood there looking so eager, so innocent, so clueless that Skye's stomach heaved.

"That's it? You want to be friends? Well, you can turn around and leave. Because no, just no."

And since Amy, as usual, just stood there waiting for things to go her away, Skye turned and walked down the hall, into the kitchen, and out the side door.

"Hey, where are you going?" Hildy asked, a hot Dutch oven held in both hands.

Straight to hell, thought Skye and let the door slam behind her.

Chapter 2

W ell," Roxy said, finally recovering her voice. Really, she must say something. She couldn't very well throw the little troublemaker out on her arse without at least saying hello-goodbye.

What came out was, "You really should have called in advance."

"Why? So you could turn off all the lights and pretend you were on a cruise somewhere?"

"I get seasick. I suppose I should ask you in."

Amy nodded vigorously and turned not to pick up a—dare Roxy think—hostess gift but to motion to someone who had parked his chinos-clad butt against the side of a blue sports car. "It's all right, you can come in."

Before Roxy could form the words, *Don't bother, stay right where you are,* two things happened.

Hildy came out of the kitchen and bulldozed her sturdy little body down the hall toward them. Her cheeks were bright red from the heat of the kitchen or consternation at losing her most complimentary and beloved dinner guest.

The man pushed away from the car, leaned into the back seat, pulled out two suitcases, and sauntered over to the porch.

Roxy frowned at him. Clean-cut, nice looking. More than an Uber driver, less than a husband? Was he backup, love interest, or manipulator-in-chief?

Roxy supposed she should find out.

"Just what's going on?" Hildy demanded, waving her red dishcloth like she was expecting Ferdinand the Bull.

"We appear to have guests."

Hildy pushed the gold-rimmed glasses that had been riding her forehead down to where she could squint at the newcomers.

"Is that—?"

"Skye's half sister, Amy."

"What's she doing here?"

"Haven't a clue. She says she wants to make it up with Skye."

"I'm standing right here," Amy said petulantly.

Hildy blew out air enough to douse a hurricane lamp. "Took her time," she said *almost* under her breath.

By now the man had reached the threshold and took a tentative step into the hallway. He didn't put down the suitcases. Just stood there like a very handsome bellhop waiting for a room number.

Roxy growled; she supposed she would have to put him up, too. If she sent them packing, they'd just get a room in town or out on the highway and be free to wreak havoc without constraint.

And Roxy knew that was exactly what Amy would do. She really would like to believe that the rift between the two sisters—half sisters—could be mended but she didn't see a snowball's chance in hell. Which is what their life would be if Amy was left to run roughshod over them as she had always done.

And now of all times, when the town's future was resting on Skye's Discover It Weekend. Roxy's internal disaster alert erupted.

"You're probably hungry. Why don't you leave the bags here." *While I think.* "Amy, show your friend to the parlor while Hildy and I see if we can rustle up something for you to eat."

It was a stupid and rude thing to say. The house was redolent with the aroma of Hildy's brisket.

Amy's companion half smiled, or maybe it was a smirk, but he slowly lowered the cases to the floor. Stuck out his hand.

"I'm . . . Connor Reid."

Roxy looked at his hand, clean and manicured; she touched her fingertips to it but retracted them before he could shake. He dropped his hand to his side.

"We haven't met before, but . . ."

No, but the name did sound familiar. "Are you one of the Phillip Reids from Newport?" Roxy didn't even know if there were Reids in Newport but she just felt like busting this guy's chops purely for his association with the little termagant he'd accompanied.

Beside her, Hildy sucked in air, possibly the same air she'd just expelled a few seconds before, because it was definitely getting harder to breathe standing here in the hallway.

"It's so good to be back," Amy said and gave Roxy an impulsive hug before trundling Connor Reid down the hall.

Hildy opened her mouth, but Roxy put a finger to her own lips then pointed toward the kitchen door.

As soon as the door shut behind them, Hildy said, "Is that really Amy?"

"Yep. Actually she hasn't changed that much from when she was a five-year-old."

"Well, I wasn't around too often when they were visiting. But I did recognize that boy's name. I'm surprised you didn't." Hildy gave her such a look, the kind of reprimand that only a short person could wield over a tower like Roxy.

"Oh shit," Roxy said. "Connor. *That boy.* I was so shocked to see Amy, and trying to figure out what to do with her, that I totally blanked. Now what do we do?"

"Don't look at me. Why did she bring him? You don't suppose they're a . . . a . . . Lord, I can barely bring myself to say the words. A couple?"

"How could they be?" Roxy asked.

"No wonder Skye's upset," Hildy said. "She stormed through the kitchen with a look I've never seen before; well, at least not for a long time."

"I don't think she even saw him; she barely took in Amy before she bolted."

"Double whammy of nothing good." Hildy glanced over the table at the Dutch oven, covered and sitting on a trivet waiting to be served. She sighed. "I suppose I can set another place at the dining table. Or we can save this until after they leave. I think we have some peanut butter and store bread somewhere."

Roxy cut her friend a surprised look and snorted out a laugh. "Remind me not to ever make you really mad."

"Oh, you do all the time. But I, unlike some people I know, know how to contain myself."

"Very funny."

"Are you going to let them stay?"

"As opposed to letting them have free rein of the town? You know what they say?"

"What?" asked Hildy.

"Keep your enemies closer."

"They, whoever they are, are fools. I'll set another place."

SKYE DIDN'T THINK about where she was going or wonder how she could leave Roxy and Hildy to deal with *her* baggage. They hadn't even known Amy except for a week or two each summer when the "family" deigned to descend on Roxy's hospitality.

It hadn't lasted long since Karen, Amy's mom, and Roxy were at loggerheads from the first day. And soon Skye and her father made the trip alone, until only Skye was sent to spend most of the summer with her mother's sister and by then, Hildy.

Ever since that last horrible year in high school when Skye had run away to Roxy, she'd made a permanent home here, first with Roxy, then after college when she opened Imagine That, in a one-bedroom apartment above the store.

And now, just when she thought she'd left the past behind

her, Amy shows up. Wanting to be friends? Fat chance of that happening.

Why now? When Skye was at her busiest, exhausted with the prep for Discover It Weekend. When her nerves were tight, praying that nothing would go wrong . . .

Something had just gone wrong. Big-time.

Maybe Roxy would get rid of her, though it was selfish to put Roxy in that position. Skye should probably go back, find out why Amy was really here. She hadn't visited since she and her mother had stopped coming for summer vacations. And Skye had made no attempt to change that in the fifteen years she had lived here.

Amy had made a few timid overtures over the years, usually by text, when she graduated from college and needed money, was between jobs and needed money, needed a new car; when her mother, Skye's stepmother, had remarried for the second time and Amy needed money for an apartment. . . .

Skye had always come through, mainly just so Amy wouldn't harass their father.

It hadn't taken Skye's father long after Skye had left home to come to his senses; he'd divorced Karen and left Pennsylvania for Florida. But too late to help Skye. She didn't resent what had happened. Her father, a dreamer, devastated by the loss of his first wife, had taken all his friends' advice. *Skye needs a mother.*

She did, but not Karen Fields.

Skye shook herself as a chill swept through the warm summer air and settled in her bones.

She'd apologize to Roxy and Hildy tomorrow, once Amy was gone. Because surely Roxy would send her packing. Her aunt wore her loyalty on her sleeve as well as in her heart.

Skye risked one look back over her shoulder. The car, some kind of sports model, was still parked at the cottage. Amy must be doing well for herself. It looked expensive.

She turned away, hesitating on whether to take the drive back to town and her friends at the pub. But Maya and Jack would know immediately that something was wrong, no matter how hard Skye tried to hide it. And tonight was Maya and Sonny's night.

And if Skye did that, she might risk running into Amy and her companion on their way out. Of course, if they did leave, she could double back and still enjoy dinner with Roxy and Hildy.

She couldn't take the chance.

Skye headed down the path past the cove to Jack's. She was tempted to text him and ask him to bring her takeout, but she didn't want to cast a damper on the celebration. Maya and Sonny had waited three long years to get pregnant. They should have their moment. Skye should be there with them, not walking alone and angry, running from her half sister, running from the bitter taste of her past.

Skye slowed, realizing that she'd come to the wall where the path overlooked Cove Beach, a small crescent of sand at the base of a scree of boulders. It was a quiet, peaceful place, used mainly for contemplation and fishing since the riptides were often too strong for serious swimming.

Usually when she was passing, she'd stop to sit on the wall to watch the sunset, which was in full progress, the sun blaring its last hurrah before sliding gently behind the sea. But tonight even that couldn't tempt her.

She reached the fork in the path and veered off down the sandy track that led to Jack's front porch.

Jack had inherited the cottage from his grandmother. He had also spent vacations here. There was a paved drive from the main road to the end of the point, but it was way out of the way, so most people just used the path going back and forth to town.

She and Jack must have passed each other's cottage a hundred times back then and yet they had never met. In those days life was lived in the bubble of your own little community. Your side of the cove.

It wasn't until several years ago, when he had moved to the cottage permanently, that they'd met through their mutual friends, Maya and Sonny. The four of them had been inseparable ever since.

Skye was practically running by the time she stumbled up the steps to the porch.

She sat down on the glider. It squeaked as she set it in motion. Across the cove she could see Roxy's kitchen lights on. Were she and Hildy sitting down to brisket? They would have called her if Amy had left. She must still be there with them.

Why? Why now? Why ever?

Skye pushed one foot along the floor, the glider creaking as it moved back and forth, back and forth. The sun went down, and Jack's cottage wrapped its warmth around her.

The cottage itself looked like most of its neighbors, brown shake covered, spacious but cozy. Inside, it was a mixture of old-fashioned granny and sleek modern furnishings. Sort of like Jack himself.

It didn't bother him to watch sports on a state-of-the-art smart TV while he sprawled in a squishy chintz-covered easy chair. He didn't even remove the crocheted doilies until Skye put her foot down and banished them to the linen closet.

The sun went down with Skye thinking about those doilies. She was still sitting there when she saw a light turn on in the living room and she knew Jack was home.

"THAT WAS DELICIOUS, thank you," said Connor Reid with a smile toward Hildy and Roxy. Fortunately Hildy had a rotisserie chicken to replace the brisket she'd planned to serve.

Roxy returned his compliment with a tight smile. He had a charm that was hard to resist even for someone twice his age, like her. She could see why Skye had thought him her soul mate. Just the right mix of intelligence, sociability, and awareness that kept Roxy from tossing him out on his ear. That and the fact that it had become apparent rather quickly that he and Amy were not a couple, at least not a serious one. He seemed to barely tolerate her.

So what exactly was he doing here?

"Coffee?" Hildy suggested. She'd managed to hide the brisket *and* the peach crumble. It was Skye's favorite. They could have store-bought pound cake if they wanted dessert.

"No," said Amy. "I think we'll go into town and check out if there are any decent bars."

"We just polished off a bottle of Ms. Kyle's excellent cabernet," Connor said. "I think that's enough for tonight." He smiled at Amy. "At least for me."

"Oh, you're no fun. I can't imagine why everyone said you were such a free spirit. You're pretty much a stick in the mud as far as I'm concerned."

Roxy began to like Connor Reid a smidgeon more than she had a moment before.

"Most places close early on weeknights until summer is in full swing," Roxy said, lying through her teeth, but she didn't want that girl running around, spreading venom and causing dissension.

"Besides, you probably could use a good night's sleep and get an early start home in the morning," added Hildy innocently. About as innocent as Al Capone's answers about tax evasion.

"I'm not leaving until Skye talks to me," Amy said. "It's not my fault that everyone blamed her for what happened. And it was so long ago nobody remembers it anyway. It's stupid for her to keep punishing me."

"Skye remembers," Roxy said. "So I suggest you just leave well enough alone and go home and get on with your life."

"Why does she blame me? I didn't do anything." Amy sniffed. She seemed close to tears.

Crocodile tears, Roxy reminded herself.

"Maybe because you're the one who accused her of starting the fire."

"Did she tell you that?"

"Yes, and I have no reason not to believe her. But it's water under the bridge, so I suggest you just move on."

"How can I? I can't even walk down the street without people staring at me. The sister of the arsonist."

Before Roxy could point out that she'd just said everyone had forgotten, Connor stood and dropped his napkin on the table. "Oh just shut up, Amy. Go upstairs unless you want to help me with the dishes." He picked up his plate and glass and carried it to the kitchen.

Hildy began collecting plates and silverware and followed him.

"Ugh." Amy scowled and stood up.

Roxy stood, too. "Come get your suitcase and I'll show you to your room. Will you need one room or two?"

"Two," Connor called from the doorway to the kitchen. "Or I can get a room in town."

"That won't be necessary," Roxy said, trying to ignore Hildy's bared teeth behind him.

Not until she found out more about why he was here with Amy and how soon he planned to take her away.

Chapter 3

Skye sat in the darkness wondering if she should tap on the sliding door to get Jack's attention. Or wait until he wandered out onto the porch and let him find her. She suddenly felt unsure of herself. That maybe she'd overreacted seeing Amy and immaturely leaving Roxy and Hildy to deal with the situation.

And she was afraid she might sound whiny and— The door slid open and Jack stepped out. The first thing he did was turn his head and see her sitting on the glider.

"Okay," he said, not moving closer.

"Is that a question?" she asked.

"More like an encouragement for you to explain why you're sitting here in the dark. How long have you been here? Usually Roxy and Hildy keep you late."

"I didn't stay."

Now he crossed to her, eased her feet off the glider, and sat down beside her.

She gratefully snuggled into his outstretched arm.

* * *

JACK WRAPPED HIS arm around Skye's shoulders, lightly, trying not to feed whatever was causing her so much distress. She always amazed him. Lightning on a calm sea, calm waters in a storm. Sometimes fierce in her energy, and sometimes as fragile as a gull's feather. But always trying to be all things to all people.

Now she was still. So still that he could feel her heart beating; occasionally a tremor rolled through her body.

He waited.

And amid the rolling and crashing of the waves below, the rustle of a breeze in the grasses around the cottage, her stomach growled.

"Are you still hungry?"

"Didn't eat."

He turned to face her. "What happened?"

She shook her head slowly as if testing the movement. "You won't believe it."

"Hildy burned the brisket."

Skye laughed softly and settled back into the crook of his arm. Not back to normal but closer.

"I don't think Hildy has ever burned anything in her life."

Another shudder rolled through her and he knew. You didn't normally have to be careful with Skye. She rarely flew off the handle, pouted, or played the poor-me card. She was a force unto herself, sometimes scarily so.

But fire. Just the mention of it—sometimes—could set her off, but not in a panic. Skye never panicked. Never succumbed to hysterics, just a momentary acknowledgment of something in her life not quite reconciled. He knew the story, of course; Skye was nothing if not open. Like the sky.

He cringed at his thinking. She could make him halfway poetical in a clunky, never-should-attempt-it way. If he had any talent at all, it was in his hands.

"It's wonderful about Maya and Sonny," she said.

"Sure is. Maya is over the moon and Sonny's quaking in his boots."

Now she turned to look at him. "Why? I thought he would be ecstatic."

"He is, but he's also worried about another mouth to feed."

"The business is going great."

"Yeah, but those kinds of fears are never totally rational. Having a kid is a big responsibility."

"They'll be great parents." She smiled up at him, heartbreaking in its delight. "And they have a goldendoodle."

"Perfect family."

"Hmm. Amy showed up at Roxy's door tonight."

It took him a while to make the leap. He started to ask who . . . then remembered. *Amy. The half sister.*

"What did she want?"

"To be friends."

Jack barked out a laugh.

Skye's head jerked up.

"Sorry. But a little late." He frowned. "Why now?"

"Just what I've been sitting here wondering."

"I take it Roxy didn't throw her out and that's why you're sitting here unfed."

"I didn't wait to find out. It had been such a great day, and with Maya and Sonny's news and with everything . . . I was so shocked, I just turned around and left." She rubbed her face with both hands, ending with her fingertips resting on her chin like a gesture of prayer. And as far as Jack was concerned, he'd add his to hers.

He'd never met Amy and he could tell Skye was careful not to bad-mouth her sister—Skye had always blamed Amy's betrayal on a lack of judgment, or immaturity, or some other excuse that Jack, not having as optimistic a view of people as Skye, didn't buy for a minute. He thought it might have actually been predicated by pure menace, if not evil.

Of course he'd only advanced that opinion once. Skye's reaction had been swift and strong, and he knew in a flash of understanding that she depended on Amy's actions not being intentional in order to keep that one little window to her family open.

Jack didn't see why it mattered so much. She'd grown up with a stepmother who sounded like something right out of *Desperate Housewives*, not that he actually ever watched the show. And a father who, from all accounts, lived with his head in the clouds and his heart in the past.

A spirit like Skye didn't have a chance in that household. Fortunately, she'd had the courage to chuck it and leave. She found fertile ground to grow in with Roxy. For which Jack, for one, was intensely grateful.

He shifted away from her. "Why don't you call Roxy and find out what's going on, while I find you something to eat."

"I'm not really hungry."

"Well, your stomach is."

He peeled his arm away and stood up, setting off the creak of the glider. He really should get that fixed. He stopped at the doorway. "Call her."

"She'll call me when the coast is clear."

He looked back at her. For a successful, independent, confident thirty-two-year-old, Skye couldn't quite manage to put her family where it belonged. Or at least where Jack thought they deserved to be.

Not that he was a paragon of family forgiveness. He stepped inside and closed the door.

"COULDN'T SLEEP?" ROXY asked when a tousle-haired Connor Reid slipped into the kitchen around midnight. Hildy had just poured them a cup of decaf coffee.

"Not until I knew Amy was asleep," he said. "I thought you deserved an explanation."

"That would be nice," Roxy said. "Care for a cup of decaf or would you prefer something stronger?"

"Stronger, much stronger."

"Oh deary," Hildy said. "I have just the thing." She hurried out of the kitchen.

Connor eyed the closing door suspiciously.

"Don't worry," Roxy said. "What doesn't kill you makes you strong."

"That's very reassuring." He pulled out a chair across the table from her and sat down.

So this was Skye's young Lochinvar. Heavens, he was a good-looking man. But he'd better not be riding to the rescue with Amy, the betrayer, in tow. Skye didn't need to be rescued. Not from here.

Though Roxy had to confess that she was dying to hear Connor Reid's side of the story that had driven Skye from home in the first place, and why he had decided to come now, since he hadn't bothered to communicate with Skye once in all the years since. At least not that Roxy was aware of.

Hildy returned with a bottle of Chivas and a glass that she placed in front of Connor, and another bottle of Tia Maria. "I thought we could use a little help in our coffee tonight."

Roxy slid the bottle closer. "Rather defeats the purpose of decaf," she said and splashed a healthy dollop of the liqueur into her coffee mug.

Hildy sat down and did the same, then both women looked at their guest.

He took a sip and set the glass down. "I know you don't know me."

"You'd be surprised what we know," Roxy said.

Connor glanced up, giving Roxy a sharp, appraising look.

"But you only heard Skye's side of the story."

"We only need Skye's side."

"But are you sure that's where the truth, all the truth, lies?"

Roxy wanted to say, *If you'd found that child, soaked with rain, shivering and hungry, huddled at the kitchen door, you wouldn't have to know anything more.* That was a truth she'd never forget. But she held her tongue. She wasn't about to give either of these interlopers a word of information about Skye.

"Well, I guess that puts you ahead of me," Connor said. "Because I'm still not sure what happened. There seems to be no objective reporting of the actual events of that night."

"Oh, I don't know. I'm pretty sure Skye was around for the repercussions."

"True." He fingered his glass of scotch, stared at it—organizing his thoughts or looking for answers? "She blames me for not being there for her."

"She has every right to."

He shook his head. "I was hoping you'd . . ."

Roxy gave him a look that said her patience was growing short. "Don't tell me I'm prejudiced, I know I am."

"And you won't change our minds," Hildy added.

"I have no intention of doing so. Well, actually . . ." He sucked in a breath, let it out. "Oh hell. Where shall I start?"

Roxy poured herself more Tia Maria, forgoing the coffee this time, then topped off Hildy's. "As tempted as I am to say at the beginning, it's past my bedtime and fifteen years must be a long story. How about what you're doing here with *her*?" Roxy lifted her chin, indicating the Sleeping Beauty upstairs. She knew she wasn't being objective but she collected Social Security; she was now old enough that she didn't have to keep an open mind.

Connor huffed out a quiet sound that might have been a laugh or a sigh. "I work for the State Department."

Hildy's eyes rounded in appreciation; Roxy kneed her under the table.

"I was on leave before my next assignment and decided to pay a visit to my parents.

"I hardly ever get back, but I hadn't been there two days when Amy was knocking on my door. Harrisburg is still a small town and news travels fast.

"She said she was going to make things right with Skye but she needed a ride. And she thought I should go with her.

"I told her no, but the fact is as soon as she mentioned it, I knew I had to come."

"After fifteen years?" Roxy asked incredulously.

"Yes. We—Skye and I—had never . . . I tried to call her, the day after the fire. She wouldn't answer her cell. I didn't know it had been destroyed in the fire. I figured they'd confiscated her phone, because Amy had told on us, that we were planning on running away together. I even called the house phone, but they said she couldn't talk. They meant they wouldn't let me talk to her. I didn't know how bad the fire was or that Amy had accused Skye of starting it.

"And yeah, I was pissed that she didn't find a way of getting in touch. My parents had made me pack for military school that night. We left early the next morning. They'd been planning to send me, but they were so anxious to get me away, I knew they had heard of our plans, too.

"By the time I got home for the holidays, Skye was gone and no one knew where she was."

Roxy snorted.

Connor held up a hand. "No excuses, I know. I tried to set the record straight that Skye and I had been together and seen the fire from the hill above their house. But with Skye gone, it didn't seem to matter. So I went back to school. Then life happened. I saw her social media posts occasionally and I was curious, but I was still upset.

"Coming here was the furthest thing from my mind until Amy showed up at my door and finagled a ride—God, that girl can talk.

"I don't even know why I came. Well, yeah I do. It was a window, and as a diplomat, you take one when it appears whether you're ready or not. I probably shouldn't have come. I just . . . I thought . . . I don't know. I'll try to get Amy to leave in the morning. It's obvious that Skye doesn't want to see me."

"Actually I don't think she saw you at all," Roxy confessed.

IT STARTS AS *a burst of light down the hill below them.*

"What's that?" Skye is frightened, it isn't normal light, not a porch light, not any kind of light that should be there.

"Fire!" she screams and pulls away from Connor. He doesn't let go. They're running away, getting married; no one can stop them. But it's fire below them. She pushes at him. He holds on.

"I have to go," she says, because she knows. Fire. She can see it fully now. Lapping up the side of her father's workshop. "Call the fire department." She screams it, she's afraid the words didn't come out, but Connor is reaching for his cell.

And she is running, tripping, careening down the hill toward the huge torch in the night. Why does no one come out to see?

Her lungs are already seared from the smoke when she reaches the door. Everything her father loves is inside.

"Dad!" She doesn't think. She just has to get inside. She pulls open

the door, burns her hand on the latch. The door whooshes open, knocking her back. The flames leap out to pull her in and she goes.

She can't breathe. Nothing is left, she can't see. The roof falls at her feet, casting molten sparks on her clothes and skin. She backs away. She has no choice. She can't breathe. "Dad!"

She stumbles outside as more building crashes behind her.

Amy, her half sister, is standing on the porch steps to the house.

A car drives up and stops. Their car. Her dad and stepmother jump out and run toward her.

Amy runs toward her. "She did it, she did it. She tried to kill Daddy." Amy is pointing at her.

"No," Skye yells over the roar. "It wasn't me."

But no one listens. She can hear the fire engine's siren in the distance. It's too late. Too late.

And her dad does nothing.

Someone is pulling her away. Yelling "Put it down." She is clutching a metal engine in her hand. Her father's prize collectible. "Put it down!" But she can't let go. It's fused to her palm.

Someone is holding her.

"Skye. It's okay. Just a dream."

Arms fold her in, pull her close, so familiar. So safe.

"Connor?" Skye whimpers.

She opened her eyes.

Jack.

Chapter 4

Jack had left for work by the time Skye's phone woke her at seven the next morning. She vaguely remembered him leaving, even more vaguely remembered the nightmare. She didn't have them often, so she could lay this one squarely at Amy's feet.

She knew dreams were not really about what they portrayed, but merely symbols of something else, or just random stray images that hadn't been filed in their appropriate memory cells. But fire did play a major role in her nightmares and for a real reason.

Skye replayed that gut-wrenching panic of looking down the hill to see her father's workshop on fire and thinking he might be inside. Her father had always been a little different. A dreamer, Aunt Roxy said. Eccentric was the general opinion.

To Skye he was quiet, self-effacing, except when he was in his workshop, where he spent hours with model trains. He provided for his second wife and his children, but he was only really himself when among his trains.

Skye thought they were magical. Not the trains themselves, but what they did to her dad's persona. It was his escape. From a world that had taken his first love from him and that offered no comfort in return. Skye loved spending time in the workshop; Amy thought the trains were boring, didn't like the musty oily smell that permeated the air, but still resented Skye for the time she spent there.

It was only after the fire that Skye learned that he'd stored all her mother's things in a locked storeroom at the back of the workshop. He'd always told them it was locked because it contained dangerous chemicals, but outside of a canister of spray oil and some paint thinners, the fire department found no combustibles anywhere in the workshop.

Skye touched her palm, the outline of the metal engine etched indelibly into her skin.

Enough. She slipped out of bed, quickly made it up, and hit the shower. There was a store to open, work on the retreat to be done, a prodigal half sister to send on her way. Busy day ahead.

When she opened Jack's closet, she realized that her clothes were quickly taking over. She decided not to theorize about what that might mean. She dressed in her daily uniform, a pair of black, stretch ankle trousers, added a gray heather tee over a persimmon tank top that she found in "her" drawer.

She pulled her hair back in a ponytail, taking a minute to look at it, straight and sort of dishwater blond with only a hint of her mother's auburn and none of Roxy's red. Amy was a true blonde with curls like her mother, Karen, which was fine with Skye. No one was ever confused about whose mother was whose.

And Amy resented that, too.

Skye grabbed a deconstructed jacket, sent a quick text order to Main Street Coffee Connection, and headed out the door.

TEN MINUTES LATER, carrying a superlarge sweet coffee and an egg white and avocado bagel, Skye unlocked the front door to Imagine That.

"I'm back here," Maya called from the depths.

Skye went to the back to the small receiving room where Maya was standing behind the counter unloading a box of an alternative publisher's children's books.

"You didn't lift that, did you?" Skye admonished.

Maya threw up her hands and looked at the ceiling. "Don't you start, too. Sonny's already acting like an overbearing mamma. I'm four months, what will be will be." Skye glanced automatically at Maya's belly, but with her tunic falling in soft folds it was impossible to see if there was a baby bump yet.

"Well, just tell me if it gets to be too much; I don't want to be on Sonny's bad influence list."

Maya laughed. "He'll calm down as soon as he gets used to the idea." She looked down at the box. "At least I hope he does. He's already talking about me quitting."

Skye waited for the wave of panic to pass. "Well, it's important to take care of yourself, but you should also have a say in how to live going forward."

"Exactly what I told him. Now, don't worry."

Skye opened the tab on her coffee cup. "I wasn't sure if you were doing caffeine. Do you want some?"

"No. Coffee and me haven't been the best of friends lately."

Skye parked one hip on the desk. "How did I not notice this?"

"Maybe because you've been really busy. In fact, you look exhausted this morning. Maybe *you're* doing too much."

"Nah, not me."

"Okay, full disclosure. Sonny called."

"And?" Skye asked.

"Jack told him that Amy showed up at Roxy's house last night."

Skye sighed. "And he told Sonny to call and make sure I hadn't fallen apart?"

"No-o-o. He told Sonny she was here, and Sonny took it on himself to call and give me a heads-up. You're very good at taking care of everyone and pushing yourself to last."

"I apologize to Jack in absentia. He's very good about not . . ." Skye shrugged. "Encroaching? No, that's not what I mean."

"You mean becoming a total part of your life."

"No, I don't."

"Do you love him?"

"What? Sure. I mean, we have a sort of something that works for us."

"Oh ick, that is the most noncommittal answer I've ever heard."

"I've got a lot on my plate these days. Can we just leave Jack nicely in place?"

"Sure, he said the same thing to Sonny."

"How come you know everything that Jack says to Sonny, but I don't know anything about what Sonny says to Jack?"

Maya opened her eyes wide, shrugged. "Think about it. You both keep your own counsel. But now tell me about Amy."

"Hopefully Roxy sent her home. If not, I'll deal with her. Now it's after nine. Shall we set up the blue studio for the Change Your Space class?"

"Penny came in early to set up, because she had a dentist appointment but said she was sure she'd be back by ten."

Penny, a formerly shy preteen, had learned her activity chops as a kid in the Imagine That Build a Story hour.

Now a junior in high school, she ran that group and helped out in the other activities. She had blossomed from a blushing, stammering tween into an enthusiastic facilitator as well as arbiter of the inevitable spats and "stupids" that occasionally cropped up.

Penny came in ten minutes before ten, and at ten they opened the doors to eight excited eight- to ten-year-olds. Smocked them up. Showed them the materials they would have at their disposal for changing their space. Held them back to recite the only rules. "Share. Don't judge. Help others."

And they were off. Some to grab chunks of washable chalk, some to choose skeins of colorful yarn, others to use the geometric rubber shapes to make things that sometimes had no recognizable geometry.

Skye left Maya and Penny to it and went into her office, hardly larger than a closet but where she could work and watch out for customers who came into the book and toy side of Imagine That.

She had about twelve minutes before they began to pour in

and she left her office to help out. It was still early enough in the summer for parents and children to be looking for things to occupy their time when they weren't at the beach or involved in all the other activities that beckoned to them.

Soon, several children were sitting on beanbag chairs reading. Two puzzle tables were occupied. And several mothers stood around the new books table discussing things that mothers discussed when their children were happily occupied.

Some left a few minutes later without purchasing anything, but that was okay. That was the point. Enough people made purchases to augment the income of the workshops and make IT and IT2 profitable while still managing to employ a handful of local residents and contribute to the town's occasional fund drives.

Skye had just found a paper airplane activity book for a father when the door opened. She glanced up to see who had entered. And froze.

Amy stood just inside, not bothering to close the door, and in her mind, Skye heard her stepmother, Karen, saying, *Do you want to cool the whole county?*

She finally closed the door and Skye made a beeline for her half sister.

Seeing Skye's intentions, Amy veered off to the side and ended up at a row of books on climate.

Skye came up beside her. "Please, this is a place of business and I really need you to leave."

"Is this your store?" she asked, in a voice that made heads turn. "It's so cute!"

Not exactly what Skye was going for, but at least Amy was being positive.

"Is that story hour?" She slipped past Skye. "I used to love those."

Skye hurried after her. "It's also a quiet place," she said and diverted Amy away from the children, who had all turned their heads to see what was happening.

"It doesn't sound like it. What's happening back there?" Amy plowed toward the door to Imagine That Too.

"It's where we hold activity classes."

"There's more?" Amy slipped past her and strode through the connecting door.

Maya shot Skye a concerned look.

At least Amy is out of the store, Skye thought, hurrying after her. "Amy, stop."

Amy *had* stopped at the door of the Change Your Space session.

"Oh, my God. What a mess. What are they supposed to be doing?"

Several kids turned to look.

"They're inventing a new space."

Amy rolled her eyes. "It looks like they're making a mess to me. Is that girl in charge? You should get someone better at keeping order."

Penny heard her and red suffused her face.

"She's the best," Skye said, her teeth clenched so tight that her jaw hurt.

Amy cocked one hip to the side with an *oh, please* expression that erased fifteen years and brought out the worst of Skye's feelings.

"Okay, that's it. Out." Skye gestured to the door.

Amy crossed her arms. "Not until you talk to me."

Skye didn't answer, just grabbed Amy's elbow and pulled her out of the room and into the hallway toward the back delivery door.

"I was just trying to help."

"No, you weren't, Amy. You just know how to hurt people and make things harder. I don't know why you decided to come here now. But I'm not going to talk to you. We are not ever going to be friends. It is what it is. Accept it."

"Why is everyone always against me?"

Skye had to force her eyes not to start spinning like cherries on a slot machine. "No one's against you. I just need to run my business and you're preventing it. I'll escort you to the door, and no scene, please."

Amy just stood there.

"I would hate to have to call the police."

Amy's mouth fell open. "You'd do that?"

Skye would like to dump her out back in the alley but couldn't bring herself to stoop that low. She steered her toward the front door.

They'd attracted the attention of the mothers and several of the children.

"Do not say another word," Skye said under her breath. She could feel the atmosphere of the space being tainted by the tension between the two of them.

Just as Skye and Amy reached the door, it opened and a man stepped inside. He stopped abruptly.

"I'm so sorry," Skye began, smiling at the newcomer. "I didn't mean t—" The rest of her sentence died midword.

Amy took the opportunity to shake off Skye's grip.

"I—" the man began. It was as far as he got.

Skye just stared, not quite believing her own eyes. It was him. Connor. After all these years. Here . . . with Amy? Why? *Connor.* It was as if she'd conjured him in her dream.

"Sorry. I . . . uh . . . I'll take her." He took Amy's arm and catapulted her out the door. The door closed behind them with Skye standing there still trying to find her voice.

The store had become very quiet; now it erupted back into sound and Skye breathed at last.

She turned to see everyone in the store watching her. She pasted on a smile. Shrugged. Hopefully indicating *It takes all kinds.* Her knees were wobbly, her stomach sick, and her ears jarred by the sound of glass breaking. Fortunately it was meta-phorical glass, an easy cleanup.

Skye almost laughed and knew she needed to get to the back, regroup. But not in a rush. Take it slow. Calmly. She made herself stop by the reading area, ask the kids how they liked the books they were reading. Stepped through the door into the hallway and peeked into the activity room where geo-metric palm trees, dinosaurs, ice cream cones filled the walls.

Jordan Ramey, a seven-year-old regular, held several balls of yarn. More yarn stretched across the room wall to wall in a cat's cradle of multicolors.

"Wow," Skye said.

Jordan shuffled over trailing yarn behind him. His eyes were bright with accomplishment.

"You know how space is made up of energy, but you can't see it?"

Skye nodded, wondering where this was going.

"This is the energy you can't see," Jordan explained. "But now you can."

"I see," Skye said in an awestruck voice.

Jordan laughed. "It's cool, isn't it?"

"Very cool," Skye agreed and backed out of the room.

The energy you can't see. But now you can. This is why she'd worked so hard to get the two Imagines up and running. This is why she was dedicating an entire weekend for family discovery.

She was tired but stoked, stressed but excited. And she didn't need her aggrieved half sister hijacking her life. And she certainly didn't need Connor Reid . . . at all.

It seemed like eons before Skye at last sat down in her desk chair. Her brain didn't seem to be able to put a logical explanation together. Amy *and* Connor? Maybe the man with Amy just looked like Connor might have looked. Perhaps she'd been mistaken, like a bad dream where nothing was what it should be. Maybe she was still dreaming. A couple of well-placed pinches convinced her that this was real.

Connor Reid had come to her door. To get Amy. Without a word of explanation. Not even a *Nice to see you.*

Maya poked her head in the door. "Are you okay?"

Skye slowly nodded. She wasn't really, which was stupid.

Connor and Amy were her past, not her present, and certainly not her future. She needed to be okay. "I guess."

Maya slipped in and closed the door. "That was Amy? What an obnoxious little twit. I was about to call Sonny to come and evict her when her husband—boyfriend?—came in. Poor guy. I don't know how he stands her."

Skye didn't, either. "It was Amy, but it's worse." Skye picked up her coffee cup. The coffee was cold. She drank it anyway.

"All right. Get your nose out of that cup and tell me what's wrong. You can't be that upset just because she was mildly disruptive this morning. Jordan said she wasn't 'woke.' I managed not to comment."

"That Jordan," Skye said. "What a unique kid."

"So are you worried?"

Skye sighed. "Of course I'm worried. I thought last night's dream was bad, but I just experienced my worst nightmare ever."

"Amy? She's not going to try to cause trouble, is she?"

"She already has."

"Maybe you should have a word with the guy she's with. Explain to him that she has problems with you."

Skye shook her head.

"Why not? He seemed perfectly rational, even if he is her boyfriend."

Skye sucked in a breath. "That guy might be her boyfriend now, might even be her husband for all I know, but he was *my* best friend—I thought my soul mate—until he let me crash and burn."

Maya's jaw slackened and her hand went to her belly. "That's Connor?"

Skye nodded.

"Oh my—you didn't tell me he'd come, too."

"I didn't know."

"Holy moly, what does it mean?"

"I have no idea, but it isn't good."

"WHY DIDN'T YOU wake me up?" Roxy said as she poured out two mugs of coffee.

Hildy looked up from the flowers she was arranging in a white milk jug. "I was in the garden picking some flowers to put in the guesthouse. The tenants will be here this afternoon," Hildy said. "Besides, I thought you were up."

"Well, you shouldn't have gone out without making sure."

Hildy snatched the safari hat that she used for gardening from the table where she'd just tossed it. Shoved it on her head and marched toward the side door.

"Where are you going? I thought you wanted coffee."

"I do but without your attitude." The door slammed.

"Then I'll drink them both," Roxy yelled after her. She shouldn't have brought out the Tia Maria last night. She had the devil of a hangover and that was so not age appropriate.

Her cell rang. She reached in her shirt pocket. Lifted one hip, checked her khakis pocket, looked around the table. It kept ringing. She saw it by the coffeepot.

She lunged and snatched it from the counter, just as it stopped ringing.

Skye.

Roxy carried the phone back to the table, took a couple of sips of coffee while she wondered if Skye was calling for an update, or whether Skye was about to give her one. She hoped for the former. Only one way to find out.

Skye answered before Roxy could even take her finger off the screen.

"What the hell is going on?" Skye demanded.

"Is that the way I taught you to answer the phone?"

"You didn't teach me to answer the phone. But I'm sorry. It's just I can't believe they're still here."

"I take that to mean Amy sussed you out, and you found out Connor was here. That's on me. I indulged in the Tia Maria last night and overslept."

"What? You mean they stayed with you and Hildy?"

"Yes, did you want them running around town without leashes?"

"It didn't really prevent her from showing up at Imagine That this morning being totally rude to the children, raising eyebrows from the parents, until Connor appears in the doorway and, without even saying *long time no see*, hauls her out to the sidewalk."

"Good boy," Roxy said and reached for her coffee.

"He's not a good boy. He's a grown man and there's nothing to say he's even good."

"Fine. You want me to kick them out? Knowing Amy she'll just find another place to stay. And I had a long talk with Connor last night, hence the Tia Maria. You can ignore Amy, but *him* you should talk to."

"I won't. There's no going back. It's over. I won't be dragged back into it again."

"Suit yourself, but you may not have a choice."

"I can't."

"It's all right, Skye. Now I've got to go apologize to Hildy before she digs up all the carrots."

"Apologize? Did you have a fight?"

"We don't fight. We kerfuffle. But this one's on me. Try not to worry. And I'll see what we can do."

Roxy ended the call, poured out two mugs of fresh coffee, and shouldered her way through the kitchen's screen door. She could see Hildy stooped over the early zinnias.

She reluctantly walked through the row of tomato plants toward her old friend.

God, she hated having to apologize. She didn't do it very well. But she'd learned a long time ago it was best just to eat crow with the people you cared about. If you didn't, you ended up eating alone.

Chapter 5

J ack put down the sanding block and pulled off his protective goggles. "I need breakfast."

Sonny looked up from the pieces of a drawer frame he'd been dovetailing together. "I'm glad you suggested it. I'm starving." He finished adjusting the frame and stood upright and stretched. "I swear Maya's pregnant, but I'm the one gaining weight and getting backaches."

Jack laughed. "Sympathy symptoms?"

"I guess. But it's pretty nutty. Just stop me if I start ordering pickles and ice cream."

"I don't think women really do that," Jack said and held the door open for Sonny to pass.

"Hell, how would you know?"

Jack shrugged. "Just what my mother used to say."

They cleaned up, walked through the showroom, a mixture of cabinetry examples along one wall and a museum display of furniture for sale taking up the center of the converted warehouse space. They didn't have a lot of walk-in traffic. Their furniture was handcrafted and expensive and their cabinets were custom-made. But there had definitely been an uptick since Skye had convinced the town to install plaques at each corner advertising the businesses that were located off Main Street.

Jack turned over the BACK IN A FEW sign and they stepped out into the sunshine.

"Millie's?" Jack asked as Sonny locked the front door.

"Yep."

Millie's Luncheonette was half a block away on Main and was their go-to place for breakfast. It had fed the residents of Sunny Point for a good thirty years, and Jack had been coming since he'd been a boy visiting his grandmother for the summer.

Jack and Sonny stopped just inside the door to read the day's specials on the chalkboard. Millie as usual had the air conditioning pumping to arctic freeze. "You wouldn't complain about the cold if you were standing over a grill twelve hours a day," she would say when any of them mentioned it. Of course it was Millie's husband, Vinnie, who stood over the grill, and Millie wanted to keep him happy. Both as a cook and a husband.

And as long as their "home-cooked" breakfast came out hot and delicious, nobody complained.

"Ummm," Sonny said, studying the menu. "Breakfast pizza or blueberry whole-grain pancakes?"

"Good morning," said a bright chipper voice behind them.

Jack and Sonny turned as one person and frowned at Leanne, Millie and Vinnie's oldest daughter and single mother of two, who never meant to have to wait tables for a living, and didn't like it all that much.

"Good morning?" Jack returned. Usually you had to go through physical gyrations to get her to bring menus and coffee.

Leanne moved closer to them. "There's something weird going on over there in booth two."

"You're having a problem with a customer?" Jack asked.

Beside him, Sonny puffed up his chest and perused the room.

"Not exactly, but they're saying some things. . . . Well, she's saying some things and he's trying to shut her up but . . . but it sounds like maybe they're talking about—I don't know. You listen and see if you think it's weird." Then she said in a louder voice. "This way, please."

"As if we can't remember how to get to the same booth we've been sitting in for years," Sonny said.

But instead of leading them to their regular booth near the back, Leanne plunked two menus down on the first booth near the entrance.

Jack got a brief glimpse of a young blond woman with a heart-shaped face and big blue eyes before he sat down. He couldn't see much of her companion.

Leanne waited for them to sit down, then surreptitiously pointed to the booth behind them and mouthed, *They're right there.* And went off to get them coffee.

Sonny looked a question at Jack. Jack shrugged, he had no idea. But on the other hand, maybe he did. Jack had never met Skye's half sister before, hadn't even seen a photo of her except online. But he was pretty sure she was sitting in the next booth.

". . . hated my father for marrying my mom. Resented me being born. Always resented me, you know that."

"No, I don't know that; it's your own twisted sense of self-worth."

"That's why she did what she did."

"She didn't do anything," the man said.

"She did. She had a fight with him that morning because you two were planning on running off together."

"Which you made sure to tell him," the man said.

"So. Someone had to warn him. And then she did what she always did, got back at him."

Leanne came back with two mugs and a coffeepot. She poured out the coffee, leaning over the table to make a face at Jack. He shook his head at her and she retired to watch from the counter where Rhoda Sims was having her daily Danish and coffee.

"Lower your voice," the man said. He lowered his until he was practically hissing. "That's so much bullshit and you know it. If you just conned me into bringing you here so you could throw out more false accusations, then we're leaving today."

"She could have killed him." The woman's voice was tearful and Jack didn't believe her emotion for a second. "I bet she wished she had."

"Give it a rest, Amy,"

Jack and Sonny exchanged looks. Definitely Skye's sister, and Jack was getting a sinking feeling about who the guy might be.

"How long can you keep harping on the past? She didn't set that fire. . . ."

"Yes she did, I saw her."

"You mistook what you saw or else you're lying about it. Have lied about it all along. She didn't do it. I know she didn't because she was with me, and we saw the flames together. I was the one who called the fire department."

Jack froze, his hand gripping the coffee mug so tightly that he could have crushed it to smithereens. *Aw jeez. Shit.* It *was* Connor. The man whose name Skye had whispered in her sleep last night. She hadn't mentioned he was here, too.

And Jack grew cold inside. With rage and maybe just a bit of *holy shit, that's what I'm up against.*

"You're lying. She could always twist you around her little finger."

"Didn't we just have this conversation? Five hours of it. I'm done. I should never have let you talk me into coming. It was a stupid idea. And if you think you're going to screw up Skye's life now, I won't let you."

"What the hell?" whispered Sonny.

Jack twisted around, trying to get a better glimpse of the people sitting in the booth behind them.

Leanne came up with their breakfast, and they both jumped like guilty schoolboys.

She slid their plates in front of them. "You know those two?" she asked, careful to keep her voice down.

Sonny shook his head. Jack didn't know what to think.

"Well, I'm going to find out." Leanne hefted her coffeepot and put on a smile as she moved to the next booth.

"Wait," Jack hissed, but Leanne moved on to the booth behind them.

"What's going on?" Sonny mouthed.

"Care for more coffee?" Leanne said brightly.

Jack pressed back against the upholstery to hear better. Sonny leaned across the table until his shirt was in danger of being covered with his breakfast pizza.

"You folks staying in town or just passing through?"

"Just—" The man's—Connor, Jack reminded himself—next word was cut off.

"We're here visiting my sister," Amy said. "Maybe you know her. Skylar Mackenzie."

"Skye? Of course. Everybody knows Skye." Leanne's enthusiasm was going over the top and into red alert. Leanne could go from *I'm your best friend* to a right hook in the winking of an exclamation point. "You're Skye Mackenzie's sister?"

Half sister, Jack thought just as Connor Reid said, "Half sister." At least they both seemed to feel the same way about Amy—but what about Skye?

"Well, you must be *very* proud of her. She's the heart and soul of this community. We just love her to pieces."

"Oh, I don't doubt it," Amy said. She sounded positive and innocent, but Jack stiffened for the rest. Because he knew better. He might not have met her, but if the things Skye told him were even a quarter true, he knew her.

"She's always so likable, helpful, charming, and useful . . . She's been trying to get me to visit for ages. But I just can't get away from the office."

"Could we have our check, please?" Connor's voice.

"So she's made friends here . . ." Amy continued.

"Why wouldn't she?" Leanne asked, a bite to her voice that had made grown men quake in their coffee mugs.

"No reason," Amy said in a singsong kind of voice that made Jack's skin creep. "It's just—"

"Are you finished?" Connor asked. "Grab that last piece of toast, Amy, you can eat it on the way."

"But I'm not—"

Jack could see Leanne take a step back, but she couldn't resist cutting a look toward Jack and Sonny.

"I was just going to say that she has a hard time making friends," Amy continued. "You're always taking her side."

Jack assumed this was directed to Connor. Why was he with her? Had he traded in one sister for the other? That didn't sound like the person Skye had told him about. And she *had* told him about Connor. Which had made him think their teenage love affair was long over; now he wasn't so sure.

"I'm not the one with a problem," Amy continued. "I know firsthand—"

"Okay, that's it."

Leanne took a sudden step back as Connor Reid surged from the booth. He was tall. Not as tall as Jack. Lean. Not as muscular as Jack. Perfectly trimmed black hair. Jack pushed his own overlong hair back from his face. Strong jaw, damned good-looking. Stylish. Of course he would be.

Leanne certainly thought so the way she was staring at him.

Connor reached in his back pocket, took out his wallet, and placed a bill on the table.

Jack was on his feet before he thought of the ramifications.

"What are you doing?" Sonny hissed. "Sit down."

Jack sat. What was he doing? Was he going to confront Connor Reid here in the diner and say what?

"Get your purse; we're leaving." Connor didn't wait for a reply but strode to the cash register where Deni Inglath stood ready to take his credit card.

It seemed that Connor's voice had gotten the attention of the entire place. All heads were turned toward the door.

Amy took her time about getting out of the booth, straightening her shorts, sashaying past their booth, slowing down just long enough to give Sonny a flirtatious smile, then she continued on her way.

As soon as Amy reached Connor, he took her firmly by the elbow. No one lifted a hand to stop him and the door slowly closed behind them.

Leanne put her coffeepot on the table, then shooed Sonny over, before sliding in beside him. "Holy moly, what a nasty little . . . I can't say what I really think or Rhoda Sims would give me a supreme lecture about cursing in a place of business. Here she comes now."

Rhoda Sims had had coffee and a Danish at the same counter stool at the same time every morning except Sunday for as long as Jack had been coming in and probably long before. She took exactly thirty minutes every day—nineteen minutes to eat, leaving one minute to pay her bill, and the other ten for the walk to and from the First Baptist Church, which was several blocks away and where she'd been secretary for decades.

She was nice, but punctilious, and frowned on anyone who

talked too loud, used vulgarity, or didn't act appropriately, which was most of the town in Rhoda's mind. She turned a disapproving eye on the three of them before sliding off the counter stool and making a brief stop at their booth.

"Did I hear right? That was Skye's sister?"

Jack and Sonny said nothing. "Seems so," Leanne said.

"What a pretty young lady. I'm sorry I didn't have a chance to say hello." Rhoda gave them a tight smile before continuing on to the cashier.

Leanne made a face at her back, then turned back to Jack and Sonny. "Okay, call me a gossip, but what does Skye's sister think she did that we don't know about?"

Sonny looked at Jack.

Jack just shrugged, no way was he going to get into that fight. "No idea." Skye and her father had come to an understanding several years ago. And it didn't need to be drudged up all over again.

"Well, somebody oughta tell her to put a sock in it. She won't find any traction in this town."

Millie came out of the kitchen on that pronouncement and made one of her own. "Leanne, table four's breakfast is waiting."

"Oh shit," Leanne said, clapped her hand over her mouth, slid out of the booth, picking up the coffeepot along the way, and hurried back to the food window.

She came back balancing four plates and narrowly missing Herb Pritchard, who was making his way toward the cashier, and whose rambling, dilapidated family camp was being used as the venue for Skye's Discover It Weekend.

Herb nodded as he passed Jack and Sonny.

"Morning, Herb," Jack said.

Herb grunted and shuffled up to the cash register.

Jack really wished he'd just sold the damn camp and retired before the chamber of commerce had talked Skye into using it as her home base instead of the nature conservancy a few miles away.

The chamber's board thought using a venue adjacent to town would help boost the town's economy. And God knew they could use it. But Jack was afraid it was going to be more expensive to "spruce up a bit" than to pay the hefty rental fee for the conservancy.

The camp had stopped functioning as a family vacation spot years before. And Jack was pretty sure the costs that the discovery weekend and the chamber of commerce had assumed in exchange for the "rent free weekend" were already over budget.

But that was Skye. Always looking toward the greater good. And Jack was hit by a sense of needing to protect her so intense that it scared him.

She was more than capable of taking care of herself. But damn, the weekend was her idea, her project, and she didn't need to be hampered by a struggling town with a flagging economy and an old man who had given up trying to keep up years before.

Herb, who had been hard enough to convince in the first place, was still skittish about running into more debt and not being able to sell. But after Amy's display this morning, would he get cold feet? How much had he heard? How much could he have understood? And how much would he believe?

"So that's Amy Mackenzie," Sonny said, tearing off a piece of his breakfast pizza and losing a piece of egg, mushroom, and bacon on the way to his mouth.

"Yeah," Jack said.

"Did Skye invite her?"

"No."

"Didn't think so." Sonny washed his bite down with a gulp of coffee. "Then what's she doing here?"

"Doing what she does best," Jack said. "Causing trouble."

CONNOR MARCHED AMY down the sidewalk.

He'd known this was a rotten idea from the get-go. He also knew that Amy was determined to make the trip and he couldn't let her go alone. He, arrogantly as it turned out, thought he could facilitate the meeting of the two sisters. It's what he did. Rising in the ranks of the diplomatic service so quickly must have addled his brain. Because so far this was a disaster.

And all his experience hadn't been any help at all.

After the six-hour drive of Amy talking and harping and whining nonstop, he'd been ready to dump her by the side of the road.

Pretend she's a country, he told himself after the first hour. But he already knew that the *Let's see if we can find common ground idea* was not going to work.

Skye was a dreamer, a doer, an imaginer; optimistic and freewheeling. She was pretty enough, smart enough in school, ordinary to most people, but not to Connor. Her mind was a fertile playground. And when her face lit up with an idea or an escapade you could see the light, be energized by *her* energy; she could become the brightest star in the firmament.

Amy had always been the pretty one, dressed and pampered by her mother, and given everything she could possibly want. And it was never enough, as if she were built with a hole somewhere that siphoned off every positive thing and left her hungry and resentful.

Connor would kid and say Skye always dressed like Cinderella before the ball. She didn't, or at least she didn't have to, but she wore crazy combinations of clothes because she liked the colors, or they were comfortable. She seemed so powerful to him, not needing the attention of her stepmother, or her father, who was a remote being, living in his own head without much interest—it seemed to Connor—in his family.

Unlike Connor's own father, who was determined to shape him up and ship him off to a military career. Skye was like a breath of freedom, a grand adventure, and he loved her with all his heart and soul. His family forbade him to see her, like it was the 1800s or something. It just made him want her more. He and Skye had planned to elope, but the morning after the fire, his parents had driven him off to military school, only telling him that Mr. Mackenzie had not been in the building. He'd tried to call Skye before he left, but her cell was turned off. Probably confiscated by the stepmother, whom he'd come to hate on Skye's behalf.

"So? You're giving me the silent treatment now?"

Connor started. He'd forgotten Amy was walking beside

him. He was still holding her by the arm, propelling her along, and he didn't even have an idea of where they were, since he'd been deep in the past.

Amy sniffed and yanked her arm away just as he saw his rental car ahead. He didn't try to stop her. He'd agreed to drive her, and now that they were here, he didn't know how to make her leave.

Mr. Quick-Thinking, Glib-Tongued, Up-and-Coming Junior Attaché had bungled this assignment big-time. He'd had better results with tribal water rights.

It wouldn't take Amy long to figure out that maybe Connor's coming hadn't been all about keeping the peace but about seeing Skye, and she would be doubly hurt and feel betrayed. Because nothing seemed able to assuage her need for whatever it was that she needed.

The body count was bound to start piling up.

"And you let that waitress be rude to me and you didn't do anything about it."

Connor stayed mum. It didn't work to try to explain things to Amy; it only made her more desperately vindictive. Twenty-six and lost as surely as if she were in the desert without a compass.

And now that he thought about it, maybe she was. However, what she needed was a therapist, not a diplomat. Maybe he should call her mother and have her come get her. Of course Karen had remarried and moved to Palm Springs. About as far as she could get from Harrisburg. Even she didn't seem to have much interest in her only daughter.

Connor slowed down as they neared the BMW. Amy had managed to sneak out of the house this morning even though he'd been determined not to let her go anywhere alone. He'd been so freaked to find her gone that he'd jumped in the car and driven the few blocks straight into town. It took him a few minutes to locate Skye's store, Imagine That, and another couple of minutes to find a parking place.

"You drove into town?" she said incredulously, ending the sentence in a big eye roll to let him know what she thought of that.

"Look, I have some work to do; why don't you take the keys, go out to the mall? We passed a pretty big one a few miles back on the highway. Then I'll take you over to Newport tonight for dinner."

Amy settled into one hip and gave Connor a look.

She was really pushing it, and he was holding on to his finely controlled temper with difficulty. He pulled out his wallet and slid out a bill. "Take this."

She just looked at it. "A hundred? What can you buy with a hundred dollars?"

"Well, you're nuts if you think I'm giving you my credit card. Don't you have any money?"

She pouted her lips and shook her head.

And damn if he didn't feel sorry for her. Not for not having money, she probably did. And not because she looked so forlorn. He wasn't falling for that. But because she thought she had to. Poor girl was willing to go through all sorts of gyrations for . . . what? Control? One-upmanship? Attention?

What the hell. Anything for a couple hours of peace and time to figure out what came next. He went to extract another hundred; changed his mind. "Fine, you can window-shop." He started to put the bill back in his wallet, but she snatched it out of his hand. Relieved him of the keys and jumped into the car.

The engine started, and just as he began to have second thoughts, she said, "Ciao," swerved the car into the street and sped away.

Connor breathed a sigh of relief. He figured he'd have at least a few hours before being back on duty. He'd like nothing more than to give Amy a one-way ticket anywhere, just to give himself some peace and save Skye from having to put up with her nonsense. But that would really enrage Amy and cause further resentment. *Be the facilitator not the impediment*, he reminded himself.

For better or worse, he was stuck with her, and for what? To facilitate the sisters' reconciliation? If he was truthful—and he tried to be—he thought Skye was better off without Amy in her life. He'd agreed to drive her because he'd needed to see Skye. He was the one who needed reconciliation. Maybe more than just reconciliation.

He'd pictured this first meeting so many times in so many ways. None of them included him, shocked and tongue-tied, standing next to the one person he should never have been seen with.

He needed to figure out how to get Amy back home where she belonged. As for himself, Connor had no intention of leaving before he'd had a chance to make up with Skye.

Chapter 6

Skye managed to keep busy and her mind mostly off Amy. Though she had to admit curiosity was beginning to overpower her shock at seeing Connor again. How awkward was that? Face-to-face and then he was gone.

By the time the Change Your Space class finished for the day and was documented by copious photos, Skye was fidgeting with unease.

She had the biggest event of her life coming up in several weeks, and she needed all her attention and energy focused on making it a success. The whole town was depending on her.

She didn't have time to deal with Amy—or Connor—right now. She knew one day she would have to deal with Amy. But not today. Skye had hoped that as Amy matured she would change, but her behavior in the store today had disabused Skye of that notion. Selfish, spoiled, and still blaming others for her lack of whatever, she'd managed to sabotage the peace of Imagine That within two minutes of coming in.

Never once had Amy approached her with *Let's talk* or *What really happened?* Or *Sorry, I jumped to conclusions.* Or to just tell the truth, which Skye was afraid might be the reality, *I hated you, so I lied.*

But Connor. He'd been the last person in the world Skye ever thought to see again. Why now? Why ever? Why with Amy? The same questions ran over and over in her mind. Without an answer in sight.

Skye had struck him off her list of people she could trust years ago. And yet she had to admit she had a desperate need to know why he had come.

She'd learned along the way that he hadn't really betrayed her. According to her dad, when he'd come home for Thanksgiving vacation and heard what had transpired, he'd attempted to set the record straight. But Skye was already gone. And Amy's version was implanted in people's minds.

Connor hadn't even called after he left for school. To be fair, she'd lost her cell phone to the fire and her father and Karen were not inclined to buy her a new one.

Connor could have called the landline or emailed. But there had been nothing, zip, crickets, nada. He had tried to connect on Facebook a few years later but Skye had still been too hurt and betrayed to be interested, then he'd dropped off her radar.

Which was fine by her.

As curious as she was as to why he was here, she knew it was best not to even start down that road to the past. It hadn't been easy, but thanks to Roxy and her friends and Jack, she was well planted in the now.

No going back.

"Skye!"

Skye jumped. Maya was standing two feet away from her.

"What?"

"He's here," Maya said in a whisper. "He came in a minute ago. Asked if you were available. He's waiting in the bookstore."

Skye's mouth went dry. "Who?" Stupid. She knew who.

"Connor, who else. What a sweetie."

Skye screwed up her face.

"Well, go out and talk to him."

"Tell him I'm busy."

"Skye."

"I haven't figured out what to say to him. I'm not prepared."

"Then you'll have to wing it." Maya pulled her out of her chair and nudged her toward the door.

Skye nervously brushed a strand of hair away from her face.

"You look great, now go."

Connor was standing at the new book table, a copy of *The Fine Art of Doing Nothing* opened in his hand. And Skye's heart—or maybe it was her stomach—tightened. It was odd, the lanky, agile boy she'd known had developed into a svelte, fit, sleek man. Dressed in khakis and a polo shirt, he looked very put together.

Skye wasn't sure she liked it.

She was no slob—she dressed for success—but her success meant she had to sometimes get down and get dirty. She felt at a slight disadvantage.

Skye only made it halfway across the room before Connor looked up. The book snapped shut and he put it down on the table.

Her step stuttered, barely, and she kept going. Did she shake his hand? Give him a friendly hug?

He waited while she continued toward him, his lips slowly forming a smile that arrived at full wattage as she came to stand in front of him.

"Connor. What a surprise." Really, was that the best she could do?

His smile widened to show perfectly even teeth. The product of braces through middle and high school.

The tightness burst into a pang of remembered feeling. *The devil is in the details*, Brendan Wraye, their LEGO docent, always said. Memory was in the details, too. And suddenly Skye realized how much she had missed Connor, all the little things that made up the person.

"Hi, Skye."

And he was hugging her, and even though he had changed, she knew him in that hug. She pulled away first.

"I just wanted to say hello, but if you're busy, I completely understand," he said before she could think of something to say.

"I'm not." *Of course she was.* "I mean—"

"She's not," Maya said from the doorway. "Why don't you go to lunch. Take your time."

Considering they never really stopped for lunch, much less went out for it, always catching a bite on the sly, Skye just said, "Thanks," and turned to Connor. "Is now a good time?"

"Perfect."

Maya had disappeared, but now reappeared, carrying Skye's small crossbody bag.

Skye slipped it over her shoulder, sneaking an OMG look to Maya.

"Have fun," Maya said and wafted away.

Skye started toward the front door before Connor could put his hand on her back or open the door for her or do any of the other things he'd been taught from childhood to do. But she could feel him walking a step behind her, no longer all arms and legs and slouching, but confident. It seemed to Skye that except for the military uniform, he'd turned out just like his dad had planned.

"So would you like to have lunch somewhere?" he asked.

"Not unless you're hungry."

He laughed. "I just had breakfast."

"Where is Amy?" Skye just blurted it out. She'd meant to be more in control, more distanced, more mature, but she had things to do, schedules to plan, a town to save, so best to get right to the point.

"I bribed her into going to the mall. I wanted to have a chance to catch up. Just the two of us. You've really come into your own."

"I do okay."

"Imagine That. I like it. It's . . . you. I can tell you've really found your place here," Connor said as they started down the sidewalk.

"I have," Skye said. "I studied business in college."

"You?"

"Yeah, I can be down-to-earth when I need to be, and I knew I'd have to find a way to do what I do best and make a living at it."

"I love the name," Connor said. "But how do you manage a store and a workshop?"

"I have help. Maya, who you just met, is my best friend and a whiz at everything."

"Aren't you worried about hiring your friends? I've seen friendships cave over working disagreements."

"We run an idea store—other people's ideas, we just facilitate. And the worst situation we've had so far is the adults and children fighting over the LEGO room. We solved that by renting a steam cleaner—cleaning LEGOs by hand got old quick—and running twice as many sessions.

"But organizing an entire weekend of discovery is a stretch. I wanted to create an intensive experience for people to explore their surroundings, looking in new ways, trying new things, seeing differently, with guides and facilitators but not teachers, you know? But not on quite such a grand scale as it has turned into. But the chamber of commerce—of which I'm a member"—she thumped her chest—"thought I could help them revive downtown."

"Have you convinced them to hop any freight trains to see where they went?" Connor laughed. It was a sound she knew so well, and the past came flooding back.

"Where would you go if you could hop on the next train?"

"Anywhere," she'd said. "Anywhere and everywhere."

He'd laughed that same laugh and said, "I would go away and away and away."

They'd had great dreams back then. Both of them, made even

more exciting when they were together, just imagining where everywhere would be. They had ditched school to find out.

Skye laughed. "Where did we end up?"

"Grounded for two weeks."

They bumped shoulders and the years fell away and they were two dreamers, skipping school and following the next adventure. "Actually it was in the stockyards outside of Pittsburgh somewhere. Do you have a significant other?"

Skye tripped over the sidewalk. "What does that have to do with Pittsburgh?"

"Nothing, I was just curious."

Actually she and Jack had settled in to something unnamed, but he was definitely significant. And since she didn't feel the need to see anyone else . . . "I do."

"Serious?"

"I don't know. Yeah. I guess. Do you?"

Connor shook his head. "I was married." He stopped to smile at her. "For a minute. Unfortunately, she thought the diplomatic corps meant fancy cocktail parties with visiting heads of state. Instead she got an apartment in an embassy compound in a desert. To her credit, she lasted a couple of years, but she'd built up a pretty big resentment by then." He shrugged. "I can't really blame her."

"Hit you for a bunch of alimony?" Skye clapped her hand over her mouth. "I'm sorry, it's totally none of my business."

Connor barked out a laugh. "That has never, in all the time I've known you, ever stopped you from doing or saying anything."

"I've learned a lot since then."

"Well, don't let responsible-citizen Skye knock out the dare-to-dream Skye."

Skye smiled back at him. "Never." She linked her arm through his. It was as natural as it had ever been. "His name is Jack. He designs and makes furniture with Maya's husband. They have a business in town."

"Creative, then. He a local?"

"Summer person, then he inherited his grandma's house and he moved here full-time."

"So you've known him for a long time?"

"A while." They'd come to Shore Road; they crossed to the seawall.

"Connor, why are you here, besides, I assume, that Amy somehow conned you into it?"

"Is there someplace we can talk? Preferably without interruptions."

"How are you about sand?"

"Fine, I just spent the last three years in the Sahara."

She knew just the place. Not the public beach. Not Roxy's beach, but her favorite think place, Cove Beach. "What were you doing there?" she asked as they turned right along the sidewalk.

"I work for the State Department. Foreign service. I was a staff member at the consulate there." He shrugged. "It was that or a military career—or being cut off from my family." A cloud passed over his face, a reaction she knew so well.

Unlike her, Connor had been given a choice, Skye thought. "Dad and I reconciled long ago."

"I know. I've kept up . . . well, I did for a while. Why didn't you—"

"Don't," Skye warned. "I don't want to go back to the past. So let's just catch up on what's happened after that."

Connor fell silent as she knew he would. Diplomacy actually was a perfect job for him. He'd always been a good listener. He could also attack an argument from any direction and usually ended up getting his way without ever raising his voice. Which brought her back to wondering why he was here with Amy.

She led him past the drive down to Roxy's, veered off the sidewalk and through a stand of trees, and ended up on the path above the cove.

"NO SWIMMING ALLOWED. RIPTIDE. Riptide, huh?" Connor said, reading the warning sign stuck in the rocks behind the stone wall.

"So don't go in above your waist or you'll find yourself in Massachusetts, if you survive."

"I'll just stick to Roxy's beach. It's safe?"

"Almost always. They put up a sign if there's a storm." She threw her leg over the wall. "You good with a little rock climbing?"

"Try me."

Skye swung her other leg over and came to balance on the granite on the other side. "There's kind of a path here." She glanced back at his shoes. "Good to see that diplomats wear sneakers."

"Ha, want me to go first?"

She grinned back at him. Damn, he'd gotten her. Pulled her by that challenge right back to where she didn't want to go.

"I'd say race you, but you might hurt yourself," and she started down the boulders, her feet automatically finding the footholds of years of familiarity. Connor kept right behind her and they were both a little out of breath when they reached the sand.

"This is beautiful." Connor kicked out of his shoes. Rolled up his khakis. "I just have to get my feet wet."

"Really?"

"Yeah. Sand, I'm used to, but it was a desert. Not even an oasis in sight. Race you." He ran across the sand and into the water. Skye ran after him but stopped at the edge, fists on her hips, trying not to laugh as she watched him cavort around in the surf.

"Man, this is fantastic." He pirouetted in the water and nearly fell. "Hey, is that Roxy's house over there?"

"Yep," Skye said. She didn't mention that Jack's cottage was just on the opposite side of the cove and both houses had a view of the beach.

"So no skinny-dipping, I guess."

"You still haven't told me why you came."

Connor sighed. "It's a long story."

"Then you'd better get started."

He came out of the water, walked to where the sand was dry, and threw himself down on it. "Do you know there are places where the sand at midday is too hot to stand on even in shoes?"

"Connor."

"Oh all right." He patted the sand next to him and waited for her to sit down.

"I'm between posts. I'm off to Thailand in a few weeks. I decided to make a stealth visit to my parents. Dad hasn't been all that well lately and you never know. Anyway, I was there less than two days when what to my wondering eyes did appear, but Amy in four-inch heels, ringing our doorbell. Oh and by the way, she let me know that she pronounces it *Ah-me* now. *Ah* as in me, me, me."

"Not in this lifetime," Skye said.

"Nor mine," Connor agreed. "I swear that girl has a sixth sense. I didn't even know she was in town. Not that I ever knew where she was, I never inquired, didn't care.

"Anyway, she started telling me about her mother and your dad divorcing—which I already knew—then her mother's new marriage and that divorce. Ugh. I got the full version on the ride here, I'll spare you the gory details."

"Thanks."

"And that she'd been meaning to come see you, to reconnect, even though . . ." He made air quotes. ". . . 'It wasn't her fault, and she didn't know why everyone got mad at her.' Then she went off on how no one understood her, and if you and she could just be friends again . . . because she needed a sense of closure and acceptance. She's been going to some class to get in touch with her inner self, but her boss doesn't understand anything about business, and nobody . . . Lord, the girl can't hold on to one thought long enough to get it out."

Skye felt a tremor rumble through her. Evidently her half sister was still the master of manipulation.

"Acceptance? Closure? I'm sure she made the whole thing up

on the spot just for your benefit." So far the only contact Amy had made was to ask for money.

"Oh, no doubt about that; if she's had one thought about anyone but herself, it wasn't for you or me or, hell, anyone else we know.

"I told her to back off, in a very diplomatic way. That I thought it was a bad idea, and she should reconsider alternative options for going forward—diplo talk—but it just pissed her off and she flounced out of the house.

"I deliberated and decided to try again. I grabbed my car keys to go after her, which was hubris on my part, because she was still outside my house, leaning against the neat little BMW I'd leased for the month just waiting to reel me in."

"And you bit."

He paused, cocked his head to look at her. "I figured I'd better come along and try to do some damage control. Maybe talk her out of it on the way."

"So much for diplomacy."

He grinned. "I confess I didn't try all that hard. After we started out, I couldn't stop, not because of her, but because after having shoved you to a dark corner of my . . . mind for so long, I suddenly needed to"—he shrugged—"to do something. Just talk maybe.

"I tried that before many times, if you recall. I got crickets, so I'm done with overture. If you want to hear what happened after you left, I'll tell you. If not, I'll just get back in my car and drive home. And you're on your own."

"Oh no you don't. You brought her here. You take her away.

And soon. I've got a major weekend coming up and she'll figure out a way to wreck everything. If not through malice aforethought, out of sheer boneheadedness."

"Aren't you going to at least talk to her?"

"Why would I? So she can finally confess that she lied and somehow manage to also blame me for her story unraveling? Thanks, but as they say, no thanks."

Connor had been resting on one elbow, but he sat up. "I think she's desperate. From what she said on the ride here—all six hours of it—"

Skye groaned in sympathy.

"It tested my diplomacy skills to the max. She's lucky I didn't slow down long enough to toss her by the side of the road. Not really. She's needy and manipulating and prickly, and she made a big mistake, one that came close to getting you killed."

Skye stood up. "Which is why I don't intend to give her another chance to do it again." She needed to get back to the store where she felt competent, independent—and safe.

He jumped to his feet as she started past him and grabbed her arm. "What about us, Skye?"

"Us? There is no us. Us died the night my dad's workshop burned."

"It didn't have to. Why didn't you return my calls? Let me know you were okay?"

"Maybe because I didn't know you called me."

"I did, countless times."

"Well, too bad, because my phone died with the flames." *And my life*, she added silently.

"I called the house. Left messages. Karen said you didn't want to talk to me. I knew you didn't have your own computer, so I wrote you a letter. Many letters, but you didn't answer. I never knew any of the details until I came back for Thanksgiving break."

"I know that . . . now. I didn't know *then* about the calls or the letters. My dad told me a few years back." Skye bit her lip. He'd known about them all the time, but he hadn't told her. That had been the hardest hurt of all. "He also told me you set the record straight when you came back. Told everyone what had actually happened, that we'd been together when we saw the fire. For what it's worth, he said he was sorry."

"You knew my parents took me away the next morning. I meant for you to follow me."

The last vestige of a long-forgotten hope flared and died.

"What do you want, Connor?"

"I don't know. I thought maybe I could just set the record straight, maybe see if it's not too late for us."

"To do what?"

"I don't know. Aren't you curious?"

Skye opened her mouth, closed it. What could she say to that? Her curiosity had always led her into trouble. It also had led her to a successful business and life. She wasn't sure she wanted to find out where curiosity about Connor Reid would lead.

Chapter 7

Skye didn't say anything, just started back toward the path; Connor grabbed his shoes and followed her.

"You want to see something?"

"Sure," Connor said, brushing the sand off his chinos.

Skye led him back up the rocks, climbed over the stone wall, had to wait a second for him to push sandy feet into his shoes, then set off down the path, not back to town but past Jack's house, to where it rejoined the main road. A few yards later, they came to a wooden frame whose painted PRITCHARDS' FAMILY CAMP had been covered over with a big For Sale sign.

"This is the venue for our Discover It Weekend. In a few days the retreat sign will go up. Afterward it will go back up for sale." Skye turned into a drive that opened onto a large parking lot whose pavement had been recently patched.

"Generations of families used to come here. You had to reserve space a year in advance."

Skye stopped to look around, trying to see it as it could be and not what Connor was seeing now. A few acres of run-down wooden cabins, a small beach, a bathhouse once painted sky blue that was in the midst of plumbing repairs. And a mess hall that had dry rot at one end and whose concrete block foundation was weakened in several places.

It suddenly seemed like an overwhelming undertaking.

"Herb Pritchard and his wife, Edna, own the place. It's been in their family for decades. Unfortunately, it's gotten old and doesn't have the amenities of the modern hotels, condos, and Airbnbs that have sprung up. A few families still come, but the older ones are dying off and their children have moved away or are so busy all year, they just want to be pampered on their two weeks off.

"I'd like to think that this will give the camp a kind of rebirth, but I imagine it will just become another teardown." Skye sighed. "A shame. It's old but holds so many memories and experiences. You can still feel them, can't you?"

"I can hear hammers and saws," Connor said drily.

"That's coming from the mess hall. Let's take a look."

Skye started across the parking lot to the long rectangular building that served as meeting house, mess hall, and multipurpose room.

"It's a perfect venue. Right on the edge of downtown. Herb and Edna are still living in the caretaker's house." Skye pointed through the trees to a white-framed house sitting at the edge of the camp where it abutted the privately owned cottages of Sunny Point. "We're just using this first cluster of cabins for workshops, storage, a canteen, and meeting points."

"You have your work cut out for you."

"You should have seen it a few weeks ago."

"And this was your idea, of course."

"Not originally. I was going to rent the nature conservancy for my headquarters. Really expensive but for a good cause. But that meant that the venues were really spread out. Then the chamber of commerce asked me if I couldn't find a place closer to downtown, so the businesses could reap some of the benefit of the extra visitors. What could I say?" She smiled up at him. "I kind of fell for the camp. It's perfect. At least it will be. I guess you'd say it picked me."

"Why don't you buy it and then you could run weekends all year-round."

"I've thought of it, but it's way too expensive. Luckily it's covered by strict zoning codes because it abuts the county nature park and is within a single-home residential area. So no replacing it with multistoried condos. Still . . ."

"You could figure out a way to do it." He pushed a strand of hair behind her ear. "You have a limitless imagination."

"Wish I could say the same for my funds."

"The selling of ideas is not so lucrative?"

"Oh very. But, strangely enough, there is a very high overhead on ideas.

"Come on, there's someone I want you to meet." Skye led Connor across the parking lot to a spacious rectangular building that until a week ago had been sagging so badly that they were afraid it would have to come down. Now the sound of buzz saws and hammering reassured her that work was proceeding.

"This is the old mess hall. It was in bad shape, but we

needed a place large enough for group projects and extra space if the weather got so bad that the outdoor activities had to move inside."

She stepped onto the wooden floor where Brendan Wraye, a retired architect who had volunteered to oversee the project, stood with a roll of paper stuck under his arm, talking to Herb Pritchard. Brendan was a tall man with wavy silver hair and slightly stooped shoulders, an odd contrast to Herb, who was short and still muscular even though he was in his seventies.

Brendan saw Skye and raised his mechanical pencil in welcome. Herb shoved his hands in his pants pocket and the two men waited for them without speaking.

"Hi Brendan. It looks like things here are really shaping up." She turned to Herb. "Brendan and the guys have done a great job, haven't they?"

"So far," Herb said as if the words were dragged from him.

Skye glanced at Brendan, who lifted both eyebrows.

"We're running close to budget and we keep finding dry rot. Herb's getting a little nervous that we'll run out of money before we finish the rehab."

"No worries," Skye said. "It will get done. And it will drive up the resale value." *Besides*, she thought, *you're not paying for it. The town and I are.*

"I suppose." Herb ended the sentence with a frown that threatened to bring down the rest of his face with it. "Just hope you know what you're doing and don't leave me with half a rotten building." He nodded abruptly and slumped off toward the caretaker's house.

Brendan leaned over to shake Connor's hand.

"Sorry," Skye said. "This is my friend, Connor Reid, we went to school together. And this is Brendan Wraye, LEGO docent and architect extraordinaire."

"Nice to meet you," Connor said.

"What's wrong with Herb?" Skye asked, watching Herb's slow progress across the yard to his house.

Brendan scratched his head, his fingers disappearing into a patch of gray hair. "I think Edna's worrying about the future. She's got it in her mind they have to be gone by the end of the summer. Must be hard to work your whole lives and then have to give up the only thing you have to show for it. It won't be easy for them to leave everything behind. Family legacy is sometimes a heavy weight."

Skye could sympathize. "Well, it will be over soon, I guess."

Brendan shrugged. "Anything in particular you need?"

"No, I just wanted to show Connor the site."

"Then I'll get back to it. Nice to meet you." He went back inside.

Skye and Connor left a couple of minutes later. Skye thought about what Brendan had said. It had been bad enough to leave her childhood and family behind, but she'd had her whole lifetime to start fresh.

Not the case for Edna and Herb Pritchard.

"Well, Mr. Wraye seems competent," Connor said. "But LEGO docent? I was afraid to ask."

"He's a godsend. You didn't see the other half of my store; it's divided into spaces for creating and playing. We have a designated LEGO and building block room, which has become so popular that we've had to add separate sessions for the adults."

"Adult LEGO-ers?"

"You'd be surprised."

"At what people do? Maybe, but what can you convince them to do? Never. Thus LEGO docent."

"I swear I didn't even have to strong-arm him. He came into the store one afternoon to buy a present for his grandson. He said he was a retired architect, and I showed him our LEGO room where a kids' session was being held. I thought maybe he and his grandson might like to come for one of our all-ages sessions," she explained.

"He walked into the room, looked over the activity, then picked up one of the plastic blocks and stuck it to another. He attracted the attention of Jimmy and Cole Westin, two imaginative but energetic brothers, who came over to see what he was doing.

"Jimmy picked up a triangle and said, 'Use this one next.' It was enough to set Brendan off on an explanation of how to structure a building. I watched in amazement as his explanations, rather than mystifying the boys, fell on fertile ears, and soon the three of them were building a skyscraper of epic proportions.

"I hired him on the spot and Imagine That had its first LEGO docent."

"Brilliant," Connor said. "Way to rope in talent. And let me guess, he was the first but not the last?"

"What can I say. It's amazing the talent in this town. At first they were mainly volunteers who came in for the company or tea and cookies. Others for the free marketing it sent to their own businesses. A few I hired outright, like Brendan."

"You have docents for everything?"

"Pretty much." They'd reached the street, and Skye stopped. "It was great seeing you, but I'd better get back. Maya is pregnant and probably starving by now. Do you know where you are? Turn right and you'll come to the drive down to Roxy's."

"Thanks." He turned toward the sea walk.

"How long are you planning to stay?" she called.

He glanced back over his shoulder. "That depends on Amy." He stuffed his hands in his pants pockets and continued on his way.

Skye could swear he was whistling.

THE STORE WAS filled with lunch hour browsers when Skye returned a couple of minutes later. She hurried over to Maya. "Sorry. Are you starving? Go on your break. I didn't mean to stay out so long."

"I ate in between customers. Now I want to hear everything. Is he like you remember him? I hope he isn't planning to lure you away."

"Not a chance," Skye said, "though after the initial awkwardness, it was nice to see him again. Are you sure you don't want to take a break? Get off your feet?"

"Don't you start. Sonny is already making me crazy. If you join him, we may have to fall out."

Connor's words rang in her ears. Never go into business with your friends. "Okay. Just tell me if I get too obnoxious. We're all just so excited. I'm going to be the aunt that I always wanted to be. Maybe I'll take up knitting . . ."

Maya held up a finger to stop her and hurried over to the game table where a man was looking over the board games. Maya helped him pick out two and she rang up the sale. As soon as she saw him to the door, she came straight back to Skye.

"So what about Connor?" Maya asked in low tones. "Why is he here?"

"He brought Amy. Evidently she feels like we need to come to an understanding or have a reconciliation, or wants me to forgive her, which I'm sure he misunderstood. More likely she's at loose ends, broke, and has nowhere else to go. The few times she contacted me, she ended up asking for a 'loan.' I sent her a few hundred here and there, knowing I'd never see it back, which I didn't."

"Maybe she's come to pay her debt."

"Fat chance, and we could use the money."

"What? We did well last month, and with the big weekend coming up . . ."

"Yeah, but the camp renovation needs are multiplying. I know the budget is beginning to get stretched. If it keeps up, I'll have to take out a loan."

"Ask the other businesses for more money at the meeting tomorrow night. The burden shouldn't be on you."

"My pig, my farm," Skye said.

"But they'll all be eating the bacon."

"Cornball," they exclaimed, and high-fived.

Maya gave Skye an impulsive hug. "I got your back, just remember that."

"And vice versa," Skye said and returned her hug.

"And I made blueberry muffins."

"Perfect. I'm starving," Skye said, motioning to Penny to watch the front, then she and Maya headed for the back.

"So you and Connor had a long heart-to-heart?" Maya asked, peeling the wrapper from her muffin.

"I wouldn't call it that. But we kind of caught up. He did tell me the only reason he came was because Amy found out he was visiting his parents and hit him up for a ride. But when I asked how long they were staying, he said it was up to Amy. Which is kind of weird. I mean he works for the State Department, what's he doing chauffeuring Amy around?"

"Maybe they're . . . ?"

"I don't think so, but I didn't ask what their relationship was."

May raised both eyebrows. "So why *did* he agree to bring her. I bet it was to see you."

Skye didn't answer. She didn't want to admit it, but he'd pretty much told her that.

"I almost forgot. Jack called while you were out." Maya grimaced. "Twice, actually."

"Jack?" Skye said. "Why? What did he say? Does he want me to call him back?"

"No. He just said he was taking a break and thought he'd call to see how things were going."

Skye frowned. Jack didn't often call for no reason. "Did you tell him where I was?"

"I just said you'd stepped out for a minute. I didn't know if you wanted him to know."

"Of course. It's no secret. Connor and I are old childhood friends."

"Do you think Jack's jealous of Connor?"

"Of course not. I can't even imagine him being jealous."

"You? You can imagine anything."

"I only imagine good things," Skye said. *Mostly*, she added to herself.

Maya whooshed out a breath. "Good, because I'd hate it if you and he— But what about you and Connor? I mean, I shouldn't even ask this, I feel like such a traitor, but was the old fire there?"

Skye nibbled her muffin while she thought about it. Something was still there. She didn't think she should name it and she certainly didn't want to pursue it. She had enough on her plate without that kind of disruption.

"It was awkward at first. But then it became just like the old days. I took him to see the construction at the camp. Brendan was there talking to Herb, who was awfully brusque. He's afraid we're going to abandon him midproject. Don't know where he got that idea.

"And then we left. Connor went to Roxy's and I came back here. That's all." Skye tossed her muffin wrapper in the trash. "Now I need to prepare the latest financial data for the committee meeting tomorrow night. As soon as I get through that, I'll deal with Amy and send her on her way."

SINCE CONNOR WAS taking Amy to Newport for dinner, Roxy called Skye and invited her and Jack for brisket. Now it was going on five o'clock and Amy still wasn't back.

Roxy, Hildy, and Connor all sat on the porch, sipping iced tea, listening for the sound of a car.

"How much damage could she do with a hundred bucks?" Connor wondered out loud. "I was expecting an hour max."

"I just hope she doesn't run into my tenants on her way back," Hildy said. "They should be arriving soon."

The sound of a car crunching along the gravel drive outside brought them all to attention. "Finally," Connor said. "I'll hurry her along so I can get her out of here before Skye and Jack arrive for dinner."

"Tell her to park next to Roxy's Toyota and leave the place next to the cottage for the tenants," Hilda called after him.

"Will do." Connor was just getting up when the sound of a second car joined the first. "Sounds like your tenants have arrived, too."

"Good heavens," Hildy said. "I'll just see if they . . ." She followed him out.

They reached the door just in time to see Amy jump out of the car and shake her fist at the startled man who was getting out of the car.

His wife was peering out the window looking concerned; three children were already out and huddled near the car door.

"Dammit, it's the Jensens," Hildy said and hurried outside.

"You can't park there," Amy shouted. "This is private property, you'll have to find someplace else."

"S-sorry," the man said. "Isn't this 5 Sunny Lane? We were told to park where it says tenants." He pointed to the newly painted sign that read TENANTS.

Amy slouched into one hip.

"Can that girl do anything without causing trouble?" Roxy said.

"Amy!" Hildy strode toward the confrontation.

"These people took my parking place," Amy complained.

"What a terrible way to start a vacation," Roxy told Connor under her breath.

"I'm on it." He took off toward the others. Roxy decided to stay out of it; she was too near blowing her top and embarrassing Hildy in front of her guests by shaking Amy until her neuroses fell out.

"Amy, you're mistaken," Hildy said. "This space is for my guests, you'll have to park next to—"

"Over in the visitors' lot," Roxy called out. "Down at the far end of the drive," she added, pointing to where the street dead-ended a good six houses away and where spaces for six visitor cars had been grudgingly carved out. A bit of a hike and there *was* room to squeeze a small car in next to Hildy's garden, but dammit, she'd just about had enough of Amy's attitude. A little exercise wouldn't hurt her.

"Well, no one told me," Amy groused and flounced back to the car.

"Sorry," Connor said, jumping into the fray. "My bad. Roxy asked me to tell you this morning but I forgot. Why don't you go inside and get dressed? I'll drive it down and park."

"I'll do it," Amy said. "But someone should have told me." She got back to the car, slammed the door, and drove away.

"Well, well," Roxy said to him under her breath. "You know I told you no such thing."

Connor shrugged.

"Sorry for that little mix-up, Mr. Jensen," Hildy said. "She's the daughter of a friend of a friend," she explained, managing to distance them all from Amy and her rude behavior. "She's visiting for a few days and we forgot to tell her not to park there." Hildy had taken Mr. Jensen by the arm like everyone's favorite grandma, when Roxy knew she felt more like grabbing Amy and wrestling her to the ground. *Hildy could do it, too,* Roxy thought maliciously.

"And you must be Mrs. Jensen."

"Carol, please," said the woman, who was finally extricating herself from the car.

"I'm Hildy Bloome. We talked over the phone. I'm so sorry for this mix-up." She turned a full wattage smile on the boys, one about thirteen looking sullen, one still in the chubby pre-teen stage, who was looking around as if he expected alligators, and the youngest one clinging to his mother's leg and smiling shyly at Hildy.

"You must be Bill Jr., Terry, and Malcolm," Hildy said. "You're going to love our beach."

The entire family visibly relaxed, even the teenager.

Roxy watched with satisfaction. Hildy always knew how to diffuse a situation, make everyone feel at home. Two feats Roxy had never managed without extreme effort and even then with varying success.

"Now you all go on inside and settle in. I've left some goodies for you to enjoy. There's coffee and cream for the morning, a list of restaurants and shops and nature venues on the table. Just let us know if there's anything you need, we're right next door. Otherwise we'll leave you to enjoy your vacation."

With a smile she nodded goodbye and started back toward the house. Connor strode off down the street toward the visitors' parking area probably to check on the state of his car, and hopefully to give Amy a lecture about insulting other people's guests.

Roxy followed Hildy back to the house.

As soon as the door closed behind her, Hildy exploded. "That girl is a menace."

"I couldn't agree more," Roxy said. "How about a nice afternoon cocktail?"

"Grrr," answered Hildy. "Make mine a double. I'll join you on the porch as soon as I check on how the dinner rolls are rising."

Roxy made a pitcher of margaritas, filled the ice bucket, and took glasses, pitcher, and bucket out to the porch where she placed the drinks on a wicker table that sat between two shell-backed wicker chairs.

She poured herself a glass, added a couple of ice cubes, and went to stand at the window to enjoy the view. Today the sky and ocean were a Tiffany melding of blues and greens as far as the eye could see. A perfect beach day.

Except there was hardly anyone on the beach. Roxy enjoyed the solitude all year long, but summer surely was meant to be filled with the annoying squeals of happy children; the occasional wayward Frisbee that ended up in Hildy's garden; the too-loud parties, accompanied by louder music and the inevitable drunken madness. Today she was even missing them.

And Roxy found herself thinking about her own sister. How her first instinct had been to dissuade her from marrying James. It was obvious she adored him and he worshiped her, but almost from afar without ever becoming fully engaged. It seemed to Roxy as if part of him just couldn't come fully down to earth. Certainly he couldn't nurture a young daughter. Could never totally free himself from the memory of her sister to embrace life or his family. And Roxy felt a little sad for them both.

"You're getting old, my friend," she told herself. Actually she wasn't that old. She'd been much older when she'd found Skye huddled at her kitchen door some fifteen years before. Flynn had been dead for several years and the spark had just gone out of her life.

She'd never had to worry about Flynn not being totally engaged. He loved life, every messy bit of it. He challenged her, irritated her, laughed too loud, worked too hard. But he'd never been distant, not for a moment.

He'd dropped dead in the garden with no warning. Roxy still had problems going out there even to pick lettuce for dinner. She always expected him to pop up and say, *You're picking that too soon. It hasn't developed enough nutrients as yet.* So much for nutrients. His heart had given out at fifty-one.

The garden had pretty much gone to seed after that, until Hildy's Emmet followed Flynn to that great golf course in the sky and Roxy convinced Hildy to move in with her.

Now Hildy had pretty much taken over garden duty. Raising Skye had filled the big holes in their lives, but neither one of them had completely forgotten. There were times when they were reminiscing and they would both turn away as if to comment to the missing men. Then realize what they were doing, and sheepishly pretend that it hadn't just happened.

People always told Roxy, *It will pass. You'll meet someone else.* But that wasn't true. The pain changed, the emptiness filled with activity. She'd met plenty of someone elses. She enjoyed having fun, but people didn't understand. It wasn't that she couldn't get over losing Flynn, she couldn't get over losing the partnership that made both of them more than they were alone.

What Skye called your soul mate.

Whatever it was called, Roxy knew you kept those feelings for life. And she wondered what this appearance of Connor Reid might do to Skye's long-fought-for peace.

"What are you frowning about?" Hildy asked, coming into the room wiping her hands on a tea towel. She tossed it on the arm of her chair and sat down.

"Nothing. Thinking about Skye. How are the rolls coming?"

"Fine," Hildy said and sighed.

Roxy didn't have to ask what she was thinking. After all

these years, the two old friends could practically read each other's minds.

They both fell silent, heard the door open and close and the voices of Amy and Connor. Neither moved until it was clear that the two guests were continuing on their way upstairs, then Hildy relaxed back in her chair and Roxy poured her a drink.

When sometime later they heard footsteps coming down the stairs and the sound of the front door opening and closing again, Roxy stood up. "Free at last."

"For dinner anyway. I have to say, I wish they hadn't come and I wish they would just leave, though I do rather like Connor. He seems like a nice man."

"Hmmm," Roxy said. He was certainly polite, but she didn't trust his motives—not one little bit.

IT WAS AFTER six when Skye turned the store over to Nat Lieberman and the night shift. They stayed open until nine five days a week along with many of the downtown retail stores during the summer. It was the only way to compete with the malls out on the main highway.

She waved good night and opened the door—and ran straight into Jack.

"Am I late?"

"Nope, I'm early." He kissed her.

She pulled away and looked at him. He was not usually a demonstratively-affectionate-in-public kind of guy. And today he'd called several times during the day to see if "they" needed anything.

"I meant to call you back, but we got busy. Roxy and Hildy invited us to dinner. I guess Hildy refused to serve Amy and Connor her brisket and peach crumble and packed it away until today."

"Are they gone?"

"Nope, but—"

"Then thank Hildy profusely but say—"

"Connor is taking Amy over to Newport tonight for dinner. And there's peach crumble." Skye ended her sentence on a tempting upward swing.

"Fine. Actually you had me at brisket. But I wish they would leave for good."

Skye gave him a quizzical look. "I agree, but fat chance of that. Amy's digging in her heels and Roxy thought maybe we should come up with a strategy. Though fat chance of that, too. You can't have a strategy with Amy, she's got a one-track mind. Me, me, me."

"You, you, you?"

She smiled against her will. He always had a way of making things seem less awful. "No. Her, her, her."

"I think you're right, but you, you, you are going to have to deal with her, her, her, and the sooner the better."

"Why? I have nothing to say to her."

"She and that guy Connor were over at Millie's this morning. She was talking smack about you and people overheard."

Skye stared at him while the words clicked in. Then she got it. Her stomach tightened convulsively.

"Don't worry. Leanne put her in her place. But Herb Pritchard and Rhoda Sims were there, among others."

"Damn." Skye blew out air, sending her anxiety and general annoyance into the air, then quickly batted the air around her to disperse the bad feelings.

"Better out in the atmosphere than bottled up inside," Jack said, knowing exactly what she was doing. "Shall we go? I'm sure they have the cocktails ready." He offered his elbow and she laughed.

"Does this mean we're not dressing for dinner?"

"My tux is at the cleaners."

She laughed again. "That explains the Sundance 2012 T-shirt. I can almost still see the logo."

They strolled companionably down the sidewalk toward the sea. This was the worst time possible to have to deal with her half sister and her neuroses, but at least Skye had a support group. People she could depend on. Of course she'd thought the same thing fifteen years before. A shiver of memory passed through her and was gone. *That was the past, this is now.*

And this is where she belonged, and where she would stay.

Chapter 8

Skye scraped the last of Hildy's crumble off the dessert plate and savored the last crumbs.

"There's more," Hildy said and reached for the pan.

"I couldn't. I'm beyond stuffed. I think this brisket is even better than your last brisket."

"It had a day of sitting," Hildy said straight-faced.

"Thanks to you know who," Roxy added.

Skye sighed and leaned back in her chair. "Okay, let's talk about the elephant not in the room, but make it fast. We hate to eat and run, but I want to be gone before they get back." She held up her hand. "I know I have to talk to her. And I will. But I have a huge amount of paperwork to do before the committee meeting tomorrow night. We're already over budget and there are certain people who are going to balk.

"I'll talk to her, but not tonight, or tomorrow. If you can put up with her for one more day, I promise I'll see what she wants and send her on her way."

"Fine, but I'm getting the distinct feeling she won't be as

easily paid off this time," Roxy said. "Besides, why should you keep doling out money to the little witch when she just comes back for more and isn't even grateful."

"It was just a few times. And if that's all it takes to keep her at bay, I'm willing to do it."

"It's blackmail," Hildy said.

Good loyal Hildy. She sometimes seemed more upset by what she perceived as wrongs, especially by Skye's family, than Roxy seemed to be. Skye appreciated her intensity. A person couldn't have a more supportive group of people surrounding her, and she was grateful.

"I suppose it is," Skye said.

"Well, hallelujah," mumbled Jack.

Skye cut him a look. "I do listen to you."

"It's not the money," he said.

They'd had this talk several times before. Jack said Skye was enabling Amy to not take responsibility for her life. He was right. Skye knew he was, but it was so much easier to hand over a few bucks every few years than to have to talk about the past, to hear Amy's complaints and accusations and slights she'd endured because of Skye.

Skye had long ago tired of being the villain in Amy's mind. She wasn't a villain. She didn't know why after all this time Amy couldn't just accept that.

The truth had finally come out. Well, enough of the truth that it freed Skye of any responsibility. There was still no definitive reason for the fire. It was finally chalked up to faulty wiring. But that had taken time and by then Skye's life had changed forever.

And as it had turned out, for the better. She had no desire to rehash the past.

This would be the time when she would finally cut Amy loose to sink or swim in her own misery. And Amy wasn't even alone. She had a mother and a father.

"Fine," Roxy said. "The girl's a menace. She insulted Hildy's paying guests before they were out of the car."

Hildy snorted. "*Her* parking place, she said. As if she was moving in."

"Not until Stagnant Pond freezes over," Roxy said.

"Don't say that," Hildy said. "I remember when it froze over in 1982."

"Yeah but they drained it two seasons ago because of the mosquito problem. And good riddance."

Jack stood. "It's getting late. This strategy meeting is adjourned. You two man the battle stations long enough for Skye to get through the chamber of commerce's Jump-Start July committee meeting and then she'll go in for the kill."

"Jack!" Skye exclaimed, but she followed his lead and stood.

He gave her a look. "She's twenty-six, spoiled, irresponsible, and a few other things. But the *poor little me, I accused my sister of arson, and now nobody likes me* attitude is getting a little tiresome. Sounds like she was an awful child. She's certainly an awful adult. She proved that today."

All three women stared at him until he stretched his neck. As close as Jack ever got to squirming.

"Well, it's true, isn't it? We're in the last leg of getting this weekend experiment running—the future of the town could easily rest on it—I don't think that's hyperbole. Skye is busting her butt, trying to do everything while keeping everyone happy and calm.

"It could all go up in smoke—" He broke off. Winced. "Sorry. Poor choice in analogies. But really. Enough is enough."

Roxy picked up her glass, "Here, here," she said and downed the rest of her wine.

"I DIDN'T MEAN to do that," Jack said as they walked along the sea path toward his cottage.

"It's okay." It wasn't often that Jack lost his cool. Skye was glad when he did on her behalf. She didn't always know where he stood when it came to their relationship. Though if she were soul searching, she didn't exactly know what her position was, either.

They were good together. She knew that. There was passion in all the right places. Understanding most of the time. Fun, seriousness, all the things that should be there.

She glanced over to him, his profile silhouetted by the night stars. *Good cheekbones*, she thought. It was the first thing she'd noticed when they'd met several years ago.

Another year went by before he asked her out. He was friends with Sonny and Maya, but they were both seeing different people at the time. He was still transitioning from a nomadic life to life at the shore and she'd been busy deciding how to use her brain and her imagination and make a living at it.

They eventually got together and it seemed to be working. But seeing Connor again . . . It was like they had never been apart. The buzz in the air between them sprang back to life, but was it real or was it residual memory from a past that had moved on?

"Why didn't you tell me there were overruns in the budget?" Jack asked in the dark.

"I just found out from Brendan today. I guess the floor is worse than originally thought."

"You're talking about a few concrete blocks and square feet of lumber."

"Well, it was enough for Brendan to mention. And Herb is getting anxious. I don't know why. He agreed wholeheartedly when we finally talked him into it. Do you think it might be anything that Amy said?"

"I don't think so. Like I said, Leanne put her straight pretty quick."

"But what did she say?"

Jack stopped at the stone wall of Cove Beach to look out at the sea. And Skye realized, except for her few minutes on the beach with Connor that morning, she hadn't even thought about the things she loved most: just watching the waves with Jack, lying out on the sand with Maya, lazing in the heat of the sun. Sometimes Jack and Sonny would join them after work and they'd walk into town to the Dog and Pony. They hadn't done much lazing this summer. Zero in fact.

August, she thought. When August comes, life will be slower, and the beach will still be there. And Amy would be long gone.

"What did she say?" she asked again.

"I don't know. It took a few minutes for Sonny and me to figure out who was who and then it was snatches of an argument they were having. It wasn't anything. We heard your name, and Leanne went over to put Amy in her place. Then the guy, Connor, I guess, got mad and made her leave."

"He was mad?"

Jack's head snapped toward her. "Yeah, I guess. Sounded like it. But we were working without context, so . . . Don't worry about it."

She leaned into him, rested her head along his bicep, strong, muscular, reassuring. "Thanks."

"Come on. You need your sleep if you're doing double duty tomorrow."

THE NEXT MORNING came all too soon. At least Skye had slept fairly well, and she was surprised to find Jack still in bed when the alarm went off. He didn't look like he'd slept much at all.

"Is something wrong?" she asked immediately.

"Huh? No, I made coffee, then you looked so comfy I decided to come back and call in late."

She snuggled into him. "Too bad we both can't call in late today, but . . ."

"Yeah, me too. August," he said, unwittingly echoing her thoughts of last night.

"August," she said and climbed reluctantly out of bed.

CONNOR HAD TAKEN his second cup of morning coffee out to the beach in front of Roxy's house. Hildy's tenants had already settled in for the day, the kids running from beach chairs to surf and back again. Other families had set up little tent camps along the sand. Neighborly with enough room not to get in each other's space.

He should be enjoying this. The heat of the sun tempered by the sea was welcoming after the scorching dry heat of the desert. His face and arms were already pretty adapted to a sunny climate, but the rest of him was in need of the sunscreen Hildy had insisted he take down along with his coffee, which she put in a thermos, then added a blanket, a bag of cookies, and an aluminum chaise longue.

He staggered toward the beach trying to decide if she was being motherly or trying to get rid of him. Neither she nor Roxy had mentioned their dinner with Skye. Merely said that she was going to be very busy today because of an important town meeting. He was good at code. They were telling him to stay away today, and he could only suppose this meant Amy, too.

He was perfectly willing to do his part, as far as it went. And he fought his desire to pin them down. Ask if that meant Skye planned to talk to Amy after the meeting. Or if she planned to ignore Amy until she gave up and left.

Good luck with that. Connor was pretty sure Amy was broke. He'd asked about her job and she said she was on vacation.

He'd made the decision to take her at her word. It was none of his business. This visit was about Skye and Amy and he should stay out of it.

Who was he kidding? It wasn't just the desire to prevent trouble that had him driving Skye's talkative, egocentric sister six interminable hours to seek a meeting.

He couldn't even blame curiosity. Not innocent curiosity. He started out telling himself he could facilitate the confrontation. But he couldn't cling to that excuse for long. No. He was here for sheer self-interest.

He'd jumped at the chance to come because, dammit, he wanted to see Skye again after all these years.

Their relationship had loose ends, and even though Skye seemed happy in her new life, he couldn't help but wonder what if . . . The closer he and Amy had gotten to Rhode Island, the need to see Skye became almost unbearable.

And for what? There was bound to be a scene between the sisters. And then it would be over, for him at least. He'd drive Amy home, finish his visit with his parents. He had a life, a career that he loved. He was doing well in the world. He didn't need this. And yet, he just had to see for himself.

"What are we going to do today?"

Connor looked up. He didn't really need to. Amy's voice was unmistakable. And even though she was a mere silhouette block-ing out the sun, he had no illusions about what she had in mind.

And he wasn't going to play. Skye deserved more than this.

"I'm going to sit on the beach and read."

She crossed her arms. "You're no fun."

"I didn't come for fun."

"I know. You came to see *her.*" Amy pushed his legs over and sat on the chaise facing him. "Didn't you?" She leaned into him. Not in an aggressive way, but . . . *was she flirting with him?*

"I came because I felt slightly responsible for not being there to stick up for her when you accused her of arson. I thought you two should finally deal with it. That's the only reason and I'm ready to leave anytime, so if you want a ride . . ." Connor stopped. *Never force the other side into a position from which they can't escape.* And that included him. He wouldn't leave her here to cause whatever havoc she would—and yet he knew he had to leave.

He'd realized that at the beach with Skye yesterday. Many things in their lives had changed, but one thing in his hadn't. And that was something that could have no good outcome. He knew it. Yet here he sat.

He closed his book, postponing the inevitable. "What do you want to do?"

"Something fun."

Something fun, and preferably out of town, Connor thought. Not Newport. "How about we take the ferry to Martha's Vineyard?"

"Martha's Vineyard? That's where all the rich people go, right?"

"Yeah," he said, already regretting his suggestion.

"Famous people?"

"Yep."

"Good restaurants?"

"What do you think?"

"Okay. I'll get dressed." She stood up, nearly upsetting his chair. And definitely upsetting his peace of mind. He could be sitting on any beach he wanted, relaxing and enjoying the amenities of anywhere, but he wasn't. He was here, with Skye too close and too much temptation—and that was on him.

ROXY HEARD THE screen door slam. "You didn't last long," she called out. "Want more coffee? I just made a fresh pot."

She turned and an involuntary "Oh" escaped her lips. "Amy, I didn't know you were awake."

"Well, I am. I was going to talk to Skye today—"

"Not today," Roxy said. "She has to plan for an important meeting tonight. The whole town is counting on her, so this isn't a good time to distract her."

"Distract her? You sound like she doesn't want to see me."

"*I* don't want you to bother her today."

"Well, I can't anyway. Connor's taking me to Martha's Vineyard."

"What a great idea." Roxy knew she sounded condescending, but at least she'd managed not to roll her eyes. Could the girl be this clueless? Either that or purposefully obtuse? *Girl?* The way Amy was acting had Roxy thinking of her as a child instead of the adult that she should be. And that was a mistake.

"I know you don't want me here at all. Nobody in this family ever wanted me."

Roxy forbore pointing out that Skye and Amy's father was "this family," and she'd been the one to drive Skye away from her own father. And as far as Roxy was concerned, no, she didn't want Amy here. But that seemed gratuitously cruel. The girl—young woman—was obviously lost.

Amy's lip quivered, soon the tears would leak out. Roxy remembered the same expression from twenty years before, when James had still brought both daughters for a few weeks each summer. Amy had been five years old.

"I just want to make amends," Amy said.

"You have a funny way of showing it. Skye said you disrupted the store yesterday."

"I did not, but, Roxy, it's a god-awful mess."

"It's supposed to be, that's the freedom of creativity. And you were heard saying not very nice things about Skye at the diner."

"That was a private conversation. I was upset. She'd just practically thrown me out of her stupid store."

"Then you should have your private conversations somewhere private."

Amy dropped into a kitchen chair, the tears leaking down her cheeks.

Roxy sighed. Poured out a mug of coffee and placed it on the table in front of Amy.

Amy looked up from glistening lashes. "Cream and sugar?"

Suppressing a groan of annoyance, Roxy went to the fridge, got a carton of cream, snagged a spoon from the drawer, and placed them both firmly on the table in front of Amy before sliding the sugar bowl, which was already on the table, toward her.

Amy picked out several hard cubes and dropped them into her mug. Poured in the cream and spent an inordinate time stirring.

Roxy leaned on the table to face her. "Tell me, Amy. Why did you decide that this would be a good time for a surprise visit?"

"I just . . . just thought it was time."

"Maybe because Connor was visiting his parents and you saw, shall we say, a perfect opportunity?"

"He wanted to come."

Roxy raised an eyebrow but managed not to comment.

"He begged me to let him drive me here."

Roxy knew that there were at least two sides to every story and that the truth usually lay somewhere in between the two versions. This was pushing the envelope. But she'd also seen the spark in Connor's eye when he talked about Skye.

What a mess.

"Look, you want to make up with Skye? Then either put your actions to your words or leave her alone."

"But she's my sister."

"As far as I'm concerned, you forfeited that right years ago."

"How? I didn't do anything."

"You lied. Made everyone believe that Skye intentionally burned down her father's workshop. I wouldn't be surprised if you set that fire yourself."

"I did not. That's a horrible thing to say. I saw her."

"You saw her coming out of the building where she was trying to put out the fire, and she has the scars to prove it."

Amy pushed her coffee away. "Well, I can see she's convinced you."

"She didn't have to. Connor was an eyewitness. And if you've suffered a few nasty looks along the way, you have nobody to blame but yourself."

Roxy turned away, grabbed the first and only dish she saw, and began to scrub it at the sink. Turned on the water until it splashed against the porcelain. Maybe she had taken sides, but anyone would have if they had come home one night to find a shivering teenager huddled, muddy and drenched to the bone from the heaviest September nor'easter they'd seen in decades, her hands bandaged in gauze so filthy that Roxy was amazed infection hadn't set in.

But it had in fact set in, and the shivers were as much from fever as from chill.

Roxy and Hildy, not Skye's father or stepmother, had nursed Skye as she was ravaged first by infection, then pneumonia and then memory. She and Hildy together had nursed her though the delirium, where truth wove itself into nightmares. Roxy and Hildy had helped Skye look away from her broken life toward a hopeful future.

Skye had done better than Roxy could even imagine. And though she still carried the faint scars of the model train car on the palm of one hand, the rest of her had recovered . . . mostly.

"Skye's a well-loved and respected resident of town," Roxy said, staring out the window. She was too angry to even turn around. "She's gone more than the extra mile to help the other retailers. And many of their futures depend on her success. If you try to undermine her . . . this time she has many, many friends on her side."

The screen door slammed shut, and Connor stepped into the kitchen. "You're not ready yet?" Then he looked from Amy to Roxy. "I'll just go change."

Chapter 9

Skye managed to run upstairs to her apartment to change before the meeting. It had been touch and go until the very last second. It seemed like the days you most needed to do quiet work, something always went wrong. Today it was the LEGO steamer. Fortunately it was still under warranty, but it wasn't a common item and parts had to be ordered.

Until then, they would have to use hand washing and the portable steamer that they had started out with.

Fortunately Penny and Nat were able to come in early to take over the cleaning duties, since after half an hour Skye was afraid Maya might faint from the heat.

"You're sitting down right now. Or do you need to go home?"

"No, no, I'm fine," Maya insisted. "It's just I didn't get much sleep last night. Heartburn."

"Ugh," said Skye. "No more Mexican food for you until Baby Daniels is born."

"And even after," Maya said. "I don't want to give Baby heartburn, either."

"Oh yeah. I hadn't thought about that." Actually Skye hadn't thought much about babies at all. It was not a subject that came up often while building a business. Plus she still had plenty of time to decide what she wanted to do and with whom. Was it Jack? They hadn't discussed the future. Because they were content to live in the present or because . . . ?

"But I'm all right now." Maya stood up.

"Well, you're not going back into all that steam. You can manage the store today, if you really think you're okay."

"Of course I am. Don't you start, too."

"Sonny still being a little overprotective?"

"A lot. And cranky. I think he's worried about supporting both of us."

Skye's blood somersaulted in her veins.

"But I told him I was going to keep working."

Skye's heart started pumping normally again. She would deal with whatever Maya needed. Maya really was like the sister she'd always wished she had, unlike the one encroaching on Roxy' s hospitality at this very moment. And whom Skye would have to deal with soon. Instead of mooching off Roxy, Amy could have been the one getting overheated in the workroom now instead of Maya. Like that would ever happen.

Skye reached over and squeezed Maya's arm. "Whatever you need."

"I need things to be normal." Maya brushed at her eyes. "Sorry, it's the hormones."

"Hormones are fine. They're what make things work. We'll cope."

"Right," Maya said. "I'm fine, really. Go finish updating the financials."

And Skye had. Shut up in her cubicle office for most of the afternoon, finessing her reports on the coordination of special events and retail coupons that thankfully had a committee of its own. The status of housing in the local motels, inns, and B and Bs. Brendan, bless him, had agreed to come to report on the construction progress and back her up on the cost overruns.

Discover It Weekend had been Skye's idea. It had started as her individual business expansion, an opportunity for individuals and families to develop their quiet inner time for longer than forty-five minute blocks of scheduled time. She'd decided on a mid-July weekend, after the distractions of the Fourth were over and before people turned their attention to the coming fall. When she'd added it to the town calendar of summer events, interest was immediate.

The whole weekend? Where were the participants going to stay? Where were they going to eat? It was obvious to everyone that they could capitalize on Skye's event. Which was exactly what the town needed. A group effort to shore up the local businesses. They'd formed yet another committee, put Skye in charge of organization. She should have said no, but she didn't.

She'd originally planned to run the weekend out of Imagine That Too. Either doing things in-house or having docents meet the participants and then traveling to the various venues.

But the interest was immediate and overwhelming. They'd

had to cut off the participants at two hundred. Had a wait list pages long. It soon became evident that it had outgrown the original venue.

Then someone had suggested the Pritchards' camp. It had once been a popular summer destination but had fallen into disuse—and ruin. Suddenly, Skye had felt her weekend slipping out of her hands, but she had agreed to talk with Herb about renting the camp—to which he had agreed with the stipulation that she didn't expect him to make any repairs.

She'd talked with a local insurance agency about the cost of adding a temporary rider to her already expensive insurance. Sent in an inspector who didn't have great news. There was some rot and other structural problems with the mess hall and several of the cabins. To make it pass inspection would cost more than she could or was willing to pay.

But it turned out to be the perfect place for what she had in mind. Large enough to accommodate people for group events and perfectly located for the small events, with its own private beach and abutting the county nature park. Still, she'd needed financial help.

She'd run this all past the chamber of commerce. Expecting it to end there.

Local businesses, through the chamber, agreed to help with the funding. All they had to do was talk Herb into postponing the sale of the camp until August. In return, they would do basic maintenance and repairs, which would in turn increase the value of the property. He'd agreed . . . reluctantly.

Skye was skeptical, Jack was skeptical, and so were Roxy and

Hildy. But they were borne along on the local businesspeople's enthusiasm, which Skye knew was also born of panic.

Several stores had already closed downtown; several others were barely getting by. They were afraid that a developer would come in and build condos. No one wanted that. There were more condos than they needed right up the road.

The weekend could save the town. Everyone was optimistic.

Skye hadn't had the heart to say, *Let's just see how this goes then maybe next year we'll go bigger.* Many of them didn't have a year to spare.

So here she was less than three weeks before the opening with the construction running in the red and way too much work to go.

Skye dressed in navy linen slacks, off-white silk tee, and a light tailored jacket in case the air conditioning was working at the Moose lodge where the planning committee was meeting. She considered heels and decided on sandals instead.

She grabbed her papers and walked the four blocks to Rock Street.

The Moose lodge was a two-story, gray-shingled building with a steep roof and white shutters. The row of parking spaces that ran along the front was nearly filled. She'd figured the meeting would be well attended. People were excited. She just wished she didn't have to give them the financial update and burst their momentary bubble of optimism.

Skye had already spent her own allotted budget for the weekend. She had a slush fund available, but she felt an effervescence of unease.

Several people were crowded around a wooden pass-through that held two urns and several plates of cookies and dessert breads. Charlie Abbott, owner of Abbott's Heating and Air Conditioning, president of the chamber of commerce, and chairman of the Jump-Start July planning committee, saw her and waved her over.

Charlie was a tall man with big features, the largest being his ears, which stuck out from his head and wore a permanent sunburn at the tips. His hair was blond and quickly receding. All this combined to give him a slightly goofy appearance, which fooled competitors and clients into complacence until he went in for a surgical kill.

He could often be heard spouting his favorite motto among his friends. "Charm 'em, disarm 'em, and make 'em sign on the dotted line."

Fortunately, he was as honest as he was competitive. It made him a good leader.

"Coffee?" he asked, giving Skye a brilliant smile. Something he was doing a lot lately. And though Skye would like to take the credit for his high-wattage reception, she knew it was just because he'd gotten his teeth capped, which freed up his normally morose expression into one of joy.

"Thanks, but I reached my limit hours ago."

Skye made herself a cup of chamomile lavender tea, and since lunch was a dim memory, took two cookies and a napkin.

"I was just showing everyone the mockup of our Jump-Start July village posters." Charlie held up a large drawing sheet.

"Very effective," Skye said, her eye going directly to the

weekly schedules and finding the Discover It Weekend slot midway through the list of things happening in the village. There were a lot of them.

Skye's stomach tightened. She'd intended a quiet getaway retreat where people could discover their inner creativity. That's why she'd scheduled it for after the Fourth of July influx. She'd expected things to calm down after that, but now the town was being overrun with things they'd never had before.

"We're bringing back our Sundae Social," Rhoda Sims announced as she came over to look over Skye's shoulder. "The day before the Fourth, so it should bring in a lot of new faces."

"You are?" It was the first Skye had heard of it.

"Why shouldn't we? We used to have it every summer," Rhoda said. Being the church secretary, Rhoda took her position of organization maven and savior of all things church with a seriousness that often gave a bite to her speech.

"It will be held at the church," she continued. "Pastor Olins has already okayed it."

"Great," said Skye. "It sounds delicious."

Rhonda sniffed. "It was always a favorite. Speaking of which, I saw your sister, Amy, at the diner yesterday. Such a lovely-looking girl. I'm sure you're so happy to have her visit."

Skye gritted her teeth. "Yes, and a surprise, too."

"Is she planning on staying for a while? It's so nice to see new young faces in the community."

"I don't think so. I'm sure she has other commitments."

"Oh." Rhoda frowned. "Don't you know?"

"Know what?" Skye asked, wondering where this was going.

"Don't you know if she has other commitments?"

"No. Actually we haven't had too much time to talk."

"Well, maybe you can get her to stay awhile. I know you're busy with everything, but one should never neglect one's family. And if she *is* going to be around, maybe she'd like to help us with the ice cream social. It's just for a few days. It's important to get young people involved. And such a pretty girl, I'm sure she would inspire the young set to participate. Does she attend church at home?"

"I have no idea," Skye said, gritting her teeth, remembering the many times in her youth when she'd had to stand by while someone complimented Karen on having such a pretty daughter. It wasn't that Skye was a troll, she was nice enough looking herself. It wasn't even for herself that she resented those compliments to Karen. But that they seemed like such a slight to her own mother, who like her sister, Roxy, had been elegantly and slightly exotically beautiful.

Suddenly it was no easier to take from Rhoda Sims than it had been then.

Fortunately the door opened and Brendan Wraye walked in, followed by Herb and Edna Pritchard and Tizzy Lane, of Tizzy's Dizzy Sweets and Ice Cream, carrying a tote bag, which she held up as soon as she came inside.

"My flavor for July: Red, White, and Blueberry." She hurried over to the pass-through to the kitchen, deposited the bag, and began pulling out cardboard bowls and plastic spoons.

Skye made a mental note to bring up the recycling situation. The local business had made strides in reusable materials, but with the added people coming in for various events over the summer, they would need to make this a coordinated effort. She took out her phone and keyed in a couple of businesses who could be pivotal in setting that up.

As soon as they all were fortified with cookies, drinks, and a beautifully colorful swirl of Tizzy's latest creation, Charlie said, "It looks like we're all here."

Everyone took a seat around a long rectangular banquet table.

"Don't forget about asking Amy to help run the social," Rhoda said to Skye before taking a seat farther along the table.

Skye didn't recall ever having agreed to ask, but she'd let Rhoda think what she wanted. With any luck Amy would be long gone by the time the social rolled around this coming Sunday.

"Before we get to old business," Charlie said. "I'd like to thank Tizzy for another winning ice cream flavor." Polite applause and exclamations. "Now let's hear from Ed Novak on accommodations."

Ed Novak, a quiet-spoken man, stood up. "Participating inns, motels, and B and Bs are reporting an uptick in occupancy for the Fourth of July weekend, which includes the Sundae Social and Beach Barbecue. The trend carries through to the following weekend, with a slight dip midweek and . . ." He paused to smile around the table. "Nearly full occupancy for Discover It Weekend."

Everyone turned to look at Skye.

"Excellent," she said.

"Restaurants are preparing for the influx of people, and offering coupons for anyone participating in Skye's weekend."

He continued on quoting figures and data and Skye's mind turned inward. She was pleased and proud to have the whole town involved, but part of her worried that the situation was snowballing out of her control.

She was determined to prevent Discover It Weekend from becoming just another passing summer entertainment. To be successful, it would have to be able to keep the participants' experience insulated from outer pressures and the allure of constant bombardment for their attention. Someone had to be in control.

And then there was the budget . . .

"NO OFFENSE, BRO," Sonny said over the music at the Dog and Pony, "but it's kind of weird without the girls."

"Skye's meeting probably won't be done for at least another hour," Jack said. "But the state of Maya's indigestion is all on you . . . Papa."

Sonny sighed. "I didn't know it would be like this."

"Man, it's a hell of a time to have second thoughts."

"I'm not, it's just the responsibility. And it's always there. We had Mexican food—we always get Tito's takeout on Mondays—and she was up all night. I thought it would be cozy. Not scary as all hell. What if I can't support them?"

"People have been having families for thousands of years. I think you'll muddle through."

"Easy for you to say."

"True," Jack agreed. "Just thinking about it . . ." He stopped himself before he said *scares the shit out of me* and substituted, "makes me envious."

"Really?"

"Yeah."

"Well, what about you and—" Sonny stopped abruptly. "Shit, isn't that Skye's sister?" He lifted his chin toward the entrance door.

Jack turned around in his chair. "Yep."

They both watched as Amy Mackenzie, dressed in a short skirt and one of those scrunchy tube tops, stepped inside the pub.

"Looking for her boyfriend?" Sonny wondered.

"If you mean Connor, he's not her boyfriend," Jack said. "Or at least I don't think he is." Though maybe he was. Having lost Skye, maybe Connor had taken up with her sister. Kind of gross, but Jack would breathe easier if that were the case. Unless Skye wanted him back. And how would Jack deal with that?

"Yo, Jack."

"Huh?"

"Where did you go just now?" Sonny asked, looking concerned.

"Nowhere special. Looks like she's alone."

"Should we ask her over?"

Jack started to say, *Are you crazy?* Then thought again. He wouldn't mind getting a closer look at the workings of Skye's sister's mind. Find out why she was here, since Skye was avoiding her. "It might keep her out of trouble," Jack said finally.

Amy was scanning the room. She made eye contact and Jack motioned her over. Then he realized he didn't have a clue as to what to say.

Sonny didn't have that problem. "Aren't you Skye Mackenzie's sister? We saw you in the diner yesterday."

"Yeah, I am." Amy shifted onto one hip, a pose that looked at once uninterested and inviting.

"I'm Sonny and this is Jack. We're, uh, friends of Skye's. She has a meeting tonight, but she'll be coming in later." He flicked a look at Jack and, not getting any support, carried on. "Are you meeting someone? We're a couple of bachelors for the time being, so you're welcome to join us."

She scrunched up her shoulders and smiled. A cute gesture that matched her clothes and set Jack's teeth on edge. He reminded himself not to have preconceptions. But she already irritated him.

Jack pushed the drinks specials menu toward her.

She dipped her chin and looked up at him. Waiting for him to say something.

"They have some decent craft beers on tap," he said. *This was a dumb idea. It is going to be a long evening.*

And it was. Amy pumped them about Skye in a fairly conversational way, but it invariably led back to herself and how she admired Skye and she just wanted to be friends.

"I don't think she ever forgave me for being born," Amy said on a pitiful sigh that made Jack want to run for the hills.

How she could even be Skye's half sister was amazing.

In between her sad rendition of childhood, she peppered

Jack and Sonny with questions about Skye and about them and somewhere along the line it came out that Sonny was married and Jack was . . . as Sonny put it, "uh, Skye's friend."

What the hell *was* he to Skye? What was she to him?

Jack hadn't thought much about it. Except that it was what it was and that was good for him, and he thought it was good for Skye. He didn't like all this disruption when his life finally seemed to be settling down to what he thought he wanted it to be.

Finally Sonny stood up. "I gotta get going; Maya wasn't feeling well tonight, and I better get on home."

Amy clasped her hand over his. "Are you going toward the beach? Could you walk me there. It's kind of dark out there, and I'm not sure of the way."

"It's a straight shot down Main to the water," Jack said. "You'll see the drive to Roxy's across the street and to your right."

"Is it safe?" she asked, turning her big blue eyes on Sonny.

Of course it was.

"Of course it is," Sonny said, echoing Jack's thought. "But I'll be glad to walk with you. It's on my way home."

"Great." Amy stood up, pulled on the hem of skirt. "Nice to meet you, Jack."

Jack nodded. He waited until they were out the door before he let out his breath and ordered another beer.

Skye came in twenty minutes later.

"I'd just about given up on you," Jack said, standing and giving her a quick kiss. She looked like she could use it. "How did it go? You want something to eat?"

"No thanks, I had cookies and ice cream."

"Not good enough." He motioned for the waitress.

Bea Clark came running over. "Hey, Skye, what can I get for you? So that's your sister. You just missed her. How long is she here for?"

Skye cut a look to Jack.

"The gazpacho is excellent tonight," Jack said.

"I'll have a bowl of gazpacho," Skye said. "And a grilled cheese on rye and a micro. I'm not sure how long she's staying. Just a short trip."

"Well, any sister of yours . . . tell her we'll give her the local discount next time she comes in."

"Thanks." Skye waited for Bea to leave before turning to Jack.

"She came in, alone, and Sonny and I figured we better keep her occupied before she flirted and insinuated herself with every guy in the bar."

"And Maya was okay with that?"

"Maya wasn't here. She was feeling queasy, so she went home after work."

"She okay?"

"I think so. Anyway, Sonny's probably home by now. He left a while ago. He was going to drop Amy off at the drive to Roxy's and then go straight home."

"What?"

"No reason for you to get upset. Sonny's a big guy, he can take care of himself."

"You don't know my half sister."

"No, but I got a good dose of her tonight."

"If she does anything to upset Maya, I won't be responsible for my actions."

Jack smiled. "You're fierce. It's one of the many things I love about you. But maybe a good sisterly talking to would do the trick."

"Do you think she's sick?" Hildy asked, playing a four/seven on her domino train.

"No, I think a day in the sun and constant talking for the last three days may have tired her out," Connor said. Not to mention two ferry rides, a day of sightseeing, and a two-cosmo lunch on Martha's Vineyard.

"Or maybe she's upstairs plotting her revenge on us for keeping her away from Skye," Roxy quipped. "Should I go check?" She played a double three, and an additional three/two on her own train, then pushed back her chair.

"No," Hildy said. "Those stairs creak and if she is asleep, best to let her stay that way."

"True," Roxy said. "But Skye really needs to talk to her soon. We're all walking around like superspies, nervous superspies, so certain she's going to make trouble. I'm beginning to wonder if we're being too hard on the girl."

"Don't let your guard down yet," Connor said. "She wears you down with her 'no one understands me, no one loves me' routine. It may be true, but it's her own damn fault."

"The question is," Hildy said, domino in hand, waiting for Connor to make his move, "are we going to give her another chance or send her packing?"

The sound of the front door opening and closing had them all on their feet.

Amy stood in the hallway, swaying slightly on her feet. She smiled at them. "Hi."

"We thought you were in bed," Roxy said.

"I was, but I wasn't sleepy, so I went out. You guys were busy with your dominoes. I didn't want to bother you."

"Where did you go?" Connor asked. It didn't matter where, it wouldn't be good.

"I just had a couple of drinks at the local bar."

"Well, I think you better take your inebriated self to bed and sleep it off."

"Want to help me?" Amy smiled up to him.

Roxy saw red. Hildy gave her a warning look.

"No thanks," Connor said. "You made it this far by yourself . . ."

"Oh, this nice guy named Sonny walked me home."

"That's it," Roxy said and picked up her phone.

Chapter 10

Skye's cell rang as she and Jack walked along the shore toward his cottage. "So much for a peaceful end to a crazy day," she said. "I just hope nothing's wrong."

Roxy didn't even give her a chance to ask. "We're all fine," she said without preamble. "But I did want you to know that Amy had Sonny bring her home tonight."

"I heard." Then, "Why are you calling so late?"

"She just got in. We'd thought she'd gone to bed hours ago. It's probably nothing, but it is after midnight, and shouldn't Sonny be home with Maya?"

"He should," Skye agreed. And it shouldn't have taken him so long to walk Amy to Roxy's driveway. "I'll open up tomorrow then come over. Don't let Amy go out until I get there. She wanted to talk. She's about to get one."

Skye ended the call, turned to Jack. "What time did Amy and Sonny leave?"

"A little after ten, I think. He was just being polite. Amy

was afraid to walk alone. He offered to walk her down so I wouldn't have to, because he knew I was waiting for you."

"I'm sure he was, but that doesn't mean Amy didn't take advantage of him."

Jack laughed.

Skye cut him a look. "Don't think you guys are so smart. Amy is a talented manipulator. She's been honing it her whole life. And if she gets Sonny to do anything that will wreck their marriage, this baby, or my friendship with Maya, I'll make her pay."

Jack pulled her into his arms so fast that her head snapped back.

"And don't tell me you love me when I'm angry," she added.

"I do. But I love you most when you aren't angry. This is not your responsibility. Sonny is an adult, just trying to do the polite thing. Nothing happened."

"Jack, don't you understand? Nothing *has* to happen. It's all about perception."

He loosened his hold enough for them to start walking again.

She rested her head against his shoulder. He was strong, calm, self-assured. All the things she was not at the moment. "What am I supposed to do?"

"I assume that was rhetorical and not addressed to me specifically." He kissed the top of her head. "You'll figure it out. I have no doubt about that."

RED LIGHTS FLASH, lighting up the night, men shouting as flames rise behind them. Her dad just stares past her to the fire.

"She did it, she did, she did it." Amy's whine hurts Skye's ears. Everything hurts. Her hand feels heavy. She tries to open her fingers but they won't move, she's still clutching her dad's engine in her hand. She holds it out to her dad, her small offering, but he just stares past her.

Dad. She forms the word but he can't hear her. Why won't he look? Karen pushes her toward the house, Skye staggers, tries to turn back, but Karen is screaming at her, horrible things. And her dad just stares past her.

"You ungrateful little bitch." Karen's words burn into Skye's soul like the engine in her hand.

SKYE AWOKE THE next morning feeling like someone had dropped the world on her chest while she slept. She'd managed to shake off the lingering remnants of her oh so familiar nightmare, but instead of relief, the daylight merely brought burgeoning budgets, pregnant associates, and demanding sisters to replace it.

She looked in the mirror, decided she needed a day at the beach or at least a bit of makeup. Considering the things she had on tap for the day . . . she reached for her makeup bag.

A half hour later, armed with folders, spreadsheets, and a latte from the coffee bar, she stopped in front of Imagine That.

There was a new display in the front window that hadn't been there the day before. Maya must have redressed the window after Skye had left for the meeting last evening. Or come in really early—

She went inside.

Maya was standing behind the main display case intently cleaning the glass and hardly looked up when Skye entered.

"You're in early," Skye said.

"Couldn't sleep. The new brochures came in. They're over there." Maya pointed toward the information table without looking up.

Frowning, Skye went over to take a look. "They're fantastic," she said. A colorful advertisement that could be trifolded and mailed. With a list of some of their programs. LEGO of My Ego, Follow Your Star, A Bug's Life, and Copy That.

"I think we nailed this. Maya?"

"Yeah."

One glance told Skye that all was not well. Maya's face was puffy, and her hair that she'd been curling lately hung limp around her cheeks.

Skye forgot all about the flyer, her financial problems, and the Sonny situation. She dropped her bag and folders next to the flyers and slipped in beside her.

"Are you okay? Everything is fine with the baby?"

Maya nodded.

Skye exhaled in relief. "You're not sick?"

Maya shook her head. Skye had to lean over to see the tears pooling in her dark eyes.

"What is it then?" But Skye was afraid she already knew the answer. And dammit, if Sonny had succumbed to Amy's machinations, Skye would . . . do something.

"Hang on." Skye hurried to the front door, turned over the Closed sign. "I'd say a cup of tea in the back room is in order."

"But it's almost time to open."

"They can wait." Skye led Maya to the tiny kitchen/supply room, plugged in the electric kettle, and pulled down a mug and tea bags from the cabinet.

"It's nothing really. I don't want to be a burden . . . and . . ."

"Stop. Right now. We're in this together. Whatever it is, Sister I Always Wished I Had. So spill."

"Hormones."

"Let me guess. Sonny."

"He didn't come home until after midnight last night."

"He was with Jack at Mike's."

"I know. But . . . why did you let him go home with Amy?"

"They left before I got there, but Jack explained everything. Evidently Amy came in alone, and deciding it would be better to keep her contained they invited her for a drink. Then Sonny said he had to go home and she asked him to walk as far as Roxy's drive with her, because she was afraid of muggers or the dark or something.

"That was all it was," Skye finished, crossing her mental fingers that there was nothing more. Why had it taken almost two hours to walk two blocks? *But really what could they have done—no, don't even think about it.*

"Your meeting was over a little after ten; he didn't come home until after midnight. He was drunk. You do the math." Maya got up and fled the room. A moment later Skye heard the bathroom door slam. At least Maya hadn't left the store.

The tea water was ready, Skye poured out two mugs and waited.

When the tea was steeped and Maya still hadn't returned, Skye went to her. She knocked on the bathroom door. "Tea's ready."

"I don't want any."

"Maya. I'm sure you're right. It's hormones. Sonny would never do anything to hurt you. He adores you. He's going to be a dad." *And if he's misused your trust, I will make sure he pays big-time, along with my conniving little half sister.*

The lock clicked. The door opened and Maya stepped out. "I'm sorry."

Skye gave her an impulsive hug. "Don't be. I'm the one who should apologize. I should have dealt with Amy the first night she came. I'm going to remedy that now. Your tea is probably mud by now. I'm going to Roxy's."

"You don't have to," Maya said. "She's your sister. Half sister. You should hear her out."

"I think we've heard all we need to hear from that quarter. Isn't Penny in today? Let's plan to have a lunch, just you and me at the bistro on the water."

"But—"

"No buts." Skye headed for the beach.

As she expected, Roxy and Hildy were waiting for her in the kitchen.

Hildy handed Skye a mug of coffee before the door had closed behind her.

"She's down on the beach. At least we can keep an eye on her from here," Roxy said.

"Can we send her packing?" Hildy asked.

"Hildy!" Roxy exclaimed. "It's up to Skye whether we keep her or not."

Skye was filled with gratitude and a sense of belonging. Roxy wore denim clamdiggers and a plaid button-down shirt, with her hair piled riotously on the top of her head. Hildy looked like everyone's favorite grandma in her seersucker gardening smock.

Two formidable women full of love and compassion and adventure and to whom Skye owed her life.

"I was just kidding, sort of," Hildy said.

Roxy snorted. "No, you weren't."

Hildy harrumphed and turned back to the pile of beans on the counter.

"But we did talk, didn't we, Hildy?"

Another harrumph from Hildy.

"Maybe since Amy's here and Connor is here, just maybe this should be the time to get it all out there and be done with it. See if we can turn Amy around and if not, saints preserve us, send her on her way for good."

"I know I should hear what she has to say," Skye said. "But it's a pivotal point in my career, the town's future. I don't have the time for her neediness. I don't have the energy to make this any different than all the other times. But the alternative is to offer her some money and wait until she comes back for more.

"I don't want to live like that. All that negative energy directed at me. The lying and the whining, it will never go away if I don't come to terms with her once and for all. I know that. It's just . . ."

"I know, hon, and if you think it's too much, we'll stand by you and throw her out."

"It's not that I want to throw her out. I just want to be free of her backstabbing, and begging, and manipulating and denying it."

"She's a mess, but she is your half sister."

"And she can't stay for much longer," Hildy said. "How many weeks do irreplaceable office managers get for vacation?"

"I hadn't thought of that," Skye said. Amy's appearance had seemed like another chapter in a never-ending horror story. "But she's here now. Maybe it's time to confront it and get on with what it's going to be from now on. Think it will take longer than this morning?"

Roxy snorted. Hildy shot her a disapproving look.

"If you want to find common ground," Hildy said, "it may take a little longer than that, so we'll have to find something to keep her busy before she drives us all crazy."

"There are chores around the house," Roxy said. "She can clean out the hall closet." She grinned at Hildy. "And Connor can take her sightseeing, but he hasn't said how long *he's* going to stay. Did he tell you?"

Skye shook her head. "We talked a little the other day but he didn't mention it."

"He's no trouble, and it's nice having a threesome for dominoes," Hildy said. "So that's not a problem."

"Well, there is one possibility," Skye said. "I saw Rhoda Sims at the committee meeting last night. Evidently she saw Amy at the diner and she told me Amy would be the perfect addition to the Sundae Social committee."

"She didn't!" Hildy exclaimed.

"She did. Rhoda said she was so pretty and kept carrying on about how sweet she was, and how they needed someone who could draw more young people back to the church. And since Amy says she's good at organizing things . . ." Skye shrugged. "It could work."

Hildy snorted out a laugh. "Well, if Rhoda Sims can't whip her into shape, I don't know who can."

Roxy laughed so hard, Skye had to move her mug away so she didn't knock it off the table.

"Besides," Skye said, when the mug was safe, "if we don't do something, she'll head to Dad's for the rest of her vacation so she can mooch off him and make his life miserable."

"In that case," said Roxy, grinning so widely it threatened to swallow her whole face, "we'd love to have our little half niece stay." She frowned suddenly. "But what do we do about Connor?"

Good question, Skye thought. She hadn't thought about him. Had *tried* not to think about him. "I expect he'll go back and finish his visit with his parents."

"I wouldn't be so sure," Hildy said mysteriously and turned to pour herself more coffee.

"I'm sure he'll be relieved to be off the hook."

"You have to admit he's a good guy," Roxy said.

"He is and I appreciate it. It took me some time to realize it, but we talked a bit the other day. We're good."

Roxy nodded. Skye didn't miss the side glance she shot Hildy. "I'm just saying he's *nice*. We like Connor. We love Jack."

"Don't worry. I'm good. As long as Amy doesn't do something to destroy my reputation." Skye played with the handle of Roxy's mug. "An ultimatum. We let her stay if she works at the church. Who knows, it *might* do her some good. And it will keep me free to work. Do you think she could do any real harm?"

"Not at all," Roxy said. "I think it is an excellent idea. And Rhoda Sims is just the person to make her or break her."

Skye stood. "Into the breach then . . ."

She reluctantly left the kitchen and made her way down to the beach where Amy was stretched out on a lawn chaise. She was wearing a tiny bikini that looked so new she might have picked it up since she came to town.

She didn't look up until Skye stood in front of her. Finally lifted her sunglasses high enough to see it was Skye. Then let them drop. "You're blocking my sun."

Skye just stood waiting. She wasn't in the mood for games, especially not Amy's kind of games.

Careful, Skye warned herself. *She's doing it to get a rise out of you.* And it was working. Years might pass but some things never changed.

Finally Amy lifted her glasses again.

"What?"

"If you think I'm going to talk to someone who doesn't give me the courtesy to sit up and take their sunglasses off, then you can start packing."

Amy huffed out a sigh and pulled her glasses off, making a big show of shielding her eyes with her hand. "The sun's in my eyes."

"Then turn around." Skye grabbed the end of the light aluminum chaise and pulled it around to face the house.

Amy screeched and grabbed the armrests. "You can't make me go. Roxy said I could stay."

"Don't count on it. Now you said you wanted to talk. Talk."

"Why do you always attack me? All I want is for you to be my sister."

"Half sister and it's a little late for even that."

"You can't keep blaming me for something that happened years ago."

"I never give that part of my life a thought," Skye said. *Only in her dreams.* And in those, the horror and the pain was just as bad as ever. "But if I did, I would say that you're the one who should be carrying the blame."

"I didn't do anything."

Skye forced herself not to turn away. They'd been here before. "No? You falsely accused me of trying to kill my father by burning down his workshop. Why would you do that?"

"I know what I saw."

"You also knew that he and Karen were having dinner out."

Amy at least had the consciousness to look away.

"You did it on purpose, didn't you?"

Amy shook her head jerkily, like a guilty child.

They'd been here before, too. With Amy refusing to believe Skye or accepting responsibility for her actions. Skye was so tempted just to walk away, but they needed to get it all out once and for all. Unfortunately, nothing with Amy was once and for all.

At least not until now. She just kept coming back, calling, emailing whenever she needed money or someone to cosign, or a shoulder to cry on.

Skye put up with the sporadic calls just to keep Amy from bothering their father, who was too easily coerced and not that capable of taking care of himself, much less his needy daughter.

As for Amy's mother, Karen, she was the mold from which her daughter was formed. She'd remarried twice and left Amy out in the cold.

Skye could almost feel sorry for her half sister if she wasn't such a pain in the butt.

But this was the last time.

She stepped closer to Amy's chair, braced her hands on the arm of the chaise. "What do you really want, Amy?"

"I told you."

"No, I mean this time. Money? How much do you need? I'm not very flush right now. Will a hundred do it? Two? Three?"

"I didn't come for money." Amy's mouth twisted into a sly little smile. "Though I could do with a little loan right now."

"Fine, and then you can go enjoy your vacation elsewhere. You can take Connor with you. How much do you need before your next paycheck?"

"We-e-ell." Amy's gaze dropped down to her hands. "Here's the thing." She stopped to straighten out the towel she was sitting on. "I don't actually still have a job?" She ended the sentence on a question, an annoying habit she'd had since childhood.

"You quit?"

"Not exactly."

"You were fired?"

"It wasn't my fault."

"Oh Amy, it never is. What was it this time? I thought you liked that job."

"I did, but they never listened to me. They're living in the Dark Ages. Do you know they still send out paper bills?"

"Most businesses do."

"No, I mean by hand. You have to stuff envelopes and everything. And their filing system, and the computers are ancient and you couldn't share data with anyone, and it was so . . . tedious."

"And I suppose you told them so."

"Of course I did. I was just trying to help, but old man Hazlitt said I was being disruptive and if I couldn't get along with everyone . . ."

"And you said. 'Oh, I'm so sorry, Mr. Hazlitt. It was just my enthusiasm taking over, and I promise to do better in the future'?"

"What? Why would I do that? He was wrong. They're just too stupid to move forward. They'll be out of business before they know it."

How did you explain to someone like Amy that no one wanted to be called stupid? Or that you caught more flies with honey, and all those other clichés? You couldn't. She just didn't get it.

Amy looked up under mascaraed lashes. "So now I don't even have an income. Unless you want to give me the money for airfare to Florida."

"So you can mooch off Dad? No thanks. I'll give you a train ticket back to Harrisburg so you can start looking for a new job."

Amy shook her head. "I don't want to go back there. I want to try something different. I know, I can help at your store."

"Not a chance. You dissed my store in front of my customers. You upset the parents and made fun of the kids."

"I was just trying to help."

"No you weren't. People who are trying to help make suggestions, not insult you and your customers."

"I didn't."

Skye just looked at her. Maybe she'd bite the bullet and call Karen, suggest she get Amy some kind of therapy. Not that Karen would give her the time of day. Skye was sure she had danced on the ashes of the workshop when Skye ran away. Especially once she'd learned what had been stored there.

"Why not? You really need someone to help out. It was a mess."

"It's supposed to be a mess. It's a creative space. The only rule is kindness."

"Ugh. That's so corny."

"Well, it's my corn. I came to terms with you and your angst years ago, but I won't have my store used as a pawn."

"No, you didn't; you won't even talk to me."

"I'm talking to you now."

"That's not what I mean."

"You mean that we're not talking about *you*. You're a black hole of need, Amy. You were loved, no, adored by everyone. You were given everything you needed, preened and pampered your entire childhood. You have nothing to complain about."

"They gave me stuff, but they liked you better."

"Bullshit. The kids used to call me Cinderella. I don't know what went wrong with you, so I don't know how to fix it, but you should really try. For now, though, I am going to talk and you're going to listen. No explanations, no excuses."

"But—"

"Quiet. Last night, I don't know what happened, but Sonny was late getting home and his wife was worried. Did you hear that? *Wife*. She's pregnant and she's my best friend." Skye refrained from saying, *Maya is the sister I wish I had instead of you*, but she was so tempted as she felt her anger threatening to boil over.

Skye didn't like being angry. It added bad energy to the world and made her physically sick. She took a breath.

"And?"

"And you will leave him alone, period. Stay away from him, far away from him."

"It was dark and I was scared." The words tumbled out in one breath.

"For close to two hours? Try again."

"He thought we should stop for coffee because I'm not used to drinking beer and I was a little tipsy. I didn't want to go home that way."

"One, Roxy's isn't your home. And two, she's seen worse. Don't do it again. This is between you and me. You're not going to start poaching on my friend's husbands." Skye turned to leave. Came back. "On second thought, maybe it would be better if you just left. Now."

Oh, she had so not meant to say that. She was supposed to be mending things.

"What about Connor? Do you want him to leave, too?"

"What Connor does has nothing to do with me."

"But I bet you'd like him to stay."

"Water under the bridge."

"Just give me a chance."

"Really, Amy? You can ask that? We've given you chances, money, even character references, and you haven't been able to make any of them work; you are the only one who can decide what to do with your life, besides using people to no good end. It doesn't even help you in the long run, does it? Does it?"

Amy shook her head. "Please. Just one more time. Or I'll hitchhike to Dad's."

"Blackmail isn't endearing, Amy."

"Oh please, Skye, I just need a break."

It was hopeless. Amy really didn't understand what she was doing wrong. How could that be possible? As far back as Skye remembered, her half sister had friends in school. Karen had doted on her, so obviously sometimes that Skye heard other mothers commenting on it. Skye still blushed at the things they'd said about Amy, about her mother, and about Skye.

Amy stood there looking contrite and eager and Skye knew not to trust it. Amy could erode your resolve with her mercurial changes of moods and manipulations.

"I'll give you one last chance to show you're serious about reconciling. One week. I'll even get you a job. It's volunteer, but Roxy and I will take care of room and board and even give you a little—a very little—spending money."

"You will?"

"On the condition that you do not screw up, do not insult anyone, do not try to steal anyone's husbands, or do anything to make me regret it. You have to promise."

"Okay, I promise. What is it?"

"You might have seen your new boss in the diner the other day."

"I have to work at the diner?"

"Oh no. Too many things could go wrong there."

"Then who? I didn't see anyone else."

"Sure you did. A nice, late-middle-aged woman, sitting at the counter. Short haircut."

Amy's face fell. "Oh, her."

"Yes. Her name is Rhoda Sims. She's the church secretary and she's looking for someone to help with their ice cream social this coming weekend."

"Church? No way."

"You can stay through the weekend, then you'll have to go home."

"That's not fair. You're just setting me up for failure."

Skye had a hard time not rolling her eyes. It's what Amy did best. Almost as if she were failing on purpose. But who would do that?

"It's your choice."

Amy slid down on the chaise. Then sat up. "I know. Why don't I help Roxy and Hildy with the B and B?"

Skye shook her head. "You already insulted their guests."

"Well, nobody told me that was their parking place."

"No excuses, remember? You have a week to turn over a new leaf. So you might want to take out your 'I'm sorry,' and polish it up a bit."

"Why do you hate me?"

"If I hated you, I would have sent you packing the night you arrived."

"Roxy wouldn't let you."

"I wouldn't bet on it. So if you want to stay and have us subsidize your visit, you'll run upstairs and change clothes."

"Now?"

"Yes. I'll take you to meet with Rhoda now and you can start today. Put some of your twenty-first-century ideas to work for a good cause."

Amy slumped so far down in the chaise that her chin rested on her chest.

She was acting like a child. Had always acted like a child. Maybe she was incapable of changing. "Or Connor can drive you right back to Harrisburg this afternoon. Fine by me either way."

"Oh okay." Amy rolled off the chaise, snatched her towel off the chair, and began shoving things into her beach bag.

"And wear something pretty," Skye called over her shoulder as she headed back to the house.

Chapter 11

"You told her to wear something pretty?" Roxy could barely ask through her laughter.

"I know," said Skye. "It was gratuitously tacky. It's what my stepmother always told me and I was just so fed up with her."

"I know. And we shouldn't laugh," Hildy said, trying to keep a straight face. "It's wrong to be so mean, but how can someone her age be so clueless?"

Skye sat down at the kitchen table. Her one little show of malice was already causing her chagrin. She just wasn't cut out to be mean. But evidently, she was cut out to keep giving in to her half sister.

"I should have said no. Given her the money to fly to Florida. Let Dad deal with her. I know he's kind of clueless himself, though, and I didn't have the heart to impose her needs on him. But maybe I'm wrong. Maybe they would be good for each other."

"In what universe?" Hildy said.

"Hildy's right," Roxy said. "Your father was never a favorite of mine, but he loved you and he loved your mother. I'm sure he loves Amy, too, in his way. But I don't think he'll be any good for her or she for him. She can stay here—"

"On the condition she stays away from my tenants," Hildy added.

"I'll make that clear," Skye said. "Are you guys sure? I'm not strong-arming you into this?"

"Not at all," Roxy said. "We'll try to help her. She's obviously a confused soul."

"I'd say she's more than confused," Hildy retorted. "Neurotic and self-centered come to mind. That girl has some real problems."

"Well, maybe having her so close will give us some insight."

Skye did not feel that optimistic, but she supposed she must try. Unless Connor could give her a better alternative.

"Where is Connor this morning?"

"He went down to the library or maybe it was city hall. He had some communications he wanted to deal with and I think he needed some alone time."

"Well, if we let Amy stay, he can go back to what he was doing before she coerced him into driving her here."

"I don't think he needed much coercing," Hildy said.

"Did you know he'd been married?" Roxy asked.

"He mentioned it the other day. I took him down to see the camp."

"Ah," Roxy said.

"I'm not sure why he's still here, except that he feels responsible for bringing Amy."

"A little trip down memory lane, perhaps," Roxy said.

"He was never here before."

"Don't be obtuse, leave that for your sister."

"I'm not reopening anything with Connor."

"Then maybe you should make sure you close it once and for all, so you can both get on with life."

"I have."

"And so has he," Roxy added. "But the past evidently hasn't let go of him . . . or you. Or Amy. This might be the best time just to duke it out and see what's left standing."

Or who, thought Skye.

The kitchen door opened and Amy dragged herself in.

"Perk up, Amy love," Hildy said. "You're about to have your audition."

Amy straightened, put on a smile that almost passed as genuine.

Well, that's a start, thought Skye. "Are you almost ready?"

JACK TORE A sheet of graph paper from the tablet, balled up the latest failed design, and tossed it on the floor. For days he'd had this idea for a corner hutch, pearlized glass front and beveled from the wall. So far it looked like a cartoon character that had swallowed a bowling ball. Or the clock from *Beauty and the Beast*.

He and Skye had actually streamed the movie one night on a whim. Jack wasn't averse to the idea of talking furniture as long as it wasn't programmed to reheat your coffee. He was a minimalist. Sleek was his middle name. There was nothing sleek about a device that talked back and never understood what you said. The idea was about as appealing as reproduction Queen Anne. Which was to say not at all.

He'd enjoyed the movie. So had Skye. And something about those petals slowly dropping inside that bell jar led to mad passionate sex in front of the TV. The credits were rolling when they realized they'd missed the end of the movie. They should have been satisfied with that, because when they reran the film to see the end, Jack was disappointed.

"I kind of liked him better as the beast," Skye had said.

"Good," he'd said. He liked the beast better, too. He could relate.

Jack leaned back against the worktable and watched Sonny hand-sanding a table leg.

After a few seconds, he could see that something was wrong. "You trying to sand that leg into oblivion?"

Sonny didn't stop, just leaned in harder.

"Hey, hold up, or you'll have to make a new leg." Jack went over to take a closer look. "What's up?"

Sonny tossed down the piece of fine sandpaper. "Maya is pissed at me. I tried to explain but she's just impossible lately."

"She's pregnant. I think you're supposed to cut her some slack."

"I do. But nothing I do is right."

"So what is she upset about?"

"About me taking Skye's sister home last night." Sonny picked up the sandpaper again.

Jack stopped his hand. "Never make furniture or food in anger. Bad juju."

"Grrr." Sonny tossed the sandpaper on the floor. It landed near Jack's crumpled piece of graph paper.

"Let's take a break." Jack dropped his notepad and walked over to the half fridge. The sound of the fridge door opening set off motion in the corner where Goodle, Sonny and Maya's goldendoodle, spent most days.

Jack took a couple of sodas out of the fridge, grabbed a dog biscuit from the box on the shelf. He propped the delivery door open so they could hear the buzzer from the showroom if anyone came in, then carried everything out to the back lot, followed by Goodle with Sonny bringing up the rear.

While Sonny hosed off Goodle's bowl and refilled it with water, Jack pulled two folding chairs into the shade. The lot was just a patch of overgrown weeds that served as scrapyard and garbage dump, but if you placed the chairs just right, you could actually see a sliver of sea between the neighboring buildings.

Jack set the sodas on an old glue drum, gave Goodle his treat, and sat down. Sonny sat in the other chair, and Goodle settled at his feet.

"We're all feeling the effects of Amy Mackenzie," Jack said. "Skye is wound as tight as I've seen her. She's under a lot of pressure because of how her weekend has turned into a town lifeline with her holding the line."

"Yeah, I've noticed that lately," Sonny said.

"Why did you even tell Maya about taking Amy home?" Jack asked. "You just took her as far as Roxy's drive, right?"

Sonny popped the top off his soda and took a long pull.

"Sonny?"

"Yeah, once we got there."

Jack groaned inwardly. "Please say you didn't do anything stupid."

"No, man. I would never. But it was weird. I meant to go straight home, but I didn't get there until after midnight."

"You left after ten. What the hell?"

"We got to the end of the street, right past the diner. She'd started to feel the effects of her beer, acting tipsy and staggering and falling into me and giggling."

"She wasn't drunk when you left."

"I know. It must have been the night air or something. Anyway, she asked if we could stop in at the diner for a coffee because she wasn't used to drinking and she didn't want to go home drunk and have Roxy and Hildy think bad of her."

"That should have been your first clue."

"Hell, I didn't know what to do with her. So I said okay. I thought she'd have a quick cup at the counter, but she went right to a booth. Leanne was closing up and she gave me a look that could freeze a man's blood.

"I said something stupid about how I'd been asked to escort Skye's sister home—I shouldn't have brought Skye into it, should I?"

"I'm pretty sure the whole town knows by now."

"Anyway, Leanne poured us two cups. And Amy started talking about how she just wanted Skye to like her. And, really, I don't see why Skye can't just make up with her, she seems nice enough."

"Looks can be deceiving," Jack said, though he only had

Skye's opinion to go on. But she was Skye's half sister and if Skye didn't know her, who would?

"Then she wanted another cup of coffee and she kept talking."

"Why didn't you just call Maya and tell her what was happening?"

"I didn't want to wake her. She's having enough trouble sleeping as it is. I was trying to be considerate and I got reamed for it.

"And I finally told Amy I had to be home. And she made some joke about me not being allowed to stay out. Pissed me off actually.

"Then when we got to the drive she said it was too dark and she was afraid, so I walked her to Roxy's door. As soon as she was inside, I hightailed it home. Maya was not asleep."

Jack grimaced. "Bad, huh?"

Sonny nodded. "Bad. I tell ya, Jack. We've tried really hard to get pregnant. But these hormones are making life crazy. I show concern, she bites my head off; I go out for a drink, she bites my head off."

"I should have taken Amy home," Jack said. "Actually I should never have invited her over to the table. I just wanted to avoid a replay of the diner. She's trouble."

"Hell, don't I know it. Though . . ."

"Though what?" Jack asked, getting a bad feeling.

"She doesn't seem so bad. I mean she's kind of self-centered and immature, but she's also kind of sweet."

THE BAPTIST CHURCH was a fairly long walk away, so when Roxy and Hildy offered to drive them over on their way to the grocery store, Skye gladly accepted. She had a huge amount of things to do today. And every minute counted.

Plus, she was eager to get back to the store and reassure Maya that Sonny was now off-limits.

Skye and Amy sat in the back just like they had as girls going to Sunday school, only then it was a Toyota Camry and their father would be driving. Karen would sit beside him, head forward, chin lifted, face pointing away from her husband. Amy, six years younger than Skye, would be wearing a dress from the high-end children's clothing store. Skye wore whatever was comfortable and closest at hand.

She actually had liked church: the music, and the pastor's sonorous voice, and the scriptures always made her feel like there was something bigger than herself. She hadn't much liked Sunday school, and often she would sneak out and meet Connor in the park where they would sit and dream or hit the pancake house to share a short stack.

Then Amy would invariably tell on Skye and Skye would be sent upstairs to think about her attitude until dinnertime.

She glanced over at Amy, now the one looking morbid and uncomfortable and like she'd rather be anywhere but here. And Skye had to keep herself from saying, *Serves you right*.

She couldn't remember a time when the sisters really liked each other. Maybe when Amy was a toddler, before she went to school and Karen began grooming her to think she was better than everyone else.

It was sad really. Cinderella Skye had made a decent life for herself. But pampered Amy was still finding her way. Finding her way? Hell, she seemed as lost as ever.

Well, Skye would do what she could, this once, then she'd wipe her hands of her half sister, her stepmother, and their self-actualizing problems.

They arrived at the church while Skye was still thinking. Roxy pulled into the parking lot of the white clapboard building with its slightly leaning bell tower. The ancient bell still rang every Sunday rain or shine in spite of being drowned out by the mechanized recordings adopted by most of the other local churches.

It seemed stuck in time to Skye, and she felt a pang for those lost moments of when real bells filled the air.

Roxy drove around to the back and stopped at the wooden annex where the church offices and hospitality hall were located.

"Good luck," Roxy called as Skye and Amy got out of the car.

And Skye had her first misgiving.

What if Amy insulted the ladies' auxiliary on her first day on the job? Skye's stomach flipped over. And she realized that she was worried not just about Amy, but for her own reputation. That didn't happen often. But between the town's summer plans, and the appearance of Amy—and Connor—she felt suddenly on a precipice of indecision—something else that didn't happen often.

As Roxy and Hildy drove away, Skye turned to Amy. "Remember what I said. Please."

"I'm not incompetent," Amy said.

"I know you aren't. I just don't understand why you seem intent on making yourself fail."

Amy pulled a face.

Skye waited.

Finally Amy smiled. "How's this?"

It was going to be a disaster.

They walked up the steps and went inside. The church, though not air-conditioned, felt cool, but damp. The office door was open and Skye poked her head inside. No one was sitting at Rhoda's desk, but she could hear the printer working in the other room.

She nudged Amy inside, then followed her into the office.

"Rhoda? Are you here?"

Rhoda's head appeared in the doorway to the back room. She was wearing a navy skirt, a flowered blouse, and a light yellow cardigan. *Caught in time, like the church building*, thought Skye.

"I brought Amy to talk to you about helping out with the social. Maybe she could also do some filing and things around the church. She's worked as an office manager and should be a big help."

"Wonderful, just let me finish up this job. Have a seat." Rhoda's head disappeared.

"I can talk for myself," Amy said.

"Of course you can. I was just . . . Fine, I'll leave you to it."

Amy grabbed the sleeve of Skye's tee. "Don't you dare."

"Fine." They both sat down, and in a few moments Rhoda was back with a stack of paper.

"Perfect timing," Rhoda said. "I just finished the mailings

for the social. Everyone knows about it already, I'm sure, but it doesn't hurt to remind the congregation. I'm so pleased that you'd like to help out, Amy. Can you start right away?"

Skye left Rhoda to explain the history of the Sunday Sundae Socials.

CONNOR STOOD ON Roxy's porch, hands in his pockets, looking out over the water. His leave was creeping away. He wasn't visiting his parents as he'd intended. He wasn't even having a relaxing few days at the shore.

So far he'd been chauffeur, babysitter, and mediator. And he was going stir-crazy. Now that they'd arranged work to keep Amy busy and out of trouble, there was no reason for him to stay. Actually there had been no reason for him to come.

Except he'd wanted to come. Welcomed the excuse, even though it had been the longest six-hour drive of his life. He'd rather have a half-dozen envoys yelling at him in disparate languages than go through that again.

But it had been worth it just to see Skye again. Once. She hadn't even suggested meeting again. He should leave. He was sure Roxy or Skye would pay for Amy's passage home. She wasn't really his responsibility. She wasn't his responsibility at all.

He'd never felt that she was. She hadn't had to try very hard to con him into giving her a ride. Once the idea of seeing Skye had gotten into his head, it took over his entire world.

Well, you've seen her. She's happy. She doesn't blame you for anything. Curiosity satisfied.

But it wasn't satisfied. He didn't want to disrupt the life

she'd built. But . . . he did. He wanted to see if there was anything left between them. He'd never found it elsewhere, and God knows he'd tried.

Diplomacy was a great career as far as careers went, but his personal life had suffered. He'd met plenty of women along the way, even married one, and what a disaster that had been.

He didn't hold out much hope of finding another one. Because truth be told, he was afraid he was still in love with Skye.

And that was crazy. She obviously had a significant other, though she really hadn't talked about him. And why was that? Was she wondering, too? Did he dare go down that road?

He could cause Skye as much trouble as Amy could, maybe even more, but for better reasons. But that wasn't fair.

But it was also not fair not to know. He'd been here four days, seen her once for a few minutes. No plans to see each other again. She didn't even act like she wanted to see him again. Maybe he should just leave.

Connor glanced at his watch. If he left now, he could be back at his parents' house by midnight. Of course he'd hit I-95 for rush hour and that would slow him down. Better to wait until the morning.

Besides, Roxy and Hildy had gone to the store. They'd probably need help with the groceries. It was the least he could do to pay back their hospitality.

And he should make sure Amy made it through her first day at the church without insulting everybody. That would be better.

If all was well, he could leave in the morning.

He heard a car stop at the back of the house. He went out to help unload the groceries and tell them he was leaving.

Roxy and Hildy were just getting out of the car. Hildy lifted open the trunk and Connor reached in for two bags while Roxy went to hold the door open.

It only took three trips to empty the car and fill every surface in the kitchen with reusable carryalls.

It was now or never. "I've been thinking," Connor began.

Roxy and Hildy both turned to give him their full attention.

"Do you think it would be okay if I asked Skye to dinner?"

Chapter 12

Skye ended the call with Connor. He'd said he was planning on leaving in a day or two if Amy's work at the church was going smoothly. So he would like to see Skye again before he left. Would dinner tonight be convenient? She'd felt a tumble of disappointment and anticipation. And confusion. And she'd said yes.

He'd sounded so formal, almost as if he'd prepared what to say. Almost like he was a stranger. Not like the boy she'd known. But Connor was no longer a boy. And Skye wasn't the girl she had been.

Being a diplomat he'd probably learned to choose his words carefully. But it had thrown her off so that she hadn't questioned if it was wise to reopen that door to the past. Their one meeting had reestablished that there were no hard feelings, that they were both successful in their careers, and she'd thought that would be the best way to leave it.

But just seeing him had set off feelings that she didn't want to examine and she certainly didn't want to pursue.

She'd said yes. She didn't say, *I'm really tired, how about tomorrow?* She didn't say, *I'll have to check with Jack first and make sure we don't have plans.* She'd just said yes.

Of course Jack rarely made plans before consulting with her. He might surprise her with a piece of sea glass he found on the beach, or a bracelet or necklace from a local artist that caught his eye. A bucket of freshly dug clams. But plans . . . ?

Skye breathed out a laugh. She and Jack had a very balanced relationship. Comfortable. Satisfying. And he never, well, hardly ever, made her question what she was doing.

With Jack, she never felt the rush of nerves she was feeling now. Of course the only baggage they shared was from the last five years and they'd worked through most of it. There were things she didn't know about him, and things he probably didn't know about her. But they hadn't been a part of those things.

Not like she and Connor.

She and Connor had grown up knowing everything about each other. Dreamed and planned together, like yin and yang, not whole without the other.

They'd shared everything. Everything but the last fifteen years.

Sheer panic spread through her.

Jack would probably think it was a good idea to find some kind of new understanding with Connor. He always said it was best to know where you stood in the world. He was so down-to-earth, so assured, so solid. Then you saw his furniture, sleek and lean and so sublime that she sometimes wondered if there was a part of him she'd completely missed.

It's only dinner, Skye told herself. *Not an existential reckoning.*

They agreed to meet at the store at six.

"Wouldn't you like to go home first?" Connor asked.

"I live upstairs."

"Oh. That's convenient. I'll see you then."

She'd immediately called Jack.

"Connor called and asked me to dinner tonight. Do you mind? He's leaving in a day or two."

"Sure, you two probably have a lot to catch up on."

She waited. Hoping for some further reaction, maybe? "You don't mind?"

"What kind of question is that?"

A stupid one, Skye realized. Was she asking his permission? That's not what she'd meant. She didn't know what she meant. "I just didn't know if you had your heart set on Sal's Pizza or something."

"I'll survive. Go have dinner and enjoy yourself."

"See you after?"

"Sure. I'll leave the porch light on."

"Was that a joke?"

"A little one. Is something the matter?"

"No. Well, I'm a little nervous."

This earned her silence at the other end.

"Stupid, huh?"

"You feel what you feel. You'll be fine. Gotta go, Sonny needs an extra pair of hands. See you tonight."

He ended the call, but Skye just sat there. Added to her

jumble of anticipation and her agitation was something she rarely felt toward Jack, annoyance.

"WHAT WAS THAT all about?" Sonny asked as Jack lifted the other end of the tabletop, balancing the weight between them.

"Skye is going to dinner with Connor tonight."

They sidestepped the heavy wooden piece until it was directly over the braced and clamped wooden frame, gently lowered it until its marks aligned, then eased it into place.

"They didn't invite you?"

Jack looked at his friend over the tabletop. "They probably just want to talk about old times and figured I would be bored."

Sonny shook his head. "You know for a smart guy, you sure can be dumb."

"This from a guy who is in trouble with his wife for walking Skye's sister home." Jack blew a few specks of sawdust from the table surface. Looked up again. "What are you saying?"

Sonny gave him a look.

"You think he's going to come riding in like Sir Galahad or one of those guys and whisk her away to foreign lands? She has her family here. Her business. Me."

"Just saying, a guy can't be too careful."

"Hell, Sonny. It's just dinner."

"Uh-huh." Sonny squatted down, his head disappearing beneath the tabletop. "A half inch toward me on the left," came his muffled direction.

Jack lifted the corner of the top to slide it gently forward.

"A little more."

Jack pushed it the merest amount.

"That's it."

Jack watched the top of Sonny's head as he crouch-walked over to the next corner. "Perfect. Check your end."

Jack crouched down, checked that the marks were in alignment.

"Good here," he said.

Sonny looked at him from underneath his end of the table. "Good here. And you're an idiot."

They both stood. "Okay, I'm a dumb idiot. You think she's going to succumb to that . . ."

"Well-dressed, handsome, debonair—"

"Not funny."

"I'm just ragging on you. You're probably right. Just two old friends getting together over drinks and dinner and . . Is it a full moon tonight?"

Jack threw a chamois cloth at him.

They cleaned off the table and took a break to let it settle before making the final adjustments. They went out back, the only place to really sit down and relax.

"Finished three days ahead of schedule," Sonny said, stretching his legs out from the battered aluminum chair. He laced his fingers behind his head and lifted his face to the sun. "If it sets up without any hitches, we should be able to deliver it next week."

"Hmm," Jack agreed, but he wasn't really listening. He wasn't thinking about furniture or the fact that the delivery truck needed new tires. He was thinking about Skye and what he would do if she left him. It was something he hadn't thought about before.

He stood up. Walked across the yard to the sagging chicken wire fencing just to get a glimpse of the ocean between the buildings. Jeez. He didn't think in those terms. People leaving each other, stealing someone, losing someone. It was so not cool. People didn't belong to other people.

Though you could never convince his father of that. Winslow boys belonged in the family and to Winslow and Sons Fine Hand Built Furniture and Cabinetry. The company had passed from father to eldest son for generations, the son not having a choice but to accept.

Fortunately, Tom, Jack's older brother, had always intended to take over. Terry, the younger brother, announced early in his teens he was going to be a vet. A disappointment, but accepted by their father. And Terry was now a practicing veterinarian. Jack's two sisters had fared better, since Winslow and Sons had never so far had to change the sign to Winslow and Daughters. That left Jack stuck in the middle, literally. He had hung on for as long as he could.

But he just couldn't go through life copying historic designs. He wanted to experiment, incorporate modern design with other cultures. His father had accepted his betrayal stoically. Wished him well, but without the caveat of "you'll always be welcome," and Jack struck out on his own.

For the next several years he had traveled from one furniture maker to another, apprenticing then moving on. He went to

Japan, Turkey, Scandinavia, and any other place on the way that sounded interesting. And when he inherited his grandma's house, he came here.

Jack wasn't alone in the world. He went home for holidays and birthdays, but he could tell his father would never be totally reconciled. It still rankled him that all his sons weren't following in his footsteps. Though it was even harder for him to understand Jack, who still made furniture, but not for him.

Skye wasn't alone, either. She had Roxy and, unofficially, Hildy, who was like one of the family. And she had him.

Jack turned back to the yard, snagging the edge of his T-shirt on a rusted piece of fencing. He yanked it away. Heard it tear. "This fence oughta come down. It's an eyesore and dangerous. Someone's liable to get lockjaw from it one day."

Sonny looked up, frowned, then he slowly broke into a grin. "I was just giving you a hard time, Jack. Don't mind me. It's all gonna be all right."

Roxy and Hildy had just settled onto the porch with glasses of wine when Connor came trotting down the stairs.

"We're in here," Roxy called.

Connor appeared and stood in the archway to the parlor.

Roxy tried not to stare. He was unconscionably handsome.

Hildy raised an eyebrow. "I hope you're not planning on going for lobster at the Crab Shack. They'll crack it for landlubbers, but I'm not sure the plastic bib quite works with that linen jacket."

"I don't think he has the Crab Shack in mind," said Roxy

under her breath. She knew exactly where he was taking Skye. "White wine?" she asked.

Connor glanced at his watch. "I'd better get going."

"Before Amy gets back, you mean."

"No, I just—"

"Too late," Roxy said, hearing the front door open. "You can run out the porch door but you'll get sand in those huarache sandals. Though I doubt they came from the local bazaar."

Connor looked down at his shoes, the rich brown of the handwoven leather. "Actually they were handmade—"

"Naturally," Roxy said.

He gave her a dazzling smile. "By a one-legged cobbler in Cartagena."

"Ironic but lovely," Hildy said. "Ah, there is Amy."

Amy must have followed the sound of their voices because she appeared in the archway, hands on hips, hair curling about her face in the humidity, her face flushed.

"Nobody picked me up."

"Oh?" Roxy said. "But it's a lovely walk. How did your day go?"

Amy came onto the porch and flopped down on the cushioned love seat. "Interminable. Those old biddies never shut up. And everything is sacrosanct. You can't move this file to there," she mimicked in what Roxy supposed was to be an old lady's voice. "We've always kept that recipe under Gillian, who . . ."

She dropped into her normal voice. " . . . who evidently created the strawberry rhubarb sauce, which if you ask me sounds hideous and besides there is a whole hanging file of recipes in the designated Holiday Event file. Ugh." She finished by reaching over Roxy and snagging two pieces of cheese off the snack plate Hildy had prepared.

She popped one in her mouth and finally noticed Connor. "Wow, what's with the outfit?" Her expression brightened and her voice slid from querulous to flirtatious. "You're taking me somewhere special to celebrate my first day on the job." She stood up and tossed the second cheese wedge back on the plate.

Hildy's lip curled.

"I'll just run upstairs and change." She hurried away.

Roxy gave Connor a pointed look and flicked her fingers at him.

He gave her the look right back, but then he sighed and followed Amy out.

Roxy and Hildy craned to listen. A muffled explanation from Connor, followed by a moment of silence before Amy's explosive "Fine. What do I care." Followed by footsteps running up the stairs. A pause at the landing and a parting shot. "And you're overdressed for the beach. You'll look stupid."

The sound of her door slamming.

Hildy and Roxy exhaled pent-up breath.

"Sorry about that," Connor said, appearing in the doorway again and looking completely unruffled. "Guess I'll go. Maybe she'll sulk in her room all night. You can leave a tray of bread and water outside her door." He started to leave, then turned back. "You don't have to keep her, you know. I can take her back to Harrisburg when I leave."

"Not that we are in a hurry to get rid of you," Roxy said. "But when *are* you planning on leaving?"

He raised both eyebrows. "That rather depends on tonight."

SKYE WAS WAITING for Connor at Imagine That, which was doing a robust early-evening business. She was tempted to help Nat out at the cash register. He was doing double duty, since Skye had sent Maya home early with the orders to take a long bubble bath, pamper herself, and do something nice with Sonny.

Two classes were being held next door. Writing What You Don't Know for Adults and Stretch Yourself: Relaxation Techniques for the Harried. Penny was due back from her dinner break for the After Dinner Story Hour.

The door opened, Connor stepped in, and Skye's first thought was, *I'm glad I decided to wear a dress.* And her good sandals.

His hair was slicked back, and he'd gotten sun since his arrival; the tan set off the soft, off-white jacket and light green shirt that turned the green of his eyes to little beacons of light.

She shook herself. It was Connor; the package may have changed but it was still her old schoolmate and friend.

"Hey," she said, coming to meet him.

"This place is hopping," he said, looking around.

"Revving up for the weekend." She waved goodbye to Nat and headed for the door.

Connor reached it just in time to open it for her.

She didn't know why she was in such a hurry to get out, but she felt uncomfortable. She hadn't thought it would feel so weird, but her customers were definitely casting looks her way. It was just dinner between old friends, no big deal. Not much bigger than an impromptu walk on the beach.

"I didn't ask where we were going. You want some recommendations?" Skye asked as Connor guided her to his car.

"No thanks, we're good."

He opened the car door and she got in. He smiled down at her for a moment before he shut the door and went around to the driver's side. He pulled out of the parking space and turned at the next corner, looped down to Shore Road, then turned left in the direction of Narragansett.

He seemed to know where he was going, so she sat back and enjoyed the ride. Ahead the sky was turning a deep mauve as the low-lying clouds reflected the last rays of sunset onto the water.

"I hope you don't mind, I got an early reservation so we would have time to catch up."

"Fine," Skye said. "Where are we going?"

"A place that was recommended to me by a friend of mine."

"Oh. You have a friend who knows the local restaurants? Is his name Yelp by any chance?"

"No, though I did read the reviews. And just so you know, I have friends all over the world."

She could believe it. The wild, carefree, exuberant boy seemed to have been finally honed into a finessed person, comfortable with himself and others. Skye didn't doubt that he was a good diplomat.

"And I think this is it, right up here." He turned into a drive lit with hurricane lamps and drove toward the Mast, the best and one of the most expensive seafood restaurants on this part of the coast. And Skye's favorite.

Skye glanced at him. "Would your friend happen to be named Roxy or Hildy?"

He laughed. "Yep. They said this is your favorite place. I hope you're not tired of coming here."

"We only come for special occasions."

"Well, I'd say this is a pretty special occasion." Connor followed the sign to valet parking and stopped before a porte cochere of hewn stone.

Both car doors were opened simultaneously, and Skye was handed out by an immaculately pressed young man. She was really glad she'd worn her good sandals.

"I'm surprised you could even get a reservation," she said as Connor escorted her up the stairs to the white-and-gray wood building.

He laughed, a sound so familiar that it catapulted her into the past—their past.

"Ah, Mr. Reid, welcome to the Mast. This way, please."

The maître d' led them across the wooden floor of crowded tables, past the huge stone fireplace to a table for two by the panoramic window.

"Isn't this beautiful?" Skye said.

"It is," Connor said, looking at her.

And Skye felt herself blushing. *Stupid, this is Connor.*

She was given time to recover her equilibrium while the waiter filled water glasses and handed Connor the wine list and left them to decide on red or white.

It took some time while they discussed the merits of body over crispness, over whether it really was acceptable to drink red with fish, and finally decided on a full-bodied Chardonnay.

As soon as the waiter had hurried off with their order, Skye laughed. "If this is the way diplomats decide on food and drink choices, it's amazing you ever eat at all."

"But I bet this will be the best Chardonnay you've had all year." His smile lingered and so did his eyes.

Fortunately, the waiter returned before the ensuing silence became uncomfortable, and the next minute or two was spent pouring, tasting, accepting, and having both their glasses filled.

They touched glasses.

Skye was glad Connor didn't make a toast. It was easier to slip into their old friendship when she wasn't constantly reminded of how long it had been gone.

Chapter 13

The wine was good, the fish fresh and impeccably seasoned as always, and halfway through dinner Skye and Connor had fallen back into the kind of conversation that had always brought them closer together. Connor kept her laughing with stories of desert diplomacy and meals that tested his most rudimentary courage. She told him about announcing her intentions of creating an idea store after perhaps one too many beers. And how it had grown into two stores and a summer weekend on the horizon.

Connor listened, commented, looked at her with a depth that should have made her uncomfortable. Instead she slipped into the safe place of adolescence when the world was before them—a time before that future was ripped from her.

Why had she rebuked his efforts to communicate all these years? Maybe she hadn't been ready. Not mature enough to not resent losing the life that might have been.

But she was ready now. At least she thought she was.

They ate, drank, and reminisced. Their plates were removed

and Connor ordered a decadent chocolate dessert that neither of them could possibly eat. She realized that he was merely trying to prolong the evening. And she was surprised that she was glad.

They leaned forward over the table, eating from the same dish. It was an intimate process, forks posed on their respective side of the moist chocolate, each bite bringing them closer and closer . . .

"Skye!" The jocular voice jolted her back in her seat. She looked up to see Charlie Abbott and his wife, Melanie, standing at the side of the table.

"I thought I recognized you when we walked in," Charlie said affably, glancing toward Connor.

Skye patted her mouth and dropped her napkin on the table. "George, Melanie. How nice to see you. And this is my friend, Connor Reid. Melanie and Charlie Abbott." Skye was sure her voice was overly bright as if she were guilty of something. She wasn't, but she lowered the wattage.

"Charlie is the president of the chamber of commerce. Melanie is a real estate agent. Connor is an old school friend . . . visiting for a few days."

Connor had risen from his seat at the first introduction. He shook hands with George, then Melanie. He looked charming and comfortable, while Skye sat with a forced smile on her face. What was wrong with her?

"Pleasure to meet you, Connor," Charlie said. "But don't let us interrupt your dinner. Hope to see you around town while you're here." He took Melanie's arm and they continued on their way, but not before Melanie shot Skye one of those girl-to-girl looks that Skye wanted to tell her was completely unwarranted.

Fortunately, they were gone before she recovered enough to make a fool of herself. Connor sat back down. Skye breathed with relief. The mood was broken. And Connor asked for the check.

"Old school chum, huh?" Connor said as they drove back to town.

"It was the first thing I thought of," she said. "I couldn't very well say, my partner in juvenile misdemeanors and larks on the lam."

"I was more than that, wasn't I?"

His change of tone completely threw her off.

"Of course you were," she said, trying to read his expression from his profile, but his features were diplomat calm. "Anyway, I didn't think it was any of their business."

"It isn't," he agreed and said no more.

They made the drive back in companionable silence, and it wasn't until Connor slowed down in front of her store that she realized he was taking her back to her apartment. And Jack was expecting her at his cottage.

She felt a moment of social panic. She should have thought about the end of the evening before she started. Should she just get out, do the *I had a lovely evening* thing? Go upstairs then turn around and go out again and walk to Jack's the long way around?

That was stupid and possibly awkward considering the way

the evening had been going. If it was a girlfriend, she'd just say *Drop me at Roxy's; I'll walk to Jack's from there.*

Connor was a friend, ergo . . . Was it rude to have the man who took you to dinner drop you off at your lover's house?

"If you don't mind, I'll go as far as Roxy's with you. I told Jack I'd drop by after dinner."

"Ah. I can drive you. I don't mind."

"Thanks but it's just a short walk from Roxy's. There is a road but no one drives, because you have to make a big loop out of the way." She laughed. "Jack usually keeps his truck parked at his workshop. I don't even keep a car, which sounds crazy I know, but Roxy and Hildy both have cars, so it's a bit of over-kill to keep another."

"Not to mention bad for the environment," Connor said with a twinkle in his eyes.

"Of course. We take our environment seriously around here."

"You always did. And you managed to instill a healthy dose of earth appreciation in me while you were at it. You haven't said much about Jack."

The non sequitur threw her off for a minute.

"Well, he designs and builds furniture. He's partners with Sonny Daniels, Maya's husband; you met her when you came into the store."

"What kind of furniture?"

She thought about it. "The usual; tables, chairs, desks, but with a twist. Jack's traveled all over the world to study his craft. It's really special, what he . . ."

"Imagines?"

She'd never really thought about it before. She'd always marveled and appreciated the product and the craftsman, but she'd accepted them both for what they were.

She was out rallying other people's imaginations and taking Jack's for granted. "Yeah. He's got a pretty remarkable mind."

"How about the rest of him?"

Skye cut him a look.

"I'm sorry, that came out weird. I mean, does he appreciate you? Is he a good partner? Maybe it's none of my business, but I still care about your well-being."

She smiled. Connor had always been deep, but transparent to her.

"Jack's strong and loving," she said, shocking herself. "But contained. No, that's not what I mean . . . he doesn't get ruffled easily where as I . . . well, you know what I'm like."

"He grounds you."

"He does, but it's more than that . . . he—"

"You sure you don't want me to drop you off?" Connor said, cutting off the rest of her sentence.

That abrupt change of conversation surprised her. It was like he was controlling the direction of what was said. Was that how diplomats worked? She looked over to him, his profile sharp, intelligent, a world of experience reflected in his expression; so much of her was a part of that. Or maybe she was just being arrogant to think it still might be.

"What? No, just go on to Roxy's. Jack's is right down the path, the one we took down to the beach and then to the camp. We walked right past his house."

"Ah."

They turned down the drive and said no more until they came to a stop next to Roxy's Toyota.

Skye could see the light of the television from the sunroom, which her aunt and Hildy mainly used to stream British comedies and watch the news.

As Hildy often pointed out when anyone commented on their lack of media, "Whenever I want to watch people doing stupid things and getting into trouble, I just look out the window."

"Are you coming in?" Connor asked, when he came around to Skye's side of the car.

"Thanks, but it's getting late. I have a load of work tomorrow."

"And every day."

"Yep, until August," she said. "Then we're all taking a couple of weeks off. Thank you for the lovely dinner." Impulsively, she squeezed his arm. "I'm so glad things are going well for you."

"This is sounding like we won't see each other again."

"I thought you were planning on leaving."

"I was, but . . . I feel responsible for bringing Amy and I think I should wait around to see if she makes it through the Fourth. If that's okay. Then I'll take her back."

Skye frowned at him, then the sense of melancholy that had begun to steal over her lifted without warning. Knowing that Connor would be riding shotgun on this Amy experiment would give her some peace of mind. Though now that she saw his expression, she wondered if he had planned to leave at all.

"You don't have to stay," she added.

"I know . . . unfortunately."

Skye suddenly had a horrible sense of the inevitable about where this conversation was going. "I'd better get going. Jack will wonder where I am." Stupid. No, he wouldn't. She'd made him sound like a jealous, untrusting . . . "I mean—"

"Fine, but I'm walking you over. It may be close and he may be standing at the door waiting with a shotgun, but you're not walking down that path alone in the dark.

"Besides, Amy is watching us from the upstairs window and I want to postpone her tongue-lashing for not inviting her along as long as possible."

Skye laughed. "Look, if you walk around that crepe myrtle, you can see me all the way to his front porch."

"Nonetheless . . ." He crooked his elbow.

"Then come along." She hooked her arm in his and they walked down the path to Jack's.

The night had turned cool while they'd been in the restaurant and clouds had begun to cover the stars in big amorphous patches. They stopped to look down at Cove Beach, where the dark water had frothed itself into white-tipped waves.

"Looks like we're in for some weather," Skye said. "I hope it doesn't slow down work at the camp."

"The camp," Connor said. "I meant to ask how your committee meeting went yesterday, besides being long and tedious, if your meetings are anything like State Department debriefings."

"I wish," Skye said on a sigh. "There was a lot of excitement over Tizzy Lane's new ice cream flavor. But my budget is almost maxed out, and the other businesses, who I might add were eager to jump on the bandwagon, are balking at paying more for the ride."

"Can you carry it yourself?"

"If it doesn't get much higher. I'll know once the weekend is over and I've collected all the fees. Worst-case scenario, I might have to beg for some kind of bridge loan. I'm hoping it won't come to that. That the other members will come through. But don't say anything. I don't want Roxy and Hildy to worry."

"And Jack?"

"I haven't discussed it with him yet. I just haven't had the time and we're not there yet. Hopefully won't get there at all."

"Sounds like a risk. What will he say?"

"Jack?" Skye shrugged. She knew exactly what he would say. "He'll sit back while I mull it through, occasionally throwing out a question or a comment that will open the argument into a new path." He was infinitely patient, she realized. "We'll discuss it and I'll make the final decisions. *If* it comes to that."

Connor smiled in the sliver of moonlight.

"What?"

"Sounds like Jack would make a good diplomat."

"Jack? I don't think so. He's even-tempered but he doesn't suffer fools lightly." She frowned. "I'm sure you don't, either. I didn't mean it like it sounds. It's just that unless the fight is really worth it, Jack would just as soon walk away. Guess that means he *wouldn't* make a very good diplomat."

"Probably not," Connor agreed. "But he sounds like an interesting guy."

More than interesting, Skye realized. "Yeah. He is." She turned from the water. It was time for her to get home. To Jack's. If he were expecting her, he would be able to see Connor and her from his porch.

"Skye." His fingers slipped around her arm and she turned toward him. They were in shadow but she knew Connor's eyes were locked on hers. And she knew where this was going. Where they were going. She wasn't ready. But she didn't move away.

For a timeless moment, they balanced on that treacherous line between the past and the present. But the past was over and her present was here. She stepped away. "It's getting late. I'd better go."

His hand fell away, and they walked toward Jack's cottage side by side.

Jack was sitting on the porch when they stepped beyond the trees and into the open. Skye waved, turned to Connor. "Come meet Jack." She took his hand and virtually pulled him down the path and across the patch of lawn to the porch.

Jack didn't come down to meet them but stayed at the edge of the porch until they were standing below him.

Skye began the introductions, but Connor stuck out his hand. "Connor Reid."

Jack stood his ground but offered his hand. He had to lean over shake Connor's. It made him look like a hulking predator. "Jack Winslow."

They dropped hands. And Skye shifted her weight, not sure of what to say next. She could practically feel the testosterone in the air. She supposed it should be flattering, but it seemed so absurd.

"Do you want to come in for a drink?" she ventured.

Jack opened his mouth. Connor said, "Thanks but I'll take a rain check if I may. Maybe the three of us could go out for a drink before I leave."

Jack made a sound like, *Huh*.

She gave him a pointed look.

"We'd love to," he said finally.

"Well, good night then," said Connor. "Skye."

"Thanks, Connor, I had a . . . good time."

"My pleasure. Good night. Nice to meet you, Jack." And with that he turned and walked back to the path.

"Jack? What the hell was that?"

Jack gave her his bland, nothing-is-bothering-me look that she'd grown to know and not love. Because she knew it meant just the opposite.

They both watched from the porch until Connor became a shadow and then invisible against the trees. Then they went inside.

IT TOOK MORE willpower than it should have to keep Connor from just one look back. Were they watching him from the porch? Had they already forgotten him and gone inside? Or were they greeting each other in that time-old way of lovers who've been away for too long?

Hell, she wasn't gone that long. It was just dinner. Not the tundra. It irked him that he was thinking thoughts that were bound to make them all unhappy—or for him, happier than *he'd* been for a long time.

The shadow moved into him before he could even react. All he could do was raise one arm to shield his face.

"Jeez! What's wrong with you?"

Connor lowered his arm. Amy stood in her favorite pose, fists on her hips, chin poked out in confrontation.

Connor huffed out a breath. "I thought you might be a mugger."

Amy twisted sensuously from side to side. "Does this look like a mugger to you?"

"Not in the mood, Amy." Connor started walking toward Roxy's house.

"For love," she crooned and scooped up his elbow as he passed. "It doesn't look like you were very successful." She turned in an over-the-top expression of innocence and looked back at the cottage he'd just left.

Don't turn around, he ordered himself. *Just don't turn around.*

He turned around. There was no one on the porch.

"You were spying on us?"

"I was just curious. That was Jack, wasn't it?"

Connor didn't bother to respond.

"It was. I recognized him from yesterday."

Connor cut her a look.

"I had a drink with him and Sonny last night; he never said he was Skye's boyfriend."

Connor didn't blame him. He'd come so close to kissing Skye tonight that he still felt the promise of it. If she hadn't stopped him, they would still be at it. And Amy could have seen it all. In the emotion of the moment, Connor had forgotten how direct the line of sight was, straight across the little cove where Skye had taken him that first morning.

For all he knew Roxy and Hildy had been watching them, too. And if they could see the two of them, so could Jack.

Damn. It had been a close call. And he couldn't even thank himself for pulling back.

He pried Amy's hand away from his elbow and walked on. She didn't follow right away.

"Do you think they're watching us now?"

He spun around to find her right behind him. "No more voyeurism, Amy. Why don't you use all that energy to make amends to your family? A conniving person becomes a lonely person really quickly."

Turning over a new leaf was not what Amy had on her mind. It was dark and Connor couldn't actually see her smile, but he could feel it.

"He's kinda hot in a countrified way. The strong silent type." In the dark her voice was cool and slightly teasing, and Connor knew why men fell for her. Too bad she hadn't managed to actually love one of them.

And something in him finally broke. "Enough. You will not meddle in Skye's relationship with Jack. I mean it."

"Why not? *You* are."

"Not true." Though he wouldn't have been upset if Skye suddenly showed interest in him. She had been so close tonight. He was sure if he'd kissed her, she would have kissed him back.

Except that she hadn't. But was it because she'd been afraid that Jack might be watching from his house or because she didn't want to?

"You know, if you want her, you should try harder. I mean Jack's nice enough, I suppose, but you are way above him. He's kind of sexy, but he doesn't dress very well, and he probably cuts his own hair. He's nothing to you, you're good-looking, suave, well dressed with a cushy job that probably pays a lot.

"I bet you could get her back if you'd just try a little harder."

Connor so didn't want to go there, because dammit, he'd been fighting not to admit the same thing since the day he first saw Skye in the store. But after tonight . . . A man can tell when another man loves a woman, and it was pretty obvious Jack loved Skye.

"Maybe I can help." Amy slipped in front of him and pressed her hands against his chest.

He grabbed them and flicked them away. "Stop it, just stop it. You don't have to seduce every man you meet, you don't have to hurt everyone you should love, you don't always have to be the center of attention. Why don't you just for a minute try being yourself?"

"I am myself."

"I don't think you know who you are. You're so busy blaming everyone else for your dissatisfaction with your life, I don't think you've even bothered to look inward. Instead of building and enjoying your own life, you're constantly hijacking yourself and taking everyone else with you. Just stop trying so hard."

"To do what?"

They'd finally reached the house and Connor yanked the back door open. Then manners took over and he held it for Amy to go through.

"I don't know. I don't think you know who you are or why you do what you do. Whether it's merely to cause trouble, or to comfort yourself, or even to hurt yourself. I don't know why you can't just be Amy."

"But I am. Who else would I be?" she asked as she squeezed past him.

"I don't know," he called after her. "But you need to find out before there's no Amy left to find."

Chapter 14

Jack didn't ask Skye how her evening was. Or if she had a good time. What kind of questions were those? He didn't want to ask. He didn't want to know the answer. If she said it was okay, it wouldn't assuage this attack of caveman mentality he was having.

He didn't have many. And hardly ever with Skye. She didn't test him in any way but straightforwardly . . . until now. If that was even what she was doing. Maybe she was just being polite. Going out to dinner with an old friend. *Like hell she was.* Going out with her "soul mate."

She'd shared enough about what she and Connor were to each other. Jack and Skye were open about their feelings. That's the kind of relationship they had. They talked about stuff. They fit. The sex was good. Sometimes it was out of this world. She challenged him, but never made him feel attacked or out of control. Played games, but only the kind that were fun, not manipulative.

Good old Connor had that honor. Watching them walking

up the path toward the cottage, the moonlight overhead, made Jack want to throw the first punch. It was crazy. He should really get himself a beer, sit out on the porch by himself, and wait for the craziness to pass.

But he didn't. He guided Skye inside, across the living room, down the hall, and into the bedroom. Once inside, she cut him a knowing smile and closed the door.

There was no fooling Skye. Ever. It was a good thing he never wanted to.

And when they finally fell asleep, sated and together, he knew he would never have to.

SHE'S OUT OF breath long before she's reached the top of the hill where she throws herself into Connor's arms, nearly knocking him over. His kiss stops the bad news from tumbling out of her mouth. And for a minute she holds on as if she could climb inside that kiss where it's safe and the fires of hell feel like the warmth of love. But she knows she can't stay in that safety.

She jerks her mouth away. "They know," she says. "Amy was spying on us and she told. They said I could never see you again. Not even to say goodbye."

"It'll be all right."

"No it won't. He was so angry. She told me I was an ungrateful bitch and he didn't say a thing. Didn't tell her she was wrong. Just stood there looking disappointed. I don't want to ever go back there, even if he is my dad."

"You won't have to."

She looks up, but his face is clouded over. She can always see right into his soul but not tonight. "What is it?"

"I have to leave for school in the morning."

"The morning? Tomorrow? You weren't supposed to leave until next week. Why?"

"Do you even need to ask?"

"Amy told Dad and Karen and they told your dad. They all know now, we're doomed."

"Hey. Have we ever failed yet?"

Skye shakes her head. She'd been thinking of the future so much she'd failed to see the obstacles of the present. "This sucks."

He puts his fingers to her lips. "I have a plan. I'm never going to be a soldier, ever. So there's no reason I should even go to military school."

"But—"

"Let's go tonight. Run away before they can stop us. There's a whole world out there. Waiting for us."

But that would mean she'd have to leave her dad alone with her stepmother and half sister. Would that be so bad? Would he even notice?

"Do you have money? We can't use credit cards."

"Yeah," *Skye says.* "I can get some out of the ATM, but only a couple hundred."

He grasps her arm. "It's enough to get started. Get your stuff together and meet me back here."

"They'll be watching us."

"Don't worry." *He pulls her close, kisses her; his lips feel hot and feverish, filled with promise. He pushes her away too soon.* "Now go, don't forget your bank card, and driver's license."

She turns to go. "What's that?"

"Where?"

"Down there." She points down the hill to where gray smoke is billowing from her father's workshop. The flick of flames. "Oh my god. It's on fire! He might be in there."

She starts to run. Connor reaches toward her but she brushes his hand away. "Call the fire department," she yells and careens down the hill toward home.

JACK WOKE WITH a start. Skye had gone rigid in his arms. Another dream. That made two this week.

Because Amy and Connor had come to town. Damn, he'd like to march over to Roxy's right now, middle of the night or not, throw them both out and send them packing.

Skye rarely succumbed to her demons.

Jack liked to think maybe he helped keep them at bay. But they were set off this week in spades.

He always knew when she was being pulled into the past. A least that particular past. Could feel when she was reliving the night that changed her life. Jack had family dreams, too, but his were usually wrapped up in strange symbolism. Textbook stuff. He rarely, very rarely, woke up in a cold sweat, heart pounding. Dreams of his father could leave him tossing in his sleep. But he rarely appeared as himself, preferring animated objects or amorphous shadows.

Skye's dreams were like instant replays, newsreels reliving every second, every moment, asking the same questions over and over.

Jack lightened his touch, gave her some room. He'd learned long ago not to try to hold her, comfort her; she only struck out if he did. So he just stayed close without encroaching, willing himself to be a cocoon and not a restraint until the past loosened its grip.

He could feel when that happened, too. Then he slid closer to her and when she turned into him, he didn't try to wake her, fought the impulse to rush it toward its end. He just waited for it to pass. He didn't like the feeling of helplessness, but he knew he was doing the right thing.

And when she finally snuggled against him with a murmured "Jack," he held her close until they both succumbed to sleep.

"STORM'S COMING IN," Roxy pronounced as she poured herself a fresh mug of morning coffee and looked out the kitchen window.

"Well, good, the garden could use it as long as it isn't too heavy," Hildy said. "Guess I'd better go reinforce the tomato stakes."

Connor looked up from where he was sitting at the table, a coffee cup at his elbow and his cell phone in his hands. "Says intermittent showers and possibly a thunderstorm or two toward evening."

He turned the phone so Roxy and Hildy could see the screen.

Hildy snorted. "I feel every one of those little green dots in my lumbago."

"Lumbago," Roxy echoed. "More likely that last ten pounds you put on."

"Could be. Regardless, it's gonna rain. How long is it lasting?" Hildy asked Connor.

He consulted his phone. "Until about midnight. Then clear through the rest of the week."

"Good. Wouldn't want the Fourth of July fireworks to fizzle."

The door swung open and Amy came in dressed in wide-legged crop pants, a tank top, and a collared shirt tied in a knot at her waist; a band held back her curly hair.

Roxy wondered if she was going for the Doris Day or Lucy Ricardo look.

"It better not rain," Amy said, coming to stand next to Roxy and rising on tiptoe to see out the window. She shrugged, poured herself a mug of coffee, and went to the fridge for her own cream.

Progress, Roxy supposed.

Amy poured out a healthy dollop and returned the carton to the fridge. "I have to get to the church, they're expecting me at ten."

"Well, you better hurry," Roxy said, glancing at the kitchen wall clock. "It's twenty till and it's a fifteen-minute walk."

"Walk? Can't somebody drive me?"

Roxy turned her back to the sink and began scrubbing her coffee cup, except that there was still hot coffee in it. *Damn.*

"I gotta pick the lettuce before it rains," Hildy said.

"It's sunny outside," Amy pointed out.

"You never know." Hildy grabbed her gardening hat from the peg and headed for the side door.

Roxy watched Amy's reflection in the window glass. Amy's

eyes scanned Roxy's back, then finally came to rest on Connor, who had buried his face in his coffee cup.

Roxy had a sneaky suspicion that Connor was putting up with Amy because he wanted to spend more time with Skye. She understood how he felt, but she didn't think any good could come from renewing that relationship. And having Amy around could only make the situation worse.

Amy came to stand over Connor's bent head. "Looks like it's you, Con."

"Really, Amy?"

"You didn't mind driving Skye wherever she wanted last night."

Connor jumped from his chair, nearly knocking it over. "All right, come on."

"Wait. I haven't had my coffee yet."

"I'm sure they have some at the church."

"Yeah, it's like colored water, 'cause the ladies can't have too much caffeine," she added in her "old lady" imitation. "Ple-e-e-ase," she continued in her normal voice.

Roxy took the opportunity to slip out of the kitchen.

"YOU WANT A ride, you come now." Connor took his cup to the sink, ran some water over it, then strode out of the room without looking at Amy.

"Oh all right," she called after him. "Just let me get my purse."

Connor didn't feel like waiting, not that he had any place to go. He just wanted to get away from her. Of course dropping her at the church would keep her out of everyone's hair for at least a few hours.

He snagged his keys off the hall table where he'd left them the night before. Went out the front door, straight to the rental car, and climbed inside. He didn't even know where he was going if she didn't come right out. He couldn't very well go back inside.

He could drive away, take himself out to breakfast. That would show her. Who was he kidding? He was anxious to get going because he wanted to see Skye.

Connor turned on the ignition and was backing out of the parking space when Amy ran out the door. He slowed down but didn't stop until she caught up and yanked the passenger door open.

"I said to wait," she said as he came to a stop.

She jumped in and shut the door.

He made a two-point turn and drove toward the street. "How do you get to the church?"

Amy looked blank and shrugged. "I don't know. Roxy was driving."

He started counting to ten. "Which church is it?"

"Methodist, no Baptist . . . I think."

He plugged Baptist Church into his GPS and turned right out of the drive.

"You don't have to be such a crab. It's not my fault that Skye hasn't come crawling back to you. What did you expect?"

Connor focused on driving.

"It's pretty obvious she's not going to. And who could blame her? You actually delivered her back to her boyfriend last night. What a wuss."

"That's it." Connor pulled the car over and parked at the curb. Turned to Amy. "First of all. You have no idea what Skye and I mean to each other. You never did, but even when you were a little girl you resented us seeing each other."

"I wasn't a little girl. I was twelve."

Something in her voice made him pull back. He tried again. "You were twelve, you couldn't have possibly understood what we were to each other."

"Enough to know that it isn't the same now, is it?"

"No," he admitted. "Not what we are now." But that didn't mean they couldn't become something else.

She crossed her arms and let out a satisfied sigh.

"Does that make you happy? Is that why you asked me to drive you here? Because you needed to bring me down a peg?"

"No-o-o," she drawled. "You're managing that all by your-self."

He just looked at her. "I don't know why you are so determined to make everyone hate you. But it's working."

He was shocked to see her eyes fill with tears.

He didn't trust those tears—he'd known people who could turn them off and on at will—but he couldn't exactly ignore them, either. "Look. I don't mean to be harsh. But why don't you try thinking before you say things; you can't be as mean-spirited as you act."

She sniffed. "I hate you."

"Fine. I give up." He waited for a truck to pass then pulled out into traffic. A couple of minutes later they arrived at the church parking lot.

"It's in the back," Amy directed.

He was too fed up to suggest she walk across the parking lot. He drove straight to the back side of the pavement where a grove of trees surrounded a flat lawn and where several middle-age-and-beyond ladies were clustered together.

One of the women held a clipboard. Her voice rose above the others as she pointed from the clipboard to a place on the lawn, back to the clipboard and then to another place, while the heads of the others bobbed up and down like ducklings as they followed her hand.

Amy jumped out of the car with more energy than he'd seen from her yet. She hurried across the lawn waving at the ladies. They all stopped what they were doing and waited for her to join them.

Connor stayed just long enough to hear her say, "Sorry, but Roxy and Hildy insisted I have breakfast before they would let Connor bring—" Connor pressed on the accelerator and sped away.

He drove straight to Imagine That. He didn't question what he was doing or why. Or even what he would say to Skye once he was there. He just wanted to see her.

He parked right in front of the store, fed the meter, and went inside. They had just opened and there was no one about.

He walked across the store to the Imagine That Too space and looked in. There were open doors but no sound came from any of them.

"Anybody here?" he called.

Maya came out of a door toward the back of the building. "Oh hey. Sorry, I was in the john. My favorite place these days." She patted her flat stomach and smiled.

Connor remembered Skye saying that Maya was pregnant. "Congratulations," he said. "I was looking for Skye."

A slight frown passed over Maya' s face. "She won't be in until later."

Connor waited while she came to a decision to either tell him where Skye was or leave him in the dark. He'd seen the same look on minor officials stuck between two bargaining dignitaries.

So he just asked. "Do you know where she is?"

"She had to go over to the camp this morning. Something about plumbing, I think. But she'll be in around lunchtime if you want to come back then. Or I can tell her you dropped by," she added.

"Thanks, I'll come back later." And he would, but first he would go directly to the camp.

SKYE AWOKE TO the aroma of bacon frying. At first she thought she was dreaming.

She glanced at the clock. Almost nine. She remembered the alarm going off, and finding Jack, who, instead of having left for work, was lying warm beside her.

When she pushed back the covers, he pulled her back and she went willingly. A good while later she drifted back into sleep. "Set the snooze button," were the last words she remembered.

Now, she threw back the covers and got out of bed. That was definitely the smell of bacon. She took a quick shower, dressed in work clothes, and scooped a pair of running shoes out of the closet. She padded barefoot down the hall to the kitchen, opened the kitchen door just wide enough to peek inside. Jack was standing at the stove, lifting strips of meat onto a paper towel.

She opened the door wider and stepped inside. "Is it a holiday?"

"Sure. What shall we call it?"

She came up to him and hugged him from behind. He was muscular and masculine and was wearing one of Hildy's old, ruffled aprons because it always made Skye laugh.

And in a flash of insight, she got it. She rubbed her cheek against his back. "I should go out with other guys more often," she teased.

He turned around. "No." He pulled her close and kissed her. She indulged for a few seconds, then danced away. "Oh no. No more fun for us. I've got to meet Brendan at the camp at ten. And I'm not about to let you burn that bacon."

Chapter 15

It was overcast when Skye and Jack left the cottage. It wasn't often these days that they got to have breakfast together. The furniture design business was hopping. Skye had more business than she could handle. And it occurred to her that maybe they were working too much.

She moved closer to him.

"Thanks for breakfast," she said. "We should try it again sometime."

"August," they said simultaneously and laughed.

They parted at the main path. Jack slipped her computer bag, which he'd insisted on carrying, from his shoulder onto hers and gave her a quick kiss. Then Skye turned left toward the Pritchards' Camp and Jack went right toward his store.

She felt the first raindrop as she turned in at the family camp's sign. Neither of them had thought to bring ponchos or an umbrella. No matter, it was summer.

She just hoped the rain didn't get heavy and impede the progress on the construction.

By the time Skye reached the mess hall, it was coming down in a fine sheet. She trotted up the steps to the porch, stopped under the eave to shake the worst of the drips off, then went inside. Several men and women were busy hammering, sawing, and scrubbing windowpanes. Brendan Wraye and another man were leaning over plans.

It was an amazing transformation. The old mess hall had been a tumbledown mess. The floorboards were sagging and warped at one end where the roof had leaked. Now the roof, at least in that area, had been replaced, and bright new boards had taken the place of the old ones. And all the old tables and benches had been stored in one of the cabins.

Skye could begin to see what it would look like finished for Discover It Weekend and a thrill shot across her. It was really happening. Over budget maybe, but it was happening.

Brendan looked up and motioned her over.

"Skye, you've met Ollie Ford?"

"Of course," Skye said. "Ford Plumbing refit Imagine That, one and two. And did a great job, I might add."

"Thank you, ma'am," Ollie said and dipped his grizzled chin to her.

"Ollie's just been explaining the plumbing situation."

"What is the situation?" Skye asked, already seeing the dollars add up. She crossed mental fingers and moved closer to look at the plan.

"Well, now, you got pipe laid in here and here," Ollie said, using his mechanical pencil as a pointer. "Town's given us the go-ahead for four additional toilets. So that's not the problem.

"Dinken's Supply is giving us a good price on the extra pipe, so that's not the problem, either.

"But the septic tank is pretty much shot. Herb had the house connected to the town's system a few years back, but he never got around to changing the camp over. Now we're gonna have to do one or the other, put in a new tank or run a pipeline to the street to connect it to the water department. Either one's gonna cost you a bundle, no way to get around that. Plus—"

"There's a plus?" Skye's mouth went dry.

"Actually more like a minus. Unfortunately, while we were replacing some of the worst of the water pipes, the main water supply line, which is connected to town water, sprang a leak. Rusted through. If you want to look out the back window, you'll see a lake forming. It will have to be replaced."

Skye didn't even want to look. "The town can't help us out on this?"

Ollie shook his head. "State's got regulations, county's got regulations, town's got regulations."

"So what do you suggest we do and can you give me a ballpark figure?"

"Well, we can try to jury-rig this old tank, but if it gives out, where are two hundred people gonna pee? If it were me and I was planning to keep this place, I'd hook both lines to the public water and call it done. But it could set you back twenty thou or more to run the appropriate lines out to the main on Sunny Point Road."

If she were to *keep* it? She hadn't even planned to use the camp at all until the town talked her out of using the nature center. Considering the prohibitive rent of the center and the boon having it at the camp would be to the town, she may have been too easily persuaded. The chamber of commerce had already kicked in a substantial amount toward renovations, but those dollars had dwindled down to a precious few.

"How soon do I have to make a decision?" she asked.

"Ummm, yesterday? Unless you just want to hang it up and rent porta—"

"No, that I do know. People are paying premium prices to attend the weekend. I want them to be able to at least pee in peace. And we'll need water for a thousand things.

"I don't think I can make this decision on my own. I'll talk to Charlie Abbott. As president of the chamber of commerce maybe he can allot extra funds. And I'll try to call an emergency Jump-Start July committee meeting."

"Okay but don't take too long. With the holiday it might be hard to find a backhoe operator who's working, and we can't do a thing until the ground's broken."

"Okay, thanks," Skye said, forcing a smile. She felt sick. That would clean out her slush fund and there were still suppliers to pay, contingencies to deal with. What had she been thinking? Even if she opened the weekend to the wait list, she'd still end up in the red at the rate she was going.

"Anything else I should know about?"

"Nope," Brendan said. "Everything else is on schedule. Cabin one has been cleaned out for the concession area, fitted out with counters, sinks, cabinets, et cetera. We're just waiting on the refrigerators to arrive. No cooking facilities as we agreed. Electrical is up to code.

"Cabin two is rewired and serving as supply storage. It's watertight, so everything should be fine there. Cabin three is being fitted out for first aid and four through six will be finished by the Fourth or right after. We've already installed shelves and cabinets and receiving desks in two. You should take a look before you go. I'd show you around, but I want to get these windows done and inspected before we have to leave today."

Just then a clap of thunder reverberated through the rafters.

"Kill the saws, guys," Brendan ordered. "Still haven't grounded all the outlets in here. Don't want anyone getting hurt or have sparks flying around all this sawdust."

Skye shivered as a past workshop fire filled her mind. "No, we don't. Did the fire extinguishers arrive?"

"Arrived and installed. We're golden. Now Ollie and I are going over to the water department and check out our options and a timetable. Let us know what you decide. Want a ride into town?"

"I think I'll just look around for a bit. I can sit out the rain here if that's okay."

"Sure. Let us know what you want to do and we'll get on it."

"Thanks, I will."

Brendan and Ollie gathered their windbreakers and made a dash for Ollie's van. Everyone went back to what they were doing except for sawing. Skye wandered across the mess hall, imagining it filled with people exploring things they had never explored before.

She wandered outside to stand on the porch, waiting for a lull in the downpour. The air was heavy from the rain and she breathed in the scent of wet pine, sand, and waves. This really was a perfect place to de-stress and let your imagination soar. Actually it would be great for a lot of things. Not just vacationing. With a little planning Herb and Edna could start making money again.

But they were retired and wanted to enjoy that retirement. They had poured their lives and the last of their vitality, it seemed, into keeping a dying camp alive. Maybe it would just be too much.

Well, Skye would give the old camp its last hurrah. Once she figured out what to do about the plumbing. She called Charlie Abbott. He agreed to have his secretary call the others and would let her know about the meeting time.

"This is getting expensive, Skye. Didn't anyone foresee this happening with the plumbing?"

I don't know, Skye thought. *The committee volunteered to handle all requirements and permits.* "That's why I want everyone's assessment before I make a decision."

"Okay. I'll get back to you."

The rain finally eased up, and she raced across the yard to the first cabin and went inside. It had been cleaned out and painted white. A counter stretched across most of the front and there were stacks of paper plates and paper cups already filling the shelves.

They had made a big effort to have a sustainable and garbage-free weekend, but total compliance would be impossible, and though they were giving away reusable water bottles, Skye had no illusions of the making it through two days plastic free.

She turned to go and saw the fire extinguisher mounted on the wall by the door. *Excellent*, she thought, feeling the faint scar across her palm. Call her neurotic, but knowing there was an extinguisher in every building—even if they never used it—would give her peace of mind.

Skye went back outside just as a sports car drove into the lot. Connor. A moment of indecision and she went out to meet him.

"Hi," she said as he got out of the car. He, of course, looked crisp and fresh compared to her in her rain-splattered work clothes. "What brings you here?"

"Just had the morning off and thought I'd come say hi." He smiled, an expression so familiar that it made her heart hurt. And for a split second, just the tiniest of moments, she wondered what might have been.

"You look worried," he said, moving closer.

"Just angsting over plumbing codes."

"Sounds serious."

She laughed, she couldn't help it. "It is. You can't have people getting their best ideas inside a porta-potty."

He barked out a laugh. "It does take some of the genius out of it." He wiped at his forehead. "Is that a raindrop? Again?"

"Yeah, welcome to bait-and-switch beach weather. It will probably be like this all day off and on, then clear overnight. It's sort of summer weather's MO."

"That's what my weather app said. As long as it's sunny for the weekend and the fireworks."

"You're staying for the fireworks?" It was definitely beginning to rain again.

"You said Amy could stay until after the Fourth and since I'm responsible for bringing her, I thought it was the least I could do to take her away again. Besides I wanted to—"

A barrage of heavy raindrops cut off his sentence and had them racing to the nearest building, cabin two. Laughing, they stumbled through the open door and burst inside. As Brendan had said, supplies had been delivered and put away in cubbies, stacked on shelves, fitted into bins.

"What's all this stuff?" Connor asked, picking up a fishing net.

"Equipment, supplies for the workshops. They'll be organized and placed in the various stations for pickup. But for now it's central storage."

Skye squeezed in between two stacks of boxes and came out with a twelve-pack of paper towels. "Aha, at least we have these." Skye brushed the rain from her face and poked a hole in the cellophane large enough to extract a roll.

"Here." She pulled off a couple of sheets and turned to hand them to Connor. He was standing right behind her, and when she turned, they were almost touching. Tendrils of dark hair dripped down his forehead and cheeks, and he felt warm in spite of the wet polo shirt clinging to his chest.

Skye opened her mouth to say something—she didn't know what—but she never got the chance. He leaned over and kissed her. And years fell away. And they were two teenagers, making plans for that future and ready to face the world together. She'd gotten lost in his kisses then and she was getting lost now.

But now was now. That world was gone. The life that might have been a mere memory.

Skye pulled away. Connor didn't let go.

She couldn't find the words to say what she was feeling. Just . . . "Connor."

He moved into her again, but she backed away.

"We can't. I can't."

"Why? Because of Jack? I get it. But what about us? Shouldn't we give us a chance?"

"Connor, there is no us. Us died a long time ago."

"No. You're wrong. We were parted but . . ."

"We've moved on. Both of us. Let's just be happy for what we were—still are—to each other."

"What are we?"

"We're different people, Connor. Let's let us be."

Skye slipped past him and out of the cabin. She wasn't sure where she was going. It was pouring, but she couldn't stay inside with Connor. It was too close. Too confusing. Too dangerous. And she so didn't need this complication in her life right now.

She raced across the yard and into the mess hall where she knew people were still working. Skye smiled and shrugged as they looked up at her bedraggled figure. Waited until she heard Connor's sports car drive away.

Then she walked, mindless of the steady rain, to her apartment above Imagine That to change into dry clothes.

"I CAN'T BELIEVE nobody picked me up," Amy complained as she burst into Roxy's kitchen.

"You look pretty dry for someone who had to walk the six blocks from the church," Hildy said, looking up from her tea.

Amy pulled up a chair and sat down. "Edna Pritchard drove me home. Where's Connor?"

"Haven't seen him since he left with you," Roxy said. She looked at the mug of tea she'd just poured, considered offering it to Amy, then sat down to drink it herself. The last few days seemed like weeks. She'd been a fool to invite Amy and Connor to stay. Amy seemed to have settled down to her idea of princess in residence, and Connor . . . Well, if Roxy wasn't mistaken, Connor was about to rock the boat big-time.

It shouldn't be any of her business. She liked Connor. He seemed like a very sincere and caring young man. But she also liked Jack, a lot. He was steady. Talented, understated, and Skye had blossomed during their relationship. And come to think of it, so had he, in his own silent way.

They were all adults, but Roxy hated having been the instigator of something that might change all their lives. What had she been thinking?

In her attempt to control Amy's ability to sow discontent, she'd paved the way for Connor to sow his. And there didn't seem to be any way to extricate themselves. Well, the Fourth was just a few days away and then they would be rid of them both.

Roxy had decided to be fair. Let things play out as they would, maybe even try to understand why Amy was so unhappy and vindictive. But even the few times she'd tried to draw the girl out, she'd danced around reality like a circus performer.

And Roxy gladly gave up. As far as she was concerned, they were just marking time until they could all get back to normal.

"The ladies of the church finally caved today and decided to set up the social so that people didn't have to wait an age to get their ice cream while the rest of their party finished theirs."

"Oh," Roxy said without interest.

"An assembly line, duh. The Model T? You set up stations, you get your bowl, next station get your ice cream, then your toppings, then the whip cream and, voilà, everybody in your group finishes within seconds of each other and you all enjoy ice cream together." Amy opened her hands in a "simple" gesture.

"Sounds like the army to me," Hildy said and carried her tea out of the kitchen.

"What's with her?" Amy asked. "She's always so grumpy. How can you stand being around her?"

Roxy raised an eyebrow.

Amy just looked back, guileless.

"Pots and kettles?"

"What's that supposed to mean?"

"Nothing. Are you enjoying your work on the social?"

"It's all right. Once they started listening to me. And I finally convinced Rhoda to let me rearrange the business office. Extension cords everywhere, she has to practically do contortions to get to the storage cabinet. They should really get a new printer . . . and computer, too. But Rhoda says the church doesn't have enough money.

"I find that hard to believe. Our church at home was rolling in it, last time I checked. Which was a while ago but still. I'm sure they could find a way to get new equipment if they just set their minds to it."

"Bake sale?" Roxy said. She started to get up, then sat back down. Hildy had had the right idea. Get the hell out. But Roxy just didn't believe that Amy was all bad. Just shallow and unthinking. Maybe it was time to try a little heart-to-heart with Skye's half sister. Maybe it was even time to hear her side of the story.

Chapter 16

When it started raining for real, Jack had doubled back to his house to get Skye a poncho. She was so overworked and stressed because of Amy he was afraid that standing in the rain inspecting the progress of the construction might make her sick.

He took a shortcut across two of his neighbors' yards and came out at the family camp just as a blue sports car pulled to a stop and Connor Reid got out.

Jack automatically stepped back into the brush pines. It was a stupid thing to do. He had every right to be there. More of a right than Connor Reid. What was he doing there at all?

Stupid question. To see Skye. Skye had come from one of the cabins and was going to him. Had she known he was coming? Had they planned to meet. Was this morning with Jack guilt sex?

He shook his head as droplets of rain hit him in the face, bringing him to his senses. He was being an ass. Skye would never—she just wouldn't.

So why didn't he just walk out and hand her the poncho? She was getting wetter standing there talking to Connor. Why didn't Connor insist she go inside?

Jack took a step. Connor and Skye turned and began walking his way. And here he was like a voyeur outside a girls' dormitory window. He slipped behind the brush just like he was guilty.

He didn't want Skye to think he was spying on her. She wouldn't. He wasn't. But he certainly didn't want to give Connor any ideas.

He'd just drop the poncho by the store and go on to work. He'd forget about being here. Seeing them. Imagining that Skye might have finally found her soul mate again after all these years.

Jack didn't believe in soul mates. People were people. You took them as they came. But he'd thought he'd found a home in Skye.

ROXY STOOD IN the doorway to the porch. Amy was sitting, knees pulled up, in the wicker armchair, staring out to sea. She'd taken the band from her hair and curls tumbled over her face, but Roxy didn't need to see Amy's face to know that she was looking at one unhappy child.

Not a child, Roxy reminded herself. Amy was twenty-six. Most young women her age were on their way to fulfilling their goals in life. Planning for a future. Enjoying being young. But Amy seemed to be drowning in her own negativity.

Maybe Roxy should just wait it out and hope that the visit

would be short. Hell, she could hide in the hall closet with the extra macs and wellies and wait for it all to pass. She knew as soon as Amy and Connor drove away, Hildy would take out the cleansers and scrub the place top to bottom. Skye would be over with a bundle of sage to burn. And Hildy, the pragmatic, would loan her the matches.

And things would go back to normal until the next time. And there would be a next time and another until something changed. For better or worse. Nope. Better to deal with it now and move on.

Roxy took a fortifying breath and stepped onto the porch.

Amy didn't look up. So without an invitation to join her—it was her house after all—Roxy pulled over a chair and she sat down, cutting off Amy's view of the beach.

Amy's frown stretched longer. "What now?"

And Roxy's good intentions flew out with the rain.

"God, you're hard to be around."

"Then why did you come out here?"

"I thought," Roxy said. "That we might have a little talk."

"What for. I know nobody wants me here."

"Well, they might change their minds if you tried acting a little nicer."

Amy glanced up without lifting her head. She was so childlike—when she wasn't being a manipulative little witch. What was driving the girl?

"Why don't we start with why you really came here?"

"I told you. I want for Skye and me to make up. You don't know what it's like when your sister hates your guts."

"True. But I wouldn't say that Skye hates you."

"Yes, she does."

"I believe she doesn't trust you."

"That's not fair."

Roxy felt her temper beginning to fray. "Of course it is. You lied to your family, to the police, and to everyone else about Skye starting the fire that destroyed your father's . . ." She started to say *refuge*, but she decided the truth was hard enough to swallow for Amy without rubbing in the fact that her father avoided her and her mother in that workshop. Surrounded by his electric trains and the memories of his dead wife, he could find a little peace. ". . . workshop," she finished.

If anyone had reason to burn it down, it would be Amy or her mother.

"She *did* burn it down. She did a bad thing, and everyone forgave her. Then they turned on me."

"Perhaps—"

"I didn't lie. I saw her. She did it, no matter what anybody says. I saw her." Her eyes pooled with tears and they tracked heavily down her cheeks.

"Okay, let's say you didn't lie, let's just say you were mistaken."

Amy shook her head. "I wasn't. I know what I saw."

"Perhaps, you saw her coming out of the building and misinterpreted her actions."

"You sound like my therapist."

"Are you still going?" Roxy asked, taken off guard.

"No, she was stupid."

And evidently had not been able to help Amy. Why was Amy so determined to hold on to her false belief for so long? And if she hated her sister, why did she keep coming back? Why was she here now? Did she really think they could reconcile while she was still blaming Skye for something she didn't do? Or was she here to finally get back at Skye?

For what? What had Skye done that was so awful that a sister—half or not—would make such accusations and spread them through the whole town?

"Let me put it this way. As long as you continue to accuse her, Skye is never going to reach out to you. If it's money you want, I'll see what I can do, but don't bother Skye with it."

"Why is everyone always on Skye's side? She was the bad one, not me."

"Then why on earth do you want to reconcile with her?" Roxy asked, balancing on the sharp edge of aggravation and exasperation.

"She's my sister. My dad doesn't want me. My mom doesn't want me. Nobody does."

Roxy's breath caught as Amy's barrage of despair hit her. "I'm sure that isn't true." Was it true? Not being a mother herself, Roxy didn't know from experience. But still she couldn't imagine a mother not wanting a child, especially not after coddling and pampering that child for her entire youth.

Skye had always been the unwanted one in that family. Roxy had seen it firsthand. She should have convinced James to send Skye to her permanently, let her raise Skye, but James had refused.

By the time Skye had shown up on her doorstep, Hildy had moved in. Between them they managed to give her niece a safe heaven.

Roxy thought Skye had let go of the past, and in truth she had in many ways. She knew Skye on occasion sent Amy money, though she never mentioned it. But now, she wondered if Skye would ever be entirely free until she and Amy came to an understanding.

Skye's reaction at seeing Amy had frightened Roxy. In the brief moment before she turned heel and ran, Roxy had felt the power of her anger.

Roxy tapped her fingernails on the wicker arm of her chair. "Do you and Connor have plans tonight?"

Amy shrugged, sniffed, and wiped her eyes on her arm.

Actually, Roxy wouldn't mind seeing the back of Connor, either. Though she liked him, she was afraid that he had the potential of upsetting their lives even more than Amy.

But things needed to be dealt with before they got worse, which they were bound to do if left unchecked. And it looked like it was up to her to get it done.

"Why don't you both stay here for dinner. Hildy and I will make something. I'll call Skye and see if she and Jack can come."

A flicker of interest, before Amy's eyes shuttered again.

"I'll take that as a yes. But Amy, you and Skye need to act decently toward each other and give each other a chance to explain your side of the story."

"Tell that to Skye."

"I intend to. Do I have your promise?"

"Yeah, I guess."

"Good. I'll just go make that call."

SKYE TOOK A long, hot shower before she changed into dry clothes and went downstairs. It wasn't that she was cold from the rain, it was summer. She wasn't even trying to wash away the memory of Connor's kiss. She was trying to restore her normal equilibrium.

She didn't like extremes of feeling. She didn't think that meant she was lacking feeling. She just believed in *balance in all things*. She'd learned that since coming to live in Sunny Point, after everything she'd believed and loved had been shattered by her own family.

Connor had been a part of that time before. The good part, although they had had their own tumultuous relationship. Not fighting and making up, but rebounding from joy to despair when they were thwarted and forced to conform, to joy again at the first sign of freedom.

Skye thought living like that as an adult would be exhausting and to no purpose. It took steadiness to make things work, to build two businesses and share her love for fulfillment with others, to be a family.

Connor must have come to the same conclusion, or why else was he a diplomat. The long hours of negotiations, the setbacks, the arguing over minutiae. The old Connor would have ditched a boring meeting and run off to convince Skye to go fly a kite or drop a jar of jelly beans in the river and follow it just to see where it ended up.

He'd talked a bit about his work at dinner. Mainly they'd reminisced. The past. It was tempting to succumb to the remembered fun, but there were also the fights with her family—and his. The trauma of being picked up by the police when they'd run away or gone too far on a lark; lectured by their teachers, and their parents. The groundings that they ignored, the phones taken away, the allowances withheld.

A part of growing up for everyone, but for two dreamers like Connor and her, the lack of freedom was torture, because no one had taught them how to use that freedom. Or how to weave the rest of their lives into it. Skye made her own kind of freedom now. Except suddenly that freedom was beginning to show some signs of caving.

She went downstairs where Penny, book in hand, was leading seven tiptoeing children between the nature table and the rainy day table.

"Billy Goats Gruff," Maya explained.

"What?" Skye exclaimed.

"Not to worry, it's the new, no-poking-out-of-eyes version. Penny wrote it herself. I read it and it's quite good." Maya sputtered out a laugh. "It's a goat of a different color for the next gen-whatever. They're tiptoeing because they don't want to wake up the troll because—get this—he gets cranky when he doesn't get enough sleep and won't want to share his grass with them."

"Okay then," Skye said. "Though sometimes I wonder if we're right to always change classic tales to make them more palatable to our . . ."

"Modern-day mores," said Maya.

"Yeah. We grew up with some pretty gruesome stories and we're perfectly fine."

"I know what you mean, but I'm surprised to hear you say so."

"Still, the Billy Goats Gruff . . ." Skye began.

At that moment, Penny's voice rose in a basso. The kids squealed. They were enjoying it immensely and Skye and Maya left them to it.

"Oh, Jack dropped by earlier with your poncho."

"He did? He must have gone back to the cottage for it. What a sweetie."

"He is," Maya said. "And don't you forget it."

Skye frowned at her. "Never," she said, pushing the uncomfortable memory of Connor's kiss out of her mind. "On a more pressing issue, the plumbing budget has skyrocketed. Oliver Ford suggested portable toilets."

"Ugh," Maya said.

"My exact sentiments. And the main waterline is leaking and flooding on the lawn. I've asked Charlie to call an emergency committee meeting. I'm going to ask them for money, which seems a waste just to have Herb sell the property."

"And is there a plan B?"

"That is plan B," Skye said. "I probably should have stuck to the nature conservancy."

"I don't think so. The camp is the perfect place. It has the woods, the beach, the ocean and bay. Plenty of room for individual exploration, it's close to the store, downtown in general, places to eat . . ."

"Stop! Stop! I agree, perfect location. And until now, a lot cheaper. But the budget is rapidly becoming a thing of the past."

Skye hadn't planned on making a huge profit on the first outing, but to clear just enough to pay for everything and everyone and have enough for a down payment on the next one. Now that was all about to go down the drain, literally.

"It's a good thing you didn't let the chamber talk you into organizing a winter carnival during Christmas," Maya said.

"Thank God for that," Skye agreed. "I felt a little bad about letting them down. But imagine trying to do all that and the store with you . . . Hey, we might have a Thanksgiving baby."

Maya smiled and her hand went automatically to her belly. "Yep. And besides, we're about exploration and imagination. Not Santa Claus and selling Christmas tchotchkes."

And there was the dividing point. It would be nice if the town could benefit from the weekend, but Skye was not interested in becoming just another hyped-up holiday tourist attraction.

She was balancing a fine line. A fragile line. She was feeling a little fragile herself lately, and that was so not like her.

And she still hadn't gotten back to the people from the ad agency. A regular, dependable large client like that could definitely free up the financial yo-yo. She planned to draw up a prospectus for them, but one that would assure her that she wouldn't be perverted by corporate needs over creative ones.

Skye's cell rang. She looked at the screen.

Roxy, she mouthed to Maya before answering. "Hey," she said.

"Now just listen. I'm inviting you and Jack to dinner tonight. Amy has been here for almost a week and you haven't made an effort to really talk to her."

"But—"

"I said just listen. I know this is a terrible time to have to deal with family but she's here and it's time. All I ask is that you are civil to each other and don't run off upset. Seven o'clock. Have a drink before you come." She hung up before Skye could answer.

She wanted to say no. At least put it off another day, but Roxy was right. It was stupid to have Amy here and ignore her. It wasn't fair to either of them, not that she was particularly worried about being fair to her half sister.

Maybe Roxy was right, and it was time to put the past behind them. But not without reinforcement. Skye called Jack. It was a long wait, and she was afraid the call would go to voice mail, when Jack finally picked up.

"Hello."

"Jack, I was just about to leave a message."

"Sorry, I didn't hear you over the saw."

"Sorry to bother you in the middle of work, but Roxy invited us to dinner tonight. She guilted me into talking to Amy, trying to normalize our relationship. I know she's right but . . . Anyway, you don't have to go if you don't want to."

"Why wouldn't I want to?" Jack asked.

"Because it's bound to be tense."

"Would you rather I not go?"

Skye frowned. "Of course not. I just thought— Is something wrong?"

"No. Sorry. Just busy."

"Then I won't keep you. Dinner's at seven. But, really, if you change your mind about going, I won't hold it against you. Just let me know."

"Okay. Later."

And she was listening to nothing.

JACK SHOVED HIS phone in his back pocket and looked up to find Sonny frowning at him.

"What the hell was that about?" Sonny asked.

"Nothing." Jack picked up the skill saw.

Sonny leaned over and pulled the plug. "Okay, spill." He shook the plug of the electric cord at Jack. "You come in here like a thundercloud this morning. You haven't taken one break. Or said anything but grunts and huhs. And now you sound like you're mad at Skye. Is that what it is? Are you guys fighting?" His expression changed comically. "She isn't pregnant, is she?"

"No."

"And you obviously can't be, so what gives?"

Jack gave up and put down the saw. He didn't really want to voice the suspicions that were bashing around in his head.

"Roxy invited us to dinner tonight."

"You're always going to Roxy's for dinner."

"She wants Skye and Amy to normalize their relationship."

"Ugh. But she's probably right. How bad could it be. Amy lives several states away."

"It isn't that."

"Then what is it? It's not like you to bail when somebody needs you. Especially when it's Skye."

"I'm not, but she sounded like she didn't want me to go."

"I kinda got that part from your side of the conversation."

"Maybe I shouldn't go."

"Whoa. Haven't you learned anything about women? They tell you stuff because they want to be nice, but if you take them up on it, they get all pissed."

Actually, Jack had observed that in his close encounters with several relationships.

"It's just . . ah hell . . . what if she doesn't *want* me there?"

"Not tracking."

Jack deliberated. Then shot his self-esteem to the wind. "Connor?"

"The ex-boyfriend?"

Jack winced. "I'm not so sure he's still ex."

"No way. They're just old friends."

"That's what she says. But they went to dinner last night, and he walked her home. All the way to my door."

"Just dinner and good manners," Sonny said, but Jack heard the ambivalence in his voice.

"And then they were together again today." Jack gave him the *Reader's Digest* version of going back for Skye's poncho and seeing Connor's sports car at the camp.

"He was probably just passing by. Besides, she hasn't had much time for him since they've been here." Sonny's expression changed. "But now that I think about it. You better go to dinner and make sure he knows what end is up."

"I'm not sure if I know."

"Bullshit. Don't try and tell me you're having second thoughts about Skye."

"Of course not. But it's not exactly up to me."

"The hell it isn't. You better claim your territory or he'll walk off with her while you're being all enlightened male."

"Oh, man." Jack sank onto an empty sawhorse. "Maybe he won't even be there."

"The hell he won't. You can bet he'll be there. He's poaching."

Chapter 17

Since Jack had left the workshop early to clean up for Roxy's dinner, Skye met him at his cottage. She could hear the shower running when she let herself in, so she went out to the porch to wait.

She could see Hildy's tenants out on the beach. Roxy's kitchen light was on and she knew Hildy would be there bustling about in last-minute preparations. Skye usually took comfort in their proximity. But tonight, instead of looking like the welcome glow of security they normally were, they took on the menace of challenge.

Calming breaths. Calming breaths. There was Amy and there were four of them. And probably Connor. He would be on her side surely.

Stop it! she warned herself. Ganging up against Amy would just make her more likely to lash out. This was supposed to be a civilized "thaw" dinner. Skye didn't hold out much hope for that one, though she was more than ready to let bygones be bygones if it would stop the craziness. *Calming breaths. Calming breaths.*

Jack came out to the porch a few minutes later.

"Wow," she said, happily startled out of her train of thought.

His hair was wet from the shower and it curled down the nape of his neck as always, but he'd parted it on the side and combed the rest straight. He was wearing slacks and a short-sleeve button-collar shirt that he never wore because he complained it was too tight. Not too tight for Skye, because it tapered in such a way that showed his chest and biceps to total advantage.

"Are you going to be comfortable in that all night?" she asked. And was surprised at the scowl she received in return.

"You want me to change?"

Skye blinked. "Not me. You look great. But . . ." She tilted her head. "Is something wrong? Do you want to wig out? I won't be mad."

"No. Let's just go."

"Not if you're going to be all surly and taciturn all night." Though she had to admit this rarely seen side of Jack was kind of scintillating.

"Sorry. Just a long day."

"Tell me about it," she said, taking his arm.

"You, too?"

Skye laughed. "Kind of, but I meant tell me about your long day."

"Just a bunch of stuff. I'm looking forward to dinner."

"You are?" she asked as they cut across the patch of lawn to the path to Roxy's.

"I'm hungry. And . . . Well, maybe this is as good a time as any to get things settled." Jack didn't elucidate, just dropped back into silence as they walked along, not even slowing down to look at the waxing moon.

It was as if they were on a mission. And maybe they were. He was right. If there was to ever be peace between her and Amy, they would have to meet each other halfway. And tonight was as good a time as any.

Jack said no more. Skye appreciated his silence in a way. She thought she knew what he was doing, giving her space to shape the situation and take control and prepare. She loved that about him . . . normally.

Jack was great at being "there" without being in the way. But tonight, for once, she wished she could just dump everything in his lap and let him handle it.

But this was her former life, her family, and she didn't blame him for not wanting to get embroiled in her relationship with Amy. Skye was willing to try for Roxy's sake, but she wasn't optimistic.

Jack did stop her at the kitchen door where the aroma of Hildy's roast pork wafted through the screen. He gave Skye a quick squeeze and she felt a ripple of confidence course through her.

Roxy's face appeared on the other side of the screen. "Waiting for an invitation?" She pushed open the door.

Jack cleared his throat. And Skye realized he was nervous, too.

They entered single file. There were no place settings at the kitchen table. They must be eating in the dining room tonight. To keep them on their best behavior?

"I wanted Hildy to make her spaghetti and meatballs but she said it was too heavy for summer and that she didn't want to have to clean up if food started flying."

"I did not," Hildy said, bustling over to pour green peas into a colander. "No throwing of food. Especially you, Jack."

Jack laughed and Skye could practically hear the ice cracking around his mood. Hildy had a way with people as well as food. She returned the pot to the stove, and Skye gave her an impulsive hug.

Roxy sighed theatrically. "I really was hoping for spaghetti. I've wanted to replace that dining room wallpaper for years."

Hildy just winked and said, "I hope you brought your appetites. Now get out of my kitchen and get yourselves a drink. Jack, there's beer in the fridge and Roxy's got a nice sauvignon blanc in the ice bucket on the porch, don't you, Roxy?" Two raised eyebrows and Roxy was herding Skye and Jack out the door to the parlor.

Connor was standing in the archway to the porch and looking out to the ocean. He made a trim, confident figure, and Skye suddenly understood why Jack had worn that shirt.

Could it be possible? She almost laughed. Almost. There was something unsettling about the very thought of Jack acting so . . . so . . . predictably male.

That was one of the many things that had drawn her to him in the first place. Steady, but not predictable. He could enjoy himself without adventure, see the beauty in the most commonplace things. He was open . . . and yet self-contained.

And for the first time, she wondered if there was a long-term place in that bubble of containment for her. And even more, if she would she be content there.

Roxy headed to the ice bucket. "Look who's here," she warbled.

Connor turned around. Smiled at Skye and fifteen years fell away. She smiled back at him, but instinctively moved closer to Jack, except that Jack had stepped forward to shake Connor's hand and Skye bumped into Roxy, who had just held out a glass of wine.

Skye took the glass. Roxy glanced at the two men, flashed her a scary clown frown complete with rolling eyes

If it had been a made-for-TV movie, Skye would have rolled hers, too. Instead, anxiety seared through her stomach. This was not funny; this wasn't what this evening was about. She wished she'd never agreed to come.

She gave Roxy a serious frown, warning her not to interfere, and went to stand with the two men. Usually Skye was the one to put everyone at ease, but tonight she couldn't get past her own discomfort. So the three of them turned to watch the ocean until they heard footsteps on the stairs and Skye knew Amy was making her entrance. And like a well-prepped studio audience, they all turned and watched her pause at the bottom of the stairs.

"Am I late?"

Roxy shook her head.

Skye silently willed her not to make any cracks. Amy was made up; her hair was swept up to one side, and her leggings were topped by an off-the-shoulder clinging blouse. She looked really beautiful.

And Skye took a punch to the gut. *Little Princess Face.* And like a hundred times in childhood, she felt herself disappearing, in the back seat of the car, at the edge of the family photo, in the background of a birthday celebration, invisible.

"Dinner's ready." Hildy's voice broke into the mesmerized group and they all reacted as if they'd been goosed. Skye breathed again. The spell was broken. She was Skye and she was happy the way she'd turned out so far.

The dining table was laid with everyday plates, a gesture that made Skye relax a little. She didn't want to have to deal with whatever came up over the lineup of forks and spoons that Roxy was wont to pull out every now and then just for "practice." And Skye wondered if she'd already used the good china just to impress Connor, the diplomat.

Roxy sat at the head of the table wearing such a smug expression that Skye wondered if she was up to something. Hildy bustled in and out refusing help while the rest of them sat there and watched her work. Skye sat down next to Jack on one side of the table. Amy and Connor sat across from them.

"Now isn't this nice," Roxy said to the empty place at the foot of the table where Hildy would eventually sit.

No one said anything.

"And how are things going for the ice cream social?"

Amy looked up. "Oh fine, exhausting with putting up with all their 'We've been doing this for twenty years' excuses. I swear you'd think no one had an idea in decades."

"Did they come around?" Roxy asked.

"Eventually. And they're going to love it once they see it in action." She smiled. "Actually I bought ice cream and toppings yesterday and made them do it my way. Needless to say . . ."

"So you're enjoying your work?" Roxy asked.

"It's okay. Trying to drag them into the twenty-first century takes some doing, but they're kind of fun once you get past the blue hair."

Hildy came in holding a platter of pork. "You know full well that none of those ladies have blue hair."

"Edna Pritchard?"

"An unfortunate miscalculation on the part of a new beautician."

"Yeah, she went in yesterday for a do-over."

"I'm sure they're glad you're helping out," Hildy said.

"They said I was indispensable."

Hildy put the pork down. It had already been carved and Skye sent a silent thank-you to her. She was acutely aware of a tension arcing across the table between Jack and Connor. Asking one of them to carve was bound to increase it. Stupid maybe, but men . . . Or was she just imagining the atmosphere between them?

"This looks delicious, Hildy," Connor said.

"As always," Jack added.

"Who wants to say grace?" Roxy asked enthusiastically.

Five faces turned in surprise. Roxy didn't care for organized religion as she let anyone who asked know.

"Just kidding. Let's eat." Roxy reached for the rice and peas, ladled a healthy mound onto her plate, then passed it to Connor.

"Jack, take some pork and pass it to Skye," Hildy said.

Jack dutifully took a piece and held the platter for Skye, who took a piece and handed it to Roxy. Roxy winked at her. It was going to be a long dinner.

Hildy was the one who had the most reason to snub Amy. Amy had interloped on her life and she wasn't even a half-family member. She'd insulted Hildy's paying guests, could have driven them away. And yet Hildy was making an effort to draw her out.

At least Skye could do her part. She took a bowl of zucchini and tomatoes from Jack. "So, Amy," Skye began, "tell us more about how you're organizing the social."

Amy looked up sharply, her face so unguarded that Skye felt a pang of compassion. She knew nothing of Amy's life. By choice, true, but was she being gratuitously and willfully mean by holding on to her distrust? Would she have mended fences with someone whom she'd liked more to begin with?

And there it was.

After Skye's mother's death, her father was distraught. Roxy had come to stay with them. Roxy, who never had children of her own, knew how to comfort an inconsolable child.

Skye had clung to her as the only motherlike security she had. Then her father married Karen, and Roxy had packed her bags and gone home. And Skye was bereft for the second time in her first six years.

It didn't take long for her to realize that she was no longer the center of someone's affection. Not her dad, who'd never re-covered from her mother's death. And certainly not her new "mother."

Then suddenly she was going to have a new baby sister.

At first her dad seemed excited at the prospect of another child, but soon after Amy was born, he began to retire more and more to his workshop. Skye had never really taken to her "new sister." And it was immediately clear to her that Amy now had her own mother and Skye didn't.

That admission pierced Skye like a hot needle. She'd *always* resented Amy. And heaven help her, she still resented her.

She felt a tug at her hands; she was still holding the zucchini bowl and Roxy was pulling it from her grip.

Skye was aware of Amy talking but had no idea what she'd been saying.

". . . ancient tablecloths. And really, cardboard bowls. So unappealing. I went right out to the party store and bought red, white, and blue plastic ones. Much better. Once they finished complaining about the expense, they loved them. . . ."

"But a good idea," Skye said way too brightly but what the hell. . . . They'd agreed to cardboard because it was biodegradable.

"Thanks," Amy said dubiously. "Edna says you're planning a big event at her place."

"Uh, yeah," Skye said. "That's the plan."

"Sounds interesting."

"Thanks." Right now it was a plumbing nightmare. And Charlie Abbott still hadn't called back about the emergency meeting. "It's been a lot of work, but hopefully, it'll be a good experience."

Amy nodded. She looked down at her plate. It was obvious

she was trying to do her part. Or was she? Skye had grown so set in her expectations, would she even recognize if Amy was being sincere or not?

"Wish I could see it," Amy said, not looking up.

Manipulation, Skye thought. She could hear it in her voice. *She wants to stay longer.* "Maybe next time," Skye said. How was that for opening a door, then closing it again.

Amy picked up her fork and moved food around on her plate. "That would be nice."

Skye risked a look at Connor, who was very intent on spearing a piece of zucchini. No help there.

They lapsed into silence again, everyone concentrating on eating with a vengeance. And into the silence Jack said, "At least the weather should be good for the ice cream social."

Skye forced herself not to do a double take, but she cut her eyes to Jack. She didn't know whether to laugh or throw her arms around him.

"Indeed," Roxy said. "Hopefully it will last through the Fourth."

The conversation clung to the weather with Connor asking about the plans for the celebrations, and Hildy and Roxy regaling him with anecdotes about the Fourths that had gone before and the annoyance over kids with illegal fireworks disturbing the neighborhoods for days before and after.

At last dessert was served. Blueberry-strawberry shortcake with homemade whipped cream. And along with dessert, Skye's cell rang. She sneaked a peek and pushed her chair back. "I'm sorry, it's Charlie about the meeting tomorrow. Excuse me." She accepted the call as she hurried into the hallway to speak in private.

It only took a minute.

"Everything okay?" Roxy asked when Skye returned.

"Yes. Just a meeting tomorrow morning." Skye could feel Connor's gaze from across the table. She refused to look at him. It was the first time she could think of that she'd wanted to keep anything from him. Of course there had been fifteen years since she'd had the choice.

They finished dessert. Skye, Jack, and Connor immediately began to clear their plates. Connor took Amy's plate, and after a look of surprise, she picked up the rice bowl and followed him into the kitchen.

Cleanup only took a few minutes, and Skye and Jack, refusing coffee or tea, said their thank-yous and goodbyes and left through the kitchen door. They didn't slow down until they came to Cove Beach, where they stopped as they often did on their way home.

"That wasn't so bad," Skye said.

Jack stretched his neck and reached for his top button.

"Told you not to wear that shirt."

"Huh," he said and kept unbuttoning until his shirt was open and he stretched out his arms. "Whew."

Skye laughed. "Was that whew, you can finally get out of that shirt, or whew, the whole dinner is over?"

"Both."

"You mean I shouldn't take this striptease as a come-on?"

"That too," Jack said. "And dinner wasn't so bad." He turned her to him for a long kiss. She reveled in the feel of him. His bare skin was warm, firm and definitely a turn-on, but it was more than passion, more than security, but a sense of place. But the feeling came to an abrupt halt when she suddenly wondered if anyone was watching them from the house.

"Come on," she said and pulled him down the path toward home. He didn't hesitate.

AFTER SKYE AND Jack left, Hildy shooed the rest of them from the kitchen. Connor went outside to get some air. At least that's what he told them, and himself. But as he stood on Roxy's beach gazing out to sea, his attention inevitably wandered to his right where he could just see Skye and Jack standing above the cove.

He told himself to look away. But he couldn't. The night was so clear he could see Jack unbutton his shirt. Surely they weren't . . . *Turn away, dammit. Just turn away.*

"I hope you know what you're doing and are willing to take responsibility for what happens."

Connor pulled his gaze away and turned to Roxy.

"What do you mean?"

"You know exactly what I mean. I just hope you are not willing to hurt everyone in order to get what you obviously want. We've had more than our share of that already."

"What am I going to do?"

"Not to sound cold, but you're the diplomat. You figure out what's best for everyone."

"I should leave. I know I should. I'm planning to as soon as

Amy finishes the ice cream social. I feel responsible to at least do that."

"Is that the real reason?"

"Do you want me to leave her here?"

Roxy huffed out a sigh. "No. But I don't want you upending Skye's life and possibly doing irreparable harm."

"You think I should back off."

"Actually, no. We all love Jack. We don't know you, but from everything Skye has said and I've seen this week, you're an honorable man. Poor Skye to have two honorable men interested in her." She held up a hand to stop his answer.

"And don't tell me you're not interested. You can't hide it. I see why you were her closest friend and confidant, but think of the future; yours and hers and Jack's. Don't start something that you can't or won't finish."

"I know, Roxy. Believe me, I know." But he was afraid it was too late to go back.

Chapter 18

The next morning came all too soon. Even Jack had trouble getting out of bed on time. When he offered to drive Skye to the church where the committee meeting was being held, she gladly accepted.

The sun was shining, and things looked fresh and verdant after the rain. They drove through downtown, which had miraculously changed overnight as bunting was unfurled from balconies and stars and streamers had appeared in store windows.

"I wonder if Maya came in early to decorate the store," Skye said. "I really should tell her to kick back a little."

"Don't," Jack said. "Every time Sonny suggests it, she bites his head off."

"That's because he's her husband, and a man."

"Thanks for the warning?"

Skye gave him a curious look. "Are you planning on scolding me for overworking?"

"Not me."

Skye tried to read his expression. Mainly she just saw fatigue. He was doing his own work, helping Brendan out at the camp, dealing with Skye's situation with Amy. And losing sleep because Skye's nightmares had started again. Jack never mentioned them, but she knew he was there for her. And seeing Connor and her together couldn't be easy. It wasn't easy for her.

"I think it's time we all take a day off."

Jack snorted. "It's not August." It was a statement said so often that it had become a bit of a joke. He didn't sound amused now.

"No. It's the beginning of July. Maybe this Sunday for the ice cream social. I'll put people in charge of the store. I don't have that many workshops and activities scheduled because of the holiday weekend. Maybe we could take the whole weekend off."

Jack stopped at a stop sign, leaned over from the driver's side of his truck, and squeezed her shoulder. "For now, just concentrate on today. Just do what you do, and you'll see your way through."

"From your lips—"

"Don't count on that. Just tell the committee what they need to do. They talked you into including the whole town. They can't expect a free ride now. Time to pay up. Just remind them of that."

"Want to come with me?"

"No way in hell." He tugged her hair. "Come by the workshop afterward. You can rant to your heart's content. The fridge is stocked with beer and apple juice, and dog jerky, though you probably don't want to try that."

"Thanks," she said. "I mean it." Silly as it was, she felt a whole lot better.

At least until Jack stopped the truck in the church parking lot.

Skye started to get out, but Jack pulled her back and kissed her. "Just don't let them push you into doing something you don't want to."

"Right." She got out, waved back at him, and walked to the entrance as he drove away. She was grateful for his support and a little bemused by his sudden frequent and overt displays of affection.

She liked it, but she didn't know whether to be gratified or alarmed.

Charlie Abbott and Rhoda Sims were waiting in the conference room, a square space in the church annex with a row of windows along one wall and religious posters on the other three. A well-worn portable chalkboard had been rolled into the room.

"Good morning, Skye," Rhoda said. "There's coffee over on the counter."

"Thanks."

"Tizzy called to say she's on her way," Charlie said. "And Brendan and Herb will be here. Millie and Vinnie are also coming but will be a few minutes late. Alice Dougan said she would try to stop by. No one else could make it, but I asked Brendan to bring Ollie Ford so he can explain just what we need to get the plumbing up and running."

Skye nodded. She hoped the lack of turnout wouldn't prevent them from deciding on a plan and enacting it.

"Your sister is a godsend," Rhoda said. "Such a delightful girl and so clever. I don't know why we haven't met her before."

"She doesn't get away from work often," Skye said. The fact that Skye had never invited her to visit was none of Rhoda's business.

"And she's been helping me with finally getting the office in order. These religious men are just too busy to be interested in earthly organization."

Skye thought the fact that the Reverend Olins was on his way to eighty-five and Rhoda never let anyone touch her office arrangements might have something to do with that. But she just smiled and nodded and silently willed Brendan or Tizzy to walk through the door.

Which they didn't.

"Well, we're trying to talk her into staying for the bake sale we're having during your weekend. She is such a good organizer."

Another two weeks. They'd all be in bedlam by then. Then again, dinner hadn't been a total fiasco. . . . Maybe Skye should back off, let Amy stay. She was bound to get bored with the church. And if Skye didn't force Amy to leave, Amy couldn't hold that against her in addition to all her other perceived slights.

What was she thinking? The mere idea pushed her mind into self-destruct mode.

"She already came in early today and I left her with Edna

Pritchard. They're planning a seating area for a Bake Sale Bistro, like a coffee bar so people can enjoy their baked goods on-site as she calls it, as well as the ones they take home. I didn't think Edna would go for it, you know how she can be, not the easiest to get along with, but those two get on like a house afire."

Skye flinched as Rhoda babbled on, oblivious. "I don't know if she can stay that long. She has to be back to work," Skye lied, falling back on Amy's original story. "She only had two weeks off and I know she has important duties." They only had Amy's word for it that she had held a very important position. Skye didn't actually know what Amy did, besides that she'd worked for some business in Harrisburg.

Maybe she should have tried harder. Then again, why should she? Amy hadn't done anything this trip besides help Rhoda with her ice cream and cause trouble for Skye and her friends and family.

Finally the door opened and Tizzy, followed by Brendan, Herb, and Ollie, walked in.

Ollie had brought plans that he stuck on the chalkboard. He was just finishing when Edna hurried in. "Sorry, I was busy in the office. Skye, your sister is a wonder."

Edna had barely closed the door when it opened again and Millie and Vinnie Garda bustled through the door.

"Sorry we're late," Millie said. "Did we miss anything?" They hurriedly took the two remaining chairs.

Charlie called the meeting to order. He explained the situation to the others and turned the meeting over to Ollie. It didn't take long for the mood to change. Questions about practicality, financial obligations, and time considerations were fired one after the other.

"Our budget is already being eaten up faster than predicted," Charlie said. "If we continue at this rate, there will be nothing left. And now we have this waterline emergency. Anyone have any suggestions?"

No one did. They all turned to Skye. She'd expected that. It seemed they turned to her for a lot of answers. She just didn't have one that wasn't expensive.

"You should have checked on the plumbing earlier," Rhoda said.

Ollie broke in before Skye could answer. "Skye did. The plumbing is accounted for in the budget. We didn't know the septic tank was going to fail inspection. It doesn't make sense to install a new system, since it can now be hooked up to the town water system. And we didn't know that the waterline was corroded. They both have to be dealt with."

He turned to Herb. "It will up the sale value of the property."

"I don't have that kind of money. Why do you think I'm selling?"

"Herb," Edna exclaimed.

"Well, it's true."

"It's just getting to be too much for us to take care of," Edna said.

Herb chewed on his bottom lip.

"Well, it is, Herb."

"Can we just get on with this discussion?" Herb said. "The

children are coming in with the grandkids this afternoon and I want to know they'll have someplace to take a shower and do their business while they're here."

"Herb!" admonished Edna.

"Well, it's true." He turned to Skye. "You can't leave me high and dry. Literally," he said.

"Herb, I'm not leaving you anywhere. We have a contract; we just need to make a decision."

"We're all counting on you, Skye," Charlie added. "The town has put a lot of money behind this."

"Merchants and restaurants, too," said Vinnie. "If things start falling apart, we could lose our shirts. We've already got orders in. Hired extra staff."

"Vinnie Garda!" Millie exclaimed. "Of course we did, because we knew a good thing when we saw it. We're all planning to reap the benefits from Skye's hard work."

"That's right," Tizzy added. "We jumped on it and left Skye to figure out how to make it work." She turned to Skye. "What do you think we should do?"

Skye thought that she had a huge amount of work to do before the weekend, and she didn't want to spend what little time she had worrying about plumbing. "I just need to know what funds are available, and what Herb wants to do, then I'll consult with Ollie and take care of it."

She ignored Brendan's look of alarm.

"I don't want you turning off my water," Herb said. "This is the last time the kids will get to spend their vacation here. And I don't want it to be a horrible experience."

Edna reached over and patted his hand. And Skye began to wish she had never involved the town at all.

"Herb," Ollie said. "We hooked your house up to the municipal water system when the point went public a decade ago. Remember? Hooking up the camp to the town won't affect you at all."

"But it *will* affect your resale value," Brendan added. "Not to mention that without it you won't pass inspection and you'll be stuck with having to fix it yourself."

"Oh," said Herb. "Well, in that case, if you can pay for it, go ahead."

THE MEETING BROKE up shortly after, with Charlie doling out most of the committee's funds and promising to ask the full chamber of commerce for additional money. Herb had made it clear he couldn't contribute. And it was hard not to blame him for pure mismanagement.

Skye knew she would have to pick up the tab for the rest. She had no choice—it was too late to change venues now. She'd take out a loan if she had to. There was money in the bank and she'd taken out insurance against having to cancel due to circumstances beyond her control. But she didn't want to spend the entrants' registrations until she had paid her outstanding bills.

She walked down the sidewalk, hardly aware that the sun was shining from a cloudless sky, the streets were filled with activity as shoppers came and went, and the town had placed flags on lampposts along the main street.

And for the first time she wondered why she had ever thought a discovery weekend would be a good idea.

She opened the door to Imagine That to find Maya, hands on her hips and surrounded by stacks of boxes.

Skye hurried toward her. "What's all this?"

"More supplies for the weekend. Evidently there was no one at the camp to sign for them."

"They were all at the meeting. I guess I'll have to ask Jack to help me truck them over."

Maya nodded, frowning. "How was the meeting?"

"Not that great. We need a girls' afternoon off."

"Are you crazy? Look at all this stuff."

Skye *was* looking at it. Suddenly it all just seemed like too much. *Now is not the time to waver*, she reminded herself. *Just take care of a day at a time.* There was always a time in every project when it seemed like a total disaster, when things seemed like too much trouble, or just too difficult to even attempt. Evidently this was one of those times.

She knew that it would pass. But it would pass easier with a long lunch and lie out on the beach with her best friend, *the sister she'd always wished she had.*

"We hardly do anything together these days," Skye said.

"We're busy."

Skye looked more closely. "Are you okay?"

Maya nodded.

"Don't hold out on me. What's the matter?"

"There is something, and maybe it's none of my business . . ."

"But you're going to yell at me anyway?" Skye asked, only half joking.

"No, but Sonny and I were talking last night."

"And he wants you to slow down. I totally understand." But she didn't know how she would manage without her.

"It's not about me. It's about you."

Skye stilled. "What about me?"

"Sonny is worried; well, actually he's pissed." Maya paused.

Skye waited.

"About you and Jack and Connor."

"Oh."

"I wasn't supposed to tell you about what he said, but it's important."

Skye looked around; it was still a few minutes before it was time to open. "Okay, but let's go in the back for a quick cup of something."

There were two bottles of cranberry juice in the fridge. Skye brought them out and handed one to Maya and they sat down in their usual places at the tiny tea table.

"We love you," Maya began.

"Okay, thanks?"

"And we love Jack."

"I do, too."

Maya's face convulsed. "But do you love Connor more?"

"What?"

"I mean I'll support whatever you want to do, but Jack is Sonny's best friend. And I don't know . . ." Maya trailed off and her eyes filled with tears. "Not hormones," she said. "I mean it. What's happening with you two?"

"What two? There's only me and Jack."

"Skye, this is serious. Why is Connor still here? What does he want from you?"

"I think he feels responsible for bringing Amy here and thinks he should hang around until he can take her away."

"That's all?"

"He kissed me."

"Oh no. I mean, whatever you— Did you kiss him back?"

"Yeah, but I think it was because I turned around and he was there and it happened before I could react."

"And?" Maya leaned over the table clutching the sides as if she thought it was going to levitate between them.

Skye twisted off the top of her juice. She didn't really have an answer.

"Skye? Was it like it always was before?"

Skye thought about it. "Yeah, only better. No, that's not what I mean . . . more developed."

"Developed? What does *that* mean? Did you fall in love all over again? Would you leave all this . . . us . . . Jack . . . and go with him, if he asked you?"

"He hasn't, so don't worry."

"But if he did?"

"But he didn't," Skye said. "Besides, this is where I belong, with Roxy and the store . . ."

"And Jack?"

"Maya, take a deep breath. You're blowing this all out of proportion, there has been no suggestion about anything further." At least not much and it was pretty much all on Connor's side. "He wouldn't leave the service and I won't leave my work. It's a fait accompli."

"But I want you to be happy. Do you still love him?"

"I don't know."

"I'll support whatever you want, but, well, who do you love more?"

"It's different. When Jack and I got together, most of our baggage was from our individual pasts. Connor *is* my past. Apples and oranges. Now stop worrying. Nothing is going to change."

Except something obviously already had. "What did Jack tell Sonny?"

"You know, his usual. 'She'll figure it out.' But Sonny said he's been acting weird. Kind of distant. Maybe he's just jealous."

"Jack?"

Both of Maya's fists came down on the table, rocking the two juice bottles. "Yeah, Jack. Sometimes you really piss me off. Of course he's jealous. And hurt, though he'd never admit it. And he has every right to be if you're encouraging Connor to move in on him."

"Okay, stop it, you're going to give Baby Daniels agita. What we need is a girls' afternoon off away from all this. We'll go down to Stella's at the beach for lunch, my treat. Then we're going out to shop for baby clothes."

"No, we're not, we have a Discover It Weekend docent orientation meeting this afternoon."

"Damn, I forgot. Then tomorrow."

"Ice cream social," Maya reminded her.

"Then the next day," Skye said, barely clinging to the possibility of getting a break.

"Fourth of July," Maya said

"At least you and Sonny will come to Roxy's for the Fourth."

"Of course, we always do."

"But soon we're going to take a day off, just the two of us, completely away from work and significant others, and responsibility."

Skye stopped and looked at Maya. "In August," they said together.

AT LEAST THE *orientation meeting went off without a hitch*, Skye thought as she closed up Imagine That well after eight o'clock that evening. The docents were in place. A dozen locals had volunteered to be greeters and guides and they were organized and run with precision by Leanne Garda and her mother, Millie. The meeting ran almost two hours, but by the end, logistics were clear, and everyone was enthusiastic and up to speed.

Now Skye only had to deal with the plumbing problem. And possibly Jack. He hadn't seemed distant to her when he and Sonny had come that afternoon to pick up the supplies and moved them to the storage cabin at the camp.

Of course, they were in a hurry, so there wasn't much time to engage while they were hauling heavy crates to the truck.

She tried to remember the morning ride to her committee meeting, but she couldn't recall any of their conversation or, to be honest, even if they'd had a conversation. Evidence of how distracted she was between Amy, Connor, preparing for the meeting, and the Pritchard camp plumbing.

She stood in the middle of store, now dark, and just breathed. Soaking in the feeling of her surroundings, trying to remember why she'd thought this was a good idea in the first place.

But she knew, beneath the angst, and the unsuspected, and the unknown, was her dream, the fruition of her life. The way she was. Her inner self.

It was also the monkey on her back. Skye walked to the door, and after one last look around, she locked the door and stepped onto the sidewalk.

And realized she didn't know where she was going.

She and Jack usually got in touch to plan their evening. She stopped to check her phone, found no texts or missed calls.

For the first time in a long time she wasn't sure where she should go. And she didn't miss the symbolism of that. She called Jack and waited for him to answer.

Chapter 19

By the time Skye and Jack finally met up at his cottage it was late, and they were both tired and cranky.

Skye didn't volunteer any information about the committee meeting other than they had convinced Herb to let them go ahead with the plumbing repairs. She didn't tell him any of the details and he didn't ask.

They scavenged the fridge for leftovers, then sat in front of the television while they ate. Skye was suddenly too exhausted to wonder if there was something brewing besides general exhaustion, and when Jack announced he was going to bed, she went, too.

She was asleep before Jack got out of the bathroom.

SKYE AND JACK met Sonny and Maya for brunch at Millie's the next morning. Since they'd slept later than usual, they had to stand in line waiting for a table. A good sign for Millie because they didn't usually have to wait, which meant the tourist traffic had picked up considerably. Not so great for the four of them.

It hadn't been the congenial brunch date of most Sunday mornings. Maya was feeling queasy and picked at dry toast and tea. Jack had carried his frigid mood into the diner, and Sonny and Skye were left to carry on conversation as best they could.

Even Sonny seemed pressed for something to say, though, and Skye wondered if he was mad at her because of his perceived idea that she might be . . . what? Cheating on Jack? Treating him badly? Not paying enough attention to him?

She should probably just ask Jack outright and get it over with. But she just didn't want to risk one of their infrequent arguments, not when she was dealing with so many other anxieties.

Now they were standing in line, stuffed with breakfast, and not really wanting ice cream but determined to do their community duty. And though the sun was shining and it was a beautiful day, it seemed to Skye that Jack was carrying a thundercloud above his head. She linked both her arms around the crook in his elbow. "Hey," she said.

He looked over at her. "What?"

"You okay?"

"Sure." He smiled, definitely as an afterthought.

"Good. Because . . ." Because she needed him to be okay, she needed—wanted—them to be okay. Because he was her better half. Her stronger half. Consoler in chief. Did she give him anything in return? "I appreciate you."

He sighed, extricated his arm, and pushed her forward in line to where Alice Dougan was holding out a plastic bowl to her. "Choose your flavors at the next station," she said with a smile, and they moved on.

"Well, Amy was right about one thing," Skye said a few minutes later. "Our ice cream is barely starting to melt and we've all got our sundaes. That's a first." They sat down with Roxy and Hildy at one of the tables scattered across the church lawn. This year all the tables had been covered with new red-checked tablecloths.

"Well, you have to hand it to that sister of yours," Hildy said. "Very efficient and the look is much more festive." They all looked around at the long row of sundae-making stations; the red, white, and blue banner that was stretched above their heads; the cashier at the gate; the new tablecloths and little flag decorations that adorned each table.

"And a good crowd," Roxy said. "Praise the Lord. I quaked just wondering if she would manage to piss everybody off and ruin the church's comeback."

It's not over yet, Skye thought. "Where *is* Amy?" she asked.

"Inside running the operation," Hildy said. "Keeping the supply chain going, Et cetera. She even conned Connor into helping. I have to say, she does know how to get a bunch of old broads who can never agree on anything to put on the best social they've had since I can remember.

"Well, that hit the spot." She heaved herself out of her folding chair and picked up her trash. "Coming, Roxy? We've got stuff to do, groceries to buy, grills to clean. And we'll see you two around 6:00 tomorrow—or earlier if you want to spend the afternoon at our beach before the fireworks."

Roxy stood, cut her eyes to Jack and then to Skye before gathering up her bowl and napkin. "See you tomorrow."

Skye turned to Jack. "So what do you want to do now?"

"Don't you want to go by Imagine That?"

"No. Penny's there, she'll close at six. And there are no workshops or open classes scheduled for today or tomorrow. I'm all yours."

"The beach," Jack said. "The Point Beach, not Roxy's."

"Perfect."

CONNOR COULDN'T BELIEVE that he'd let Amy con him into schlepping for her during the ice cream social. He could see Skye and Jack standing in line while he was stuck in the kitchen opening boxes of plastic bowls and spoons. An environmental garbage dump if you asked him. But nobody asked him.

He should have left days ago. There was only one reason to hang around here, and that was to see Skye. Try to figure out if she was really happy with her life, happy with Jack and her store.

It was hard to tell because there was so much tension between Amy and her. Not a normal environment for decision-making. But environments never were.

Usually Connor knew what he or his superiors wanted and he went about making sure it happened. He was now pretty sure what he wanted, but he didn't think any move he might make would be honorable. And how would he live with himself if he enticed Skye away and he couldn't make her happy in the long run?

God knew his track record was pretty bleak.

He should leave. But still he made excuses to stay.

"Connor, hon, Amy says she needs more napkins, ASAP."
Rhoda Sims, wearing a red apron over a blue-striped blouse,
reminded him of one of those elongated American Gothic carv-
ings in souvenir stores.

He slit open the box of napkins and followed Rhoda outside.
He just didn't get it. Amy was competent, innovative, had even
gotten a bunch of squabbling church ladies all on board. And
yet he knew that there was still a good chance that she would
manage to screw it up before it was over.

And Connor intended not to stick around in case it came at
the end of the day.

He saw Roxy and Hildy walking toward the parking lot.
Maybe they needed him to help with something.

He deposited the napkins and turned to Rhoda. "You're all
set, there are more bowls in the kitchen if you run out. I'm
afraid I have to leave."

"Well, you were very sweet to help out," Rhoda said. She
grabbed a handful of the napkins and headed to the end of the
row of tables.

Connor tucked his head and hurried to the parking lot and
freedom.

SKYE AND JACK changed into swimsuits, gathered up their
beach gear, and walked the two blocks to the far side of the
point where Point Beach stretched in a narrow strip of smooth,

white sand. It was a great place for swimming since the waves were tempered by an inlet to the river.

There was something private and intimate about the point's beach despite the handful of families already set up for the day. And today it was just what she and Jack needed. A few hours away from Amy and Connor and work and indecision.

Skye was unbelievably relieved that she'd managed to get through the ice cream social without having Amy lose her grip and insult someone or make a blunder.

Not your responsibility, she told herself, as she snapped open the beach blanket and let it float to the sand. Next came books, the paper, a bag of carrots and celery, bottles of water, no phones, and a Frisbee that she didn't think either of them was interested in throwing.

They plopped down on the sand. Jack stretched out, his hands behind his head and his feet stretching beyond the blanket's edge. Skye looked up at the sun, decided it was too late to bother with sunscreen, and lay down beside him.

She didn't open her book, Jack didn't open his. They just settled into a day-at-the-beach silence.

Skye didn't know how much time passed, just that the gulls wheeled above their heads, and the waves lapped at the shore, and the stress that had been building for the last few months began to ease.

She could have easily fallen asleep except Jack jumped up, grabbed her hand, and pulled her toward the water. The surf was cold on her ankles, but he didn't slow down until they were waist-deep in the water. Then he fell slow-mo back into the water, his hair floating out from his face like in a Pre-Raphaelite painting.

He would laugh at the comparison. Connor wouldn't. Connor evoked those kinds of comparisons.

A sudden spray of salt water brought her back to the present.

"What are you looking at?" Jack said.

"You," Skye said and dove in to overturn him in the water.

When they finally got out, the sun had turned the sky red and orange. They gathered up their gear and headed back to the cottage where they showered together in the outside shower stall and ran into the house wrapped only in their towels.

"I'm thinking pizza delivery," Jack said sometime later.

"Excellent idea. Oh, damn, I forgot to go to the grocery."

"I went for you."

"You did?"

"Yeah. Yesterday, but only because I wanted to make sure there was plenty of potato salad for tomorrow."

She raised her eyebrows at him.

"Well, Sonny had to go pick up some stuff for Maya so I figured as long as he was going, I might as well go and pick up the stuff for potato salad. I left you a note."

"Thank you." She grimaced. "I guess I didn't see it."

"You were preoccupied with the camp situation."

"Ugh. Don't remind me. Promise me if I ever get any more bright ideas after a couple of beers, you'll tell me they won't work."

He gave her a curious look, but before she could figure it out, he was on the phone to Point Pizza.

They ate on the porch, devouring a Point Pizza Special of pepperoni, sausage, olives, mushrooms, onions, no anchovies, picking up the pieces when they fell off the overloaded slice and tossing them into each other's mouths. Washed it all down with a local microbrew.

When they were stuffed, they sat back on the glider and watched the sea as the sky turned from blue to mauve to dusk. The families on Roxy's beach gathered up their things and went inside. There was no one below them in the cove.

Skye leaned back against the glider and soaked in the starlit sky. Breathed deep and was startled by a loud bang that rent the air.

"Now it starts," Jack groused. "I don't mind the noise one night a year—at least that comes with a display of fireworks— but the other stuff for days before and after just pisses me off. Let's go inside."

He didn't wait for her to agree but took his plate and beer into the house. The mood broken, Skye grabbed her empty plate and bottle and followed him in.

Skye totally agreed about the illegal fireworks, but she had a feeling that his abrupt decision was due to more than just the noise.

She glanced across to Roxy's beach and saw that one lone figure stood on the sand. Of course. She hadn't seen him come out of the house, but she bet Jack had. Was he the source of Jack's bad mood lately?

Should she even mention it? Was she willing to go where that might lead?

Roxy stood on the porch watching the beach. Hell, watching Connor on the beach.

"That boy's got it bad," Hildy said.

"He isn't a boy."

"Anyone under forty is a boy to me."

"What a mess."

Hildy came to stand beside her. "You don't think anything will actually change, do you?"

Connor was just standing there, not moving, and Roxy felt a stab of compassion. "It already has. I just don't know in which way."

"I don't know why they came in the first place," Hildy said. "Amy and Skye haven't made any real reconciliation, far from it. And Connor has managed to upset everyone without even trying. We all had a perfectly lovely life here. Jack and Skye are good together."

"But Connor is special."

"Special?" Hildy said. "So is Valentine's Day. Until you see the five pounds you gained from eating all the candy."

Roxy snorted and sat on a porch chair. "What kind of analogy is that?"

"Hell, I don't know. I'm just saying that 'special' doesn't see you through life."

"You just hate it when things change."

"No, I'm just careful about changing things."

Roxy stood up again; she couldn't seem to get settled. "He's planning on leaving the day after tomorrow. And taking Amy with him."

"Good, I like him well enough, but I'll be glad when they're gone."

"I know what you mean. I should never have encouraged them to stay, I just thought that I might be able to help facilitate a reconciliation."

"Instead we're just sitting around waiting for the other shoe to drop."

"True," Roxy said. "And it always does with Amy. Uh-oh. Here he comes."

Hildy turned as if she were going to make a dash inside for the parlor. "Too late," Roxy told her, and they both turned to face Connor as he stepped onto the porch.

He smiled at them both.

"We were just going to refresh our drinks," Roxy said, trying to pretend they hadn't been caught red-handed spying on him.

"Thanks, but no. I think it's time for me to leave. If Amy wants a ride, she'll have to come with me."

"When?" asked Roxy.

He smiled a little ruefully. "Tomorrow morning early enough?"

"No. What I meant was you can't leave tomorrow. It's the Fourth. Do you know what traffic is like on the Fourth?"

"So the day after. Thanks for your hospitality. I know it hasn't been easy." He walked past them, stopped, turned back. "I'm sorry I brought her, it was for totally selfish reasons. Tell Skye I'm sorry. I'll just go pack."

"Tell her yourself. She and Jack are coming for the Fourth."

The look he gave her was so bleak that Roxy had to look away.

They watched him walk through the house, tall, determined, and it broke Roxy's heart. "He shouldn't leave this way, not again. I feel terrible."

"Huh," Hildy said. "At least it will soon be over."

"Will it? I just don't know what to do."

"You should go fix us another drink and let Skye broker this mess."

"I hate for her to lose him again. But I'd hate for her to lose Jack, too."

"Stay out of it. She came to you before because she was given no choice. I for one am thankful for it. But give her the chance to be the one who controls her fate this time."

Chapter 20

The morning of the Fourth broke overcast and chilly. *Not a good sign for the fireworks*, Skye thought. When Jack announced he had promised to make a delivery that morning and took off before nine, she knew it was going to be a long day.

She spent the morning making her grandmother Kyle's Fourth of July potato salad. Skye had made it every year since they'd been celebrating the Fourth together at the beach.

When she'd finished boiling and chopping and mixing, had returned a huge bowl of potato salad to the fridge, and washed all the dishes, it was just after twelve and Jack still wasn't back.

Skye opened her laptop, pulled a few figures out to look at them. Everything looked good except the renovation fund. And that was within an affordable overage. Only the plumbing decision was still up in the air. She would talk to Newton Tyndale at the bank. Maybe take out a short-term loan. Just get the plumbing done, and hope the chamber would pay for it after the fact. Not a brilliant move, but she was running out of options.

And for what? So Herb could get a better sale price, and all the money that she could have reinvested in new programs or even a permanent site would have gone down the drain.

When Skye finally heard Jack's truck in the drive around three o'clock, she was more than ready to leave.

"What took you so long?" she asked with more bite than she meant and added, "I missed you."

"I had a flat on my way back. The spare had a flat. I need four new tires. I knew it and I should have dealt with it, I just let it slide."

"Did you get new tires?"

"No, a plug. I promised to go in . . ."

"In August," they said together.

"We're going to be too busy in August doing the fun stuff we didn't get to do all year."

"Yeah," Jack said and gave her an impulsive kiss. "Let me take a shower and we'll go."

He left her standing in the kitchen wondering what "yeah" meant.

Skye paced the kitchen, feeling slightly uneasy. She was tempted to take a quick trip to Imagine That just to make sure things were running smoothly, though she knew there was no need.

She was a hands-on manager but not a micromanager. She had no qualms about other people being just as competent as she was. She considered that one of her strongest assets. She could recognize talent when she saw it, and lately she'd been leaving the day-to-day managing to Maya and others.

They didn't seem to mind, but she wondered if she'd been taking advantage of them, too busy or distracted to mind her own enterprises.

Well, it couldn't be fixed in a day, not today anyway. She went back to the bedroom to change into her swimsuit. She'd just stripped and was stepping into the bottoms when Jack came out of the shower.

"I'm in no hurry," he said and dropped his towel.

"They can't eat without the potato salad," she said, batting halfheartedly at him with her swimsuit top.

"We could send the salad over and stay here. There's leftover pizza."

Normally she would be tempted, but not today. Because she was hearing more than he was saying. Had been for a few days. He was tired of dealing with Skye and Amy's volatile relationship. That much was obvious. And who could blame him? So was Skye. Another reason to make sure her half sister left town.

As far as Skye knew, Amy would abide by Skye's intention for them to leave tomorrow. Even Skye wouldn't send Amy and Connor off in Fourth of July traffic.

Then her duty would be done. They had come to no détente. And as long as Amy continued to claim Skye had started the fire, they never would; Skye refused to nurture a relationship that was based on a lie.

She wasn't quite as eager to see Connor leave. They'd barely had time to spend together. That was probably a good thing, because it was setting off a whole lot of insecurities and second-guessing on Skye's part—and among her friends.

She cut a quick glance at Jack, who was sitting on the edge of the bed, not making a move to get dressed.

"Is something the matter?"

He practically jumped at her words. "No. Why would there be?" He stood and went to the dresser for his board shorts.

They both stuffed clothes for later in a spare backpack and went to the kitchen for the famous potato salad. And his question hung in the air between them all the way to Roxy's house.

Fortunately the haze had burned off, and the day had turned sunny and warm. The beach was crowded with residents, visiting families, friends of families, and a few local residents. Picnic tables had been dragged out; the smoke from numerous grills billowed with each gust of breeze; and the smell of barbecuing meat filled the air.

Skye and Jack were met with a crowd in the kitchen, Roxy, Hildy, Amy, and Connor all cutting, mixing, and stacking plates and silverware to be taken out later to their own picnic table that had been set out on the front lawn.

Hildy immediately handed Jack a platter of burgers and sent him out to man the grill.

Maya and Sonny arrived just as Jack declared that the burgers were done. Sonny was carrying a massive watermelon over one shoulder; Maya was struggling with a pile of beach towels with a plate of brownies balanced precariously on the top. Roxy took the plate and Skye took the towels.

"Chow's on," Hildy announced, and everyone filled their plates, got drinks, and went outside to crowd along the benches on either side of the table.

Next door, Hildy's tenants waved from their own table. They had made friends with another family renting for the week with children of similar ages and seemed to be having a great time.

There was the usual initial silence that occurred at Hildy's meals, while everyone savored the deliciousness. But after they slowed down, the chewing was overtaken by sighs and compliments, and gradually conversation began to pick up.

"Lovely ice cream social yesterday, Amy." Hildy smiled a benevolent smile down the table.

"Thanks. The ladies were pleased with the results. They made a bundle compared to the ones before."

"That's good," Skye said, making the effort. "I'm glad you could help them out."

"How was the committee meeting?" Roxy asked Skye. "I haven't had time to ask you."

"Not the best," Skye confessed. "The septic is almost full. That we anticipated, but the main water pipe to the street is corroded. Don't ask me how. Herb managed not to mention any of this before we signed the contract. Though to be honest maybe he didn't know."

"So what's the plan?"

"So far? None. I asked the committee to come up with more cash, but they're balking at spending more money on property that's just going to be sold. And who can blame them. Someone suggested portable toilets."

"Ugh," interjected Amy.

"Exactly. And that doesn't take care of the corroded pipes. I suggested Herb and the town bite the bullet and replace the pipe. It's necessary for more than the weekend, but Herb says he can't afford to put in any more money, not that he's put in a dime. That was what deciding to use the camp as a base was about in the first place, at least partially, to help him out with the sale. And cheaper in the long run for me . . . until this week anyway. Still, it will have to be done. We can't do without water."

"You should buy it," Amy said.

Everybody turned to look at her.

"With my pocket change," Skye said.

"No, really. Edna took me by to see it yesterday when she drove me home. Since no one else waited for me." She cast Connor an accusing look that he ignored.

"Anyway," Amy continued. "Since you haven't told me anything about what you're doing, I asked her and she showed me the camp.

"It really wouldn't be half bad if you did a little landscaping. Rustic chic is in these days. You could do weddings and family reunions and photo shoots and make a bundle. You'd have to change the cabins into dressing rooms. They'd have to be gutted and redesigned. All upscale rustic, not shabby. And you'd definitely have to get real plumbing. You can't ask brides to pee in a porta-potty."

Roxy snorted.

"I guess not," Hildy added.

"That sounds nice," Skye said. "But I don't have that kind of money. And I don't think the Pritchards are up to that kind of work, much less that kind of expense, even if they wanted to, which I also doubt. But it's good to know they're considering their options . . ."

"Oh, they aren't. Edna got all teary and said it would be a perfect place for her granddaughter to get married, but then we left. Weird. Her granddaughter is like twelve or something.

"I mean, Edna probably won't even be alive to see her get married anywhere."

"Amy!" Roxy exclaimed.

"Well, it's true."

"I hope you didn't tell her that," Skye said.

"Of course not. I would never say that to her. You're the only person who thinks I'm a monster."

Skye stifled a sigh. "I don't think you're a monster."

"No?"

"No."

"Then why did you say that?"

They'd almost made it through dinner without a fight, thought Skye.

"You hate me. You've always hated me."

"Stop it, Amy. I don't hate you and I don't think you are a monster. I do, however . . ." Skye felt Jack squeeze her thigh, but she was too far gone to play nice. "I think you're self-destructive and determined to take others with you."

"Oh yeah?" snapped Amy. "You're the one who brings everyone down. With your stupid weekend that you can't even pee at."

"Just shut—"

"Girls, stop it, we're celebrating today."

"You celebrate." Amy slid off the bench and stomped off to the beach.

"Sorry," Skye said. "But she can never leave it alone. Why does everything have to be a confrontation with her?"

"Go after her," Roxy said.

Skye hunched down in her seat.

"Go. Apologize whether you mean it or not."

"Why am I the one who has to apologize?"

"Because you're the better person." Roxy pinched her cheek, a gesture that was so uncharacteristic of Roxy that it still carried shock effect. The first time she'd used it was when Skye had first arrived all those years before. It had surprised Skye's anger right out of her and made her laugh because it was such a stupid thing to do. She didn't laugh now, but she did give in.

And feeling like a reprimanded teenager, she rolled her eyes and stomped off across the lawn toward Amy.

Amy saw her coming and moved farther away. Skye gritted her teeth and ran after her.

"I'm sorry if you got the wrong idea," Skye said.

"Did I?" Amy spat out the words, but at least she slowed down.

"Yes. I don't think you're a monster. I even think you may actually believe I started that fire, even though I didn't."

That stopped her. Amy turned on her. "I—"

"Sit down," Skye said. "Let's sit down . . . please."

They sat facing the water shouldered slightly toward each other.

"This thing between us started before the fire," Skye said.

"You were always blaming me for something, telling on me, getting me into trouble. Some of it I can pass off to being a younger sister and spoiled. But sometimes it was just outright malicious."

Amy hung her head. "I was unhappy."

"You?" Skye blurted before she could stop herself. "You had a mother and father who both doted on you. My mother was dead. I had nothing left."

"Not true. Dad didn't even notice me. He just went along to keep Mom off his back. You're the only one he spent time with."

Skye sighed. Wondered why she hadn't seen that before. "Amy, he didn't spend time with me. He let me sit beside him while he worked on his trains. I wasn't allowed to touch anything."

"He shared them with you."

"He *showed* them to me." *Not shared.* Skye had realized that long ago. Her father wasn't really connected to any of them. He stayed in that workshop to be close to the only thing he really loved. Skye's mother. Did Amy know this? Did Karen? Surely she must have guessed when they found the remnants of her mother's things in the ashes of the storage closet.

Now that Skye thought about it, maybe her father hadn't even believed she was responsible for the fire. Maybe he'd just withdrawn wherever he always retreated to. The place where this world didn't matter. Where he didn't feel the pain of loss. Maybe they'd all misread his reaction.

Oh Dad. You could have saved us all so much suffering.

Skye looked over at her half sister, who had turned away to look out at the waves. They would never be close. Their life together had only taught them to compete for a love neither of them would ever completely know.

Not even Skye, who was the closest James would ever get to his first wife. But even as a child, Skye had looked more like Roxy than her own mother.

She hadn't even been able to give her father that.

That's why he'd seemed so distant and slightly confused when they'd finally reconciled years afterward. Because he wasn't holding the fire against Skye; he was holding her not being her mother against her.

She even felt a little compassion for her stepmother. Maybe she'd had good intentions marrying James Mackenzie. And she'd been given a rude awakening.

Amy glanced at Skye. "I guess you're never going to accept me, are you?"

"Why is it so important? It never was before."

"You're wrong; it was always important to me."

"Selective memory, Amy."

"No really, you just never noticed."

Ouch. She was right about that one. After the initial cute baby stage, Skye had made a conscious effort to ignore her demanding half sister.

"I'm sorry you're so unhappy, Amy. But I can't fix it. Only you can." Skye stood. "I'm going for a swim before it gets too late."

Maya, Sonny, and Jack were already in the surf. Skye slipped off her cover-up, dropped it to the sand, and ran in to join them.

Horseplay and splashing ensued. And after that the four of them stood braced against the waves talking and laughing like people without a care between them.

As the sun began to set, they all plodded out of the water, grabbed towels, and headed to the house, passing Connor settled in a beach chair, engrossed in an unfamiliar-looking newspaper.

Skye should have thought to ask him to join them. Amy, too. They both had to feel a bit awkward. Skye knew she did. She pulled her cover-up closed as they passed his chair.

It was a ridiculous thing to do since she'd been cavorting around in her bikini all afternoon. And a silly false modesty. They'd swum in the nude as teenagers. There were no secrets between them. Only the ones that had appeared in the intervening years.

They all showered and changed, and, while Jack and Sonny arranged beach chairs and towels for viewing the fireworks, Maya sat down with Roxy and Hildy on the porch, and Skye, seeing an overlooked dish on the picnic table, retrieved it and took it to the kitchen.

And ran into Connor, who was at the sink filling a glass from the tap.

Skye sucked in a startled breath.

"I—" Connor began, then put down his glass. "I guess we'll be leaving tomorrow. I was hoping to see you . . . alone . . . for a minute before we go."

Skye didn't say anything at first. Part of her wanted him to go, part wanted him to stay. But to what end?

"I'm sorry I didn't have more time to . . . see you. It's just the busiest I've ever been."

He stepped toward her. "Come with me. I'll put Amy on a train and you can come with me."

She stared as the meaning of his words sank in. *Come with me.*

"Connor, no."

"Why not?"

"I just can't. I have a life here, a business."

"Jack?"

She didn't really "have Jack." They were just what they were. "I can't."

"You can start a new business anywhere in the world."

She shook her head.

"Or I'll stay here, though I suppose that would be awkward; we could go somewhere else, somewhere new."

"Hop a freight train and see where we end up?"

"Sure, why not."

Because of a thousand things.

He moved closer; she didn't move away, but she felt her world tear a little.

"Connor . . ."

"There you are." Roxy bustled in. "Leave the dishes."

Skye noticed that the dishes had all been washed and put away, which Roxy must have known.

"The fireworks are about to begin. Hurry up, you don't want to miss the beginning."

They followed Roxy outside where she stopped at her usual beach chair next to Hildy. Amy sat on their far side as if keeping out of sight. Connor sat down in the grass beside the two women.

Skye joined her friends on the beach, fitting in between Jack's legs and resting her back against his chest. He put his arms around her and the first fireworks began.

They all crooned their obligatory *ooh*s and *ah*s as the brilliant colors and designs filled the air one after the other, sometimes in clusters, exploding high above them, sending out more bursts of color, growing smaller as they drifted to earth.

And all the while Skye wondered if Connor was watching her or the fireworks. She could feel his energy across the darkened air. It had always been like that.

She pulled Jack's arms closer around her and tried not to see the fireworks exploding above her as an omen of things yet to come.

Chapter 21

S kye didn't sleep very well that night, despite the sun, the
food, the beach—all of which normally would have sent
her into heavy oblivion. Too much was going on in her head,
in her life. Several times she'd been tempted to kick Jack "ac-
cidentally" so that he'd wake up and ask her what was wrong.

But she didn't because she didn't know what was wrong. Except Connor had asked her to come with him. To what? She'd
never let him get that far. To a new life? To the life of a diplomat's wife? Girlfriend? For a rollick and a spree before they
both got back to their own separate lives?

Easy for him to do maybe. He was going to a different place,
working with different people. How would she be able to come
back here? Pick up like nothing had happened?

It wouldn't be possible.

But she hadn't given him time to explain what he meant.
Which seemed ironic, since they'd never had to explain things
to each other before.

You were kids, she reminded herself and turned over for God only knew how many times that night. And still Jack slept. He could do that. Just turn off, shut down at night. He never shut down with her, only took a few *I need a minutes*. Though he had been acting odd lately. Because of how busy they both were? Or because of Amy and Connor?

Her half sister was enough to drive anyone nuts, but Connor? Was it possible Jack saw Connor as an interloper? Well, of course he did. Hadn't Sonny complained to Maya about it? So why didn't Jack say something?

Why did he act like they were all just fine? They weren't all fine. She wasn't fine.

Jack wasn't normally obtuse. He must know that something was going on. Even if it only consisted of one stolen kiss, and an offer to run away. She turned again.

Jack's arm dropped over her. "Sleeping with you is like wrestling an octopus."

"Sorry," she said. "Maybe I should go home."

"You are home," he said drowsily. And she heard no more. Soon after that she fell into sleep.

IT WASN'T SURPRISING that Skye woke with a stiff neck and grainy eyes the next morning. Jack had made coffee and gone to work. She padded around the empty cottage trying to pull reality from dreams. Had Jack said she was home last night or had that been part of the tape loop of fragments floating around her erratic sleep?

She walked out to the porch, looked across the cove where the beach was empty. Everyone was still asleep or just waking up in the houses along the shore. Skye was tempted to just sit down and enjoy the quiet, the slight breeze off the ocean that sparkled blue against the sky for as far as she could see. The feel of the wooden porch floor already warm beneath her bare feet.

But duty called. And the call was urgent. Was it too early to check in with Charlie Abbott about the decision of the board?

She went inside. Made calls to the county parks office to confirm that they would be using their covered picnic pavilion for yoga and that all the park's facilities would be open to the participants. Check.

Ollie Ford, who promised they were ready to move on her say-so. Check.

Charlie Abbott. "They're still dithering," Charlie said. "I'll stay on them but you'd better make sure you have a plan B."

Skye hung up. *You. They.* What had happened to *we*?

She called the nature conservancy next to confirm they would be using the nature trail that ran past the town into the marshes then to the state park farther inland.

Still no decision on the water situation.

This was not how she wanted to spend her days before Discover It Weekend. She should be fine-tuning the scheduling, smoothing out any overlaps or conflicts, organizing supplies, which were at this point stacked in the order they'd arrived inside cabin number two. Not thinking about where people were going to pee. Or if there would be safe, running, potable water to drink.

She called Maya to tell her she would be a few minutes late, poured the rest of her coffee in the sink, and got dressed.

Instead of walking directly to the store, she cut across the point to the back of Pritchards' Family Camp. There had once been a fence around the property. Until a few days ago it had mostly fallen into disuse, missing or beaten to the ground in some places.

Skye's grounds team had torn out the worst places and replaced it with signs that said: PLEASE RESPECT THE RESIDENTS. NO TRESPASSING. Because even though they'd searched for a less abrupt term, *no trespassing* was exactly what they meant.

She walked along the side of the Pritchards' house and the smell of bacon that wafted out the kitchen window. She didn't really know why she had come, maybe just to make sure there were no other surprises in store and try to visualize the camp filled with people discovering new things and filled with wonder.

As she stepped into the clearing, five children of various ages, led by a boy holding up a sparkler evidently left over from the night before, ran up from the beach. They crossed her path without slowing down and ran in a big circle before disappearing between the first two cabins.

Herb and Edna's grandchildren. Skye was glad to see they were having a good time.

Herb stood on the beach, hands in his pockets, watching them.

Skye walked down to join him.

"You know," he said, watching the children reemerging from behind the cabins and running to the mess hall, "having our kids and their little ones here has made me realize how much this place is home. We had some good years here."

He chuckled. "Some pretty bad ones, too. The green fly summer, that was a bitch. And there was the summer it poured for two weeks straight, and three women including Edna went into labor at the same time.

"Three new human beings from right here. Cabin one, cabin five, and the main house. Herb Jr. was one of them. His boy Herb Three is about to make me a great-grandpa. Some good times." Herb's voice cracked and he ran a hand over his face.

"I guess sometimes you just have to leave a place where you've spent your whole life to see how much of a life you've had."

Skye couldn't begin to imagine what Herb and Edna and maybe their whole family were going through. Leaving everything, friends, home, family, the day-to-day habits that made a life. Starting in a new place with no memories to build on.

She'd lost her home at seventeen. Roxy and Sunny Point had become the place where her memories would be made, and Skye would have her whole life to make her own memories here . . . if she stayed.

But generations of Herb's family had lived right here, and it was sounding like Herb was having second thoughts.

"Do you want to go?"

"Of course. It's . . . the smart thing to do. Look around." He said it but he didn't look around. Maybe it was too painful. "The camp is going to rack and ruin. People don't come anymore. The kids think we should go. That it's too much for us. And they're right."

"What about Edna?"

"Edna says it's time. That we deserve to retire and have some fun. Fun. Wasn't this fun? Hell, if I wanted to play golf, I could do that here. Except it's too expensive. I can putter around the camp for free."

"You might be surprised," Skye said. "There are probably a lot of things to do in Florida."

"I'm sure you're right. Anyways, it's no use griping. I can't afford to stay. Can't run the camp. I can't even pay the taxes, much less heat the house or pay utilities on the rest. What can I do but sell?"

Stay out of it, Skye warned herself. *Don't interfere.* But something Amy had said at the table had stuck.

"Look. I don't want to try to change your mind, but there might be other ways to use the camp. I've been in talks with some people at Lexington Advertising Agency in Hartford. They're a big company and they're looking for a program and possibly a venue to provide de-stressing and creative prompts for their execs and program teams. One of them was here and had expressed interest in further talks.

"They might be interested in using the camp several times a year. Things would need to be upgraded."

Herb looked back at the camp. "Lot of work. Lot of money."

"True. And like I said, I'm not trying to change your mind. I'm not even sure it's feasible.

"But my half sister, Amy, said that rustic weddings were all the rage and that the mess hall has the potential to be a venue for ceremonies, receptions, and photo shoots."

"You're kidding. Couples would want to have their wedding in the mess hall?"

"Well, it would have to be spruced up a bit. 'Rustic chic,' she called it, is very popular these days. The camp would be the perfect spot. Just a thought; I haven't crunched any numbers or anything."

"Do you know how much it would take to fix this place up?"

"Probably a lot. I just thought I should mention it as an option. Also you might mention it as an option to interested buyers."

"And they might not tear it all down after all?"

"I can't say, Herb. I probably shouldn't have mentioned it. I'm sure you've discussed this before."

"No. Actually we didn't discuss it at all. Edna and the kids just decided it was time we took it easier. She's right, but Florida?"

The grandkids made a sudden appearance, quiet this time, sneaking up from behind Herb, then jumping on him squealing and yelping with delight as they surrounded him. "Grandpa, Grandpa, Grandma says it's time for breakfast. Then Dad's taking us to get real fireworks like they had last night."

Herb shooed them away, his face animated with laughter.

"Okay, you go tell her I'm on my way, and wash your hands and faces, you hooligans."

They ran off toward the house.

"And no shooting off fireworks without your father!" Herb called after them.

Skye and Herb both watched as they swarmed up the porch steps and into the house.

"Hate to think of them not having this place to come to anymore, even if it's only for a couple of weeks in summer and

at Christmas. I always thought I'd pass it down to the next gen-
eration, but they'll probably be just as content with the money
from the sale."

He winked at her. "If Edna and I don't spend it all first.
Well, I best be going. Was there something you wanted to talk
to me about?"

"No, I was just going to check out the supply cabin and see
what work needed to be done."

"Have time for breakfast? Blueberry and banana pancakes
and local bacon."

"Sounds wonderful, but I'm late for work as it is."

They parted at the parking lot, Herb to the house and his
pancakes and Skye continuing on to check the state of supplies,
the foundation, the plumbing, the . . .

IT WAS ALMOST eleven when Skye got to Imagine That.

The store side was pretty free of customers, which was often
the case after a holiday when visitors left and the locals took a
few days to recover and get back up to speed.

"Supplies all in?" Maya asked.

Skye noticed she was sitting on a stool behind the counter.
"Yeah. It's pretty crowded in there. We may need to separate
out some of the large equipment. I'm not sure storing the telescope in there is such a good idea. Brendan swears it's water
safe, but with the humidity, I don't know."

"That's for Dennis and Follow Your Star, right?" Maya asked.
"I'll give him a call and ask him if he'll store it at his place.

"And remind me why we ordered two dozen fishnets."

"Butterfly nets?" Maya suggested.

"Are you sure? They looked like fishnets to me."

"I'll check the inventory." Maya started to get up.

The front door opened.

"Customers," Skye said and turned around to see Rhoda Sims and Edna Pritchard push through the doorway.

That was a surprise.

"Good morning, ladies," Skye said. "Great Sundae Social this weekend."

"Yes, it was," said Rhoda, stopping in the center of the room and looking around.

Edna stepped past her, cutting off Skye, who was coming forward to greet them. "This is the best social we ever had and it's because of *your* sister."

"I'm sure you all worked very hard," Skye said, beginning to get a sinking feeling.

"It was all Amy's doing; it was her idea to use the separate stations, and she made us buy fresh tablecloths and utensils."

"And she's reorganizing decades' worth of church files," Rhoda added. "She's a godsend."

"I'll be sure to tell her. Though I imagine she'll come by to say goodbye before she leaves." *Which with any luck would be in a few hours.*

"That's why we've come to talk to you," Edna said.

"We want her to help us with our bake sale and our back-to-school clothing drive," Rhoda said before Skye could nudge them toward the exit. "She has such good ideas. And she manages to get all the ladies working together for a change. And more younger people came to the social this weekend than in years. Young people are important to the spirit of the church."

"So true," Edna said.

Rhoda cleared her throat. "Which brings us to the reason we came to see you."

"We'd like to talk to you about Amy," added Edna.

"What happened?" Skye asked, bracing herself for whatever was coming.

"Nothing," Rhoda said. "She's a dream."

"Quite frankly, it's you," Edna added.

"Wha . . ." Skye couldn't even form a complete sentence.

"She told us you're making her leave today."

"Skye, do you really think that's fair?" asked Rhoda. "I know you don't come to church, but everyone respects you . . . at least . . . Well, you're normally more compassionate. And should be to your sister. Especially after what she gave up for you."

"Half sister . . . and what did she give up for me exactly? This is the first I've heard of it," Skye said, already knowing that whatever Amy told them would be a stretch of the truth if not an outright lie.

"She probably didn't want you to worry," Edna said.

"Or feel responsible," added Rhoda.

"Responsible for what?" asked Skye. "Rhoda, I have no idea what you're talking about. I saw her last night at the fireworks and she seemed perfectly fine. What is it that she's supposed to have given up for me?"

"Her job, Skye. She told us the whole story," Edna said. "We had to drag it out of her. But she said she knew you needed her, but would never ask for her help, so she gave up her job and that nice young man Connor offered to drive her here to lend a hand."

Rhoda put her hand on Skye's arm. "She was willing to give up her livelihood to help you. That's what a sister does."

Skye eased away, her surprise turning to a seething anger. "She didn't give up her job. She was fired."

"See, that's just what I mean," Rhoda said. "You have a burr in your heart when it comes to Amy. Why can't you accept her generosity?"

"She got fired for insulting her boss and ridiculing his business. And she came here . . . I don't know why she came here. For all I know, she thought you needed help with your ice cream social."

"Don't be sarcastic, Skye. It doesn't become you."

"I'm not being sarcastic, Rhoda."

Rhoda pursed her lips. "Amy had a choice, keep her job or leave it and be here for you. She chose you, Skye, she chose you and family."

"She's your sister," Edna said. "It's not like you to hold a grudge."

The two women moved closer. It was everything Skye could do not to step back.

"She told us what happened." Rhoda was so close, Skye could smell her eau de cologne. It was stifling. "About the fire. When you were kids. I'm sure you didn't mean to do it, but you can't blame her for telling the truth. She was just a child, and one who, I'm sure, was taught to always tell the truth."

Skye barked out an involuntary laugh. "Amy? The truth? The truth about what?"

"About you starting the fire because of the argument with your father."

Skye pulled away. "That's it. I didn't start the fire. Amy knew I didn't start the fire, and she lied because she was a hateful child. And *that's* the truth."

Why was she trying to justify herself to these women? Because she had to live with them. And she wasn't about to let Amy's lies taint her friends' and neighbors' opinion of her.

She took a breath. Slowly let it out. "I'm sorry she's convinced you of her innocence. And my guilt. And maybe she made an innocent mistake, but I'll say this once and once only. I didn't start that fire. I saw it from a friend's house and I ran down the hill and into the workshop to make sure my dad wasn't there.

"Fortunately he wasn't even at home. But I barely made it out alive. I live with this as a reminder."

She held up hand, revealing the lattice scar left by the metal engine across her palm.

Both ladies stared.

Skye felt Maya ease up beside her.

"Oh, I remember that summer you came," Edna said, thawing a little. "You were very ill."

But Rhoda was made of sterner stuff. "We both are sorry you suffered. But Amy has suffered, too. You've cut her off and refused to see her. That's really cruel, isn't it, Edna?"

"Oh, yes . . . and . . . And after all Herb has done for you, allowing you to use the camp free of charge, you can at least be kind to your own sister."

An explosion of surprise escaped Skye's lungs. Free? She'd put thousands of dollars into the buildings—was about to spend thousands more on the outdated plumbing—all to help the town and give Herb a better sale position. She was such a fool.

"That poor girl lost her job trying to be a good sister and if you're going to throw her out without so much as a helping hand, you're not the person we thought you were."

"That's right," Edna added. "And to make things worse, you're trying to talk Herb into paying for that new pipeline to the town by giving him false hope about turning the camp into a gold mine. You should be ashamed of yourself."

"Now wait just a minute, Edna. I'm not trying to cheat you and Herb. How can you even say such a thing?"

"Well, that's what my son said it sounded like."

"Well, I'm not. I don't want your money. Herb just sounded so unhappy about leaving this morning, I told him about the corporate interest, and using it for weddings. The weddings were Amy's idea.

"I thought it was unfair that you and he had to move if you didn't want to. So I passed on the possibilities to him to give him some options. I don't want your money. I'm fulfilling my side of the contract, and then it's over. You can do whatever you want with the property on the Monday after the retreat."

"What about the pipe?"

"I will take care of it. So don't give it another thought. You can be in Florida in two weeks. Or go now. I'm sure whichever real estate office you're using will be glad to show the camp in your absence.

"Now if you'll excuse me, I have a business to run." Skye forced a smile and went to the back room.

She'd barely made it through the door when she heard Maya say, "Really, Edna? Rhoda? After all Skye's done for you and this town. *You* are the ones who should be ashamed. Excuse me. Oh, and by the way, if you want to know the truth about what happened, though it isn't any of your business, ask Connor Reid. He was with Skye when the fire broke out."

Skye leaned up against the wall, trying to breathe and willing her shaking knees not to collapse. She was still standing there when Maya stormed past, nearly knocking her over.

Maya whirled around. "Sorry, but Baby Daniels made me do it. Ugh, those two. What got into them?"

Skye blew out several long breaths. "Amy must be up to her old tricks. She was the golden girl of the weekend; why can't she just rest on her laurels? Instead she has to spread shit about me. Why does she keep lashing out like that?"

"Beats me," Maya said. "She should try being nice. It might have better results."

"Amy? She just can't leave well enough alone. Ever. But telling those two . . . By afternoon the whole town will think I'm a cheat and a scoundrel." Skye's throat closed painfully.

"Nobody will believe them."

"They'll all turn against me."

Maya stared at her. "No, they won't. Why would you even think that?"

Skye blinked at the stinging in her eyes. "It's what happened before."

Chapter 22

I'm sure that won't happen," Maya said. "Everyone here de-pends on you."

"You heard Edna and Rhoda. They believed Amy's lies over knowing me for fifteen years because she weaseled her way into their good graces by lying and manipulating like she always does. And it fell on fertile ground. Well, this time I won't take it lying down. Can you watch the store?"

"Sure," Maya said. "But what are you going to do?"

"I'm going to the bank."

Skye went back to the office, made a quick riffle through her files, and took out a folder. She tucked it under her arm and strode straight through the store to the front door.

Maya ran after her. "What are you going to do? Don't do anything crazy."

"Have I ever done anything crazy?"

"All the time, but usually for the best. Why are you going to the bank?"

"I'll tell you when I get back."

And with that Skye let herself out the front door and walked the block and a half to First National Bank and Trust.

Newton Tyndale had helped Skye with her loan for the first Imagine That. She'd paid if off with time to spare. He was heavyset, past retirement age, and perfectly content to work forever as he often told customers who came to ask for advice.

He seemed a little surprised to see her.

"And what can I help you with today, Skye?"

"I need a short-term loan, or a second mortgage."

"Oh? Those are two very different things. Why don't you give me some background?"

"You know my Discover It Weekend is just a couple of weeks away."

Newton nodded, templing his fingers on the desk.

"The camp's water main to the street is rusted and leaking and I don't know what else. But I have to have water. Ollie Ford estimates it will cost from twenty to thirty thousand, depending on the extent of the damage and to get it in working order in time for the weekend, and since I need water . . ."

"What about the chamber of commerce?"

"They haven't come to a decision about increasing their outlay. They're worried about spending any more money.

"Once the weekend is over and I can see exactly what is outstanding I should be able to pay it back." She hesitated. "But if there's a hurricane or some other natural disaster, or I have to cancel for some reason, I don't want to use registration or town money for this."

"But who's going to pay *you* back for the pipeline?"

Skye bit her lip. She was a better businesswoman than this, and she knew she was having a knee-jerk reaction at Edna's accusation, but she didn't have much of a choice. She should have kept her original plan of using the nature center as a base. But it was too late now. If she ever had the chance, she wouldn't make this mistake again.

"Worst-case scenario. No one."

"And you will have upgraded Herb Pritchard's property out of the generosity of your heart and a hefty amount of money to pay back."

"I don't see that I have a choice."

"You might consider asking your aunt for a temporary loan."

"No. She would be more than generous. But I got myself into this and I don't want . . ."—*to drag her down with me it if comes to that*—" . . . to impose on her."

Newton shook his head. "Well, I would advise against it. Interest rates aren't great right now. But I understand your predicament. Would twenty thousand be enough?"

Dear God, I hope so. She handed over the file. "My monthly income from both spaces. The first mortgage is paid off. I'm in good standing with Imagine That Too."

He suggested several options, recommended one that she agreed to.

"I should be able to get this processed fairly quickly. Come back in the morning to sign the papers, and I'll have the bank deposit it directly into your business account."

Skye stood up, feeling like she might throw up before she made it outside.

She forced a smile. Shook his hand. "Tomorrow then. Thank you."

He walked her to the door of his office, and Skye could feel him watching her as she walked to the exit. Was he already expecting her to fail?

She didn't go back to work but went straight down to Roxy's, only stopping on the sidewalk long enough to call Ollie Ford.

He answered on the fourth ring. "Hey, Ollie, if you can get the permits and get the job done in ten days, long enough to test the system for a few days, you're hired. But you need to get started right away."

"Oh good," said Ollie. "I already talked to them, just to get a jump on things. They can expedite the permits and we should be able to get the line installed in that time frame if you can get the money."

"We're good."

"The finance committee came through then?"

"Not yet, but I'll pay for it if they won't."

"Not to be encroaching, but do you have the money?"

Skye's fingers tightened on the folder that, in addition to her financials, now also held a copy of the loan agreement. "I will tomorrow."

Skye ended the call and continued on to Roxy's. She was practically running when she let herself into the kitchen.

Hildy looked up from whatever she was making, which consisted of dough and lots of flour that she'd managed to sprinkle down the front of her apron.

"Morning, this is a surprise. There should still be some coffee in the pot."

"Thanks, but I've come to see Amy."

"She's down on the beach. Connor's upstairs packing. He says they're leaving after lunch. She's dragging her heels."

"Thanks," Skye said through gritted teeth.

Hildy wiped her hands off on a dish towel and tossed it aside. "I'll just put on a fresh pot."

Skye walked back out the door and took the path along the house through the yard and down to the beach.

Amy was stretched out on an old Adirondack chaise on the sand as if she didn't have a care in the world.

Maybe she didn't, but Skye had more than her share, and she was going to at least unload a few, starting with her half sister.

Skye walked straight through the sand and didn't slow down until she was standing at the end of Amy's chaise.

At least from this distance she couldn't reach Amy's neck.

"You're blocking my sun," Amy said.

"This will only take a minute, then you can burn yourself to a crisp." Skye cringed at her own words, swaying slightly before pulling herself together. "I guess you're pretty proud of yourself. You've become the darling of the church ladies and managed to put the screws to me all in one weekend. You must be so happy."

Amy put on a face that Skye would love to wipe off. She couldn't think of anyone, not even Rhoda or Edna, who could make her this angry.

"I don't know what you're talking about," Amy said.

Skye snorted. "I knew this would happen. I was willing to give you a chance, but you just couldn't leave things alone. I should have known you hadn't changed. And you never will."

Amy huffed out a sigh. "What am I supposed to have done now?"

"You've been telling people I'm an arsonist and a liar; you've been feeding them the same old bullshit about me starting the fire. It's been years. Why can't you just give it a rest? Live your own life and stop trying to destroy mine. What is wrong with you?"

"I didn't tell them that." Amy bit her lip. "At least I didn't mean to. I was just so upset, and Edna and Rhoda have been so kind."

"So kind?" Skye mimicked. "The same old biddies that wouldn't try anything new? And you lied about leaving your job because you wanted to come help me out? That's a laugh. But they bought that, too, because they don't know you."

For the first time, Amy's expression lost some of its assurance, and a flicker of apprehension showed in her eyes.

"What did *you* tell them?"

"The truth," said Skye. "That you were fired because you were rude, disrespectful, and not a team player. You in a nutshell."

"It was different here."

"It's always different. Until you get bored, or somebody doesn't do what you want them to do, then you'll do the same thing to them that you did to your last boss, to me, and God knows how many others."

"You're wrong. I told them what to do and it worked." Amy lifted her chin, which on an ordinary person would indicate a show of pride in a job well done, but only managed to look defiant on Amy. "I felt like I'd found my home at last."

Skye's blood froze. "Oh . . . no . . . this is not your home. You have an apartment and a car in Harrisburg. I put up the security deposit and made the down payment on the car, remember? It's time you went back and started looking for a new job so you can afford to keep them.

"But I'm done with you. No more pretending to be sisters ever again. It's over, Amy. Really over."

Amy jumped out of the chaise, sending a bowl of grapes and her beach cover-up flying. "You tried to kill our father!"

Skye stared at her half sister. Had the girl lost her grasp of reality? Had it moved beyond selfish and spoiled to pathological?

For the first time in her life Skye wanted to do physical damage to Amy. She had never felt such anger before. Not even when she left her home and family because of Amy's lie.

The intensity of the desire frightened her. She abhorred violence, she didn't even like arguing. She could only stare down at Amy while she thought about Jack and imagined him in her place. *Calm. Strong. Calm, strong, calm . . .*

Skye stepped back, more in control now. "Amy, you know that isn't true. You made up that story, or you misperceived it, but you never even tried to find out the truth. You just clung to the lie and told everyone else what you wished was true was actually true. Because you wanted to get me in trouble.

"I wasn't even nearby when the fire started. I was with Connor as you well knew, since you'd been spying on us nonstop. You're the one who told Karen and Dad we were going to run away. You knew we were going, and you just couldn't stand it."

Amy flinched as if Skye had slapped her.

"I suppose you want me to leave."

"I think we can both agree about that. But you've taken care of that, too, haven't you? You've placed me very nicely in the middle. Edna and Rhoda begging me to let you stay, as if I had any sway over what you did. Nor would I care to.

"But I can't very well make you go now. I'm damned if I do and certainly damned if I don't. If I insist you leave, Rhoda and Edna will spread it around town that I'm hard-hearted and unforgiving and not worthy of the town's respect."

Amy shook her head.

"So you've won this round, you get to stay or leave. It's not up to me." Skye started to turn away, but turned back. "I don't understand why you can't do good work, be complimented for it, and accept it without causing trouble in spite of your success. It's not only counterproductive but it's self-destructive."

"So I don't have to leave?" Amy whined in her most nasally Amy voice that brought years of annoyance back in one fell swoop. They could have been children again.

"Don't bother to ask me," Skye said. "I have nothing to say in what you do. And I want nothing to do with you. But if Roxy allows you to stay, you will stay as a paying guest. That's the one thing I won't allow, that you continue to sponge off her and Hildy and Connor."

"I'm not sponging. They're family."

"No, they aren't. Roxy's my mother's sister, not our father's."

"It doesn't matter. I feel like she's my aunt."

Delusional, Skye thought. Did Amy need professional help? If she'd been anyone else's relative, Skye might feel sorry for her.

"Well, I'm staying," Amy said as if Skye had just agreed to something which she hadn't. "Maybe I could get a job here."

Skye's head dropped back in exasperation. "Well, don't expect a recommendation from me."

"I don't expect anything from you. I just want you to be my sister."

"Half sister," Skye corrected.

"Okay, half sister," Amy pleaded.

"You've forfeited even that."

"Well . . . Could you—"

"No. No more money."

"I was just trying to help . . ."

But Skye was way past listening. She turned and marched back across the sand toward the house. She wasn't sure what had happened, except that nothing had been resolved and she was still consumed by an overwhelming rage.

"I'll never forgive you, Skye."

The cry was so plaintive that Skye stumbled in the sand.

"You'll be sorry. You think you're so great, but you'll be sorry."

CONNOR STOOD AT the open window of his bedroom. He was stunned. He'd meant to listen for a bit just to get some context and then go play arbiter. But things had gotten out of hand so quickly that he'd been unable to move, much less arbitrate.

By the time he recovered enough to step back from the window, Skye had stormed away and Amy had flung herself on the chaise, curled up in a fetal-like position.

He walked quietly to his door, stood in the hall listening to see if Skye came inside. But after a few minutes of no sound from downstairs, he decided she wasn't coming in and that it was time he took Amy away.

With Amy's parting *You'll be sorry* still ringing in his ears, Connor stole downstairs.

He found Hildy and Roxy in the kitchen standing together at the counter. They were making tea, not talking, just standing, mutely waiting for the water to boil. They both turned when they realized he was there.

"You heard?" he said, keeping his voice low since it felt like things might shatter at the least instigation.

Roxy nodded. Hildy turned away and began rummaging through the cabinet behind her.

"I think this experiment has gone on too long," he said.

Roxy nodded.

"I'll let Amy know we're leaving. I shouldn't have let it go on so long. I just . . ."

Roxy nodded her understanding. She didn't try to dissuade him.

Connor made himself walk across the kitchen and out the door, down the path to the sand. He didn't want to leave like this. He didn't want to leave at all. Not unless Skye went with him. For the second time in his life he felt his future slipping away, powerless to do anything about it.

But he wasn't powerless now. He just needed to get Amy out of the way. Could he put her on a train and stay for a few more days without her angst tainting everything?

He couldn't trust her not to get off at the next station. And come back. Why couldn't the girl just let things go? Why did she still blame Skye for everything wrong with her life?

And why did Connor still think Skye was the reason for the emptiness in his?

SKYE HAD STORMED past Roxy and Hildy, who were standing dumbfounded at the kitchen door. She saw them but she didn't acknowledge them. It was pretty obvious they'd heard. She couldn't face them feeling so angry.

She couldn't go back to Imagine That and subject them to her negativity. She headed to Jack's, knowing he wouldn't be home, but hoping his energy would be enough to calm her down.

She slowed as she passed by Cove Beach. Usually, when she had things to sort out, she went down there to think. It was private, mostly. She would never swim nude there, but still it was a haven.

But not today. She stood in the middle of the path, suddenly indecisive. She felt toxic with all the bad feeling between her and Amy. She hadn't thought about how strong it actually was. It was so easy to push her feelings into the back recesses when not confronted with her half sister in the flesh.

Amy never made overtures unless she needed money and there hadn't been that many of those. Now Skye realized she had kept options open in Amy's mind by giving her money.

What Skye didn't understand was what Amy wanted now. Why did she allegedly want to reconcile and be sisters? They'd never been sisters. Amy had been the golden child, literally. And Skye wasn't.

Skye had chafed under that humiliation. She hadn't even missed the love, because she knew even then that no love could replace that of her mother's. And frankly, her father had never seemed taken with Amy any more than he was taken with Skye. Her father only had eyes and heart for Skye's mother.

She understood that now, too.

She and Amy never had a chance, not with both of them vying for what little affection James had to give. And Amy must have felt the burden of her mother's overbearing attention, because, Skye thought, with the clarity of a light bulb suddenly popping into her mind, Amy's mother was denied his love, too.

It was so pitiful. All wanting the love of one man who couldn't give it. They could have come together, carried on, but instead they competed for his attention. And ended up hating one another.

Skye could see that now. She hadn't been the perfect sister. She she wasn't even a good sister. She was still traumatized by her mother's death when Karen suddenly became her "new" mother. And a year later, when Amy became her "new" sister.

She had tried to be good—at first. Amy was just a baby who cried and ate and slept. Skye didn't mind the *ooh*ing and *aah*ing. It's what people did over babies. But then Amy got older. Demanded more and more attention.

Even from Skye. She remembered Amy following her around, watching her every move. Skye would come home from school and find Amy in her jewelry box, her makeup smeared on her face, her lipstick smashed and broken, necklaces and bracelets tangled into knots or broken and lying on the floor in pieces. And Skye would get in trouble for putting Amy in harm's way.

At first Skye brushed it off as an annoyance, then the spying and tattling began. And Skye's consequent punishments. She'd learned to escape into her imagination and to sneak out to visit Connor, who lived just up the hill. Finally, when life at home became overbearing, she stayed away except to sleep and to spend a few choice hours with her father alone in his workshop.

Now she had to admit the truth. Her father may have loved her, but he'd only tolerated her in his sanctuary. He'd never donated or thrown out any of her mother's things, merely locked them all away.

Every single thing.

It was there he felt whole again, not because of Skye, but as a conduit to his memories, where her mother, his one true love, was still alive.

After the fire, Skye had been so distraught over Amy's accusations, her father's complete withdrawal, and her own physical pain and emotional despair that she hadn't thought about what they must have felt, Amy and Karen. She hadn't really thought about them since.

She thought about them now.

They must have felt betrayed, too, when the remnants of those possessions came to light. And when they realized what it meant, they did what they did best. They turned their hurt and anger and humiliation on Skye.

Skye had fled.

Her father left Karen and moved away. And then there were two. Karen remarried and Amy got a new family, until that one fell apart. Now Karen had remarried again. And Amy had nowhere else to turn.

What had Amy yelled? "I'll never forgive you."

For what, Amy? Not being the sister you wanted. For not loving you? For leaving you behind? Well, thought Skye. *I'll never forgive you for driving me away.*

Skye swayed as the realization hit her. Driving Skye away was the best thing that Amy could have done.

Because Skye had found her home. Her real home. In fact, she'd forgiven Amy a long time ago. Not forgiven. But accepted. Amy was the one still suffering. And Skye was sorry for that.

Unfortunately, Amy was determined to make Skye suffer, too. And Skye couldn't let that happen.

Chapter 23

A my slowly looked up to where Connor stood, hands on hips. "Oh, it's you."

"Yes. Me. The idiot that brought you here. And the one who is taking you back, today. So get up and go finish packing."

Amy gave one of her exasperated sighs. A reaction that had become so annoying that it made Connor want to smack her, not that he'd ever hit anyone. He was a diplomat after all, but still . . .

"You can leave if you want, but I'm staying."

"No, you're not. So get your butt off that chair and get packed. You have an hour. I'm done with your games and so is everyone else. We're leaving as soon as you've gotten your stuff together."

"You can leave. You certainly have blown any chance you had with Skye. But I'm staying, Skye said I could. So have a nice trip to wherever you're going."

Connor dropped his hands by his side. "I doubt if Skye wants you here."

Amy shrugged.

Connor willed himself not to clench his fists.

"She said it was up to me."

"And?"

"I'm still deciding."

"Well, you'd better decide within the next hour; that's when I'm leaving. And you'd better make sure you have the money to get home, once Roxy and Hildy throw you out."

Amy scrunched up her face in some kind of smile that Connor couldn't begin to read.

"Oh, they won't."

"Don't be so sure."

"I can be. They won't do anything that Skye doesn't want. I figured that out soon enough. And Skye wants me to stay."

"I don't believe you."

"Oh yes, she told me, herself."

"And why did she have this sudden change of heart?" Connor asked.

"Simple. Because everyone likes me so much, that if she made me leave they'd tell everyone in town how badly she treated me."

Connor just stared at her. "You mean you'd make sure that they spread that piece of garbage. What is wrong with you? You've had all the advantages of life and you're like a bitter old woman."

Amy's face turned bright red.

He knew he was on dangerous ground. But she'd pushed him as far as he was willing to go. Until now he'd vacillated between being annoyed at her, feeling sorry for her, being horrified at the things she did, and wondering why anyone could be mean when they so desperately wanted to be loved.

"Goodbye, Amy. You'll have to settle for your own misery to keep you company from now on."

She lifted her chin defiantly.

And for the first time in a long, long while, Connor Reid gave in to impulse. He grabbed the arm of the chaise and dumped Amy onto the sand.

SKYE HAD GIVEN up trying to work and was in the kitchen preparing dinner when Jack came in from work.

"You're home early," he said.

Skye stopped with the bag of lettuce in her hand. She let the fridge door ease shut. She'd been so tied up in knots that she hadn't thought about what she would tell Jack about all the things that had happened that day.

"I took out a bank loan today," she blurted out. It seemed like the most important thing at the moment. The rest would follow. She didn't want to have to explain. She was already feeling stupid for being so easily manipulated. She should have sent Amy packing the night she'd arrived.

But she'd run just like all those years before, and that one moment of cowardice was now hurtling her toward possible disaster.

"Why?"

Such a simple question. So impossible to answer. So she just poured out the whole terrible encounter with Rhoda and

Edna; Edna's accusations; and her trip to the bank and then to Amy.

Jack listened in silence, finally succumbing to head shaking as she continued on and on and on.

And when she finally stopped for breath, he said, "Have you lost your mind?"

Skye shook her head, stunned by his reaction. "You don't know what they said to me, they think I'm an arsonist, and a cheat, and a liar and they'll tell the whole town."

"So what if they do? They're just a couple of old ladies with too much time on their hands. And it's Herb's own damn fault if he can't afford to run the camp. If he'd bothered to repair and update as he went instead of ignoring every sign, he wouldn't have this trouble. He could still be in business, but no one wants to spend time in those ramshackle, mice-infested lean-tos he calls family cabins." Jack shot his hands through his hair, walked away, walked back.

"And now you're risking everything you've worked for to connect his dump to city water, costing you a fortune and lining his pockets when he finally sells. If he sells."

"He was so sad. And he didn't think I was trying to cheat him. I only mentioned that Amy had suggested it would be a good venue for events if it got fixed up."

"Amy." Jack spat out the word. "She's done nothing but cause you grief your whole life, now she's trying to destroy you. Can't you see that? This is pure manipulation. And you fell for it."

Skye dropped the bag of lettuce on the counter. Rubbed her

face with both hands. "I don't know. I kind of feel sorry for her, but I want her to go away."

"Then call Roxy and tell her to throw her out."

"I can't. Don't you see? Then Rhoda and Edna will spread it around that I heartlessly threw her out."

"So? To hell with them. What are you afraid of?"

What was she afraid of? A week ago she would have said nothing. But now, in Jack's kitchen, she was afraid of everything.

"What is it? Why are you letting everyone push you around suddenly? What's next? Are you going to walk away from everything you've worked for?"

Skye shook her head. "Walk away? No—I . . ." She wasn't, but she didn't know what was happening. A week ago she was exhausted but excited and optimistic; tonight she was tied in knots trying to explain to the one person who she thought would understand.

She was wrong.

"It's like I don't even know you." Jack slipped past her, took a beer from the fridge. "I need a minute." And he walked through the house and out to the porch.

Skye didn't follow. His reaction had been so intense that it surprised her. It also frightened her.

Jack didn't often walk away from things. And when he did, she knew he was shutting her out. Because he needed time to think things through. What she didn't know was why now? If it was because of her or because of him.

Skye got the salad bowl down from the cabinet, opened the

lettuce, and dumped half of it into the bowl. Closed the bag and returned it to the fridge. Got out a cucumber. Sliced it and returned half to the fridge.

She just kept making dinner, almost afraid to stop, listening for Jack to come back inside. But he didn't. It felt sad to be in the kitchen alone. When they ate at home, they cooked together.

Home. She'd taken home for granted. *Together*, for granted. But they were tenuous things. And she was in danger of losing both.

She kept moving, from fridge to counter to cabinets to fridge. To drawer to table, hardly aware of what she was doing. And when everything was prepped, Jack was still gone and she put it all back in the fridge.

Skye took out a beer instead and walked through the house to see if maybe he was on the porch.

He wasn't, but she could see him on the beach below, sitting on a rock, and she wondered if she should go down and try to explain.

I need a moment. Jack's time to regroup. She respected his need to be by himself. She considered drinking the beer, but her stomach revolted. She placed it on the floor and sat on the porch rail. And as she sat down, Jack stood, and her heart did a little somersault, which surprised her almost as much as her surprise when he climbed the rocks to the path and turned, not toward her but in the opposite direction toward town.

SKYE IS RUNNING. Running. Where's Connor? She's running to . . . no . . . away. She's running away, but her backpack is too heavy.

She's sweating but it's cold, too cold. And she's running. But not going anywhere.

She's running away, but nothing seems right. Her backpack is too heavy. Her hands hurt. She can't feel her fingers, her hands look like paws—big white paws.

They all think she did it. Because of Amy. Amy Little Princess Face. Amy the perfect. Amy the little liar. Amy the perfect little liar. . . . Skye stumbles. She needs money but her fingers don't fit on the keys of the ATM. She can't get the keys to work. She tears at the white stuff on her hands with her teeth, frees a finger. Gets the money. Lets it fall into her backpack. She should get more but it seems like too much trouble. She tries again, drops more bills in her backpack. Hears someone cry out in pain.

Her backpack is too heavy. But she's escaped. Back of the bus. The flames of hell behind her. There's a buzzing in her ears, a droning, a rumbling, then nothing—flatlining. And when the sound starts up again, she can't move.

Hey! Wake up. This is Providence.

Providence. Is this heaven?

Are you on drugs? Get outta my bus.

Skye's legs don't work. She falls from a long height. But she knows what to do.

What to do to get to Connor—no, Connor is gone, to Roxy. . . .

AN EXPLOSION. SKYE awoke with a start. Sat up. She was on the glider on Jack's porch. "Jack?"

Another explosion. Kids setting off firecrackers. Jack was right. It was annoying. She got up feeling stiff; her hand was asleep, and the tingling as the blood flow returned was particularly painful. She didn't remember lying down. Just Jack walking away.

Skye checked her phone. Almost eight. No texts; no voice mails.

Jack was gone.

But she could see Roxy's light across the cove. She slipped her cell in her pocket and headed down the path.

"IT'S NOT THAT I think she can't handle it," said Jack over the noise of the Dog and Pony. "I just don't understand why she didn't consult with me, or somebody, before she put her whole business in jeopardy." Jack's anger zeroed in on Maya. He knew it wasn't her fault but he couldn't help it.

"She just panicked a little bit," Maya said. "No, it was more than that. It was hurt. If you could have heard those two carrying on about how sweet Amy was and how she'd sacrificed for Skye and how unappreciative Skye was. It was enough to make me sick, even if I wasn't pregnant.

"At first Skye didn't even try to defend herself. I could see this thing overcome her. Like a cloud. By the time she tried to defend herself, they'd already made up their minds. They'd already made them up before they even came in the store, the busybodies. It was awful and Skye said the past was happening all over again."

"The past isn't going to happen all over again," Jack said and gulped down a good bit of his beer. Not if he could help it, it wasn't. He just didn't know how he could stop it. Skye hadn't been the same since Amy and Connor had come to town. What Jack didn't understand and what he distrusted most was how much of Skye's change was because of Amy and how much because of her old "soul mate."

He put his beer bottle down harder than he'd meant. He'd be damned if he'd be cut out by a soul mate. What the hell was a soul mate anyway? How was it any different than two people on the same wavelength who completed each other, who fought and reflected and came round to each other's feelings in the end? Skye had never called him her soul mate.

"Ridiculous," he mumbled.

"What?" Maya asked.

"Nothing."

She reached across the table and took his wrist. "It's not that she meant to cut you out, if that's what's worrying you. It's just . . . Maybe it's a girl thing to gather your strengths inward. Not to exclude anyone but to make yourself more prepared." She glanced at Sonny. "I've been doing it myself, lately.

"It's a part of nesting, when you're getting your home ready to accept something new into your life. Something you're responsible for."

"Lost me," said Jack, so Sonny wouldn't have to. He could tell by his friend's expression that Sonny had no more clue than Jack did about nesting and withdrawing and shit.

Maya sighed and released his wrist.

"And don't say, just like a man," Sonny warned her. "Jack's in a fix."

"Then go home and fix it."

"If I knew how, I would."

"Look, we've all been overreacting to things," Maya said. "Me because of hormones, Skye because she's exhausted and stressed with the responsibilities and the demands the town is making. Sonny's nervous about supporting a family."

"Am not," Sonny said.

"Are too." Maya turned to Jack. "And you're afraid Skye's going to fall in love with Connor and leave you."

She stopped, her features slackened as a black hole of silence fell over their table.

Am not, Jack wanted to say. It was so not cool to think that way. To feel that way.

"Jack, I meant—"

"I know what you meant. Is she?"

"No. Of course not. At least I don't think so. I mean, why would she? You're—"

"—so screwed," Sonny said, followed by an "Ouch," as Maya kicked him under the table.

"WELL," ROXY SAID, plunking an iron trivet down in the middle of the kitchen table. "If Amy expected us to wait for her. She's out of luck."

Neither Hildy nor Connor bothered to comment.

Connor reached for his wineglass. He was on his second glass and they hadn't even started dinner. It had been a roller coaster of an evening. Starting with Amy stalking back to the house, informing them that she had decided to stay, and they couldn't kick her out because Skye said she could.

Then Roxy and Hildy informed Connor that if Amy was staying, so was he. And Roxy opened the first bottle of wine.

An hour later, Amy had come downstairs wearing a flowing summer frock and announced she was going out.

That was fine by Connor, except that Amy out was bound to lead to Amy in trouble, or causing trouble, and wreaking havoc on the town and his nerves. He took a sip and then another of his wine, put his glass down.

"Maybe I should go look for her."

"Dinner's ready," Hildy announced, taking a big casserole out of the oven, virtually stopping his flight.

"I know you're worried," Roxy said. "But I'm at the point of letting Amy do her worst. She's obviously been nursing whatever her grievance is for years. Now that she's actually here, I think it's better we get it out in the open once and for all."

"It has to be more than Skye cutting her off," Connor said. "I mean, Amy was terrible back then. By the time I got back from school, she'd convinced the whole neighborhood that Skye had tried to kill her father. I put them straight. Not everybody believed me at first, but they finally came around, or so said my mother. I was back at school by then. Skye was here, she'd cut me off entirely, and I never really went back to PA much. No reason to go back except parental visits. And those were no picnic.

"Ugh. I should never have let Amy talk me into bringing her here."

"Doubt if it took that much persuasion," Roxy said, looking at him over the rim of her wineglass, lowering her chin but still managing to look down her nose at him.

Connor didn't bother to deny it.

"And don't even start with talk about leaving. You've been saying you were leaving practically since you got here. One, you're not leaving without taking Amy with you. And two, you need to come to terms about why you're here in the first place." Another one of those looks that Connor was beginning to think of as the Roxy "wither" look. "But first we need to end this sisterly feud once and for all."

Hildy placed a platter of lobster mac 'n' cheese on the trivet.

"But where did she go?" Connor said.

"A restaurant? The Pub? The movies, the mall?"

"She doesn't have any money." Connor lifted an eyebrow. "Unless . . ." He rolled to one hip and took his wallet out of his back pocket. His credit cards and cash were still there. He raised his eyebrows at Roxy. She immediately went to the cabinets and pulled out a cookie jar in the shape of Tweety Bird. Looked inside.

Connor laughed. "Really, Roxy?"

"Well, normally I don't have crooks staying in the house. Besides, it's all here."

"So we're back to, where could she go."

Hildy reached over and placed a bowl of salad next to the mac 'n' cheese. "Maybe Rhoda invited her to dinner."

"In that dress?" Roxy said. "I don't care how wonderful Rhoda thinks Amy is, she'd send her packing after one look at that see-through skirt.

"Though I wouldn't put it past those two old birds to be plotting trouble. Well, not Edna, she was fine until the last couple of years, when the real state of their finances came out. Poor as a church mouse and Edna as proud as a lady of the manse. Of course miss nose-in-everybody's-business-Rhoda Sims cozied up to her and it's been downhill ever since."

"I wouldn't put it past Amy to be smarming up to those two," Hildy said, thrusting a serving spoon into the mac 'n' cheese with gusto. "Rhoda ought to keep her nose in the church books—hell, in the good book—instead." She paused to grin at her own joke. "You'd think she'd be too busy and too thankful for what she has to be meddling in things she knows nothing about."

"Thank you, dear Hildy," Roxy said approvingly and with her own bit of gratefulness. "Now let's eat."

Roxy filled Hildy's glass with wine, topped off her own. "She won't get this kind of wine or cooking with Rhoda Sims."

"I can just see them, sitting at her Depression-style dining table, surrounded by inches of dust and the smell of moth-balls . . . Connor, hold out your plate." Hildy scooped into the mac 'n' cheese and a waft of aromatic steam rose in the air; Connor held out his plate.

"Don't ever cross our Hildy here," Roxy said, starting on the salad.

The kitchen door opened.

"If she thinks she's getting—" Hildy began.

"Skye, you're just in time," said Roxy. "I'll get another plate."

Chapter 24

Jack walked back home feeling worse than when he'd first called Sonny and asked him to meet him at the Dog and Pony. Talk about your knee-jerk reactions. He hadn't even texted Skye to tell her where he was. He'd left her making dinner.

He stopped on the sidewalk to text her now.

Sorry, I ran into Sonny and ended up having a beer and burger at the Dog and Pony. He pressed send.

Okay, so he didn't run into Sonny, where would he have run into Sonny? But what the hell. He wouldn't have had to lie if he'd manned up, gone back home, and told her—what?

Fortunately his phone pinged, saving him from having to figure out what he would have told her. Skye had texted him back.

I'm at Roxy's. Ate here. We can't find Amy. Did you happen to see her at the pub?

He hadn't. He hadn't been looking, but Jack was pretty sure she would have made herself known if she'd been there.

No, he replied. *Maybe she's with Connor.*

Not too transparent, asshat.

Connor is here.

So that told him what he didn't want to know.

I'll keep an eye out. Home soon.

Thanks. We're going to look and make sure she's not hurt. See you later.

K. He returned his phone to his pocket. That was the best he could do? *Okay?* He could have offered to come help them look. He should have. But the thought of Skye and Connor out looking together made him stupid.

He pulled out his phone.

Want me to help?

No. It's OK. Later.

He didn't keep an eye out for Amy on his way home. He had no intention of scouring the town looking for her. She was probably enjoying the attention immensely. He made himself walk past the drive down to Roxy's and turned into the path that led directly to the path that led past the cove.

And that's when he saw her.

"Do you really think this is necessary?" Connor asked. He for one had no doubt that Amy was purposely staying away in order to get attention.

Roxy shoved an industrial-size flashlight at him.

"I won't have Rhoda Sims spreading it around town that I offed Skye's half sister."

Connor blinked and took the flashlight.

"That was a joke, sort of," Roxy added. "Still, we would feel bad if she's lying hurt somewhere."

Roxy and Hildy took the beach and Connor and Skye walked down to the end of the drive to make sure Amy hadn't taken the car. Connor knew she hadn't; the keys were still on the sideboard in the hallway. But he was glad just to get out in the night air, alone with Skye.

The car was there. As he knew it would be. They turned back toward home.

Roxy and Hildy met them at the door. "Nothing."

"Us either," Skye said.

"I'm sure she's fine," Roxy said. "No reason for you to stay, Skye. We'll let you know when she deigns to show up, probably drunk on the arm of some local."

"I'll walk you to Jack's," Connor said, ignoring the look Roxy shot him. "Roxy, if she gets here while I'm gone, please keep her downstairs. I have a few things to say to her."

"Shall we?" he offered Skye his elbow like some guy in a nineteen fifties musical. And looking a little bemused, she took it.

They walked down the path and Connor reveled in their closeness. And he silently thanked Amy's bad manners for bringing him and Skye just a little closer.

"Amy!" Jack called.

She was sitting on one of the boulders near the beach. Her hair created a nimbus around her in the moonlight, her pale shoulders bare except for the tiny straps of her dress.

Sitting, he noted. She didn't look like she was in distress or injured in anyway.

"Are you okay?"

She stood up but didn't turn toward him. She didn't even seem to hear him. Just began walking over the sand toward the beach.

It was like she was sleepwalking. Maybe the girl really did have serious psychological problems.

He reached for his phone, but before he could get it out of his pocket she broke into a run toward the water.

"Amy, come back!"

Dammit, what was she doing? Surely not thinking about a late-night swim.

He bounded down the rocks, surefooted until he reached the sand, which shifted beneath his weight and it took him a second to regain his balance.

By then Amy had reached the water's edge.

"Dammit, Amy, stop. It's dangerous."

Now she turned. Her skirt was billowing in the night air. She was up to her shins in the water, and she reached down to splash it.

"It's dangerous, come out. Now!" Jack broke into a run.

Amy just kept splashing herself until her dress was clinging to her body.

He stopped at the water's edge. "Come out. People are worried about you."

She flung her arms in the air and turned around.

He automatically reached out, to steady her, but stopped himself.

"This is not funny."

"No, but it can be fun, Jack. Come out and get wet. It's lovely." She moved back farther into the water until the waves pushed against her calves.

"No. Get out now."

"Make me." She stretched out her arms to him and she staggered against the tide.

"Amy, you could drown, didn't you see the sign? There's a riptide right across the point."

"But you could save me, couldn't you, Jack?"

"No, no one could save you once it gets you." That seemed to slow her down. She moved slightly as if to come back to shore.

He wasn't taking any chance. He went out to get her before she could change her mind.

But just before he reached her she leaned over, pulled her dress over her head, and tossed it toward him.

It was pure reflex that made him catch it. And reflex that made him drop it to the sand. The moonlight glistened over her wet skin; she was entirely naked except for a tiny thong, and it if had been anyone other than Amy, he would have been tempted.

For an eternity he could only stare, ankle-deep in the surf, water soaking the denim of his jeans.

"Come on, Jack, you'll like it, I promise."

The momentary paralysis broke.

"You're wrong. Get dressed and I'll take you home."

"Really, Jack? Really?"

"Really." He backed out of the water. She came toward him,

teasing him, her breasts pert and tight. He leaned over to pick up her dress and she launched herself at him.

Before he could react, she threw her arms around his neck. Wrapped her legs around his waist, locking her ankles together to grip him tighter.

Jack stumbled back from her weight and just managed to keep from going down. He grabbed at her hands, attempting to pry her loose

"Off!" he managed, before she covered his mouth with hers.

"I'M SURE SHE'S okay," Connor said, as he and Skye walked along the path toward Jack's cottage. He didn't want the evening to end. Dinner had been fun without Amy there. Skye had been more like her old self. They reminisced and told Roxy and Hildy about the antics they'd gotten up to as teens.

Roxy had opened the third bottle of wine and they were all feeling fine until they realized that Amy still hadn't returned.

"She's probably fine," Skye agreed. "But call me when she does get home."

"It's a nice night for a walk at least," Connor said. "Do you have to go back?"

"What?"

"I mean, do you need to go home now? I feel like we've hardly had time together, just us."

"Because you—" Skye stopped, staring past him out toward sea. Her breath caught.

"What?" he asked alarmed. "Is it Amy?" He turned to look down at the beach.

It was Amy all right.

And she wasn't alone.

He automatically reached out to Skye.

She stumbled back.

"Skye," Connor said.

But she didn't look at him, just down on the beach where Amy and Jack were standing like one writhing, copulating creature. Didn't they know everyone on the point could see them?

"Skye." It was all Connor could think to say.

But she just kept backing away, her eyes fixed on the couple on the beach below.

"I'm sure there's an explanation." God, did he really say that? There was only one explanation. Skye's boyfriend and half sister were having sex on the beach.

Skye turned and ran back the way they'd come. To Roxy's.

Connor should follow her, but he couldn't tear his eyes away. He told himself it was because he wanted to give Skye time to tell Roxy what had happened and, God forgive him, so he could force himself not to hope that this had been the opening he'd been waiting for. The one that would bring Skye back into his life. But not like this.

The raw pain in her eyes told him everything he'd dreaded. She loved Jack with all her heart.

Connor dragged his eyes from the scene on the beach and walked slowly back to the house. He didn't go inside but sat out in the side yard surrounded by Hildy's vegetables. And wondered for the first time in a long time just what kind of man he was.

JACK FINALLY MANAGED to extricate himself from Amy's grip. She was like a limpet sucking into his very pores. But he'd finally pried her arms from around his neck and her legs responded. As soon as he was free he pushed her away with such force she fell on her butt in the sand.

"Ow," she said, with what was more of a pout than a grimace of pain.

The sand was soft, he knew she wasn't hurt. Keeping one eye on her, he grabbed her sodden dress and tossed it toward her.

"Put it on."

"Oh, Jack, don't you want to have some fun?" She tilted her head, her knees bent and spread apart, attempting to be sexy? It just made her look needy.

"I'm not even tempted. Now get dressed." He backed away from her, looked out to sea. To give her some privacy? That was a laugh. She was still flaunting her body at him as she got to her feet and made a big show of flapping out the dress.

It seemed like an eternity before she was dressed again, and though the fabric clung to her like a second skin, instead of enticing, she just looked bedraggled.

"Come on."

She didn't move, so he leaned over, grabbed her by the arm, and started dragging her up the beach.

"I just—"

"Shut up. Don't say anything. You'll only make it worse. You're a spoiled half-formed woman. I feel sorry for you, but I'm not attracted to you."

He felt her stumble on the rocks. But at this point he didn't care. He couldn't remember being so angry since the night his father told him to toe the family line or get out. And Jack had gotten out.

Amy was dragging her feet like a recalcitrant child. Jack said, "Keep moving. I know what you're up to. You're not interested in me. You're just trying to cause trouble. Do you know how pitiful that makes you look?"

She started to cry.

He nudged her up the rocks, keeping an arm's distance. When they were back on the path, she hesitated.

"Nope," he said and gave her a push toward Roxy's. "I'll watch you from here just to make sure you get back inside. And that you don't come out again. People have been looking for you all evening. They were worried about you, though I can't for the life of me figure out why."

"You're horrible," she cried and broke into a run. He watched until he saw her run past Hildy's garden and up the path toward the kitchen door. Then he took out his cell. Called Skye. She didn't pick up. So he left a message.

Found her, she's back at Roxy's. Come home.

SKYE HELD HERSELF together most of the way back to Imagine That. She hadn't meant to come here. She hadn't meant to do anything but get away. Unsee what she had seen. Make herself believe that it wasn't what it was.

She didn't stop at Roxy's but ran to the place that was hers, all hers. But she didn't let herself into the store or workshops. She wouldn't bring the horror and disgust and sense of betrayal into that space. That space was for good things, for growing things. And right now Skye felt none of those.

She felt sick. She went straight upstairs to her apartment. Fumbled to fit the key to the lock, and when she finally got inside went no farther than to shut the door and lean back against it as if she could keep the hurt and betrayal outside.

Skye would have never believed that Jack would succumb to Amy of all people. She still didn't really believe it, couldn't, wouldn't believe it. But she'd seen it with her own eyes. Her half sister, naked, her arms and bare legs wrapped around him. And him—he—he had his arms around her. Ugh. She shook her head until her brains rattled.

Flipped on the lights.

And it hit her. No one lived here. Not really. She could see a layer of dust on the table where weeks of junk mail were stacked. The air was heavy and stale. She crossed to the windows that faced Main Street and pushed them open. Leaned out.

There were few people on the street. It was late even for summer. One group was coming out of the bistro, and a couple walked along the sidewalk looking in the store windows. It should have been a peaceful summer night. Skye should have been peaceful here.

She swallowed a sob and closed the window, then went into the bedroom where a queen-size bed took up most of the space. Tonight it seemed absurd to have such a big bed. She threw herself on it.

It doesn't matter, she thought. *None of it matters.* She wanted to cry, but she was too numb. Of all the people . . . not Jack. Not because he belonged to her. He didn't. They'd never even discussed what they were, had just slipped into a relationship that worked. It had worked, sure it had. If it hadn't, she wouldn't be feeling this big black hole.

Had she taken him for granted? Had he always been seeing other people? No. She would have known—hell, she spent most nights at his cottage. But what about the nights she didn't?

What the hell was she thinking? Screw her personal life. It was the least of her problems. She had responsibilities. A whole event to get up and running. A plumbing installation to oversee. A weekend to ease people into a world of exploration.

And she wanted to die. Her breath caught. No she didn't. That was crazy.

She'd been depending on Jack to help her. Jack and Sonny and Maya. Could she possibly ignore her feelings, pretend like she didn't know, hadn't seen? She was pretty sure Connor would stay mum. Maybe even make Amy leave. Or would he desert her, too?

She sat up. "Get a grip. You're not the whiny one." She kicked off her sneakers, went into the kitchen, and poured herself a glass of water. Opened the fridge just because that's what people did when they were not thinking clearly, when they were bored, when their life had just imploded; they walked into the kitchen and stared into the fridge.

The air was cool. So she stood there, hanging on to the handle, staring at a carton of yogurt whose expiration date was somewhere in the past until the tears finally came. She'd never thought about this happening with Jack. Had never imagined it. And now it had. And she hadn't even had a clue.

Had she missed something? She'd been so busy. But so had he.

She returned to the bedroom, stripped out of her camisole, felt her pocket buzz as she stepped out of her shorts. Someone was sending a text. Later. Right now Skye MacKenzie couldn't deal.

She pulled back the summer quilt and climbed into bed. Pushed the quilt down to her feet. It was hot and she was sweating, but she didn't seem to have the energy to get up and open a window. And really, did it matter?

Amy had said Skye would be sorry. Well, she was—in spades.

JACK SHUT DOWN his phone, leaned on the porch rail. The cove beach was empty now but he still had the bad taste of that scene in his mouth. He should have let the girl drown.

And now that he'd finally gotten rid of Amy, Skye was MIA. She wasn't answering his texts or his calls. Was she sitting in Roxy's kitchen with Connor and the others, relieved that Amy was back and breaking out a bottle of wine to celebrate?

What was wrong with him? Skye wouldn't do that. She'd have called him to let him know they'd found her and . . . So why hadn't she called? Why hadn't she answered his texts?

And why didn't he just call Roxy and ask what was going on?

Good question. He knew the answer. He didn't want to find out that she was there and was ignoring him.

Because ever since Connor Reid had come to town, things hadn't been the same.

Jack had felt it. He just wasn't sure what it was.

If Skye was at Roxy's and knew Amy had been found, why wouldn't she call him to . . . unless Amy had told her . . . What? Jack's stomach went south.

It would be just like Amy to make up some story about them on the beach. Not that he'd gone to stop her from swimming and she'd stripped and tried to seduce him.

She'd have to mention it, because she knew Jack would. She wouldn't tell the truth, she never did. He moved away from the porch rail. Walked to the end of the porch and looked out to the sea. The moon was still shining; the stars had made a brief appearance scuttling in and out of the clouds.

He shot his fingers through his hair, but they caught in the tangles brought on by the altercation, and the ocean air. He was such a fool.

No, Amy would turn the whole episode around. Not content to just leave out the part where she humiliated herself, but turn it so Jack was the bad guy. She might even accuse him of trying to seduce her. Or that he'd attacked her. That was a popular revenge technique. A twofer. One to get back at Jack and one to humiliate Skye.

Skye would never believe that. So where was she?

He called Roxy, but ended it before she picked up. He had a better idea.

He grabbed his wallet and windbreaker and headed toward the path. Roxy's lights were still on. Skye was probably there. And Connor. And Amy.

He stopped when he reached the fork in the path waiting for, willing, Skye to be walking toward him from Roxy's. But no one came.

At first, he'd thought Amy was just out on a lark, just causing her usual trouble. But now a darker more insidious thought weaseled itself into his brain. She'd set a trap in order to seduce him, somehow waylaid him on purpose, not to hurt Skye but so Connor and Skye would be pushed together.

His rational mind refused to accept that. But he wasn't listening to his rational mind right now. Reluctantly he turned down the path toward town.

Both Imagine That spaces were dark, but the light in Skye's apartment was on.

He stood on the street looking up at her window, willing her to look out, come down. Explain that she just had to pick up something and she was coming home.

Nothing else made sense. If Skye wanted to see Connor, there was nothing stopping her. They'd never made any promises.

They shouldn't have had to make any promises; it had been perfectly clear. At least to him. Of course he hadn't known that Connor the childhood soul mate would someday come galloping into town in a hot little BMW.

Hell, it wasn't the car, or the style of the man. It's what Connor meant to Skye. He was her soul mate. And evidently Jack was not.

Fine, he'd get over it. It wasn't the first time he'd been fooled in a relationship, but damn he'd thought this was different.

But if it really was different, Skye would be at home with him and not upstairs in her apartment. And if it wasn't different, there could only be one reason why she was not with Jack. She was with Connor.

He fumbled for his phone. He had to know, but as he heard the first ring, her light went out.

Chapter 25

Connor was still sitting in the garden when Amy passed by looking more like a drowned rat than a femme fatale.

"Well?" he said.

She jumped, screeched, and whirled around. "Oh, it's you."

"Who did you expect?"

"Nobody."

Connor stood.

"I have to go inside."

"Sure you do. But just so you know. Your little parody of a seduction was witnessed."

"I have no idea what you're talking about."

"Did you plan it?"

"Plan what? I was out on the beach, thinking, when Jack came down and put the moves on me."

Connor closed his eyes. In a way he was amazed at her stamina, how she could hold on to something in the past that didn't even happen and build her whole reason for being around it.

"Where were you all evening? Lying low, knowing at some point we would begin to worry? That even Skye would worry and that eventually we would come looking for you? All you had to do was sit there and wait for it all to come together.

"But snagging Jack. That had to take some work. Did you just sit around for hours in the hopes that he would walk by or see you from his porch? Or were you just lucky?"

"Lucky? I had to beat him off."

Connor snorted. "You went a bit too far. The dress gave it away. You were the one with your bare butt shining in the moonlight. Not Jack."

"And I suppose you're going to tell the whole town I tried to seduce him?"

"Only if you start spreading tales about him forcing himself on you."

"I won't. I wouldn't."

Connor raised a disbelieving eyebrow. He doubted if she could see it in the moonlight.

"Now, I'm going inside." She started to walk toward the door. Connor watched her pick her way across the dirt, carrying her shoes in her hand. And thought, what a waste of talent and imagination.

She stopped under the porch light. Gave him a slow smile. "Just wondering, did it work?" And she opened the door and slipped inside.

Connor didn't follow her in. He didn't want to hear what lie she'd tell Roxy and Hildy, who he was sure would meet her at the door. He just sat there wondering what was happening with

Skye. Had she already confronted Jack with what she thought she saw?

That's what she would have done with Connor, if he'd ever cheated on her, which he hadn't—not in thought, word, or deed. And look where it had landed him. Fifteen years later and no closer to being with her than he was the morning his parents had driven him away to military school.

Maybe this was his chance. He used the technique in every negotiation. Look for the tiniest crack, the slightest weakness, and drive a wedge—he cut back a laugh. Wasn't that just what Amy was doing, though she created her own cracks before ram-rodding herself into the situation?

God, what an abhorrent thought. That the two of them might actually be alike. In more ways than he wanted to admit. He'd been carrying his own disappointment, grudge? For all these years, just like Amy had. Only his feelings for Skye hadn't stunted his progress, hadn't kept him from having a successful career. Unlike Amy, he'd gotten on with his life.

Then why was he here?

Okay. Most of his life. And he had to admit the temptation had been too great not to come; he'd just wanted to see if there was anything still there between him and Skye. There was, definitely on his part; she was harder to read. Something he'd never had trouble doing when they were kids.

But they weren't kids. And she had a successful career and maybe relationship. He hadn't seen that much of Jack. Skye had not done anything to bring the two of them together. Why was that?

Was she unsure about her own feelings?

And if she was, what had tonight done to drive them in one way or the other? And was he going to do anything about it?

He could work it to his advantage if he chose to. But he knew a pact founded on a lie was bound to fail. He could try to convince himself otherwise. After all, this wasn't two countries, it was the woman he maybe still loved. And if Jack was collateral damage . . . well, all was fair in love and war.

SKYE KNEW SOMETHING was wrong when she woke up in her own apartment alone the next morning. It took another couple of seconds for the whole horrible scene on the beach to come flooding in. She pulled the covers over her head as horror twisted inside her.

She still couldn't believe it. Jack would never. He was much too up front about things. If he wasn't happy with the way they were, he would have said something.

He had been acting a little distant lately. She'd thought it was because he might not like Connor around. Maybe she should have introduced them when Connor first arrived. Let them sniff each other out as men did. But it seemed so absurd.

Besides, seeing Connor again, even under these circumstances, had been more unsettling than she wanted to admit. And a little enticing. Had Jack noticed? Did he even care?

Hardly, thought her baser self as the image of a naked Amy exploded in her mind. Jack's arms around her—their mouths . . .

She squeezed her eyes shut, trying to block out the image,

but it just grew more focused in her desperation. He'd still had his clothes on, hadn't he?

Now instead of trying to block out the scene; she tried to focus to bring out the details. But now that she wanted to remember, the image faded away.

God, she was such an idiot. She should have stood up to Amy the first night. But she'd run, just like she had fifteen years before. And she woke up today just as devastated as she had been then.

Her cell rang. She sat up, groped for the phone that was hidden in the summer quilt. She snared it on the fifth ring. Jack had texted and called her several times last night. To make excuses? To break up with her?

Instead of answering, she checked caller ID. Not Jack, but Ollie Ford. He'd left a voice mail. "I'm here with my crew, but I need a retainer check."

Skye called him back.

"I'll be over within the hour."

"Man. Are you sick? Summer cold? You want me to come pick it up at the store?"

"No, I'll come to you," Skye said and ended the call.

She showered just long enough to get clean and shed a few tears. Always better not to keep tears pent up, because when they finally did break, it was major. Better to let your emotions seep out little by little. Nothing cataclysmic, just a slow-burning grief.

But it took Skye longer than usual to pick out something to wear. Most of her clothes were in Jack's closet at the cottage. How would she get them back? Maybe she'd just leave them all there. Start over with a new wardrobe. It made her think of her mother and all her clothes stored in her father's workshop.

She swayed, leaned her forehead against the closet door.

What was happening to her?

How could it be happening to her—and now? Jack and Amy on Cove Beach in the moonlight, Amy's bare butt. Skye had seen them. She couldn't pretend it away.

She groped blindly for whatever was nearest. Put on a pair of black slacks and a floral print shirt. Couldn't even remember the last time she'd worn them. And that made her think of Jack wearing that stupid uncomfortable shirt to dinner. She'd thought it had been to compete with Connor. She'd thought it was so sweet. Now she wondered if had been merely to impress Amy.

The sun breaks through her window, the day is different, her life is different. Her hands don't work. She's wearing gloves; no, mittens; no, bandages. The fire. She nearly falls out of bed. Goes to the window. Dad's workshop is a jagged silhouette against the sky. She thinks she can see smoke still rising from the ground.

Why didn't Connor come? Because he's gone. He won't come back. It's too late for them.

And now she was alone again, Skye thought, and she went downstairs to get her checkbook.

Maya was already sitting on her stool and looking glum.

"Well?" she said, turning as soon as Skye opened the door. "Oh man, you look like hell." Maya stepped past her and turned the Open sign over to Closed. "All right, I'll make coffee and you tell me what happened."

"I have to take a check—"

"Not until you tell me what happened. Are you upset with Jack? He said he was going home to talk things out."

Skye coughed out a laugh; her face twisted. She turned away.

"Oh, sweetie, you didn't break up?"

Skye couldn't begin to speak. A cataclysmic breakup and she didn't even know that Jack knew it yet.

Skye could hear Maya plugging in the electric kettle, opening the fridge for the coffee grinds, the cabinet for the filters. She couldn't seem to go forward or back, her feet planted to the floor. With a gigantic effort she propelled herself into the staff room.

"I thought coffee made you sick."

"I'm fine." Maya stood on tiptoe to get cups off the shelf above on the counter. She turned back, holding a cup in each hand. "Why won't you talk to me? Did you have a fight? Are you still in love with Connor?"

Skye so didn't want to have this conversation. She didn't know what to say. The whole situation that had happened was too humiliating to even tell the sister she wished she had.

"But make sure before you break Jack's heart. Because, well, just be sure." Maya gulped and broke into crying.

Skye stood helpless, wanting to comfort her friend, tell her that nothing had changed. But something had. And there was nothing she could do to stop it. So she left Maya sobbing into her hands and went to write out a check to Ford Plumbing.

JACK FELT LIKE shit. He hadn't slept; now Sonny was badgering him with a hundred questions he didn't know the answer to, and he was about to lose his shit.

He took a slow breath, let it out. Relaxed his fingers and carefully placed the tamo inlay he'd been polishing on a chamois cloth.

Never work wood or cook when you're in a bad mood. The most important thing he'd learned in all his travels and all his apprenticeships. *Never unleash bad juju on an act of creation.*

He'd plan to just concentrate on his work. Make himself scarce. Give Skye a chance to come around. Jack didn't want to confront her about what might be going on, or put her on the defensive, not with the responsibilities she had. And to be perfectly honest, he didn't want to have it out, take the chance of her telling him it was over, because that would end everything and how were they supposed to carry on if that happened?

So he'd just get by, wait until Discover It Weekend was over. August. And then—God, what if she left before then?

"You know, you're really beginning to piss me off." Sonny glowered at him over a burl wood coffee table.

"Look, shit happened. All I know is she didn't come home last night. She stayed at her apartment. She didn't answer my calls or my texts." *God, just say it.* "I think she was with Connor."

"What? Jeez, Jack, don't be an asshole. Skye would never do that to you. She'd be up front." Sonny waved the sanding block he was holding in Jack's direction.

Jack had to concentrate on not dodging in case Sonny's exasperation got the better of him and he let the block fly.

"Did you see them together?"

"No, but I saw her light on."

"And you didn't go up?"

"Really, Sonny? Show up at her door and say, 'Hey Connor, my man. Are you shagging my girl?'"

"Christ!" Sonny flopped down on the nearest sawhorse and tossed the sanding block onto the worktable. "All because you went into town for a burger?"

"Because I shut her out."

"Hell, it's what you do. Everybody puts up with it."

"Well, I guess this was the time she didn't. Maybe she was just waiting for an excuse."

Sonny sighed. "And I thought pregnancy hormones were bad."

They sat in silence for a bit. "And there's something else."

"Oh, man. Hit me with it."

"Okay," Jack said. "But just let me tell the whole thing before you go off on me."

"Sure, nobody's stopping you. What else did you do?"

"She took out a bank loan to pay for the water main at the camp."

"A personal loan?"

Jack nodded. "I sorta said she'd lost her mind. And then I told her I needed—"

"To take a minute. Yeah, I get it. That's your MO."

"So I did, then I called you because I knew I wasn't seeing things clearly."

"You can say that again."

Jack suddenly felt claustrophobic. The workshop was crowded at the best of times, but it seemed oppressively so today. He walked to the other side of his workbench, turned back.

Sonny was eyeing him from behind templed fingers. On

another day, under different circumstances, it would have made Jack laugh. He looked very smart and wise and not like Sonny at all.

"There's something else."

"I figured there might be."

"So after I left you guys, I was walking home and Skye texted to say she was at Roxy's, Amy had disappeared and they were out looking for her."

"That girl is nothing but trouble," Sonny said.

"Yeah, so I see her down on Cove Beach."

Sonny sat up. "Was she hurt?"

"No, it looked like she was going for a swim."

"In the water off Cove Beach?"

"Yeah, so I yelled at her to stop. But she didn't. Long story short—"

"No long-story-short, tell me what happened."

So Jack told him. Every ridiculous humiliating part. "I swear to God, I think she must have lured me down just to try and seduce me."

"And you fell for it?"

"Dammit. No. She pulled off her dress and jumped me. She's stronger than she looks. I finally got her off, threw her the dress at her. She put it on and I sent her back to Roxy's." Jack took several steps away, came back. "Why would she do something like that?"

"'Cause you're a good-looking dude?" Sonny said.

"I think she did it on purpose. Planned it."

"To get back at Skye?"

"Or get me out of the way so Connor could move in."

SKYE KNEW SHE looked awful, but she had every intention of claiming a summer cold, as Ollie had suggested. She'd just drop her check off and try to leave without breaking down.

Suddenly water pipes and discovery weekends didn't seem nearly as important as they had a day ago.

This too shall pass, she reminded herself. Just look where she'd started. She sniffed. No more thinking. Skye marched down the driveway into the Pritchard camp grounds.

She could hear the machinery at work before she could see it, so she followed the sound behind the trees to where an orange one-man backhoe was digging up the ground, while Brendan Wraye and Ollie Ford stood watching.

Skye joined them, smiled the best she could, and handed Ollie the check.

"How's it going?" she asked. Her life was falling apart and she really didn't care about water pipes in the slightest. She would willingly chuck the whole—no she wouldn't. This was her life. Love affairs came and went, but this was her calling. She bit her lip hard enough to make her pull herself together.

She did care.

"—about Thursday," Ollie was saying.

"Ah," Skye said. She had no idea what he'd just said. "I'll leave you to it then." She turned to go and saw Herb Pritchard hurrying across the parking lot.

She sighed, slowed down long enough to say, "Not to worry. I've paid for it. You won't owe a thing." And she kept going.

By the time she reached the street, she was jogging toward Imagine That.

And Maya was still waiting for her.

Skye had barely walked in, but she noticed that Penny, with a chalkboard on an easel beside her, was in the middle of Build a Story Hour. Little girl, Dog, and Space Invaders were listed on the board. Beach, Thunderstorm, and Treasure were written beneath. As Skye closed the door, one of the kids shouted out, "They're being chased by giant, monster lightning bugs." Penny dutifully wrote down his suggestion.

"Should be interesting," Skye said as she reached Maya.

"Come to the back." Maya didn't give Skye time to answer before she turned and strode toward the office.

Skye was on overload. Just watching Maya's movements was painful. Every time she moved her eyes, it was like they passed over sandpaper, which made her think about Jack, and that made her hurt even more.

She could turn around and leave the store, but hell, it was her store. She reluctantly followed Maya to the back.

Maya turned on her. "Sonny called and said you're dumping Jack."

Skye grabbed the back of the desk chair, which was fortunately right by her hand. "I—I never said that."

"Jack thinks you're sleeping with Connor. Is it true? You didn't even tell me?"

"I'm not. How could you even think that?" Skye swiveled the

chair and sat down so hard her teeth clicked together. "What's happening? Everybody's acting crazy."

"And you're not?"

"I'm not doing anything but trying to get through the next two weekends. Trying to get to August when——" Skye broke off. When what? Things would get back to normal? Would things ever be normal again? Hell, she couldn't even remember normal.

"If only you'd been my sister," Skye said, her voice quavering out of control.

"I am. I'm your real sister. If sharing everything, supporting each other, lifting up, not tearing down is what real sisters do."

"Everything has gone haywire since Amy came. I should have gotten rid of her that first night. I know what she's capable of. I don't know why she won't just leave me alone. Why does she have to keep trying to wreck my life? And this time she's really done it."

"No, she hasn't. We won't let her."

"She already has. She and Jack . . . she . . . Connor and I saw them on Cove Beach."

"What were they doing there?"

Skye hiccuped a sound that didn't even sound like it came from her. "What do you think?"

"I don't know. Wait. No. Jack wouldn't do anything like that, if that's what you mean. Not with her. Not with anybody."

"She was naked and was wrapped around him like—he was . . . they were . . . Ugh. I'll never unsee that."

Maya dropped to her knees beside Skye's chair. "I don't believe it. There has to be some explanation."

"Trust me, I've spent a lot of time trying to rationalize what I saw. There's no way to make it anything but what it was." Skye didn't want to try.

Jack had been Sonny and Maya's friend longer than she had been. Would this mean they would have to take sides? They would have no choice but to take Jack's.

What had he done? Didn't he know that Amy was mercurial at best, but manipulative most of the time? Even if Amy had instigated it, which would be no surprise, was a one-night stand in the sand worth the heartache it would cause, not just to Skye, but to Maya and Sonny, Roxy and Hildy? Everyone who saw them as a couple, even if they hadn't really made a conscious effort to declare themselves "together." Even if he'd stopped caring about Skye, how could he end it this way?

Would Skye lose them all? Not Roxy and Hildy, but everyone else. They would feel uncomfortable when they saw her, look the other way. That's how it would start . . . that's how it had started before.

Skye stood up. "There's no use sitting here crying over what can't be helped. It is what it is and I'll have to deal with it."

Maya looked so unhappy that Skye felt guilty for being so unhappy herself.

"I'm sorry. Maya. This is supposed to be a happy time. We should be out buying baby clothes and silly stuffed animals and diaper bags." Skye reached out and touched Maya's little baby bump. She hadn't even noticed when it first appeared. What kind of friend was that? "What must Baby Daniels be thinking about us?"

"He or she is thinking that we're going to be fine," Maya said, giving Skye a hug. "Somehow. It's going to work out. It just has to."

Chapter 26

Connor stood outside the door of Point Fine Woodworking and Cabinetry. *Substantial* had been his first thought when he'd rounded the corner and seen the redbrick building. A former warehouse, maybe; there were two plate-glass windows and he could see the shapes of furniture inside. A showroom of sorts, though it was hard to tell through the glass and bright sunshine behind him.

He hesitated at the door. He was still not sure of what he was going to say—not the best position to be in for negotiations. But he was resilient, he'd just go with the flow.

But first he would lay down the facts.

Connor went inside.

And found himself in a large showroom with recessed lighting that spotlighted the various pieces on display. Not your ordinary showroom of rows of coffee tables and sofas. More like an art gallery.

He wondered whose hand had shaped that. It had to have

been Skye's work. From the little he'd seen of Jack or his partner, Sonny, neither of them struck Connor as the artistic type.

No one came out to help him, so he looked around on his own. The space was filled with amazing pieces. Large and small, bold and delicate. From the grounded to the sublime.

This was a surprise.

He stopped by a heavy low table, its top constructed from a single cross section of wood. Substantial, sturdy, the kind of furniture that could withstand use and yet at the same time demanded appreciation.

Connor read the calligraphy card folded on its surface. Sequoia Table by Sonny Daniels. There was no price tag.

Connor wasn't surprised. But he was surprised at the maker. Sonny Daniels, the little he'd seen of him, was a big jovial guy who Connor thought would be happy wearing a flannel shirt and hanging out at the local bar with his bros.

He moved on to the next piece.

At first he wasn't sure what it was. A chair? A chaise. Two wooden curved pieces polished to a sheen, balanced on four curved legs and filled in between with a thatched leather sling. The lines seemed to move and meld without seams.

Connor would be afraid to touch it much less sit on it. A bronze side table next to it held the same calligraphy card. Walnut Chaise. Jack Winslow.

He wandered over to the next piece and the next.

The whole room was alive with energy and movement. Sonny's constructions were sturdy, practical, utilitarian, yet inviting.

Jack's were soaring, dipping, and elusive. Sleek, simple, with an almost unworldly quality, movement without moving.

Well, shit. Never in a million years would Connor have expected this. Jack seemed nice enough, kind of quiet, down-home, steady, but uninspiring.

Boy, had Connor missed on that. The guy had talent, skill—and a vision. Connor looked away, but everywhere he turned was evidence that he'd underestimated both men.

Comes from dealing in rarified circles, he told himself. In treaty negotiations everybody was on the make, trying for the best deals, for good causes often, but self-interested always. He'd almost forgotten what it was like just to let your mind fly with no ulterior motive . . . except maybe to make a chair or a table.

There was more to Jack Winslow than met the eye. Except that Skye had obviously seen it. And suddenly it hit Connor with painful clarity just what he was up against.

Fine, know your enemy. Not that he considered Jack an enemy. A competitor.

He hadn't decided how to play this, not completely. Every fiber of his emotional being was saying play it hard and win her back. Amy had given him a perfect opening. He didn't for a minute think she hadn't set up the whole scene on the beach. What he wasn't absolutely sure of was whether Jack had been willing to be seduced or not. It had seemed that he was more angry at her than interested. He'd practically thrown her off.

Connor probably should have stayed longer to make sure.

But he just couldn't do it. And Amy had returned to Roxy's in record time. There was no real way Connor could make that scenario work. It was clear Jack hadn't been interested.

And he didn't think Amy was, either. Connor was sure she'd set the whole scene up because someone somewhere was bound to see them. Even if it hadn't been Skye, the news would have spread and Amy would have achieved exactly what she wanted.

Whatever that was. To humiliate Skye? To hurt her.

And could Connor really be a part of that, even take advantage of the situation to get what he wanted? He'd convinced himself that Skye couldn't possibly be happy with Jack. But now he was not so sure. She could re-create her "imagination" spaces anywhere, but was that enough?

"Sorry, man, I was back in the workshop and I couldn't—" Sonny stepped into the room and stopped, a cleaning cloth grasped in one hand. His expression changed from friendly to wary. "Can I help you?"

Connor took a breath. "I came to talk to Jack."

"Oh, man," Sonny said and left the way he'd come.

SONNY BURST INTO the workshop. "He's in the showroom."

"Who?" Jack asked.

"Connor, he wants to talk to you."

Jack glanced toward the back door. He could just walk out the back and around the loading dock and keep walking. And stop where? "Shit." He covered the inlay he'd been working on for days and went out to deal with whatever was going on.

Connor was looking at one of Jack's pieces, but he turned

when Jack came in. He didn't say anything and Jack had no idea what to say, so they stood there for a really long awkward moment until Connor finally said, "I saw a pub down the street. Is it too early for a drink?"

The Dog and Pony was the last place Jack wanted to duke it out with this dude. Though at least he would be on friendly territory. It could also be really humiliating. Then again, if Skye left him and drove off in Connor's little blue sports car, the whole town would know anyway.

"Sure." Jack stuck his head into the workshop. "I'll be back."

"Want me to come with?" Sonny asked.

"Thanks, but no."

Connor was waiting by the front door and Jack noticed he was half a head shorter than he was. Primitive maybe, but it made Jack feel just a bit better.

They didn't talk until they were seated in a booth at the back of the bar.

Mike came over, flashed a curious look at Jack, nodded to Connor, then took their orders and hurried off.

Jack watched him go. Finally turned back to Connor. He had no idea where to start. He didn't want to talk to this guy, he didn't want a beer. His insides were shards of glass. The feeling threw him off. Things didn't usually hurt like this. He was good at absorbing shit. Not this time.

Mike brought their beers and left again, moving to the far side of the room and taking out a cloth to wipe what had to be a perfectly clean bar top, since there was no one else in the place.

Jack waited. He wished the guy would get to what he wanted to say. Jack knew whatever it was, he wasn't going to like it.

Connor took a sip of his beer, put the bottle down on the table. "Skye and I—"

Jack gripped his beer bottle, not knowing whether to lift it to his mouth or bash Connor over the head with it.

Connor took a pull at his beer. Put the bottle down. "There's no good way to say this, so I'll be blunt. Skye and I saw you and Amy last night."

"What?"

"Yep, I was walking her to your place. She'd had dinner at Roxy's since you were dining elsewhere."

God, he was an officious prick. "Skye . . ." Jack couldn't even go on. His throat was tight.

"We got an eyeful."

"It's not what you think."

Connor sighed. Leaned back against the banquette. "I didn't think it was."

Jack waited. Did he actually think Jack was going to do an instant replay for him?

"So what was it?"

Jack pulled at his beer. Set it down, carefully. It wasn't too much to ask, he guessed. Still he hated to . . . ah, hell. "Skye called me to keep an eye out for Amy. I saw her on the beach. I called out and told her to come away from the water. That it was dangerous to be there at night. She said something about swimming. The sign clearly says NO SWIMMING, because the riptides can be really bad past the point."

Connor shook his head. "So you went down to stop her."

"Exactly. Then she starts with this come-on, pulls the dress over her head, and jumps me."

"What kind of idiot are you, to fall for Amy's shit? I thought you were smarter than that."

"I was trying to keep her from drowning."

"Well, you better explain that to Skye."

"She doesn't think— She knows I wouldn't."

"Are *you* so sure?" Connor lifted one shoulder. "It was a pretty convincing scene."

Jack glared at him. If his eyes had been lasers, he would have finished Connor right there. He took a breath. Held it. Man, this was so not like him. He hadn't thought about fighting anyone in years. Even when they deserved it.

"She wouldn't believe it, unless you helped convince her."

Connor's hand came up so fast that Jack flinched, but he only jabbed one tapered manicured finger at him. "You're a complacent son of a bitch. If you don't care, I do. And if she means that little to you, then tell her. I'll be happy to step right in."

"What are you saying? Were you together last night?" Jack closed his eyes. He couldn't believe he'd actually asked Connor that. And he dreaded the answer.

"We had dinner at Roxy's. That's all. Not that you seem willing to go out of your way to fix things with her."

"I don't think she wants to talk to me."

"Well, really, Jack. Do you blame her? You leave her when she's making you dinner, don't come back. Don't call. Then she finds you in flagrante on the beach with her sister."

"Half sister," Jack interjected. "And I wasn't in flagrante. I was having a hell of a time extricating myself from the little barnacle."

"Then tell Skye. If she wants you, I'll bow out. Either fight for her, or I will."

"Like pistols at dawn?"

Connor stared at him.

"It was a joke. How am I supposed to fight?"

"Hell, you figure it out. I get the big civil servant bucks to help countries understand each other; you and Skye are somewhere I don't want to go. Do you actually care about her, or not?"

"Of course I do."

"Or is she just convenient for while it lasts?"

Jack was out of his seat before he knew what he was doing.

Connor brought him to his senses by merely lifting his hand. He looked like a damn traffic cop. But Jack sat down.

"I really didn't even want to give you a heads-up. I wanted to just let things get out of control—so out of control that you lost out. But that's not the way I roll. But I need to know if you care enough for Skye to figure this all out. Because if you don't, I do. I always have. I always will. And I'll take advantage of your stupidity and make her a better offer if you are going to just sit there and let life take its course. Capisce?

"Now I'm done. It's every man for himself." Connor slid out of the booth. "Thanks for the beer." He strode out of the pub.

"Hey," Jack called after him. "You invited me." But Connor was long gone.

Mike appeared to take Connor's half-full beer away. "Was that the guy who brought Skye's half sister to town?"

"Yeah," Jack said. He reached for his wallet.

"On the house," Mike said.

"Thanks. I have—"

"Something to do," Mike finished for him. "Yeah, I figured as much. Good luck."

He stepped back as Jack slid out of the booth and headed for the door.

Once outside, Jack stood on the sidewalk making sure Connor was gone. He saw him walking toward the beach. Or toward Imagine That. Connor would have to pass it on his way back to Roxy's. As long as he passed it and didn't go inside.

Connor slowed down at the door of Imagine That.

Jack willed him not to go inside.

Connor hesitated then walked past the store toward the corner. Jack breathed a sigh of relief. It was only momentary. He had no idea how to make this right.

Skye should have gotten rid of Amy and Connor the night they arrived. Or Roxy should have. Or he could have said something. But he didn't. Because he didn't want to be overbearing like his father had been. It was just what he was about to be now.

The thought jolted him. Jack always made sure he wasn't like his father, a good enough man but controlling. It had cowered his children. It had subdued their mother. She was smart and savvy and she was kept at home, because Thomas Winslow could take care of his wife and children. His father was proud of that. It's what men did in his family. Which was a good thing, but it also held them back from being what they might be.

Jack swore he would never do that. And look at him now. Still single, childless, and about to lose the one person who made it all worthwhile. Now he would do whatever he had to do to make Skye understand.

He arrived at the store way sooner than he was prepared for. Couldn't be helped. He opened the door and went inside.

Story hour was over. There were only a few people in the store. Maya was ringing up a woman and her little girl at the counter. Jack waited for the customers to take their package and walk past him to the door. He was left looking at Maya, who didn't look pleased to see him.

"She's not here," Maya said.

"Do you know when she'll be back?"

"No."

"Did she say where she was going?"

Maya sighed, bit her lip. "Quite frankly, Jack Winslow, I wouldn't tell you if I did. Oh hell, Roxy and Hildy came by and took her to dinner. They insisted. They'd just said good-bye to Hildy's guests at the B and B. And they decided to take the night off. Roxy said they needed something fried and they pretty much coerced Skye into going with them."

"Did Skye—"

"Tell me what happened? Of course she did. And you are a-a-a . . ."

"I don't know what Skye told you, but it isn't true."

"I know that. Sonny already called. That doesn't keep you from being a-a-a . . ."

"Jackass?"

"Yeah." Maya's mouth twisted. God, she was going to cry. Jack might just join her.

"If she comes back, will you at least tell her I came by?"

"I guess, but I'm leaving soon. I'll tell Nat to tell her. *If* he sees her. They'll probably be late. Roxy was on a tear."

Jack had no doubt. "Fine. Thank you. I'll be at home."

Jack turned and stalked out of Imagine That; he pulled out his phone and called Sonny.

"I'm calling it a day. Will you lock up?"

"Sure," Sonny said. "Glad to. Uh, does this mean you and Skye have made it up?"

"No, but thanks for asking." Jack ended the call. His throat was suddenly too tight to even say goodbye.

He turned toward the beach and home. It was the loneliest walk he'd ever made.

THERE WAS A breeze coming off the river when Skye, Roxy, and Hildy came out of Smitty's Whale Watch Café. The local favorite, Smitty's had been packed when they arrived, and it was still packed when they left after having eaten to their hearts' content, including Skye, who had finally seen the light.

It had taken two beers and Smitty's stuffed flounder special, but she was feeling more rational, calmer, and slightly embarrassed that she'd jumped to a conclusion that even as she saw it she knew couldn't be true.

Roxy waved the keys to the station wagon at Skye as they walked across the crowded parking lot. "So we're dropping you off at Jack's and you're going inside and getting this all straightened out. Right?"

"I said I would," Skye said. "But you don't have to drop me, I can walk from your house."

"Oh no. I'm not giving you a chance to chicken out on your way. You jumped to the wrong conclusion and now you're going to tell him you did. And apologize. And get all lovey-dovey, and—"

Hildy snatched the keys from Roxy's hand. "And I'm driving. You had one too many Manhattans with your lobster."

"It was the battered fries not the Manhattans," Roxy groused, but she handed over the keys to the car.

She climbed in the passenger side, and Skye got in the back. Part of her couldn't wait to see Jack and get it all out in the open. She felt so stupid to have carried on like she had. Jack was nothing if not up front about stuff. He would never go behind her back. She knew that. Something crazy had taken hold of her. How could she have been so mistrusting?

Hildy moved the seat up, started the station wagon, and they screeched out of the parking lot and onto Sunny Point Road.

Skye sat back looking out the window trying to command her thoughts. *Just apologize and . . . apologize and . . . and take it from there.*

As they drove along the river to Jack's side of the point, Skye's stomach started doing somersaults. She wished she, like Roxy, could blame it on the battered fries, but she knew it was nerves. What if Jack didn't forgive her? What if he was angry and could no longer trust her because she hadn't trusted him? What if—

They passed the county park where in less than two weeks participants in Discover It Weekend would meet for nature walks and leaf rubbings.

Past the fish and tackle shop. Skye's insides began to quake, definitely nerves, not the fries or the microbrew.

Past the entrance to Pritchards' family camp.

"Holy cow," Hildy said. "That's one humdinger of a barbecue."

"Where?" asked Skye.

"Up at the Pritchards' house. See, right there through the pines."

Skye pulled her seat belt away from her shoulder and leaned forward. "That's not the Pritchards' house. That's the camp. The camp is on fire!"

"Oh shit," Roxy said.

"Hold on," Hildy ordered. The station wagon screeched to a stop, backed up, and sped through the camp entrance.

Chapter 27

Connor marched Amy over the path to Jack's house. He was on overload, but he knew what he had to do.

"I don't know why you're making me do this," Amy said, hurrying to keep up. "I'm packed and ready to go. Why can't we just leave?"

He stopped long enough to take her arm, not to be polite but to make sure she didn't bolt and run. "Because you've never taken responsibility for anything in your life, and now you've dragged me into it." And brought all the old feelings he thought he had grown out of back again. There were some things you could never really leave behind.

"And we're not going to sneak out of town until you've owned up and apologized to Jack about setting him up in the most despicable way." Not like the last time, when Connor gave in to his parents and left Skye to face the recriminations and humiliation on her own.

"I don't know why I have to apologize. It takes two to tango."

She did that little shoulder squeeze that she thought was coy. But was just irritating as hell.

"You weren't dancing, and he didn't want any part of it. You forget, I was watching."

"Naughty you."

"Amy, just stop. You're like a child wearing dress-up clothes. I don't believe any of it and I'm beginning to wonder if you do. But regardless, you've done enough damage for one trip, which, by the way, you're going to make your last trip."

"Fine."

"But not before you set the record straight on what happened with Jack and apologize to Skye for once again trying to hijack her life. And then to me for being a pain in the ass for as long as I've known you."

"If you're so sure I broke them up, why do you think she'll be at Jack's?"

God, he hated that singsong voice when she got huffy. "If she isn't there, we're going to find her and you're going to explain everything to her and promise that you're never going to screw up her life again."

"I didn't screw up her life. She screwed up mine. I'm the one that always got the short end of the stick. As far as Jack goes, which isn't far if you ask me, you can tell she takes him for granted. I just wanted her to appreciate what she has. And to help you.

"Not that you'd appreciate it. You gave up fast enough. And I practically handed her to you."

Connor clenched his fists. He hadn't wanted to hit anyone

so much since learning that Amy had accused Skye of starting the workshop fire in the first place. And then he'd only broken three fingers punching his dorm room door.

Tonight he just gritted his teeth. "No man, no decent man, wants to get a woman that way."

Amy slowed down and Connor realized that they were just above the beach where Amy's clumsy seduction had gone down. The same beach where Skye had brought Connor to talk, and where he'd felt his old emotions rekindle after all the years they'd been apart. The same beach where Amy had tried to ruin it all.

Well, it was too late for him. Even if Jack had damaged his relationship with Skye beyond repair, Connor couldn't take advantage of her, not when he couldn't promise to make her happy in Jack's stead. And after seeing them together, he wasn't sure he could. He knew when to accept a loss, extricate himself before he lost more. He'd tried every honorable option he could think of, but like in a treaty about to fall apart, he knew when to ease off.

"Hmm," Amy said. She'd slowed down and was looking down into the cove. Connor looked, too, but it was empty; only the moon, fat and full, shone on the waves beyond the point.

"Don't," he said.

"Don't what?" Amy said, not bothering to look at him.

"Whatever you're planning now."

"I'm not. Why is everyone so mean to me?"

"Because you ask them to be."

"Huh?"

It was hopeless. The girl was clueless and probably always would be. She would just have to learn to get along in the world. He'd given it his first and last shot.

A life of unhappiness and sense of being slighted—all over a burnt-down hobby room. *And a distant father*, he reminded himself. And a sister who got the blame and lost her home and family. And Amy was the one who felt slighted.

Once past the cove, Connor veered off the path to the sand track that led to Jack's front porch.

Jack must have been sitting on the porch in the dark, because he came down the steps and walked out to meet them. Skye didn't seem to be with him. Connor waited for Jack to reach them; he didn't want to encroach on the man's space any more than necessary. The path would do for what they had to do.

"Amy has something she wants to say," Connor said without preamble.

They both turned to Amy, who was looking off down the path. "Amy?"

"Look!" she said, pointing down the path. "Is that smoke?"

Connor and Jack both looked.

"It's at the camp," Jack said. "Call nine-one-one." And he started running.

Connor only waited long enough to make the call, then he ran after Jack.

"Wait for me," Amy cried. But Connor didn't slow down. He was afraid of what might be waiting for them.

* * *

HILDY BRAKED THE car at the far edge of the parking lot. The car was still rebounding when Skye jumped out. Zeroed in on the mess hall. No smoke there.

Scanned the other buildings and her heart sank. Cabin two was on fire. Everything for her weekend was stored inside. Flames rose from the roof. Smoke billowed out the front door. Someone must have opened it.

A small group of people stood at the edge of the parking lot. Edna and her daughter-in-law, Darla, and the children. Skye ran up to them.

"He went in there!" Edna cried. "Herb's inside!"

Skye didn't think. She took off toward the cabin. All she could hear was the crackling of burning wood. Someone calling her name. Roxy. But Skye just kept running—right into the past.

Call nine-one-one.

She knew he would, then he would come after her to help.

But now she was thinking only one thing as she stumbled and slid down the hill, that her father was in the workshop.

The heat hit Skye first, a wall that knocked her backward, paralyzing her momentarily. Then smoke rolled into her lungs and she choked. She turned her back, gulped in what air she could, then bending her arm over her face, she ran up the porch steps and inside.

"Herb!" She couldn't see anything but a glow of flames behind the thick dark smoke. "Herb!" She wasn't sure it came out loud enough. Tried again. "Herb!" She didn't see him, maybe he wasn't inside after all. Something fell, sending a shower of sparks toward her, like Fourth of July fireworks. She stumbled back, tried to take a breath.

The flames had consumed one corner and now they were rushing toward her. *Herb! Dad?*

Skye spun around, losing her orientation. *Away from the fire. Move away from the fire.*

It was all going up in flames, she couldn't save anything, and she couldn't find Herb. She stepped back and tripped over something on the floor, fell to her hands and knees.

Herb Pritchard lay in a heap on the floor.

She scrambled around on all fours, pushed to her feet, her face and hands and back burning from the heat. He was lying facedown; she grabbed at his arms, tried to pull him along the floor, but he just fell back into place when she had to let go to get a better grip.

She grabbed the straps of his overalls and pulled with all her might. The fire was no longer a crackle, but a roar. A wall of fire confronted her, smoke billowed around her, thick and acrid and . . .

Away from the fire, she had to get away from the fire. "Help!" she screamed, but the sound was gobbled by the flames.

And suddenly Skye's foot touched the threshold. They were going to make it. Then Herb stuck; she yanked his coveralls but he didn't move. She yanked again, desperate to get him out.

"I've got him. Get away from the building. Now!" She was shoved aside.

Jack. Herb's body slid past her as Jack dragged him toward safety. She didn't follow. She had to save something. She couldn't let it burn. She went back the way she'd come.

JACK GRABBED HERB by both armpits and shuffled backward until they were on the porch. Dragged him toward the stairs where someone grabbed Herb's other side. Connor Reid.

Together, they dragged the unconscious man onto the ground and away from the cabin, just as a wail of sirens and whirling lights burst through the drive opening, and a fire engine followed by two ambulances swung into the parking lot.

Jack waved both arms; the ambulances made a beeline for him, and Jack doubled over in a fit of coughing.

Then Roxy was shaking him.

"Where's Skye? I don't see her. Where is she?"

"What?" He couldn't understand her over the wailing of the sirens. He was hit with another paroxysm of coughing. He was barely aware of someone running past him toward the cottage.

Jack grabbed the person out of pure reflex.

Amy. She struggled to free herself. "Skye's inside! She went back inside!"

"What? No, she came out."

Amy fought against him. "I saw her. She went back inside!"

Jack shoved her back toward Roxy. He heard the firemen shouting orders, the hoses being unwound, but he couldn't wait. Skye was still inside.

He cleared the porch steps in one leap. And through the smoke, like an apparition, a specter, the most glorious thing he'd ever seen—staggering out of the cabin, her arms filled with papers and fishnets and God knew what. Skye. Trying to save what was past saving.

"Skye," he said as she collapsed in his arms.

Jack nearly fell down the steps under her sudden, dead weight.

Not dead. Please God, not dead. He struggled to his feet, moved forward, not sure of his destination, just that he had to keep moving, though his lungs felt like they might burst.

And then someone was lifting Skye away.

"No." He held on tight. They couldn't take her. Not yet.

"Jack! It's Eliot Green. She needs oxygen."

Eliot Green. EMT. They played Extreme Frisbee sometimes. Jack let go. And immediately doubled over and coughed until his guts exploded. And someone was leading him over to the ambulance and sat him down.

Skye was lying on a gurney, an oxygen mask over her face.

"Is she—?"

"She's fine. Just inhaled a lot of smoke. So did you. I'm putting an oxygen mask on you. Just breathe evenly. You were both damn lucky."

Skye stirred on the gurney. Jack pushed the oxygen mask away and lunged for her.

She lifted her hand in the air, pushed away the oxygen cup from her mouth.

"Herb?"

Jack looked back at Eliot and his partner, a woman he recognized but didn't know.

"They're taking him to the hospital."

"I couldn't get him out."

"He's going to be okay. Now stop talking." The EMT fit the mask back over her nose and mouth. And Jack sat back down. After a few minutes, Eliot removed the mask.

"Breathing on your own okay?"

Jack nodded.

"You're both going in for observation."

"I'll drive myself over in a few minutes." Jack started to get out of the ambulance. Realized a crowd had formed around the opening.

Roxy, Hildy, holding up a crying Amy. And Connor.

"You go to the hospital," Connor said. "I'll talk to the fire chief and come to the hospital later with my report."

Jack squinted at him. He didn't trust the man, first appearing for no reason at his house just in time to discover the fire, and knowing full well he would try to lure Skye away if he could. Jack was trying to make a connection between those two things, but his mind wouldn't work.

"It's the least I can do."

Suddenly he was too tired to argue. He'd have to deal with Connor Reid later, tomorrow maybe.

"Don't take long," Jack said.

Eliot eased Jack back into a seat. "Buckle up," he said and jumped down to the ground. The ambulance doors shut, sealing off everything but Skye and how close they'd come to no tomorrow at all.

Chapter 28

It was two hours later when the hospital finally released Jack and he made his way down the hall to where, Roxy, Hildy, Amy, and Connor were all waiting.

Well, they weren't waiting for him, but there didn't seem to be any way Jack could get past them without stopping. And he'd be damned if he'd leave Skye to face them alone. He planned to take her straight home and not let her out of his sight for . . . for a long time.

He was surprised to see Sonny and Maya there. News traveled fast on Sunny Point.

Jack was glad to see them, but he went straight to Connor.

"The fire's out," Connor said. "They wouldn't let me near the cabin, but I can't imagine that much, if anything, survived."

"Thanks." Jack tried to remember what actually was being stored in the cabin but he hadn't paid that much attention with all the other stuff going on. Maya would know but maybe it was better just not to know until they could see it in the light of day. "Let's keep it to ourselves for now."

Connor nodded. "Can I get you some coffee or something?"

"Thanks, but they hydrated me into the next century."

He went over to Sonny and Maya. Sonny was standing behind her, his hand on her shoulder. Maya looked small, frightened, but determined.

"They're discharging her in a few minutes," Jack said before they could ask.

"Here she comes," Maya said and jumped up.

Everyone turned to see Skye being wheeled down the corridor by an orderly, but Jack and Connor were the ones who strode toward the corridor entrance.

Connor was closest, but he pulled up short when he must have realized how it looked. Jack certainly realized it. Fortunately Skye didn't witness their desperation. She'd been stopped by Edna Pritchard, who ran out from a side door and waylaid Skye as they passed by.

The orderly stopped, and Edna grabbed Skye's arm.

Jack broke into a trot. He'd just about had it with Edna and Herb and Rhoda and the whole damn town.

"You saved Herb's life tonight," Edna said. "After all the awful things I said to you. You saved his life. I'm so sorry. It must have been the children and those awful fireworks. I told them not to set them off without their father. I don't know how we'll ever be able to repay you. Thank you. Thank you."

Skye looked over Edna's bent head, her expression horrified, and her eyes signaling an SOS plea for Jack to extricate her from the woman's effusions.

Jack put his arm around Edna, giving the orderly time to get

Skye away. "And you, too, Jack. I don't know how I can thank you both. I'd be lost without Herb."

Jack said a couple of "now-nows" and "It was nothing really" and handed her off to a nurse who was walking by. Then he followed after Skye.

She'd finally been allowed to get out of the wheelchair. And Jack was ready to whisk her away when he realized he didn't have a way home.

He'd have to ask Roxy and Hildy to give them a lift. He'd ask Sonny, but he knew Roxy would insist on seeing Skye safely home. Preferably, *her* home if Roxy had her way, except that with Connor and Amy still there, Skye would be better off with Jack.

After promising to talk to Maya the following morning, seeing Amy and Connor off, and waiting for Roxy to cross-examine the attending physician, they finally all climbed into Hildy's car.

"I want to drive by the camp," Skye said as Hildy drove them out of the parking lot.

"They won't let you in," Jack said. "It's still an active investigation."

"Investigation?" Skye said.

"Just standard operating procedure."

"But how did it start? The wiring was new. It had been inspected. Could it have been the kids? Or something else? Why?"

"We'll know tomorrow," Jack said, not knowing whether they would or not. "Now, it's home, food, shower, bed."

Skye sighed, leaned back against the seat, and closed her eyes. She was asleep before they left the hospital parking lot; Jack wondered what her dreams would be like tonight.

ROXY SAT AT the kitchen table with Hildy, Connor, and Amy. She wanted to call Skye's cell or even Jack's to see if they were okay. But every time she reached for her phone, Hildy was there to keep snatching it away. And finally confiscated it, slipping it into the pocket of one of her ruffled aprons.

"Just to see if they made it home okay," Roxy argued.

"They're home. The lights are on. We dropped them off at the door," Hildy said.

"I still think she should have come here. Where we could take care of her."

"Jack will take care of her," Hildy said and placed a plate of zucchini bread slices and a tub of butter on the table.

"I couldn't eat a thing," Roxy said, reaching for the butter knife.

Amy and Connor hadn't spoken since they'd returned home from the hospital. It was almost two o'clock, and they both looked dead on their feet.

Roxy and Hildy were drinking decaf. Connor was nursing Roxy's best single malt, which she didn't begrudge in the least. Amy sat with a glass of water untouched before her.

Roxy slid the platter of zucchini bread toward her.

Amy shook her head. Roxy was amazed that for once Amy wasn't complaining, or crying, or even gone to bed. She just sat there staring at the tablecloth.

Hildy topped off their coffee and sat down. "So how bad was the damage, really?" she asked Connor.

"Bad." He looked up. "I managed to talk to the fire chief for a minute. He wouldn't tell me anything since they have to investigate, and I couldn't get close enough to see for myself. But it can't be good. Whatever had been stored there is going to be pretty much destroyed. Whatever had survived the actual fire would have been drenched in water. I doubt if much can be salvaged."

They all fell silent after that. Roxy's mind was a blank. All destroyed? What would Skye do? What could she do?

"She didn't do it." Amy's words, though barely audible, broke into the silence.

They all turned to look at her.

And Roxy remembered Amy running toward the burning building when she realized Skye was inside. *She'd been going to save her sister.*

"Didn't do what?" Roxy asked.

"It wasn't her. I didn't understand." Amy pushed back from the table and walked out of the room.

The others exchanged looks.

"Should we be worried about her?" Roxy asked.

Connor shrugged.

"Well, I think . . ." Hildy began, scooping out a dollop of soft butter and spreading it across a slice of bread.

Connor and Roxy both gave her their full attention.

"Well?" Roxy said impatiently.

Hildy put down the knife and looked at them in surprise. "Just that if I'm not mistaken, that girl has just had an epiphany."

"Amy?" Connor said.

Hildy took a bite of zucchini bread and smiled. There was a crumb on her chin.

"What kind of epiphany?" Roxy asked. "Really, Hildy sometimes you try my patience."

Hildy finished chewing, picked up her cup. "Think, Roxy. *She didn't do it?*"

"I am thinking. She didn't do it. Who didn't do it? Do what?"

"It's probably just the hatching of some diabolical plot to make everyone miserable," Connor said.

Hildy shook her head. "If nobody is going to eat this, I'm putting it away and going to bed. I'll look in on Amy during the night and make sure she's okay." She took the platter to the counter and put a top on it. Emptied the coffeepot, rinsed it, and left it in the sink to soak.

"Good night," she said and went toward the door.

"Who didn't do what?" Roxy said as Hildy reached the door.

"Skye. The fire. She didn't do it."

"Well, of course she didn't, she was with— Oh, not this fire, *the* fire. She didn't start *the* fire."

"Like I said, epiphany. Good night." And Hildy went upstairs to bed.

IT WAS AFTER noon when Jack set a mug of coffee on the counter in front of Skye. She looked tired. But she had slept. He hadn't. He'd spent the night watching her, waiting for the nightmare, imagining the unimaginable—if Amy hadn't seen her go back in the cabin, if they'd forgotten about her in their effort to save Herb.

Herb Pritchard, a pain in the ass at the best of times. His derelict camp. Skye holding those stupid fishnets. She could have died.

"Thanks for the coffee, but I think I'll walk over to the—"

"Sit down." Jack heard himself say the words. Say? Hell, he'd just screamed at her.

She was staring at him like she'd never seen him before.

Well, maybe she hadn't.

But now he couldn't stop himself.

"What were you thinking?"

"I—"

"What would have happened if Amy hadn't seen the fire? What if I hadn't gotten there in time? What if Amy didn't see you go back inside? How would I live with that? How would any of us live with that?"

"Jack, don't."

He swept his favorite mug off the counter. It crashed to the floor.

Skye jumped up. "I'm sorry. I didn't think." She had started toward him, but she stopped. "Amy saw the fire?"

Jack just looked at her, the shards of ceramic at his feet, his coffee dripping off the edge of the kitchen island. He was shaking with some kind of emotion that wouldn't let him go. Maybe it was the lack of sleep and seeing Skye in the daylight, the dark hollows around her eyes, the way he hadn't noticed before how her clothes seemed too big for her.

He would not walk away. He would not need a minute. That was how they'd gotten here. Him walking away. This time he wasn't going anywhere.

"I'm sorry." Skye was standing next to him. He hadn't seen her slip off the stool or come around the edge of the island. But she was standing against him, her bones sharp and her breathing shallow.

"I'm sorry I didn't trust you, that I've been ignoring you, so caught up in my own ego with the weekend and Amy and Connor that I wasn't here for you. You saved my life. Last night."

"No, I didn't."

"You did. And Herb's. And I wanted you to know that . . . that . . ."

Jack turned her into his arms. Kissed the top of her head. "You don't have to."

"But I do. If I hadn't gotten so involved in me, me, me, we wouldn't be here."

"I don't mind being here," he said. He knew what she meant but he didn't want her to feel she owed him. That was the last thing he wanted. He just wanted . . . he just wanted things to be right.

There was so much he wanted her to know. That he would never do something like what she saw with Amy. And she did know it. That she was the most important person in his life. And he wanted her to stay that way. But it wasn't just up to him, was it. He didn't want a life where he set the rules, but he didn't want to face the consequences of not having his way.

"Amy saw the flames," he said into her hair. He could still smell the faint odor of smoke beneath her shampoo. "She called our attention to it. I was sitting on the porch waiting for you. I would never have seen it if they hadn't shown up."

"Connor and Amy came here?"

"Yes, he brought her to apologize to both of us for pulling those antics on the beach. It was a total setup."

"I know," she said. "I knew it then, I just got a little crazy."

"We've all been a little crazy lately. Are you ready for some breakfast?"

Skye shook her head against Jack's chest. "Not yet. I want to go see the damage."

SKYE AND JACK stood side by side in the trampled grass outside cabin two. The cabin itself was a shell, and Skye didn't have to get closer to see that nothing was salvageable.

She wished Jack would say something, anything. But after his unexpected outburst in the kitchen, he'd stayed mum.

At least he hadn't wandered down to Cove Beach. She wondered if the beach they both loved would ever be theirs again.

If Jack would ever be hers again. If he'd ever been.

He must be sick of her ambitions. Because that was what it was, wasn't it? Her enthusiasm for an idea in the bar one night. The desire to help people expand their outlooks of life had turned into a reality. Turned into a mission. Her ideas would save the town's economy. Who the hell did she think she was?

Behind them, the men were laying the new pipeline to the street, even though she would have to cancel the weekend. No reason to stop them. The money was spent. They'd already torn out the old ones and Herb couldn't sell the property without water. She'd used her stores as collateral for the new waterline because she'd also needed the water. And because she let Edna and Rhoda get to her. Her weekend would have to be canceled. And it was her fault.

"Everything," Skye said, maybe to herself, maybe out loud.

She could hear Jack breathing beside her, but he didn't move, didn't open his mouth.

"It's gone." All the supplies, origami papers, equipment, blocks, paints, compasses, fishnets, string and pencils, chalk and aquariums, paint cans and muffin tins—the telescope. All turned to ash or misshapen beyond use.

She had no choice but to cancel. She'd call Maya when they got back to Jack's. Ask her to come over to help with the cancellation notifications and returning the deposits.

Skye's heart banged to a stop, stuttered painfully, before starting up again.

She would lose the store, the workshop space, the weekend. "I've lost everything."

"You haven't lost me," Jack said and walked up the steps to peer inside.

* * *

SKYE SAT ON the porch steps at Jack's cottage. The porch itself was in the shade and she needed the warmth of the sun to keep going, so she'd opted for the hard wooden steps for her call to Maya.

"It's a bust," she said. "It's less than two weeks away. I don't think it's possible to reorder everything and have it delivered before the weekend, even if I had the money to pay for it. I don't see that we have any choice but to cancel. I've looked over the insurance policy, but I don't think we're covered for enough."

Maya was silent on the other end. And Skye had to fight back tears. Everyone had worked so hard. Her volunteers and docents were lined up and ready to go. They had such good ideas, were so enthusiastic, and now she'd let them down. It wasn't fair; some had given up other work to do the weekend. She'd have to pay them what she could.

The pain in her stomach grew so intense she barely recognized the person who was walking up the path toward her.

"Oh hell, Amy's on her way."

"Tell her you're busy. I'm coming over." Maya ended the call. Skye slipped her cell back in her pocket. And waited for her half sister to reach the steps.

Skye looked up and waited, shielding her eyes with her hand. At first Amy was just a dark silhouette in the sunlight, but Skye knew who it was. As she came nearer, Amy slowly came into focus. She looked like shit.

Well, join the club, Skye thought and wished Jack would come out to her rescue. He'd been avoiding her since they came back from the camp.

The minute they'd walked into the house, he'd declared that he was making lunch and practically climbed into the cabinet with the large pots and pans. They had both been surprised by his declaration. Jack as much as Skye.

She hadn't seen or heard from him since, just occasionally caught the sound of pans and spoons clanking against each other. He was not the neatest cook, and not the best. But what he lacked in cuisine acumen he made up for in determination.

Skye was on her own.

So she waited for Amy to say something. When she didn't, Skye said, "Do you want to sit down?"

Amy shook her head. "I have something to say."

Skye considered getting up and just leaving. Or telling Amy to leave. But it all seemed like too much trouble. Might as well let her have her say. Maybe if she got it out of her system, she would go away and leave Skye alone at last.

"I was wrong."

That got Skye's attention, but it also made her wary.

She sat up a little straighter. Forced herself to look at Amy, who was blocking her view of the cove. Fine, she didn't want to see it anyway.

She didn't think she would ever look at that beach again without seeing Amy, naked and wrapped around Jack. She shivered.

"Are you okay?"

Skye nodded.

"I was wrong. I said you did it. I saw you coming out of Dad's workshop and I thought you'd set fire to it."

"You've said this all before. I'm not going to argue with you about it. Believe what you want, fine. Now I've got a weekend to cancel and a lot of people to call. Maya will be here any minute to start proceedings."

"You're going to cancel the weekend?"

"You have a better idea?" Skye's voice was shrill. She took a breath. *Stay calm. It will only escalate.* "Yes, I'm canceling. I don't think I have any other options. So let's just agree to disagree. It's been fifteen years. It's over."

"Actually, I'm sure I could come up with a better idea. I did run a major corporation, you know."

Skye's head began to pound.

"But that's not why I'm here."

Then get on with it, Skye thought as her stomach began to churn.

"First of all. It was not Jack's fault. I jumped him. My bad. But, really, you should fight for him."

Skye opened her mouth, but Amy held up both hands. "But this is what I came to say. It wasn't you, I know that now. I knew it the minute I saw you come out of that cabin last night. You were trying to save things, not destroy them."

Skye frowned at her. "What are you saying?"

"I was angry, I overheard you and Connor planning to run away. I wanted to stop you. I was the one who told Dad. Then you and Dad had that big fight and I was glad."

"Water under the bridge," Skye said, suddenly exhausted beyond even her wildest imagination.

"I saw you running out of his workshop and I thought you had started the fire because you were mad at him. I was sure you started it. Because . . . it was what I would have done if I'd been you."

"Well, it's a good thing you weren't me."

Amy shook her head.

"Amy? What are you saying?" Skye sat up, licked dry lips. "You didn't start it, did you? They said it was faulty wiring."

"No, I didn't. I swear it. But I wanted to. I was glad when it burned down . . . because then you two wouldn't be happy anymore."

"Oh Amy."

"I hated you."

"I figured that out years ago." Skye was surprised to see tears pooled in Amy's eyes. She wasn't surprised that there were tears; Amy could cry at the drop of a hat, but these seemed different somehow.

"I wanted you to get in trouble. You had Dad and you had Connor, and—"

"Connor? Amy, you were twelve."

"It didn't matter. You had each other. You had everybody. And I didn't. I just wanted you to get into trouble. I didn't want you to leave." Amy sucked in an uneven breath. "I didn't want you to leave *me*."

"Amy, you hated me. You told everyone in town I tried to kill our father. You should have been happy."

"I know, but I wasn't."

Skye heard a car door slam. That had to be Maya, and suddenly Skye wished her friend would take her time because this
was a different Amy than Skye'd ever seen before.

"Once I started I couldn't stop. Then you ran away. And I
was scared. Everybody started acting weird. Then Connor came
back from school and told everyone that you had been with
him when the fire started. And that I had lied. And they believed him. But I didn't. I wouldn't. I *couldn't*. Because that
meant I'd ruined everything."

She took another one of those long breaths. "He had all her
things in that workshop. Your mother's. Did you know? All the
things she left behind. That's why he didn't want us to go out
there. He wanted her all to himself."

Skye nodded. She'd known as soon as she'd heard the fire
marshal talking to her father the next day. How long had it
been before Amy had made the connection? When did she realize that she'd driven away the one she was most jealous of,
wrongly as it turned out? And found herself left only with a
distant father and a resentful mother.

"Mom hated him after that. And me."

Skye considered protesting. She didn't want Amy wandering
back into poor-me territory.

"Kids aren't stupid. They can tell. He couldn't wait to divorce us. I get it. I don't hold it against him. He's always nice to
me, but he doesn't love me."

Skye held up her hand, but Amy barreled on.

"Let me finish. I won't bother you anymore.

"I've let it color my whole life. Every friend I've dropped, every job I quit or got fired from, every guy I didn't bother to try and keep. I blamed you. Hell, I've blamed everyone but me. And I didn't even realize it, well, maybe a little, until last night when I saw you go back in that burning cabin and I was afraid I had lost you again."

Maya rounded the side of the house and came to a stop. She looked from Skye to Amy and back to Skye. "Uh, should I come back later?"

"No," Amy said, shaking her head spasmodically. "I was just leaving."

"Wait!" Skye said. Everything was happening too fast.

"Really," Maya said. "I can come back. It's just Mr. Neumann from the Lexington Advertising Agency has called twice. I think he heard about the fire. I told him you'd call him back."

Her cell rang. Maya glanced at it. "It's him again."

Skye shook her head. "Tell him we're still assessing the situation but most likely it will be canc—"

Amy snatched the phone out of Maya's hand.

"What the—"

"Hello, this is Amy Mackenzie, Ms. Mackenzie's chief operating officer."

Maya made a grab for the phone, but Amy twisted out of the way and walked out of range. "Yes, we were just going to call. We have a proposal we think you might be interested in."

Maya sank down next to Skye. "We are so screwed."

Chapter 29

The next week passed in a whirlwind of activity. They hadn't stopped from the moment Amy hung up the phone from her talk with the ad company.

"They've offered to underwrite the new supplies up to ten thousand. Of course I had to agree to give them ten percent off regular fees when they book your weekends down the road. They're sending a contract. I told them our people would take a look and get back to them tomorrow."

"Do we have people?" Maya asked.

When Jack finally came out to announce lunch was ready, Skye had retrieved her laptop, Maya was typing notes into her phone, and Amy was pacing back and forth while they wrote. Jack took one look, said, "Never mind," and retreated into the house.

By that afternoon, Skye had contacted most of her vendors. Some could deliver the additional supplies, some couldn't guarantee they would arrive in time.

"We'll go local," Skye decided. "We might have to do it

piecemeal, but it's doable. But first of all I need to talk to Charlie Abbott. The chamber can do a lot of the legwork for us. And Roxy and Hildy," she said. "I know they'll want to help."

"And Connor," Amy added. "Might as well make himself useful. Can he do anything?"

"He's a diplomat, he can negotiate. God knows we're going to have to wheel and deal to get this done."

Sonny and Jack worked at their store during the mornings and helped out at the site in the afternoons and evenings.

Jack and Skye hardly saw each other except when Skye visited the site or when they fell into bed at night.

And Connor. His vacation time was quickly coming to an end and yet he stayed. He took charge of payments and invoices with Amy and dealing with vendors, new permits, and other detailed work that he knew exactly how to expedite on paper and could argue his way to success with a finesse that Skye admired.

She thought maybe Amy did, too. She was definitely learning a little subtlety from him.

Hildy had taken over canteen responsibilities, bringing sandwiches and salads to the site for lunch and cooking every night. Dinner at Roxy's became a family affair, with Skye, Jack, Amy, Connor, and Hildy and Roxy sharing the table, the food, and plans for each coming day.

One night as Jack was helping Roxy with the dishes and Amy's head was buried in her laptop, Connor and Skye found themselves alone on the porch.

"I wanted to thank you," Skye began.

"No need."

"There is," she countered. "You brought Amy here, and even though I resented it at first, it's changed my life, and hers, I think."

Connor gave her a look.

"So maybe we'll never be best friends, but she certainly has stepped up to help. I had no idea that she could do this stuff."

"I didn't, either," he said. "She's smarter than she lets on."

"She always says she's smart."

"I know, but it's the kind of bragging that people who aren't as smart as they think they are usually do."

"But in her case, she really is."

"So what will you do next?" he asked, looking out to the black ocean.

"Take August off and start again."

"It's amazing what you've done here. What you've done for this town; they look to you to get them back on track. Everyone respects you, they trust you, they love you." He hesitated. "And so do I."

She shook her head.

"I still love you, Skye. I don't think I ever stopped."

"I love you, too, Connor, but—"

"But as a friend," he said bleakly.

She slipped her arm through his, moved closer. "As my dearest friend. We were young, inquiring, full of craziness. I loved every minute of it. But we were kids."

"I haven't changed."

"We've both changed. We can't recapture it. We were different people then, unformed, passionate, but shallow of life experience.

"Let's hold on to the memory of that first love, cherish what we had, what we still have. But, Connor, you and I were the road not taken."

He smiled down at her and the years were all there written in his face. And she loved him for all of it. And she always would.

"Ready to go?" Jack said from the archway.

"Yep," she said. She kissed Connor's cheek. "See you tomorrow." And she walked away from her past.

THE TOWN DID pull together, manning cars and trucks and scouring whatever they couldn't find online, in person and on a budget. Some of the docents were able to adapt their planned classes to include fewer man-made materials and more hands-on and found materials.

The motels, inns, and B and Bs began to fill with guests. The restaurants began to stay open later to accommodate the new influx of patrons.

And Skye and her team worked around the clock.

Friday night, the first registrant showed up at the mess hall, now transformed into a rustic chic information center, reading room, and coffee bar, Amy's addition. And Skye had to admit that it added a nice touch. The big problem would be getting everyone away from the caffeine and out exploring their surroundings.

By eleven on Saturday morning, nearly all the participants had registered and the first workshops were beginning. Brendan had exchanged his tools for LEGOs and was leading the LEGO of My Ego workshop at Imagine That Too for a dozen A-types, ages fourteen to sixty-two.

Herb had set off with a ball of twine and a loaf of white bread to teach his group the fine art of crabbing. George Zenakis sat under the trees, Goodle, Maya and Sonny's golden poodle, by his side, acting out the storm scene from *The Iliad*, his voice filling the air and broadcasting to the edges of the camp.

Yoga on the beach, nature walks, leaf rubbings—knots of people everywhere were doing something they had never done before, or since they were kids, or they did every weekend but were looking at it differently than ever before.

"Whew," Skye said.

"It kind of reminds me of *Fahrenheit 451*," Connor said as he and Skye stood watching from the edge of the parking lot.

"What? After all the books were burned?"

"Yeah, but not that part. Just all those people walking in the woods memorizing the great works of literature. It makes you think. Gives you hope."

"Yeah, I guess it does," Skye said. "Do you ever lose hope?"

"I'm a diplomat. My job starts at hopeless and works up from there." He grinned. "Hopefully."

"But you're glad you do it."

"Yes. It's a thankless pain in the ass most of the time. But, hell, sometimes you get people to agree, borders are solidified, arms are rolled back, lives are saved. Sometimes it's all in vain."

"Would you give it up?" she asked.

"Would *you* give *this* up?"

"No." She swallowed a lump in her throat. "I'm glad we both found the right place to be."

"Yeah," he said. "Me, too."

They didn't mention the past or the future after that. Everyone was busy keeping things moving, dealing with unexpected glitches, and making sure enthusiasm was catching. By the time they closed up camp on Sunday, long after the last participant had packed out and headed for home or their lodgings, everyone was exhausted.

Sonny took Maya home; Skye had noticed her rubbing her back several times during the weekend, but she was smiling when they left, her belly poking jauntily beneath her Discover It T-shirt, another of Amy's ideas. Skye had been reluctant at first; she'd wanted to stay away from merchandising of any sort.

But Amy convinced her to give them away and by the end of the weekend, they had taken orders for extras, all proceeds going to the local print shop that had done the first batch at cost.

"A win-win situation," Amy said.

Two DAYS LATER, on an overcast Tuesday morning, they all gathered at Imagine That to see Amy and Connor off. Connor was due in Thailand, and Amy, as she reluctantly admitted, had "some bridges to un-burn."

"I'll apologize to old Mr. Hazlitt; maybe he'll even give me my job back or a job I can rise from, or else I'll find another one."

"Will you be okay?" Skye asked as they stood on the sidewalk saying their goodbyes.

Amy smiled ruefully. "Sure. I've never had trouble getting jobs, just keeping them."

"Who knows," Connor said. "If you can manage to keep your next one, I might set you up with an interview with the State Department."

"The State Department?"

"You'll have to pass a test."

"Me? I'm great at tests. I'd make a great diplomat."

Skye wondered whether they had actually turned a corner or Amy would fall back into her old ways. She had mentioned visiting for Thanksgiving or Christmas. "When I have a real holiday and not because I got fired."

Time would tell.

Connor and Jack shook hands. It was a very serious moment, but when later Roxy asked Jack what it had been about, Jack merely said, "It's a guy thing."

Amy gave Jack a tentative hug, and Connor hugged Skye for a little bit longer than was customary.

And then it was time to say goodbye.

Connor opened the door of the sports car, and Amy climbed in.

"Europe," said Amy. "I've always wanted to work in Europe."

Connor closed her door. "And you have to obey the rules and regulations without question." He went around to the driver's side. One last look in Skye's direction and he got inside.

"Paris. Maybe. Will I get a wardrobe allowance?"

Connor's answer was drowned out by the engine roaring to life.

Roxy and Hildy wandered off to Millie's for pie and coffee.

Maya went inside.

Skye and Jack watched as they drove away.

Amy was gesticulating wildly long after their voices had faded away.

"That is going to be a long drive," Jack said.

"One that we won't be on, thank heavens."

Jack blew out a sigh. "Do you think those two might . . . I don't know, have a future together?"

"Connor and Amy? God, I hope not."

"What about us?"

"Us?" Skye said, finally taking her gaze from the street to look at him.

"I mean, your soul mate just took off to parts unknown. Do we have a chance?"

He was still looking down the street. And Skye took the time to really study him. What she saw was everything a partner should be.

"For a future together? Oh Jack. I'm counting on it."

His fingers linked with hers and they stood side by side watching the past drive away and the here and now and future settle in to stay.

Acknowledgments

A professional willing to share their expertise, an acquaintance who offers hospitality and a tour of their neighborhood. A colleague who says, "Sure, I'll read a few pages." The many bloggers, reviewers, sale forces, and marketers, the copyeditors and proofreaders. There are so many people who contribute to the journey of a book that they could fill a whole book of appreciation.

I'm especially grateful for my book crew—my book family: Kevan Lyon, Tessa Woodward, Elle Keck, and my entire William Morrow team. Thank you all.

Reading Group Guide

1. Skye has worked hard to grow her business and help the town by holding Discover It Weekend. She's exhausted but enthusiastic; stressed but optimistic. What do you think caused Skye's intense reaction to Amy's sudden arrival? Is it just a case of bad timing or something deeper?

2. It seems that Skye has been able to divorce herself from her childhood and compartmentalize her sister, her father, and Connor into a place where she doesn't have to deal with them. Was that ability good for her growth as a person? Necessary? Or did it almost cost her everything?

3. After Amy begins insinuating herself into the town, Skye worries that she will start causing trouble, just like she always did as a child. And when several of the townspeople take Amy's side about staying for the summer, Skye is afraid that history is repeating itself and the whole town will turn against her. Does she have a good reason to feel

this way? Or is she overreacting? Should she have defended herself earlier?

4. When Skye sees Amy and Jack on the beach, she can't believe that Jack would betray her. But instead of confronting them, or pretending like she hadn't seen them, she runs away. Refuses to talk to anyone. Even though she finally comes to her senses, she goes through a lot of unhappiness and pain. Do we understand why she reacted that way? What would you have done in her position?

5. Connor brought Amy to town ostensibly to keep her from causing trouble, or so he tells himself and everyone else. Why do you think he finally admits the real reason to himself? Is he an honorable man for backing off, or should he have taken a chance and tried to win her back? What do you think the outcome would have been?

6. Skye and Jack have a comfortable, nonverbally committed relationship. At least until Connor comes to town, and then Jack is thrown into doubt. Why do you think he reacted that way? Should he have been more up front with Skye about his feelings?

7. What if Skye had decided to go away with Connor? Do you think that was ever a possibility?

8. Roxy and Hildy have made a second chapter in life for themselves. What qualities does it take to make adjustments, begin again, become surrogate parents, start a new business, and enjoy life after your life has been derailed by circumstances beyond your control?

9. Do you believe there are soul mates in the world? What qualities make a soul mate? Can friends be soul mates or do they have to be partners for life?

10. Why do you think Skye and Amy held on to their beliefs about each other for so long? Do you know people who have kept their anger burning instead of just trying to meet halfway? Can everything be resolved by talking things out?

11. Amy finally gives up her beliefs about Skye when she sees Skye coming out of the burning cabin. And later, when Skye is at the point of giving up, Amy takes over and begins to organize. Why do you think she had a change of heart and was willing to help?

12. This was probably not the summer Skye had imagined. What about you? Exotic locale or someplace close to home? Active or contemplative? Challenging or relaxing? If you could chose, how would you imagine summer?

BOOKS BY
SHELLEY NOBLE

LUCKY'S BEACH

A BEACH WISH

LIGHTHOUSE BEACH

THE BEACH AT PAINTER'S COVE

FOREVER BEACH

WHISPER BEACH

CHRISTMAS AT WHISPER BEACH

BREAKWATER BAY

STARGAZEY POINT

BEACH COLORS

ALSO AVAILABLE • E-NOVELLAS BY SHELLEY NOBLE

Stargazey Nights
Holidays at Crescent Cove
Newport Dreams: A Breakwater Bay Novella
A Newport Christmas Wedding